the keeping

the keeping

rochelle ransom

The characters and events in this book are fictitious. Any similarity to real persons, living or dead, is coincidental and not intended by the author.

Preadtend Publishing, LLC
219 Bulifants Blvd.
Williamsburg, VA 23185

Prologue

The smell hit her first. *What was that?* Musty and earthy, like wet, muddy running socks forgotten in a locker. Hey eyelids refused to release her eyes. *Okay, breathe and think. What is the last thing you remember?* Driving. She was driving to meet… *Crap!* She sat up and the sudden light and movement ignited a wave of dizziness and nausea. Eyes closed, she reached out on either side and steadied herself on the cushioned surface. Slow and deliberate she blinked to focus.

She remembered pulling into her driveway… *what time was it? Had she missed her appointment?* The cushion was a thin mattress on an elevated bed that chirped and swayed on the chains attaching it to the wall. Across the room, its twin remained clipped shut with no mattress. She performed a body check, confirming her black leggings and beige sweater she'd thrown on before school that morning were still in place. *Where was her cell phone? Her jacket?* The room was about the size of their two-car garage with gray, cold cement walls, no windows, florescent lighting, and a big metal door that reminded her of the vault she'd played in at her dad's old bank. She looked at her watch and gasped. It was after 5 o'clock. *Where had she been for 5 hours?*

Hel… lo?" she croaked, her dry throat as hesitant as her thoughts. She looked down at her running shoes, still on her feet, dangling an inch or two off the concrete floor. There by her left foot sat a gallon jug of water with a typed note taped to it.

Drink this. Then read the note on the door.

She felt her throat constrict with thirst, but feared this wasn't safe to drink.

"Hello?" her voice fell flat in the room. *Did she want an answer?* Easing herself off the bed, she stood. Her legs held steady but her stomach wavered. Her throat begged her to drink the water, but she didn't dare. Not yet. She approached and tried the steel door. The handle didn't budge. She pounded on the thick, cold metal.

"Hello? Is anyone out there? If this is a joke; it's not funny!" she yelled, hoping that was exactly what this was. *Victoria Spencer?* That girl had it in for her, and had been known to pull some pretty evil pranks.

Her thoughts turned to Dave. *Was he trying to make some grand romantic gesture to win her back?* Surveying her surroundings, it didn't seem likely. This place didn't exactly scream romance; dull gray walls and floors, a small kitchen area to her left with a few cupboards, an iron-stained, crooked white sink, and a pale laminate counter. Rows of silver steel shelves were filled with supplies. A faded, green stationary bike sat upright against the wall. Past it, a partial cement wall intersected with a tension curtain rod to form a small corner room. The newness of the plastic, creased, shower curtain sent a quick chill through her. This was definitely not a love nest. Obviously she had been drugged and she could not imagine Dave doing that.

Something other than nausea gnawed at the seams of her stomach as she scanned the shelves with the large blue containers, and discovered a reusable water bottle and another note.

Water is the key to survival. Refill and drink this 3x daily.

Her thirst clouded all other thoughts. She grabbed the water jug, opened it, and sniffed. Nothing. She dipped her finger in and brought it to her mouth. It tasted like plastic. Unable to stand it any longer, she took a small drink and then forced herself to wait for a reaction.

As she waited, she inspected the food shelves: macaroni and cheese boxes, soup and vegetable cans, bags of rice. The big blue containers held water. There were rows of them. She stopped in front of the makeshift corner room. No sound, no movement. She held her breath and poked the middle of the shower curtain. Nothing moved or made a sound.

Carefully, plastic sliding on plastic, she pulled back the cheap curtain. The coverless hole of a toilet seemed to scream back at her with its black, cold mouth. *Run!* The gnawing in her stomach grew stronger. Convinced it was dehydration, she drank greedily from the gallon jug. The water washed away the last of the drug haze, and she went to confront the note on the door.

Each line she read weakened her resolve like the hollow thud of dirt shoveled onto the wood of a casket. The jug slipped from her hand, hit the floor and sent the remaining water free to race toward the depressed, pitted areas in the cement like the fear pillaged her veins in search of its own destiny. The water pooled in a small, deep, divot as the fear exploded up her throat, across her tongue and out of her mouth in a desperate shrill wail that fell flat, in the trapped air.

Dr. Laura Hart

When I came home from work that night, I was surprised to see the kitchen was still dark and empty. Sierra was usually doing homework, cooking dinner, or reading in the chair. It was our time to debrief about the day before moving on to evening routines. We had planned a family movie night to watch the latest *Mission Impossible*. I'd picked up the DVD and some Chinese take-out after work so we'd be ready to go when Patrick got home. I called out to her as I set out the food.

When she didn't answer, I checked the driveway and realized her car wasn't there. I checked the calendar in case I had mixed up the days, but saw only Patrick's familiar scrawl reminding us he'd be in New York on Thursday and Friday. I dialed Sierra's number but it went straight to voicemail. I hoped it was just a dead battery.

I sorted through the mail in an effort to stay calm, then called Dave. I knew they had split, but they still worked together and both ran on the cross-country team. I heard the hope in his voice when he answered my call. I'm sure he was not expecting my voice on the other line.

"Hi Dave. It's Dr. Hart."

"Oh, hi, Dr. H. What's up?"

"I was wondering if you might know where Sierra is. She's usually home when I get here. Have you seen her?" I could feel a little twinge of panic start in my chest, like a small pebble interrupting the blood flow to my heart.

"No, sorry. But it's weird you ask because Max said she stopped by to get her paycheck around 11 this morning. I assumed she must have been sick and decided to take the rest of the day off school." I could hear the worry in his tone; the pebble grew into a rock and my heart pounded in my chest.

"When I tried her this afternoon, it went straight to voicemail." He continued.

"Yeah, same here. It must have died. We planned a family movie night. You know it's not like her to change plans without telling us."

"Did you try Gavin? He wasn't in school today either. Maybe they're together." My heart broke to hear the pain in his voice.

"Okay, I'll try him next. Thanks, Dave."

"Sure. Hey can you give me a call when you find her so I know she's okay?"

"Of course."

"I'm sure she's fine, Dr. Hart."

"Thanks again," I said and quickly hung up to dial Mindy, Gavin's mom. She had worked in my office for years.

Mindy answered on the second ring, "Didn't I just see you?"

"Hey, I can't find Sierra. Can you please ask Gavin if he knows where she might be?"

"Oh, Laura. Sure, hold on a sec." I waited. "Gavin hasn't seen her since practice yesterday. He wants to talk to you." A chill ran down my arms and up my back.

"Dr. H? Hey, no I haven't seen her since yesterday and she hasn't texted. Do you want me to go look for her? Have you talked to Dave?"

"He hasn't seen her either."

"Maybe she just went for a run?" Gavin suggested.

"Her car is gone, but I suppose she could have gone to the lake. Are you sure she didn't mention something she needed to do today?" I prayed we had forgotten something obvious.

"Not that I can think of. Look, I'm going to go check all of her usual running spots and then call you back. I'm sure she's fine, Dr. H."

"Okay. Thanks, Gavin. I'm going to call some of the girls."

Sierra hadn't had any close girlfriends since Tia moved. After I exhausted the short list, I called her cell.

"Hey girl, what's up?"

"It's Laura. I'm sorry to bother you but, well, I can't find Sierra." I hated how panicked my voice sounded.

"Oh God. I haven't talked to her in a few days." Tia's perky voice usually made me smile, but right now it caused a rush of anger to sweep through me. She was perfectly fine but Sierra was . . . *where was she?*

"Dr. H? Are you still there?"

"Yes, sorry Tia. I'm still here. I'm going to try her father in New York. Please let me know if you hear from her, okay?"

"Sure thing Dr. H."

"I will." I dialed Patrick's cell before realizing he was still on the plane home. I jumped at the sound of the phone ringing.

"Sierra?" I answered.

"No, sorry, just Dave. You still haven't found her?"

"No. This is not like her." I said.

"Listen, I'm going to cut out of work and drive around. Maybe she ran out of gas somewhere."

"Okay, thanks. Gavin is out looking, too. I don't want to miss a call or not be here if she comes back. Call me the minute you find her, okay?"

"I will. Don't worry we'll find her."

I debated whether or not to call the police. Maybe it was too extreme. Still, I had this sick feeling in my gut. I guess it was my maternal instinct. Besides, I knew most of the police force—their children were my patients. Surely they wouldn't mind keeping an eye out. I grabbed the phone and dialed.

Patrick Hart

I remember pulling into the driveway that night and seeing the cop car. After my time in prison the sight still gives me a sick taste in the back of my throat. But it was quickly replaced by fear for my family.

Next to the cop car, I saw an SUV and a pickup. *Dave and Gavin. It must be Sierra.* I parked in front of the neighbor's house, and ran inside ours.

When I opened the door, I found myself face to face with a framed senior portrait of Sierra. Just a week earlier, I'd felt blasts of nostalgia and pride as Laura added it to the collection on our mantle. Now it rested in the hands of a cop. I felt a flash of heat course through me and turned to Laura. Her red, tear-stained face terrified me. She never cried. As the daughter of an alcoholic, ex-wife to an ex-con, and cancer survivor, tears were carefully conserved.

"Laura." My voice caught in my throat as I wrapped her in my arms. She let me hug her, but remained rigid. "What is going on?"

"Sierra is missing."

I felt like a firm tire abruptly punctured by sharp glass. I used the wall behind me to steady myself.

"Nobody has seen her since eleven this morning. Her car and backpack are gone. Did she say anything to you?"

"No. Nothing."

Dave interjected, "We've checked all of her usual spots, sir."

He looked worse than Laura: dark circles under his eyes, a five o'clock shadow, still wearing his dirty uniform from *The Kitchen*. I'd never seen this boy look anything but perfect, but then I remembered that he and Sierra had split. I probably looked equally destroyed when Laura and I separated.

"Did you check the old Oil Springs?" I asked.

"I did, sir." Gavin spoke up from the entryway to the kitchen. "We checked the dam, the old country road, and over by the middle school. Nothing."

"We have our guys keeping an eye out for her car. We sent an official BOLO about 20 minutes ago. If she is anywhere in the area, we'll find her." The cop said. I glanced at him for the first time. He couldn't be much older than Sierra.

"Have you checked her room, her computer, her email?" Dark thoughts fought to force their way through my focused resolve.

"I tried, but I don't know any of her passwords. It seemed more important to get the police looking." Laura said.

"Gavin, this is your area of expertise. Do you think you can get into her email?" I had hired Gavin over the summer to install some protective software. I was confident he could do a hell of a lot more than I probably wanted to know.

"Sure. Anything that might help." As we headed upstairs, I noticed the helpless angry expression on Dave's face. "Dave, you come too, you may have better luck guessing her passwords."

I felt dizzy as we walked into her room. Sierra's running trophies, framed pictures of her and Tia, her and Dave, the three of us this spring; it even smelled like her. Gavin opened her laptop to try and work his magic. Dave and I hovered, praying he would find an answer in there.

Note On The Door

Do not panic. You are going to be fine. If you follow all of the instructions, you will be set free before the supplies are gone. You have plenty of food and water to survive as long as you take care of yourself and make good choices.

Food: There is a complete inventory hanging on the shelves by the bathroom. You may want to plan your meals in advance to make the most of what you have. Perishable items should be used first: fresh fruits, vegetables, and bread. Daily vitamins have also been provided.

Cooking: There is a portable electric burner that can be plugged into the single outlet above the kitchen counter. Use your electricity sparingly; the outlet, lights, well pump for your sink, and septic pump are all run by the generator.

Water: There are forty-five 3-gallon jugs of water, which is more than you should need for your stay. Still, you should be very careful with your water.

> <u>Drinking:</u> If you finish your water bottle 3 times daily you will be sufficiently hydrated.
>
> <u>Sink:</u> You can use the sink water for cooking, washing dishes, and bathing. I would not suggest it for drinking unless it became a necessity. I cannot confirm how clean it is.

Cleanliness:

> <u>You:</u> Unfortunately, there is no shower or hot water. You will need to use one of the pots to heat water for bathing. There should be plenty of toiletries for your stay.

Clothes: There are some additional items of clothing, but laundry can be done with soap and plastic bin provided. A pull-out clothesline has been installed for drying.

Linens: There are 2 bath towels, 2 hand towels, 2 washcloths, and 2 sets of sheets for the bed. There are also 2 blankets and a sleeping bag for warmth.

Lights: They will go off at 10PM and on again at 7AM.

Exercise and Ventilation: This shelter has been outfitted with a stationary bike ventilation system. **It is important to exercise daily to keep the air inside safe.** The bike even has an odometer so you can track your mileage.

Entertainment: There are many forms of entertainment provided: cards, used books, notebooks, pens, crossword puzzles, and a portable record player with a small selection of albums.

Education: Due to missed scholastic time some educational materials have been included should you wish to study: *The Series 7 for Dummies*, *The Best American Short Stories of 2006*, and *Complete GED Preparation Guide*.

Why? Wondering why you are here is a pointless waste of time. Do not fear for your safety or life. Nobody will harm you. If you simply follow the instructions and take care of yourself, you will be free to leave at the end of your stay.

Sierra Hart

I spent my first hour in the hole searching for a way to escape. I tried yelling, screaming, banging on the wall and door with a pot, but by 6:36, I was defeated. I remember that exact time, 6:36. Time soon became my enemy and my friend; taunting, but also a baseline for my sanity. At that point, however, it was still just logistics. I'd been conscious for at least 90 minutes, and lost five and a half hours before that. I sat on the bed and cried. Who would have brought me here? And why? I stared at the shelves of supplies. Our pantry at home could have been filled five times over with all of the food. I grabbed the pot and started banging on the door again.

"Hello? Anybody? Can you please help me? Why are you doing this to me? I have a family! They will be looking for me. My mom is . . . I need to be with her right now. She needs me!" I curled up in a ball on the bed, swallowed back a fresh rush of nausea, and cried myself to sleep.

Dr. Laura Hart

Patrick and I had to send Dave and Gavin home when they almost came to blows over what Gavin should and shouldn't be reading on her computer. They circled around one another like two territorial dogs defending their pack. The computer was a dead end. Meanwhile, the police had contacted the cell provider to try and track her movements. Dave's dad had used his leverage to see if we could get the records faster.

"Hello?"

"Dr. Hart, this is Officer Malone. We found Sierra's car."

"Oh, God." *Just her car.*

"Her school bag was in there, but no sign of her phone. We didn't see any signs of a struggle. The car was parked down a dirt road between route 30 and the Henderson's Farm. Officers are combing the area now."

"Can we send people down to help?" I asked. Patrick was already putting on his coat and grabbing a flashlight. I whispered the location and he headed out the door.

"That's not a bad idea, but one of you should stay close to the phones, just in case."

"I will. My husb... er, I mean, Sierra's father, is already on his way. I'm going to call around for more help. Let us know if you find anything else in the car."

"We will. If she's out there in those woods we'll find her. It's been raining pretty hard but it's not so cold that she wouldn't be okay with a coat."

I tried to imagine why she would leave school in the middle of the day. I tried to remember how she had seemed that morning. Nothing stood out. Then again, I had been in a bit of a hurry. I'd knocked over the garbage with my car. Sierra had helped me pick it up before running back in the house.

I looked at the time. It was pretty late to be calling, but I knew that Gavin and Dave would want to help. And I was pretty sure they could round up a bunch of their friends. I took a breath, and started with Dave.

Patrick Hart

I hope you never have to experience how humbling it is to walk through a thick forest in the dead of night, rain pouring down, oblivious to anything but the sound of a lifetime of friends and neighbors calling out your daughter's name. How helpless. Every shape, every sound, your mind desperately wants to believe they are her. We covered acres that night, but we didn't find a single trace of my little girl. Nothing. The group thinned around eight the next morning. Even in daylight, we had no luck. I thanked each of them for their help as they returned to their regular Saturday. I wondered if my Saturdays would ever be the same.

I didn't know what to do next. This was the last place she'd been, or at least with her car. I didn't want to leave, but I knew I needed to be with Laura. She would be waiting for some shred of hope.

As I walked to my truck, I spotted Dave's SUV. He was slumped in the driver's seat, his forehead resting on the steering wheel. I gently tapped on the glass.

He jumped, quickly wiped his eyes, and rolled down the window. He looked as bad as I felt.

"I don't understand why she would be way out here in the middle of a school day, you know? I keep trying to think if there was something she said or did that I missed. But we hadn't really been talking as much, and—"

I put my hand on his arm to stop him. "I know. I've been doing the same thing. There doesn't seem to be any good explanation. Did anyone talk to her at the restaurant when she stopped in for her paycheck?"

"Just Max. He said she looked really pale, like she wasn't feeling well. He made her sit with a glass of water. She drank it really fast and left like she had some place to be."

We both looked to the spot where her car used to be, now cordoned off with police tape. They'd taken it for evidence. I hated that thought even as it popped in my head. *Evidence*. It inferred that a crime had been committed.

"Did she meet anyone on that trip to Nantucket this summer?" Dave asked.

His questioned seemed out of left field. "Nantucket? Not that I know of. She was with us most of the time. Why?"

“Well, she started to act different when she got back. Colder. Then she just dumped me out of the blue and has been distant ever since.” He stared out the windshield as the sun finally sliced its way through the clouds.

“If she did meet someone, she didn’t tell me or her mother about it.” As if on cue, Laura rang my cell. I gestured that I needed to take it and stepped away to answer. He started his car and left.

“Nothing,” I said. “I’m sorry. I’m heading home now.”

Dr. Laura Hart

On Saturday morning, a small team swarmed our house. Detective Rock was none too happy to learn the rookie cop had let Gavin and Dave access her computer before they did. They took Patrick's office computer too. We were fine with it all, anything to find her. Still, it was awful when they took each of us into different rooms for questioning. Even more so for Patrick. He looked angry and defeated when he came out.

But of course they went there. All of our minds had. Was this somehow connected to Patrick's past? Or even more sickening, to his present? I wasn't ready to voice that fear just yet. I needed him not to be that Patrick again.

Day 2 – 10/6

It's 2:13AM and I can't sleep. I must have been able to yesterday because of the drug they gave me. Now every time I close my eyes I feel like someone is watching me. It's creepy. I'm afraid to use the flashlight. There is only one more set of batteries. Only every once in a while, when I can't stand it anymore, I turn it on and scan the room. I need a weapon. I wish I'd have thought of that before the lights went out.

In the morning, I will figure out a way to arm myself so I'm ready if someone opens that door. What would make a good weapon? I only have a butter knife. I better turn off this flashlight. But in case I don't survive the night and somebody finds this notebook—my name is Sierra Hart from Laketown, NY, and my parents are Dr. Laura Hart and Patrick Hart. Please tell them I'm sorry and I love them.

When I first met the Harts, they looked like every other couple I had encountered in my job—shell shocked, tired, guilty, and scared. From what I could tell, the local detective wasn't doing much to calm their fear. In fact he seemed to take pride in doing the exact opposite. Luckily, we were able to get him out of the house and off talking to other people of interest. Once he left, I went over the current situation with the Harts.

"I know you are scared, exhausted, and frustrated, but Sierra needs you to stay focused and keep everyone around you motivated to find her. This is very important. If the community or media see you determined to find her, they will get behind you. If you falter, so will they." Laura's gaze fell to a pair of sneakers peeking out from under the couch. I stood up to try and regain her focus.

"We set up the equipment to monitor and record all your incoming home and cell calls. We've sent out Sierra's picture and story to the media. A number of people in your community have volunteered to help us distribute flyers to local businesses. We have a tip line set up. My guys are going through her computer and yours, and sifting through her text messages from the last few days." I took a breath and sat back down on the couch next to Laura. Patrick hadn't stopped pacing the room since I arrived.

"One area we are investigating is the sex offender registry." Laura drew in a sharp breath. "There are 152 registered in this county. We ruled out 80 because their history is with family members, and another 40 only interested in younger children. For the remaining offenders we are speaking with their parole officers to rule out those with a solid alibi."

"Jesus." I heard Patrick say, to nobody in particular.

"I think you should go on TV and ask for people to help find your daughter. It helps when people make a connection with the family. And if someone does have Sierra, it may humanize her and give her a better chance."

"We can do that," Laura said, after exchanging a look with Patrick. He sat and took her hand.

"Good," I said. "I'll set it up." I stood, but Laura reached out to stop me.

"I know I shouldn't ask but I can't help it." Laura's voice caught in her throat. "How many children have you found safe?"

This was a common question, although usually asked by the father. I didn't have good news. "Every case is different. What has happened before with other children is no prediction of what will or won't happen here. Okay?"

"How many?" repeated Patrick.

"Six." I sighed, starting back toward the kitchen.

"Out of how many missing?" Laura asked.

My job was not always filled with happy endings. There was no way to sugarcoat the odds. The answers just rubbed salt on the wound. The last thing I needed was for them to lose hope. But I also needed to earn their trust if we wanted the best shot at bringing Sierra home safe. "Twenty-five." I watched their faces crumble.

"Hey," I walked back toward the couch. "I saw some quote in Sierra's room about Lady Luck. It seems fitting that she should be my lucky number seven, right?"

Day 8 - 10/12
Biked 10 Miles

The silence is making me crazy. I want to hear my mom's voice; or my dad's, or any voice other than mine. I wonder if everyone is still looking for me. Are they doing those big search parties? How long will it be until they give up? The scary part is I could be up to 5 hours away from them.

I wish I could remember what happened. I left school, got my check, went to the bank, drove home, and then what? I have gone over and over it in my head and I can't remember. They must have been some powerful drugs because everything is still a blur. But how? Did someone sneak up behind me in broad daylight and stick something over my mouth? Wouldn't I remember that? Who would dare? Maybe my neighbors saw something that will help the police find me. Did they stick me with a needle? I'd tried the first day to find any trace of a needle mark, but it's kind of hard when you don't even know where to look.

I also never realized how much I rely on the internet. I find myself wanting to Google stuff all of the time, but obviously if I had internet I wouldn't be stuck here. I wish this person would tell me what they want so I could give it to them and go home. At first I thought maybe Dave had completely lost it and was keeping me here. But he would never do this. I know Dave. He is a sweet guy. Then again, he does have the money to do whatever he wants. And access to lots of stuff. And he's been a little creepy, following me around. This was crazy. Only someone crazy locks a person in a cellar.

But one thought keeps popping back into my head and I can't get it to go away. Am I a hostage for money? Is someone trying to get back at my dad?

My dad isn't particularly special in that big picture way. He isn't a senator or a famous scientist or an actor. But something about him pulls people in. Magnetism, I guess. One of my earliest memories is when I was four. My mom wasn't around as much, then. She still worked long hours as a doctor, so it was often just me and my dad. I loved it. Don't get me wrong, my mom is amazing. But days with my dad were anything but average.

That day, my father and I walked toward our favorite ice cream place, The Dreamery, my small hand swallowed in his large one. It was one of those days when the blacktop seemed to blur with the heat, the end of a long string of them. The Dreamery was buzzing. A mother waited in line with three young boys and I remember they reminded me of the puppies our neighbor's dog had recently birthed. They crawled over everything, including one another. As an only child, I found sibling interactions fascinating. I watched, slightly envious, as they pushed and ran and pinched and laughed. Their mother had clearly had enough and kept yelling. She reached out and grabbed one by the hair, jolting him to a stop. I wanted to look away, but I couldn't. She leaned down a few inches from his face and hissed,

"Dustin, Jr., if you don't stop jimmy jackin' around I am going to pull down your pants and tan your ass right here in front of God and everyone."

Then, she turned right back around to order in a perfectly pleasant tone. The boys all shrugged and stopped long enough to choose a flavor. I looked up at my dad and he smiled down at me before dropping a kiss on my head.

Two of the boys attacked their ice cream, but the smallest still waited. The mom argued with the scoop girl. My dad approached the counter as the mom insisted she had already handed her a ten. I heard some of the bad words I wasn't allowed to say. My dad pulled a ten out of his pocket and tapped her on the shoulder.

"Excuse me m 'am, but is this yours? I think it may have blown off the counter."

I expected her to smile and thank him, but instead she snapped that ten out of his hands like he was trying to steal it and said, "I expect you can handle gettin' my Sammy his ice cream before I hand you more money to lose." I only looked away when I felt the tickle of ice cream melting down my hand. My dad sat back down and the woman huffed by us without so much as a second glance.

"I can't believe she didn't even thank you!" I whispered.

He gave me a squeeze, "We all have moments when we need a

hand but sometimes it's hard to admit. It doesn't mean we shouldn't still extend it. Besides, if we put good out there into the world, maybe Lady Luck will pay us back when we need it most."

I admired my dad and hoped I would one day grow to be like him. My friends all liked him, too, because he told funny jokes and played tag or threw us into the pool the first time we asked. And he was handsome. Maybe all little girls think their dads are handsome, but I saw how waitresses became flustered around him. My mom would tease him about it sometimes, but he just laughed it off and told her she was the real looker.

Neighborhood parties didn't really start until my father arrived. The dull monotone would transform into lively conversation and bursts of laughter. Suddenly, the moms didn't notice the missing plate of brownies we had snuck up into the tree house, or changed the channel to something the Millers didn't approve of.

As I read back over this, I feel like I make him sound like a fictional character—the perfect dad. This isn't true, either. He did have a quick temper. He rarely used it with me, but after I was in bed, I could sometimes hear my parents argue about money. I never understood why. My dad had a good job at the bank and my mom was a doctor. How could there be any problem? But then he fell right off that pedestal.

The gray sky, first fallen leaves and bite to the wind didn't feel like August. I decided to run from school to the bank to tell my dad some exciting news. The run wasn't far, probably three miles, and I smiled the whole way. At cross country tryouts that afternoon, when I finished my 1600, the coach had let out a low whistle and said, "Impressive run, Ms. Hart." I couldn't wait to tell my dad. He had been a runner in high school and college and we started training that summer. Our morning runs made me feel special. I hadn't even told him I was going to try out. The list wouldn't be posted until the following afternoon, but I knew I was much faster than most of the girls—even some of the juniors and seniors.

As I rounded the corner at the light on Main Street, I noticed a small gathering and a cop car in front of the bank. As I neared the crowd, the police came out of the building with a woman in cuffs. I recognized her as my father's assistant, Julie Myers. A chill ran up my back and down my arms, pushing each hair to attention. I locked eyes with my dad, who was also being escorted out in handcuffs. He held my gaze for what felt like forever and a millisecond all at the same time. As he ducked into the back of the police car, everything blurred. The people and town that I'd known my whole life, all melted together like an impressionist painting of a crowd in the rain. I ran. I cried and ran, because somehow I knew. By the look he had given me. I knew, and it made me sick. But I kept running, because I knew he was guilty. His face said it all.

Ironically, my father had introduced me to running: the one thing that saved me that summer. It was my escape from the whispers, angry looks, pity, and the pain of watching my father's mistake rip our lives apart stitch by stitch. After I was snug in bed, my dad had a life I knew nothing about, playing game after game of online blackjack. He was addicted to gambling. I finally understood why my parents had to argue about money. What I couldn't understand was how my dad had lost control.

And when he really got in over his head, he crossed a line. He had access to funds through his job at the bank. Later, explaining it to my mom, he said he thought if he could just borrow a little to get back in the game, he could get back on top. But apparently Lady Luck turned her back on him when he needed her most. He had been "borrowing" for eighteen months. They'd tracked him, built their case, and then brought us down. My mom tried to dip into savings, but dad had gotten there first. We lost the house, we lost our friends, and we lost our dignity. But the worst loss was him. We lost him.

He was home on bail throughout the trial. They had not yet taken the house, but it had become silent. My mom hid at work, I had never been so excited and yet so terrified for school to start. I didn't know which was worse, facing my dad or facing the looks at school. My friends didn't know what to say any more than I did. Cross country saved me. I was the only seventh grader and I attacked each workout, finding relief in the pain. If I could just run fast enough, hard enough, maybe I could outrun it all. It helped that the world was preoccupied with 9/11. I remember that time as if it were a movie. We lived in New York but farther west, near the Pennsylvania border. For me, it was further proof that the world wasn't at all the place I thought it was.

My mom attended most of the trial but I couldn't imagine listening to a bunch of people describe my father in his darkest light. In the two weeks before the verdict was reached, I frequently heard my parents talking in hushed anger.

I awoke the morning of the sentencing to find my father sitting by my bed. I don't know how long he had been there. He may have been watching me sleep, worrying about how all of this would change us; how much it already had. We hadn't been running together since the day of his arrest, but now he held out my running shoes as a silent invitation.

We ran in silence through the neighborhood in which we had spent happier times, past the nursery where we had gotten every Christmas tree since I could remember. As we passed the playground, he veered off the sidewalk. I almost ran right past him when he suddenly sat down on a swing. I stopped and used the pole to stretch. I didn't like stopping mid-run.

"I don't know what to say. I can't imagine how difficult this has been for you. Of all the people I disappointed, it's you that hurts the most. I wish I could go back and make everything right again. I really thought I could work it out." He looked away. I sat a few swings over.

"Mom says you are addicted to gambling, like her father was addicted to drinking." It came out as more of an accusation than I'd meant. He seemed to sink even lower in the swing. Some angry part of me wanted him to feel as miserable as I felt.

"Maybe she's right. But gambling is not the same thing as drinking. I would never hurt either of you like he did. Ever." He stood and kicked at the pole.

"Are you scared?" I asked, thinking of the horrible things I'd heard about prison.

"Yes. But most of all I am scared about what might happen out here while I'm gone. I can't stand the thought of missing all of your cross country meets, our daily runs, your laughter, Sunday pancakes."

"What about mom?"

"Of course I'll miss her, too," he looked me in the eyes. I saw that they were filled with tears, and looked away. I didn't want to see that. I didn't feel like he had the right to be sad. This was his fault. All his fault. He traded us for money. I jumped off the swing and ran back to our trail. He followed silently. I would speed up. He would speed up. I would slow, and so would he. I sprinted the last half mile. He didn't try to keep up and arrived as I caught my breath, stretching my burning calves on the porch steps that would soon belong to some other family.

"Impressive finish, Stub," he whistled. I focused on my shoes.

"Look, I know you are angry with me. You should be. I screwed up. But when I walk out that door today I don't know how long it will be before I see you again. I hope you visit, though I can't bear the thought of you seeing me like that. So I have to say some things and I need you to listen." He squinted into the sun.

I took a seat on the steps and turned to face him. He sat next to me.

"I know I screwed up and I am sorry. Painfully sorry. I know it's not fair for me to ask you for anything, but I need to. I need you to promise me you will do two things. First, continue to be the amazing young woman you already are. You are a bright, talented, fun person and I don't want you to lose any of that because of my stupid mistake. I know this has impacted your school life, friendships, everything. Please try and rebuild that life. Just keep being Sierra. It's okay to smile and laugh and have fun. You are supposed to be happy. So please do that. I need to imagine you out here, happy. Promise."

I shrugged. "I'll try."

"Promise."

"I promise," I said.

"The second thing is selfish and I know it might not happen for a long time, but I need you to forgive me. Every girl needs a father. I can't stand the thought of anyone else filling that role. You and your mom are everything to me. I know my recent actions may lead you to think otherwise, but it is the truth. Without you in my life, I have nothing. I know I can face what I have coming if I know you'll be here when I am released. I need to know I can always be your father."

"What about mom?" I asked.

"What about her?"

"Are you two getting divorced?" I heard my voice catch and it made me angry. I didn't want him to know how terrifying that thought was to me.

"Your mom is very angry and hurt. I've already caused her so much pain and I may be gone for a number of years. I can't ask her to wait for me."

"You can't? Or you won't?" I demanded.

"I don't have any answers for you. Your mom and I are still working through all of this ourselves. I'm sorry." He shifted on the step so he could put his hands on both of my knees and look up into my face. "No matter what happens, we both love you very much. That will never change. Okay?"

I tried to swallow the lump in my throat, but managed a nod. He hesitated before gathering me up into a big hug. For just that brief moment, I pretended that nothing had changed. I wanted everything exactly as it had always been. My mom's alarm clock demanded a reality check from inside the house.

He pulled away, looked directly at me, and said, "Promise? Two things. Be happy. And try to forgive me. Please."

And I did. I promised. He hugged me again, but I broke free and ran into my room where the tears finally made their way to my face. I never said goodbye. I never said "I love you, too." But I did promise. Twice.

My dad was sentenced to eight years in prison, eligible for parole in four. I could have been either 16 or 20 when he was released. But it turned out I was 15. As was often the case with my father, he easily won over the right people and was released on parole after three years and one month. My dad had been right about my mom. She divorced him. But she told me it had nothing to do with the jail sentence. She simply could not be married to an addict. She'd already left her father behind and couldn't do it again, nor would she expose me to it. That entire year was bizarre, as if I had been transplanted into a new family, but still lived in the same town.

The whole experience changed my mom, too. My father had brought out a lightness in her that rarely surfaced after he left. She always seemed so serious. It was as if she had only let her guard down for him. When everything went wrong, she put it back up again. I ached for our old life, but I found an escape when I ran. Eventually this life became my new normal. I went to summer camp in North Carolina for four weeks to restart. Nobody knew my story and I was free to be me again. When I got back, people had moved on from the scandal.

But enough about my dad. Let's talk about my mom. I will try and explain her as best I can. The older I get, the more I understand her. I almost think of her as two different people. The mom before dad went to prison and the mom after. The before mom smiled easily. I remember her wearing soft, flowy skirts and bright colors, and she'd put on fun dangly earrings and shoes for nights out. After, she mostly wore jeans, and comfortable shoes. She never changed her jewelry. Even her hair was different. Her hair was a natural auburn and very thick. Before she would let it down on the weekends and sometimes use hot rollers to give it a little more body.

I remember watching them get ready to go out on date nights. My dad would smell good and look crisp. He'd be ready in a matter of minutes and then leave the bathroom for my mom and me. I'd sit on the bathroom counter (something only allowed on date night) and watch as my mom stood at her mirror and applied make-up with gentle precision. She'd often be dressed in her slip or a bra and underwear, slowly dancing to music between each step. She would sometimes even give me some; eye shadow for her, eye shadow for me, and so it went. She'd have a smile on her face as she sang along. Sometimes the eighties hits would prompt stories from when she was younger. I loved it when she told me stories. She didn't talk about her childhood very often so it was always a rare treat and I clung to each and every word.

Dad would bring her a glass of wine which she'd occasionally sip but never finish. She always gave me the final say on her outfit. If I gave it the thumbs up, she stopped there. Then we'd select jewelry from her jewelry box. I loved to try on the various pieces my father had bought her over the years. I knew each of their stories. The little basket necklace he had given her for their first anniversary when they went to Nantucket, the diamond pendant he'd given her when I was born, the locket that had belonged to my dad's grandmother. It had a picture of her on one side and my grandfather on the other. My favorite was the cameo choker my mom's mom had given her on her eighteenth birthday. My second favorite was the pearl choker my mother wore on her wedding day. It was a gift from her grandfather. She saved these two for special occasions.

The best part of date night was the big reveal. I'd run down the stairs and tell dad she was ready. By then, Amy, my date-night babysitter, would already be waiting for me in the living room. We'd all stand at the bottom of the stairs as she came down, a waft of her perfume preceding her. And at that moment, when she first came into view, I would watch my dad's face light up. Sometimes he would whistle, but usually he would take her arm and lean in to whisper something into her ear. A part of me wanted to know what he'd said, but another part loved that it was just their little secret. To me, this was love. This was marriage. And I would never settle for anything less. I'd glance at Amy, enjoying the envy on her face. My stomach would tingle with excitement as they left together.

I've tried and tried to remember their last date night before my dad was arrested. But I can't. By then I was twelve and too old to watch my mom get ready. I was probably wrapped up in my own Saturday night plans. Maybe by then, their date nights had become like all the other nights of the week, tense with arguments bubbling under the surface. But even during the year before his arrest, there were plenty of happy times and laughter. My mom wore her fun clothes and jewelry and I think they still remained very much in love.

After the arrest, it seemed like my mom spent more and more time at work. It might sound like she abandoned me when I needed her most, but that was not the case at all. Even though my dad had been the one to break apart our family, I was still mad at my mom, too. She would try and talk to me about what I was feeling, but I shut her out with my headphones and went running. I was angry with everyone and everything: my dad for stealing, my mom for not catching on sooner and stopping it somehow, my friends for having normal families, strangers for knowing our darkest secrets, the divorce, and finally myself for believing in the fairytale in the first place.

So I ran and she worked. Once in a while I would visit her office and watch her. Here, she still smiled—especially with the children. She had a gentle, soothing voice that they responded to. I knew she was a great doctor. I had overheard people in passing conversation; "miracle worker," "amazing with Henry," "carefully explains," "seems to really care," "called me on a Sunday just to make sure she was feeling better."

One afternoon, a toddler's frightened shriek made me look up from my Spanish homework. The frustrated mother breastfed her infant as she helped her oldest with homework, and now tried to dislodge the screaming toddler from her leg to usher them into my mother's office. The nurse tried to help, but he remained glued to her leg. The infant lost her grip on her mother's breast and began to cry. My mother slipped into the waiting room, gently gathered the infant into one arm, and knelt down next to the clinging toddler. They both stopped crying as my mom gently wiped away tears.

"I can see by your shirt that you like Thomas the Tank Engine," my mom said, rocking the infant up and down with her arm. "Well, I have a really cool train set right through that door if you'd like to see it," she stood and reached for his hand. He released his death grip and walked with my mom through the door without a second thought. The mother sighed with relief, and ushered her older child after my mom. I remember wishing she could make me feel that safe about my future.

In the beginning, weekends were the most difficult. I had always spent Saturdays with my dad. After he went to prison, my mom made an effort to fill the hole he left. But her pancakes came out flat, not fluffy like his. That only lasted a few weeks. Luckily I had cross country meets on most Saturdays through mid-November. On Sundays, we quietly read the paper and then she would putter around in her garden or clean the house while I hid in the TV room.

I remember one freezing Sunday in February; I sat in my favorite corner of the library, trying to make my way through *Pride and Prejudice* when I overheard two mothers making plans to meet for a movie that afternoon. I thought, duh! The mall was an easy bike ride away, maybe eight miles. I had purposely avoided the mall because I knew I would probably run into kids from school. But I realized I hadn't even considered the movie theater. As long as I was careful and used the street entrance, I could probably sneak in without running into anyone. Going to the movies alone suddenly sounded like heaven; a dark escape into another world for a couple of hours. It became my Sunday ritual. My mom gave me an allowance for chores and I rarely had an occasion to spend it. I had plenty for movies tickets. I saw anything and everything I could get into. Sometimes I would pay for one movie and then sneak into the rated R one next to it, getting a little thrill from breaking the rules.

One afternoon, I made my way to my seat when I noticed my mother sitting alone about half way down on the right. I quickly took a seat so she wouldn't spot me. The movie was *Memento*, but I couldn't stay focused on the complicated plot because I kept stealing glances at her. I found it interesting that she and I had found the same escape. I wondered if there had been other Sundays when we'd both been here.

Then I realized she never did anything with her friends anymore, either. I wondered if that had been her choice, or if they stopped calling. A few of my friends had made an effort, but I ended up pushing them away. I couldn't stand their pity. Maybe I deserved it after bragging so much about how great my dad was. Now they could all laugh at me. Suddenly, they had the better dads, the normal dads. It is silly looking back, but at the time I couldn't handle being around them. Maybe it was the same for my mom. She had been married to the life of the party. Now it was just us. I suddenly felt a need to protect her from all of those awful other moms. But I had pushed her so far away. How could I get her back?

As Lady Luck would have it, the very next Sunday I wasn't smooth enough sneaking into *Moulin Rouge*. The movie had just started when a smug, overweight security guard (and I use that term loosely, I recognized him from school) told me I needed to return to the movie I had paid for because this one required parental guidance. I was mortified and started to leave, when I heard a familiar voice.

"It's okay. She's with me. I'm her mother."

The security guard and I both looked up to see my mom standing there, extending a package of Twizzlers to me. She and I both knew I hated Twizzlers, but it seemed to somehow make the picture hilariously complete. He told us he'd let it go this time, clearly disappointed he wouldn't be able to exert his authority that day, and wandered back out to pester someone else.

"Thanks," I said.

"You're welcome," she responded. And so our mutual Sunday afternoon movie escape began. She never seemed to care much about the fact that some of the movies we attended were rated "R" or not. I guess she figured at this point I knew life could look and sound ugly; cursing, nudity, and violence probably wouldn't have made a big impact either way. I guess you could say we found our way back to our new reality through fiction.

Dr. Laura Hart

I've never been a big fan of getting up in front of a crowd. Give me a sick child in a quiet office and I'm comfortable. I prefer blending in with the wallpaper. Luckily, Patrick is exactly the opposite; he was born to capture the attention of a room. He is a natural performer (clearly, he fooled me for years living two lives). But this was for Sierra. I would do anything to get her back safe. Patrick held my hand as we walked out our front door and into the tangle of cameras and reporters camped out on our lawn.

Patrick's voice was strong and steady: "I'm Patrick Hart and this is Laura Hart. Many local folks will recognize her as the pediatrician who healed your child when nothing else could. Well, now we need your help with our little girl. Our daughter, Sierra Hart, was last seen around eleven yesterday morning near the First Union Bank. Her phone's traceable location puts her not far from our home. Please, if any of you know anything about where Sierra may have gone in the last twenty four hours, call the tip hotline."

He looked to me and squeezed a little tighter as I spoke up.

"And Sierra, if you can hear me sweetheart, stay strong and just hang on. We're going to find you. Okay? We're coming for you. We love you and we want you home safe." That was all I could manage. The people with the cameras and microphones had blurred into one big, loud light. I needed to get back inside the house.

Patrick led me in and got me a cup of tea. I looked at my watch. It had been twenty-eight hours.

Day 13– 10/17

Biked 13 miles

My voice is raw and my hands are sore from yelling and banging that damn pot against the door. I don't see any possible way out of here. I have no idea who is keeping me, or why, or for how long. What happens when they are done with me? At least I am finally getting some sleep. I broke the empty marinara sauce jar and used duct tape to attach two pencils like a handle. It makes a pretty decent weapon and lives under my pillow at night. I also have a few cans strung across the opening to the door. It's low enough that hopefully the person approaching wouldn't see until it was too late. If it worked, not only would it wake me up but it would trip them.

Today is my mom's last surgery. I wonder if she will still go. I hope she does, and that nothing goes wrong. I know they will be doing everything they can to find me. I am determined to do my part. I will stay alive.

After my dad went to prison I wondered how he got through the days. He never said much in his letters or phone calls. We had both agreed I shouldn't visit him there. I didn't want to pry so I decided to look it up online. I remember reading that prisoners maintained sanity by sticking to their routines. So I have decided if I am going to survive, I need a strict schedule. The prisoners exercised, read, and wrote a lot. Some even published books. I pray I'm not here long enough for that, but I do think writing may help. This is my daily plan.

7:00AM Lights on

~~7:05–7:10—bang on the door with the pot and listen for anything or anyone.~~

7:10–8:10 ride bike for ventilation and exercise (note distance in 60 minutes)

8:15–9:15 change and wash self as best as possible, brush teeth (with toothpaste and finger because I have yet to find a toothbrush—so nasty—but I do have floss)

9:15–9:30 make breakfast

9:30–10:00 eat breakfast and read (there is a big box of musty used books—first up: *All The Pretty Horses* by Cormac McCarthy. I will close my eyes and pick one to read. Otherwise I will read all the good ones first and have only crap left when I really start to lose my mind.)

10:00–11:00 clean up from breakfast and wash out my clothes from the previous day. Hang to dry—do sheets once a week

11:00–12:00 journal

12:00–1:00 prepare, eat lunch, clean up

1:00–3:00 education—read or do something with the 2 "text books"

3:00–3:30—prepare, eat snack & clean up

3:30–5:00—journal

5:00–7:00—prepare, eat dinner, clean up (listen to records while eating—it's like company)

7:00–8:00—ventilation bike

8:00–9:00 or 10:00—read

10:00 lights out

PRAY SOMEONE WILL FIND ME TOMORROW

I can't be in here too long. I just can't. I have a life I'm missing. It's my senior year. What if this is all I get? Can my life really end here? Maybe some freaky guy is going to keep me here for years just to see what I do. I bet he has cameras. I'm going to look around for cameras.

Okay I checked; nothing here looks like a camera but how can I even know? Maybe it's hidden in the lights or something. I will be sure to change in the bathroom (more like an indoor outhouse). At least there is a lot of variety in the food supply. Not much in the chocolate department though. I could really go for a Reese's Peanut Butter Cup or Snickers.

Mom, if you ever get a chance to read this, I'm so sorry I couldn't be there for you for your last surgery. I read that some doctors think stress may be a trigger. I hate that my disappearance could make you sick again. I hope whoever this creep is knows he's hurting more than just me.

Patrick Hart

That first morning the cops ransacked our house to look for any hint of where she could have gone. It didn't bother me too much. But then they grilled me. I'm sure it's standard procedure, but it still felt like a personal attack on me as a person and a father. I hadn't encountered Detective Rock during my last run-in with the law, but he certainly acted like I'd stolen from his private piggy bank. I began to worry that maybe he was right; maybe Sierra's disappearance could have something to do with my past.

"What about cell mates or people you may have pissed off while you were inside?" Detective Rock asked.

"I mostly kept to myself and stayed out of people's way." I said.

"That's not the story I got. I heard you were a little in-house accountant, like that guy in *Shawshank Redemption*."

"Are you kidding? My daughter is missing and you're talking about movies?" I wanted to pop the guy.

"So did you maybe *not* offer help to someone who wanted it? You know, piss someone off in any way?" he said, ignoring my outburst.

"I mean there were some guys who hated everyone but nobody in particular stands out. And even if they did, why would they take my daughter?"

"Well, they all knew you worked at a bank and had a doctor wife. Maybe it's a ransom situation."

"Or what?" I asked.

"Or maybe you fell into your old gambling routine and lost to the wrong guy. Maybe he is using your daughter as collateral." He slugged back the last of his coffee.

"I haven't gambled since my arrest." I said, seething. But I was also filled with shame. I knew it made sense for him to go there. I had no one to blame but myself. My addiction would haunt me forever. I swallowed my anger and pushed forward. This was about Sierra, not me. "If there was a ransom? Shouldn't they have called by now?"

"I haven't worked too many kidnappings. But usually they make contact within 24 to 48 hours. It could be any time now. We can put a tap on your phone if you consent to it."

"Yes, of course. Let's do it now." I stood, eager to take action in any way possible. "But shouldn't we call the FBI or somebody more experienced in kidnapping to help us?"

"Already contacted them this morning. The Child Abduction team should be here by noon, and I'm pretty sure they are going to need some of the same information I am asking you. You can't spend a couple years inside without making enemies with someone."

I have to admit, there was a big part of me that tried to pretend those years of my life never happened. I had a small dark cell in the corner of my mind where I threw all of those memories. It was my way of moving forward.

"Mr. Hart?"

"I know. I'm thinking. Give me a minute."

"Sure, but you know time is a factor here. With each passing minute your daughter could be another mile away from home. Maybe you should dig deep and help her out."

I felt pressure building in the base of my skull. I wanted to strangle this asshole cop, but I knew I had to concentrate on Sierra. This wasn't about me. Then it hit me. *Sausage*. "There was this guy we all called Sausage. He had a tumor that made his feet and hands and face really big. His fingers looked like sausages—hence the name. Anyway, he didn't like me from the start. I called him out on something he said. Can't even remember what it was now. Anyway, a couple of his boys jumped me one morning in the yard. It took me a few weeks to recover but when I was back in the mix, he pretty much stayed away. Then, over a year later, he had one of his boys ask if I might be able to help with a financial issue. I figured "no" wasn't really a viable option so I agreed to hear him out. It was obvious the guy was only trying to find a way to avoid paying child support for his five children. New York doesn't let an incarcerated parent lower their payment while serving time. By the time he was released, he was going to owe over twenty-five thousand dollars to his ex-wives. I guess one of his friends had used a loophole he hoped I could help him use, too. But I wanted no part in helping him skip out on those kids completely. It was another couple of weeks in the infirmary for me. We didn't cross paths again. I don't even know his real name. That was a year before I was released. He got out a few months before I did."

"And that's it? That's all you got for me? Sausage?" Detective Rock shook his head. "And you sure there you didn't owe anything before jail time? Anyone looking to collect? A bookie? A loan shark? I need something to go on, here."

"I went in owing only the bank. That's how I ended up in the situation in the first place. I'd paid my debts to anyone that would pose a threat to me or my family. I swear."

"I get it. But if you think of anyone that we should check out; call me." Detective Rock handed me his card. "And we'll see if we can locate this Sausage guy just in case."

I pushed back my chair and stood. "Look, I know what you're thinking and I can't blame you, but I lost my great job, my wife left me, my daughter stopped speaking to me, and I went to prison all so that I could keep those people from going anywhere near my family. I paid my debts and never looked back. This has to be about something else." I wished I was as convinced as I sounded. The not knowing anything sent my mind down the darkest roads possible.

Day 14 – 10/18
Biked 18 miles

Bread's gone. Two apples and one orange left.

For the record, cleaning yourself with water and a washcloth is NOT satisfying. It's cold & impossible to rinse. At least my surroundings are clean. I haven't seen any signs of mice, cobwebs, or bugs. Pro: I don't have to think about them crawling around while I sleep. Con: Can it be good if there is nothing else living down here? I guess I just need to keep my mind off it—writing helps.

I met Tia by accident on the first day of eighth grade. In English class, my pen exploded all over my new Abercrombie t-shirt. Luckily Mr. Burdick didn't make a big deal when I dashed off to the bathroom. Although, he probably thought it was a female thing and that was even more embarrassing. As I slammed through the bathroom door, I almost crushed Tia's hand as she crawled out from underneath a stall.

"Oh my God. I knew someone was going to come in here!" her face turned crimson.

"I'm sorry. I was just, are you . . . ?" I struggled to form a sentence.

"Stuck," Tia stood up and checked her jeans for damage. "The lock on the door; I couldn't get it and nobody else was in here so I just figured I'd crawl out."

"Oh yeah; they do that. You have to pull the door toward you and jiggle the slide lock at the same time." I explained, washing the ink off my hands. She took the sink next to me.

"Thanks. I'll try that next time," she said. I stared at the stubborn stain on my shirt as if I could will it away.

"Alcohol might take out the dye." She ran her fingers through her hair and I stole a peek at her in the mirror. She had dark hair with light highlights in a cut I guess you could call pixie-ish. Her eyes were dark brown, almost black, and she had the longest eyelashes I'd ever seen. She didn't appear to be wearing any make-up.

"I'm Tia," she said.

"Sierra. I take it you are new?"

"Yep. Just moved from Syracuse two weeks ago. My dad is the new superintendent."

"Oh. Well, welcome to Laketown. And thanks for the stain advice. I'm going to go see if the nurse has any alcohol." I headed toward the exit.

"Sure, and thanks for the lock lesson." When I was partially down the hall, she called after me and asked what period I had lunch.

"Fifth," I whispered back.

"Me too. See you there?"

"Sure." I smiled. It was the first of many lunches. My exploding pen turned out to be the bit of luck I had been waiting for. The next three years ended up being pretty great thanks to Tia.

I think my mom was both relieved and a little sad when I began spending most of my free time with my new friend. But we did spend more time at our house than at Tia's. She had six-year old twin brothers who rarely gave us any peace when we were around. We usually had my house to ourselves.

Tia definitely introduced me to a whole new world. Her parents were very nice, but very strict. She was not allowed to see R-rated movies, have open access to the internet, or watch TV during the school week. However, I quickly learned she had found ways to educate herself. Online dating sites were her playground. In fact she had begged my mom to let her help set up an account so she could start dating again. I was very relieved when my mom said "absolutely not!"

Instead, Tia had made a sport of creating fictitious profiles with magazine pictures. She used these accounts to chat with unsuspecting suitors. She had two female profiles and one male, Chaz. He was her favorite.

Chaz was 28, liked surfing, skiing, and beach volleyball. She created his picture from Ryan Gosling's body and the face of a guy in our Land's End catalog. He lived in Florida and New York and he worked in finance. After chatting with various women for a bit, "Chaz" would find a way to let them down gently. Tia only used the free sites, so the prospects weren't that great. At times, I found it quite entertaining, but occasionally she took things too far and I felt bad for the hopefuls actually seeking companionship. This hobby started many dating discussions. Tia felt it was all great practice for later in life.

After watching my parents split up, I was less interested in putting myself out there. Tia saw high school as our very own dating website, filled with potential perfect matches. She had no problem finding potential boyfriends; but she wasn't so great at having real conversations with them.

One of the guys she had her eye on was Dave Braun. We had been in school together my whole life, but I hadn't really thought about him much. All that changed fairly quickly.

Dave Braun

In high school, I can honestly say I had three loves in my life: running, cooking, and Sierra Hart. There was just something about her. The only way I can begin to explain it, is to start where it started for me.

I had known Sierra for years. We grew up in the same small town and were in the same grade at school. Plus, everyone in town knew about her dad's embezzlement scandal. Then we started running cross country together. Before that, I had always played football in the fall to stay in shape for basketball, which was my true passion. Freshman year, my buddy Jack convinced me to join the cross country team with him so he could drop a few pounds. I figured why the hell not? I wasn't that into football, I knew how much Jack hated the extra weight. He was one of those guys that had to wear the "husky" sizes in elementary school. When everyone else climbed out of the ugly pit called puberty and thinned out; he didn't. I mean, he wasn't ugly. He was a good looking guy just carrying around a few extra pounds. Besides, he made fun of himself before anyone else could so people left him alone.

As it turned out, I was better at running than even basketball. I loved that I was in complete control of my performance. I could run anywhere, anytime; just me and the path ahead. I didn't really notice Sierra much freshman year because I was still seeing Julie. Plus, Jack and I mostly kept to ourselves at practice.

I suddenly noticed Sierra during our state qualifying track meet. There were only 10 team members that had made it this far, four men and six women. We had been told to stand as a team and cheer one another on. As I looked over the list, I noticed I was trying to qualify in the exact same three events as Sierra: 1600m run, 3200m run, 3200m relay.

We gathered to cheer the girls on in their 3200m relay. Like me, Sierra was the anchor. It was sunny and in the low sixties. We had gotten lucky for a New York spring day. The gun sounded and we yelled as our first two girls held their own. It was a tight race but we were solidly in second place when our third girl, Carrie, grabbed the baton. She lost a little ground as they rounded their last turn and ended up in fourth. She looked angry as she approached Sierra. We all watched in horror as Carrie threw her arm out with the baton and released the baton before Sierra had a hold on it. I felt a pang in my chest as it bounced off the track.

Sierra simply picked up the baton and bolted. They would be disqualified, but we were trained to run it out anyway. I watched her go; we all did, in awe. I don't know how I had never seen it before, but watching her gave me chills on my arms, like when you hear your favorite band live. A combination of adrenaline and I don't know what. It sounds lame, but it was beautiful to watch. Sierra ran with such ease and grace that it looked like she was barely trying. By the time they rounded the last corner and headed into the final stretch, she had moved back up to second and was closing in on first. It didn't matter that a win wouldn't actually count, we all cheered anyway.

"Go Sierra. Go. You got this." We yelled. Well, most of us yelled. Carrie just stood there sulking. And the runners approached I could see it in her face. There was no way she wasn't going to take this thing. And she did, taking the leader down right at the line. If it hadn't been for that baton drop they would have gone to states. As soon as Sierra crossed the line, Carrie was on her.

"Thanks a lot, Sierra. That was my last shot at States ever. You're just like your dad—stealing right outta other people's hands." Sierra looked like she'd been slapped. She started to speak but stopped, glancing up toward the stands. She mumbled "sorry," looked at all of us and jogged off toward the tent.

"You didn't have to be such a bitch about it," Maggie, the first runner, said to Carrie, the rest of the girls nodding behind her.

"Yeah, it wasn't exactly her fault," I said.

"What are you trying to say there, big red?" Carrie stepped towards me, but I heard the announcer call us for the men's 3200relay. Warming up, I tried to focus but found myself wondering where Sierra had gone. Suddenly, it was really important to me that she watch my race.

Lebraun had gotten us a healthy lead but our third runner had shin splints pretty bad. By the time I was up, we'd dropped to fourth. My stomach filled with butterflies at the thought of dropping the baton, too. I waited for Jack's approach. I heard him yell "stick" just as it crossed my palm. I grabbed and ran, thanking God that it went smoothly. I had the third place guy in my sights and closed in on him pretty quickly, but there was a bigger gap between me and the first two. I had to get us to second or we wouldn't get through to states. There were two seniors on our team, too. I caught a flash of my mom's voice in the stands. I felt good turning into the second 400 and decided to kick a little earlier than normal. I picked up my pace and closed the gap a bit, locking my eyes on a spot ahead of the guy in second place and pushing myself harder. As we headed into the last stretch I gave everything I had left. My chest was burning and my hamstrings were screaming, but I didn't give up. I could hear our whole team screaming for me and quickly wondered if Sierra was among them. I leaned into the finish line and prayed. My team ran up to me, clapping me on the back.

"Did we do it?" I asked.

"Photo finish," Lebraun said. "Man, where did that come from? You were on fire that last lap."

"I don't know. I just really wanted to take him. Besides, it's your senior year, right?" I flashed a smile at him.

"Damn straight!" Lebraun yelled. He fixated on the announcer's booth. I looked around and found that Sierra was standing a few steps away.

"Hey, nice run," I said, breath still heavy.

"Thanks. You too," she nodded toward the finish line.

"For what it's worth, I saw the whole thing. It wasn't your fault." I looked up and my stomach flipped when she looked right back. Her eyes were an intense hazel. Again, why hadn't I noticed her sooner?

Before she could respond, the announcer came on to the loud speaker, "The final results in the men's 3200 relay are as follows. Third place Bethlehem High School-" That was all we needed to hear. We had done it. Our relay team was going to states! We were all whistles, high fives, and fist pumps.

I turned around to see Sierra cheering right along with us. "Congratulations, guys."

"Should have been both teams," Carrie grumbled, crossing her arms across her chest.

"Give it a rest Carrie," I said. She dropped her jaw, glared at us, and headed back toward the tent.

The rest of the meet was relatively successful, especially for me and Sierra. I got two personal records, taking first in the 3200m and second in the 1600m. Both qualified me for States. My coach asked what had gotten into me. I silently thought "Sierra," but said, "Guess I'm feeling good today." Sierra won both her races with apparent ease. This pissed Carrie off even more.

On the bus ride home, I tuned out the guys and found myself watching Sierra as she listened to music and read. God, I sound like a stalker or something. Anyway, that's when it all started for me. Still, it took a lot longer to get her to notice me back.

We were down to seven people training for states; Sierra was the only girl distance runner, which was lucky for me because that meant she ran with us. I began running next to her as casually as I could. She didn't seem to mind. But I couldn't work up the nerve to ask her to hang outside of track.

All too soon, the season was over. Our men's relay team placed fourth at States, and I placed seventh in both of my individual events. Sierra also just missed qualifying for nationals with fourth and fifth place in her events. Lebraun came in a disappointing third after scratching on one of his jumps, just missing nationals. His career wasn't over, though. He had been recruited for college. He'd worked hard to become the first in his family to go to college.

Lebraun had also impressed my dad, working for him during the summer doing construction. He'd helped him get proper attention from the right colleges. Work ethic was important to both my parents; a trait passed down through generations. My grandfather worried that if he made life too easy, they would live off their trust funds. In any case, working wasn't exactly negotiable in our family. It was a given. Lucky for me, my mom had the restaurant. Otherwise, I would have spent my summer building houses or strip malls in the humidity.

Instead, I looked forward to that summer at *The Kitchen*; especially because my mom had promised to let me work as sauté chef on weekend nights. That probably sounds like a shit schedule to most people, but I loved it. Those were the busiest nights and I got a rush from the pressure. That summer was pretty sweet; if only I'd known what was to follow in the fall.

Dr. Laura Hart

When your world is shattered you don't think about mundane, everyday things like the mail. I think a small scream may have escaped my mouth when I heard the knock on the door. Patrick came running.

"Sorry, Dr. H, it's just Paul, your mailman." We heard through the door. "I'm sorry to bother you at such a bad time, but I can't fit any more letters in your box. Can I leave it out here for you?" Patrick placed his arm around me.

"Sure." I hadn't used my voice in a while. I cleared my throat and tried again. "Sure, Paul. Just leave it there. Thanks."

"We're all praying for you." We listened as his boots descended the steps. We stood there for a moment, looking at the door as if Sierra would miraculously waltz through it like nothing had happened.

Patrick finally crossed the kitchen, opened the door. The lawn came alive as the media watched. But he simply brought the mail inside. Sierra had been gone for eight days. In addition to our regular collection of bills, flyers, and catalogs, it looked like there were a number of cards.

"Is that your mail?" Sheryl seemed to appear out of nowhere. "Jesus, I thought we had someone on the mail. Don't touch it without gloves." I'd never heard her raise her voice.

She recovered quickly "Sorry. Here, it'll be faster if we all help." She held out a box of gloves.

"You think there could be something in here from the kidnappers?" I asked.

"We can't rule it out." Sheryl said. The three of us began sorting. I couldn't believe the outpouring of love and support from the local community, not to mention the people across the nation who had seen the news.

I had gotten up to get the whistling teapot when Patrick froze.

"Oh God," he said.

The typed note was on a plain white, half sheet of paper.

"He was here? That means he was here doesn't it? And it has been in our mailbox for who knows how long? What is today?" I felt a burst of adrenaline.

"It's Saturday. The drop is tomorrow." Sheryl said and looked at her watch.

Want your kid? bring $175K to Anderson arena during the soccer turnamint on sunday buy the turnamint bag and put the money in it in locker 609 in the visiters locker room by 1PM. put the BROKE sign on the locker and leeve. Mr Heart must do it.
NO COPS OR FBI!

I did the same. "It's almost 4. We can't get that kind of money in time. What do we do?" I asked.

"Just hold on a minute. I'm sorry, but I need to talk to my team before we discuss further." Sheryl walked out of ear shot.

"Why didn't we think to get the mail? Why didn't anyone tell us to get the mail?" I looked at Patrick. "They're the experts. Why are we just doing this now?" I dropped my head into my hands and all but screamed. "There is no way we can get that money in time. It's not possible. What do we do?"

"I don't know Laura. We have to just hold tight and see what Sheryl says. But this is good. It means we can get her back. She's not just gone. Someone has her and will have left a trail, made mistakes."

"But they *have* her. *Criminals* have Sierra." I stared at the pile of mail. "Surely if we can't pay it in time, they'll ask again; right?"

My mind was buzzing with ways to get the money to them today. I paced the kitchen. "When you worked at the bank did they have special rules for ransom situations? Do they make arrangements to get you money fast?" I asked.

"Sometimes, I'm sure they can make special arrangements, but we only have two regional banks here. They don't have that kind of cash to loan out to someone." He hesitated for a minute and then said, "Especially not for me." I saw what he was thinking and my stomach dropped. Of course.

"So help me, Patrick if something you've done has anything to do with this-"

Before I could continue, Sheryl came back in the room.

Patrick Hart

When you break someone's trust, you damage the spine of your entire relationship. No matter how much you work to rebuild over time, the unexpected can resurface that old injury. When we found the note and Laura turned on me, I knew she hadn't ever completely trusted me again. Could I blame her?

Sheryl told us forensics was on the way to process the note and we had to meet another agent to discuss how to respond to the ransom demand. She instructed us to finish sifting through the mail, in case any further communication had been left.

I reached out for Laura's gloved hand. It felt strange, yet fitting. I knew there was more than just latex between us. She started to pull away but I held on tighter and looked her straight in the eyes, "Laura, I swear on our daughter's life that I owe nothing to anyone. Nothing. I don't know any more about this than you do." She didn't respond but I could see the hurt and confusion in her eyes. From that point on, our missing daughter became partially my fault.

Day 18 – 10/22

Biked 18 miles

Finished first jar of Peanut Butter. One left.

Never underestimate the damage aluminum foil can do. And never underestimate duck tape—it makes a great Band-Aid. Wonder what I do if I get really hurt? Being alone is hard.

Two weeks seems like forever when you are alone. Being an only child to a temporarily single parent, I had my fair share of alone time growing up. Of course, I always felt safe then. This is different. This sucks. I don't hear any noise. You'd think maybe that would be comforting, but I think it might be worse. My screams fall flat. Not even my own echo will talk to me. Even crying seems pointless when nobody is here to hand you a tissue. But I still cry. Sometimes over strange things.

Like, one of the brands of cereal I have down here is Kellogg's Corn Pops. When I saw the box I burst into tears. I know. Crying over cereal? But it made me miss Tia. She did this research paper in health class on harmful chemicals in common foods and for a while she became a little obsessed with the topic. One morning after sleeping over, I found her in our pantry with the garbage can. She had taken it upon herself to rid our shelves of harmful foods and was appalled at some of the items an "awesome pediatrician" allowed her own child to eat. I'd pulled the Corn Pops out of the garbage and asked what harmful ingredient they contained. *Jet fuel* was her response. Apparently an ingredient shared a chemical in common with jet fuel. I think it was called BTH or BHT or something. Clearly, my keeper is not up on the latest nutritional data. I wish Tia were here right now. She'd find a way to make me laugh even in this awful place.

Dave Braun

By July 4th of that summer in 2005, I was ready for a break. I usually worked the Sunday night shift, but my mom closed the restaurant for the holiday. Jack threw a party at his family cabin that overlooked the lake. It was a perfect spot to catch the fireworks. His parents had gone to visit his sister and her new baby in Maine. I knew half the high school would be there, since there isn't much else to do in this town when you're a teenager.

His dad kept beer on tap but we all still contributed our own illegal beverage offerings. By the time the sun set and we readied the fireworks, I felt no pain. I knew I was crashing there that night so I let my guard down and drank more than normal. Jack and I had dominated at beer pong—great for my ego, not for my sobriety. As the first fireworks shot into the air, I felt someone plop down to my right on the blanket. I assumed it was one of the guys, until I realized the air smelled like oranges. I turned right into the face of Victoria Spencer and almost dropped my beer. Imagine Britney Spears in her prime. We are talking hot as shit—a senior who starred in every play both the school and the community theater produced.

"Dave Braun, right?" she asked. *Holy shit, she knows my name?*

"What's up?" I tried to sound casual, like hot chicks approached me every day.

"Well, I heard that Jack's parents have a sauna out back. And Rachel," she gestured to the friend sitting next to her, "and I were wondering if you and Jack could give it a try with us after the fireworks are over."

I was glad for the cover of darkness because I felt heat crawling into my face as visions ran through my head. I didn't know what I had done to earn this privilege, but I was so in. "Sure, I'll go give him the heads up. I need another beer anyway." I started to get up when I heard my sister's voice echoing in my head, "all women love chivalry. Manners are sexy."

"Oh sorry, do you guys need anything?" I asked.

"Actually, we don't really like beer. Do you think you could find us some rum and cokes?" Victoria asked. She looked so hot in the flash of the fireworks, a small white cover-up barely covering her black bikini. I could see rosy cleavage peeking out of the top, from too much sun during the day. She had her hair in two braids, like a naughty catholic girl out of a video. Again, I was grateful for the darkness. I was so getting hard just looking at her.

"No problem," I had no clue if there was rum, but I was willing to get whatever. Jack was going to shit his pants when I told him. Girls like Victoria and Rachel went for guys like Lebraun all the time, but Jack and I weren't usually chosen by the hot chicks. We weren't pariahs by any means, but Victoria and Rachel were at the top of the pyramid—both social and during half-time.

When I filled Jack in on our grand fortune, he busted into his mom's secret-but-not-so-secret liquor stash in the cupboard above the refrigerator to get the girls some rum for their cokes. I took them back the drinks as he set off to get the sauna ready. We didn't want the party to move in there with us, so we had to be quiet about it. Luckily it was in the far back corner of the house, away from the party.

"Here you go. " I handed the girls their drinks as if I wasn't shocked to find they were still there.

"I hope you made 'em good and strong," Victoria purred (okay it sounded like purring to me at the time). "Nobody has had anything good to drink all day and we feel way behind the party, ya know?"

"Well, there's plenty more where that came from." I heard myself say, ready to get them whatever they desired, hoping that included me.

"These fireworks are so lame," Victoria whined. "I feel like we've seen the same show since we were kids."

"Yeah, they need to crank it up a notch—spend a little more money on fun and less on crap like the tallest flag pole east of the Mississippi," Rachel added.

"It would be cool if they could set it to music somehow—you know like in Boston and New York and shit." I actually thought the fireworks were fine, but I had never really spent much time contemplating them.

"Great idea, Dave," Victoria said, grabbing my arm. I liked where this was headed.

"Maybe they could get one of the local radio stations to broadcast the music so we could all tune in wherever we are and listen while we watch." I knew they did that with the Boston pops because my mom recorded it every year for when we got home from the local show.

"OMG, you have got to suggest it to your dad and see if he can get the town board to make it happen," she said. Sometimes I forgot that everyone knew my family here. My oldest sister, Karen, used it to her advantage all the time, but my sister Izzy and I wanted people to actually respect us without the connection. For a minute I wondered if Victoria was only interested in me for that reason. But then her tit brushed against my elbow. My dick and I decided right then and there, we didn't really care, at least not that night.

The fireworks ended and I told the girls we needed to hang back a bit until the party died down because Jack didn't want everyone to find out about the sauna. They seemed cool with it. They finished their drinks and headed to the bathroom, and I ran off to get us all another round and check on Jack. The last keg had run dry and people had begun moving on.

By eleven, there were only a handful of people milling about. The bonfire appeared to be down to a manageable size so Jack, the girls and I headed to the sauna. We were all still in bathing suits so the girls slipped off their cover-ups and I took off my shirt. Jack, still very self-conscious about his body, left his T-shirt on. I have to admit Rachel was no slouch in the body department either. I couldn't tell you the color of her suit but I do know it looked good. We slipped into the room.

At this point, I think we were all pretty wasted which made it easier. If I had been sober I would probably have made an ass of myself. The girls sat together and we sat on either side of them. The room had benches on three sides which was good because as much as I love Jack I didn't want to sit real close to him while we both sweat our balls off. Victoria suggested we play I—never.

"I've never made out with a girl," Victoria kept her eyes on mine as she took a big swallow.

"That is hot!" said Jack, finishing off his beer. "But you didn't drink, Rachel. Who is the lucky chick if it wasn't you?"

We all looked at Victoria.

"This girl at summer camp; It was a dare and let's just say I never back down," again Victoria looked right at me.

"You could do it with Rachel, too," Jack suggested. "If *she* dares," he lifted his eyebrows in Rachel's direction. Rachel smiled back, leaned over, and grabbed Victoria's face with her hands. She slowly ran her tongue back and forth across Victoria's closed lips.

"Fuck..." Jack whispered. Victoria twisted toward Rachel so they were both straddling the bench, face to face. Their eyes were locked. Victoria looked at me for a beat and pulled Rachel up onto her lap so her legs were wrapped around Victoria. They kissed, just a hint of tongue slipping in and out. Rachel slid her hands up into Victoria's thick blond hair and pulled her in more. I can't speak for Jack, but all I could think was "this beats the fuck out of fireworks." It was over too fast. The girls separated, smiling like little vixens.

"Your turn, Dave," Victoria said.

At first, I thought she meant kissing, but then I realized she meant in the game. "Right, and I follow that with what-" Jack interrupted.

"How about: I've never kissed a girl on both sets of her lips?" But his beer was empty. "Shit, I'm out!"

"It's my turn. I'll go get us another round," I said, hoping the girls wouldn't come to their senses and leave.

"Actually, I'm hot. It's probably not smart to stay in here too long. Let's all get out." Victoria said. *Great*, I had ruined the moment.

"Well, then let's cool off ladies. To the lake we go! You go get a fresh round, use the facilities, whatever you need to do to keep yourselves comfortable, and I will shut this down and fire up the Gator. Don't take all day because your chariot awaits." He bowed and extended a hand toward the door like some fuckin' prince in a play. The girls laughed and headed out the door. This was why I loved Jack. He could keep a party going.

The girls seemed to enjoy the rough back-road Gator ride to the lake. The moon was almost full which gave all of us that bluish glow. I thought, this is what it is supposed to feel like to be a teenager; this sense of freedom and excitement about what might happen at any given moment. Clearly really wasted (and yes, our driver), Jack was the first to strip down and jump into the water, yelling "Happy fuckin' Fourth of July!"

Rachel and Victoria laughed, and slipped out of their bikinis. Or tried to. Rachel must have been more wasted than I realized because she kept tripping on her bottoms. They were caught in a fit of laughter and I couldn't decide whether I should offer to help or just watch. Victoria's ass looked like a moon-lit heart. I wanted to touch her, but didn't want to scare her off. I decided to follow Jack.

"Carpe Diem," I yelled and jumped in. It was chilly, but felt great. I turned and watched as the girls ran down the embankment and jumped in after us, their tits bouncing with each step. They looked like heaven.

"Dude, I don't know what we did right. But thank you, God!" Jack yelled to the sky. I laughed. The girls squealed as they came up for air.

"Holy shit. It's freezing!" Victoria yelled.

"Have you ever heard that there are a bunch of old cars at the bottom of this lake from like when people break through the ice and sink?" Rachel asked.

"Yeah, but I don't know if it's true." I said. We all remained silent for a few minutes, taking in the stars, the sounds of the lake lapping against the shore. I felt a sudden warmth surround me.

"Oh dude, Jack, did you just piss?" I whispered.

"Hey, when nature calls who am I to deny." Jack announced, shamelessly.

"Gross, dude. You were way too close; I felt the water temperature change." I quickly swam further away from him and closer to the girls. As I moved closer, I realized that Victoria was floating on her back, the full frontal shot was pretty close to perfection.

"It's beautiful isn't it?" she said, looking up.

"Absolutely," I said, although we were talking about two completely different views. The liquid courage kicked in and I swam up to her. She dropped back down into the water so she was facing me.

"Hi," she said smiling.

"Hello yourself," I said and reached out to touch her arm.

"Goose bumps."

"It's freezing," her voice shook when she spoke. I pulled her against me. She wrapped her legs around me and my whole body responded.

"Better?" I asked.

"Getting there," she said, shocking me when her hand reached down and grabbed my cock. That was all the invitation I needed. I pulled her face to mine. She tasted like strawberries and rum. We had been making out in the water for a few minutes when Rachel said she needed to get warm. None of us had thought to grab towels so we pulled on our suits and raced our frozen asses back to Dave's. Victoria and I found the closest empty bedroom, hormones raging. At that point, I don't think anyone cared where they landed. Compared to Julie, sex with Victoria was like an Olympic sport. When they call cheerleaders athletes—they are not kidding.

So—why am I telling you all of this when I am supposed to be talking about Sierra? I guess because for you to understand where all of this ends, you need to understand how it started. Everything and everyone played a part.

By the time Jack and I surfaced the next morning, the girls were gone. I figured it was just one lucky night. We grabbed breakfast at the Egg Time Diner and rehashed what we remembered from the night before. There were definitely some hazy points. I learned Jack's luck had run out when Rachel started throwing up soon after we got back to the cabin. Jack admitted he had considered offering her a toothbrush so he could still attempt some action, but his conscience was still sober enough to stop him. Gotta love Jack.

Later that afternoon, I was trying to run the alcohol out of my system when I got a text from Victoria. One of us had obviously entered her number into my contacts at some point. The text got me a little excited if you know what I mean.

Hey D. crzy nite. Bit of a blur. Take 2 at my place 2nite? 9ish. I'll b thirsty so help me out?

I didn't want to seem too eager so I made myself wait until I finished my run, showered, and ate a late lunch before responding.

> DAVE: *I'm in. J too or solo? I aim to quench your thirst.*
> VICTORIA: *Solo.*
> DAVE: *Filling your Solo solo at 9*
> VICTORIA: ☺

And that was basically that. The rest of the summer I spent most of my non-working time working out (in the biblical sense) with Victoria. I never knew a teenage girl could actually have a higher sex drive than a guy. I mean, she wasn't supposed to hit her sexual prime until she was like thirty, right? God help the guy she's with at that point. She may need more than one.

I fully expected that when school started up again, Victoria would drop me like a bad habit. I was a lowly junior non-stud and she was pretty much the hottest senior, probably even *the* hottest girl at our school. But this was not to be the case. I didn't get that lucky.

The first red flag went up right after we went back to school. Juniors and Seniors had open campus lunch privileges so Victoria and I agreed to spend our lunch enjoying each other instead of food. I, however, had the typical metabolism of a sixteen year old guy and was starving by lunchtime. We were supposed to meet at my car right after fourth period but I cut out of study hall a little early so I could duck into the cafeteria and buy a sandwich. My neighbor was the cafeteria cashier. I mowed her lawn for free so she never said a word about me buying lunch when I wasn't supposed to be in there.

It was nice out, so I decided to walk around the outside of the school to the student parking lot. As I approached the parking lot, I could hear Victoria talking to Rachel. I should have turned the corner, but I was curious to hear what they said when I wasn't around.

"...doesn't count, then?" Rachel asked, sounding pissed.

"I'm not saying it doesn't count as a number two, Rachel. I'm saying the rules are that you have to wait at least three weeks in between. We all agreed on that. Otherwise it's too damn easy. Anyone could bang their way down the list by Christmas. So Jack can count as your number two but Christian cannot count as your number three. Unless you turn around and do him again now that it's been more than three weeks. Jesus, Rachel, it's not brain surgery."

"That's bullshit. You're *still* sleeping with Dave. There should be a rule about that. How are you going to move past four if you're still with him? Or is your number four conveniently not a sex thing?" Rachel asked.

"Not your problem. Besides, you should be glad I'm with Dave. It gives you a chance to catch up to the rest of us." Victoria sounded almost evil from where I stood.

"You know V, sometimes you can be such a bitch. I gotta go. I'm supposed to meet Bess for lunch. But I think we all need to go over the rules again. And vote. This wasn't only your idea, you know." Rachel walked off.

I waited a few minutes before walking around the corner. I decided not to admit I had heard the conversation until later. It might ruin our "lunch."

Later in her bedroom, I watched as Victoria's breath slowly returned to normal. She was splayed out across my chest, her hair tickling my chin. I ran my finger along the curve of her shoulder and around to her breast. She squirmed as my finger brought her nipple to life.

"You want more?" she teased, lifting her head up to look at me.

I smiled. "How am I number four?" I hadn't meant to say it but I was too curious. I saw her eyes darken for a second.

"It's nothing, just a stupid game we came up with last year. It doesn't matter. You don't want to hear about the stupid crap we girls do for fun, do you?" She ran her finger lightly across the skin next to my hip bone. It always gave me chills.

"Well, normally I would say yes, but when I am a part of it, I kinda want to know. Are we in the middle of some fuckin' game here, V? That's pretty messed up, don't you think?" I moved her hand away and sat up.

"God, Dave. It's seriously not a big deal. Can't we drop it?" She looked around for her clothes.

"If it's not a big deal then why not tell me?" I slid my boxers on. She didn't say anything as she dressed. I dressed, too and sat back down on the edge of her bed.

"Fine; I'll tell you. But you're going to take it all wrong and get pissed over nothing." She looked in her mirror and fluffed her hair.

"I'm all ears," I leaned back onto her bed, my hands behind my head.

"Last year, I overheard my parents talking about how my grandmother had created a bucket list with some of her friends. A few nights later, a bunch of us were hanging out and I told them about this bucket list thing. We started coming up with things we wanted to be sure we did before we died. A few rum and cokes later, we decided to make a list of things we should do before we graduate. By the end of the night, we had drafted the rules to the Fuck-It List." She walked past me toward the door. "Come on, we gotta get back. I have a test in Econ."

"Then you better talk faster. I want to know what it means to be number four on your Fuck-It List. Who is number five? Or one through three?" I stood up to follow her out to my car.

"See this is exactly why I didn't want to tell you." She grabbed a yogurt out of her fridge, not offering me anything to eat. That should have been a red flag, too.

"I'm not mad, I just want to know what the deal is. Because from where I'm sitting it sounds like I'm a pawn in your little game." We got in the car and I backed out of her driveway to head back to school.

"The rules say we aren't supposed to tell anyone about the list so you can't spread this around, okay? Vault this shit."

"Whatever." I said.

"Seriously. I'll get DQ'd if they find out. And you know how I feel about losing."

"Just get to the point, V."

"So we made up six lists, one for each of us. Each list has 10 items to complete, but in a random order. The lists were folded, put in a pillowcase, and we each picked out our list. Anyway, my number four was to fuck a redhead." She flashed me a sheepish grin.

"So that was what the 4th of July was all about. You were just checking a box? And Jack was on Rachel's list?"

"Number two for Rachel was to fuck a fat guy. Sorry. Jack's fun, too."

"That's really messed up. I feel used or dirty or something."

"Listen, the whole reason I suggested the redhead thing for the list was because of you. When I saw you in that game against Genesee Valley last year, I just couldn't get you out of my mind. You have no idea how hot you look on a basketball court." We pulled up in front of the school, but neither of us made a move to get out.

"So you're saying I should feel flattered?" I looked out across the parking lot and tried to decide how I did feel about this. I realized I didn't really feel anything. *What does that say about me?* She gave me the full pout.

"It was supposed to be a onetime thing. But we had so much fun, I wanted to keep hangin' out with you and now here we are."

"Here we are. You and number four." I said.

"So now what? Are we done?" I sensed a hint of anger in her voice.

"Do you want to be done?"

"No. I'm still having fun. Aren't you?" she suggestively folded a piece of gum into her mouth.

"I don't know."

Victoria straddled my lap and flipped the seat back. Leaning in, she looked me directly in the eyes, and pulled the gum slowly out of her mouth. I could feel her breath on my face. She kissed me gently, probing at first but slowly intensifying the pressure with her tongue. Damn, she was skilled in this department for sure. I started to kiss back and she pulled away "Does that feel fun?" I was pretty sure she could feel the answer through my pants.

"You gotta get to Econ. It starts in three minutes." I responded. She shrugged, popped her gum back in her mouth, opened the door on my side and rolled out.

"So see you after practice?" she asked, reaching for her purse.

"Sure," I said. I watched as she walked away. I realized I'd never gotten her to explain one through three, or what she had planned next. Was she incapable of empathy? Wasn't that a characteristic of a psychopath? She looked back and blew me a kiss.

Dr. Laura Hart

The plan to drop the ransom money terrified me. The agents claimed the kidnapper was an amateur—most likely someone we knew. The drop money was marked and loaded with dye packs to make it traceable. They hoped to watch the drop spot, follow the money, and get Sierra back. I was terrified they would harm Sierra as soon as they got the money. We had no way to contact them.

I waited at home with a local officer and another member of the FBI's team while the operation was underway. The updates came in small sound bites. "He's on highway 86"; "No noticeable tail"; "The unmarked cars are right with him." "We've entered the arena parking area."

I tried to read the officers reactions but they were poker-faced and quiet. After they relayed that Patrick had parked, they went silent for a long time. I hated the mantle clock ticking slowly into the otherwise silent room. I panicked when the officer excused himself to the restroom. What if they needed him while he was gone? Then finally we heard; "the drop has been made." I prayed this would work. *Please let Sierra be safe.*

Dave Braun

I had promised not to tell anyone about the Fuck-It List, but growing up we had a rule that family was exempt from such promises. My birth was clearly unplanned, since Karen is older than me by twelve years, and Izzy by nine (her real name is Christy but I couldn't say that when I was little and Izzy stuck. She was more of an Izzy anyway). I basically grew up with three moms. Karen is a typical first born child; did well in school, sports, went to a great college, didn't cause much trouble or angst for my parents. She is VP of sales and marketing for the family business. We got along fine, but there was too big of an age gap to be really close.

Izzy, on the other hand, made every mistake she could. She never particularly liked school and begged my parents to let her audition for a performing arts school in Manhattan to no avail. She punished them for this decision as often as possible, dating guys out of high school, skipping school, dying her hair crazy colors, partying, sneaking out at night, and refusing to participate in any activity other than theater. In the end, this was what saved her from serious trouble. Izzy auditioned for any and all theatrical performances within a thirty mile radius. And she was really good. Her singing voice was decent but I loved watching her on stage. It's kind of crazy when your own sister can make you believe she is a completely different person. I am still her biggest fan. Izzy finally moved to Manhattan when she was accepted to NYU's theater program. But she dropped out after the first year. She said she'd rather my parents gave her that money for rent. She waited tables to cover the rest; it was a flexible enough job to attend auditions as needed. She won some lead roles in small productions, but her dream was Broadway. I understood her passion. I felt the same way about cooking. She was my biggest supporter, convincing my mom to let me start helping at The Kitchen when I was only twelve. So when I needed advice or just someone to talk to, I called Izzy.

She, of course, loved the idea of the Fuck-It List and immediately wanted to know what was on it to see if she'd checked them off before graduating herself, something I did not want to know. Izzy's sex life was a topic I actively avoided. But, as she pointed out, I had opened the door on this one.

"So, this chick, who you say is hot and popular, hooked up with you as a line item, but then realized how awesome you are and wants to keep you around?"

"Pretty much, though when you put it like that it makes me feel like her new pet," I said, watching the family dog, Tank, roll around under our apple tree. I always talked to Izzy in the back yard, out of parental ear shot.

"Seems like you answered your own question; hold on, Zach just got home."

"Wait, Zach moved in?"

"Yeah, but don't tell mom and dad. They don't know yet."

"I'll vault it."

"What?"

"Nothing. It's just something Victoria says. Secret's safe with me."

"So what are you going to do?"

"Part of me feels like I should dump her. But then I think am I crazy? This hot chick wants to hang with me, why would I ditch that?"

"First of all, you're a good looking guy Dave. I don't know why you're insecure. Maybe it's my fault for talking smack about your red hair when you were a kid. You don't have to settle for a bitch, trust me. Besides, if you had any real feelings for her, you would be pissed as hell about this list thing."

"I guess."

"What ever happened to that girl you run with all the time?"

"Sierra?"

"Yeah, it sounded like you really liked her."

"I don't know. I don't think Sierra thinks of me like that."

"Well, you won't ever know if you keep messing around with Victoria."

"Maybe."

"Okay, here it is, and then I gotta go or we'll be late for dinner: you like sleeping with Victoria but you would prefer to hang out with Sierra. My advice; get your fill of the good sex, but end it soon before Victoria squashes you like a bug. And whatever you do, don't break up with her. Make her feel like it was her decision. Otherwise, she will lash out. I've seen it time and again. Girls like that don't like to lose. Life is a game to them. K?" Izzy asked.

"Got it. Thanks." I said.

"Okay. Love you."

"Love you, too." I watched Tank chase a butterfly. "Life as a dog," I said under my breath. "Life as a dog."

Day 21 – 10/25

Biked 21 miles

Bathroom smells. Garbage piling up.

Good thing I decided to separate the recycling or it would be even worse. Going stir-crazy. I was trying to save the last fresh item for as long as I could; but I dreamt that I bit into brown mush. I ate my last apple and luckily it was still good.

I feel so helpless. Frustrated. Angry. Pissed. Trapped. Vulnerable. Humiliated. Fucked. It feels good to swear when you are mad at the world. It's like that scene in *Dead Poets Society* when Robin Williams makes Ethan Hawk's character release his barbaric yelp. Wonder what his advice would be for someone trapped in a nicely stocked cellar?

It still feels better to yell FUCK really loud. "Why am I here? Is there a point? Is this all happening for some big reason I will learn in the end? Or is this the end?"

You go through this point when you wonder if bad things happen to people because of something bad they did earlier in life. Like my dad. He did something wrong; he got punished.

But then that logic falls apart when you think about things like kids with cancer. Maybe I'm down here because I brought it on myself. I've been selfish and hurt people. Here I am busted by Karma and awaiting my final sentence. Like purgatory or that chunk of time between being found guilty and sentencing. The big question is, what to do while I wait?

Patrick Hart

The Anderson Arena, the drop location, was forty-five excruciatingly long minutes away from our house. I drove our car in case someone followed. Two unmarked cars would fall in line behind me along the route, although I don't know where. I just had to trust that they had it under control. I parked in lot B since C was closed off for buses only. I grabbed the money and went off in search of the bag I was instructed to buy. I immediately felt lost in a sea of pink, looking conspicuous in all black. As I got closer to the fields I saw a large banner with a pink Nike Swoosh that said "Help us Kick Breast Cancer." That explained all the pink.

I looked around as I waited in line, *Where are you?* I wondered. The air smelled like fallen leaves and popcorn; normally a pleasant fall smell. I was surrounded by happy families, enjoying the brisk sunny day that could become the worst in my life. Nobody looked like the type of person that would kidnap my daughter for money. But what did I know?

I finally made it through the line to purchase the tournament bag. Forty Bucks?! Obviously marked up to raise money for the cause. At least it came filled with a plethora of pink extras: a soccer ball, water bottle, adjustable shin guards, and a bleacher cushion. Everywhere I looked I saw people walking around with the same bag. I suddenly worried the agents might lose me in the crowd. Laura's words echoed in my head, "*They are experts we have to trust them.*" A local radio station blared music off to the left. The DJ had a group of people doing some sort of organized dance. There were food stands and other vendors. The facility had a number of fields with games in full swing. I prayed they could track the kidnapper through it all.

I made my way to the indoor facility to find the locker room. My hands were sweating in the biking gloves (they told me to wear them so they could print everything later). I was sure I stood out; but nobody seemed to give me a second glance. I located the doors to the locker rooms and realized there were both women's and men's. I hadn't thought about that, but I had to assume they meant the men's room.

I pushed the door and went in. There were a few boys inside, some dads, putting stuff in lockers, using the bathrooms. I found 609 easily since it was the only locker with a BROKEN note on it. I opened the door to place the bag inside and found yet another note. All it said was:

looze the zero 7-19-36

I put my foot up on the bench and pretended to tie my shoe to think it over. The last three numbers were obviously a lock combination. So that left their phonetic spelling of "*lose the zero*." I walked a few rows back to find locker 69. There was only one other kid in the row, changing out of his cleats. I fiddled with the lock until he left and then quickly unlocked the door, put the bag inside, and relocked it. I stood there for a minute as if Sierra would somehow magically appear. Nothing changed. I said a silent prayer, slipped the note in my pocket for them to analyze, and left.

I walked slowly; studying each person I passed for any sign that they had Sierra. A fruitless effort for sure, but I couldn't help myself. I wanted to walk right back in that locker room and sit vigil next to the money; it felt like my last connection to my daughter. But the instructions were clear. Obviously nobody would approach that locker with me sitting there. I had no choice but to follow the plan. I made my way back to my car and headed home, sick with fear that everything would go horribly wrong.

Dave Braun

A week after I ignored Izzy's excellent advice, I was still living life as Victoria's dog. What can I say; I let my penis think for me. Plus, I hadn't quite figured out how to get her to break up with me without pissing her off in the process. I was never any good at these relationship games. I stayed with Julie for a year and hadn't even really liked her that much, even from the start. She'd approached me one night at a party after the last basketball game of the season. I'd had a few beers and she seemed cute and interested. I was a fifteen year-old virgin, who was I to say no? A year later, she finally dumped me, claiming I never called her to do anything. She always did all of the work. That was that. She had moved on to some other guy before the week was out. But I never got the chance to work out a good break-up plan for Victoria. Sometimes life just happens to us.

Every other year, the cross country team had this meet in a logging town about an hour away. The course was hell: a mile and half up hill and a mile and a half back down. And it was literally a logging trail. We were running across little streams, big roots and branches, whatever one might encounter in the woods. It basically sucked the whole way. Even the downhill killed my knees. That year, it started to downpour about five minutes in. I normally like running in the rain, but it made this trail even more dangerous—muddy, slippery. Looking back, I think we were all lucky we didn't blow a knee or ankle or something.

In fact, I finished second mainly because I held back to avoid possible injury. The girls' raced the same course but started ten minutes later. We waited at the finish line for Sierra and Maggie. Normally our coach had us posted along the trail to cheer them on, but it wasn't really easy to do on this course—especially not in the rain. We spotted the first runners coming around the corner and toward the track.

"Where is Sierra?" I asked, not meaning to say it aloud. She was always in the first group. In fact I think she had yet to lose a race that season. But now she wasn't anywhere in sight. I got that feeling in my stomach you get when you think you are about to hear bad news. A few more girls came around the corner, through the school gate, and onto the track.

I asked one of the finishers if they'd seen our girls.

"No, but it was really getting sloppy. They may have decided to walk it down."

I couldn't imagine Sierra walking the course, no matter how sloppy it was.

Our coach went over to the other coaches, probably to see if they had anyone out on the trail that could check on Sierra. Even Maggie would normally be in by now.

A few more of their girls rounded the corner.

Their coach radioed someone on the trail. We couldn't hear the response but we saw him shake his head. Rather than making a move to find them, they were having a heated discussion.

"Coach, how 'bout I run it back and look for them." I yelled.

But before he answered, someone pulled up on a 4-wheeler. Coach jumped on and they took off. I ran after them, but the rain made it hard to look up as I ran. I heard their motor slow to a stop and looked up.

"There they are!" someone yelled.

Sierra jogged out of the woods at the base of the hill with Maggie on her back. The 4-wheeler headed back but I ran to meet them. Sierra insisted they both cross the finish line so I ran with them. Maggie had slipped in the mud and come down on her ankle.

"Luckily she fell right where the trail doubled back so I saw her go down. I cut back through the woods to help her." Sierra turned to show us the back of her legs were covered in mud. They both had it caked in their hair, up their arms, and on their faces.

"We definitely made up some time accidently sliding down part of the trail," Maggie laughed. "I have to say in all of the times I've run this course, this was the most fun. Although probably not for you Sierra. Sorry for the extra weight. And I killed your winning streak."

"No problem. It was the most fun I've ever had here, too."

We all loaded onto the bus. Unfortunately, there were no showers so Maggie and Sierra had to ride back caked in mud. They had been able to change out of their muddy clothes and into sweats, but were still covered. I sat next to Sierra.

"Sorry, "she said. "I know this mud really stinks."

"You're fine." I said. "It actually makes you seem more down to Earth."

She laughed and rolled her eyes. "Seriously?"

"Hey, it may have been a small, forced, polite one, but you did laugh" I pointed out.

"I did."

"Sorry about your winning streak." I said.

She shrugged, "It honestly didn't even cross my mind. I care more about competing against myself. Besides, like Maggie said, it was the most fun we've had on that stupid course." She pulled a towel out of her bag.

"And it was our last time on it." I reminded her.

"Yeah, next year they'll come to us. And then we are outta here." Sierra wet the end of the towel with her water bottle and started to clean off some of the mud.

"Have you started looking at colleges yet?" I asked, to distract her from the fact that I was watching her every move.

"Some," She put hand sanitizer on her hands and reached back into her bag. "What about you?"

"Well, I've pretty much had it all planned since I was like 10." I took a big swig from my water bottle.

"Really? You're lucky." She shifted in her seat and a giant chunk of mud fell off her cleat into the aisle. "Oh sorry, that is just nasty!" she said. "I feel for whoever has to clean this bus.' She peeled a banana. "So, what's the big plan?"

"CIA," I was strangely turned on by the way she was eating her banana. God, I was a total creep. I hoped she didn't notice me blush.

"Like intelligence or something?" she asked.

"Oh, no. Not that CIA. Culinary Institute of America. For cooking. I want to own my own restaurant someday." Suddenly, it sounded dumb. "But I don't want to try it until I have learned from the best. After school, I want to go study in France and Italy. You know? Learn different styles and methods. Then maybe I could open my own place."

"Kind of like your mom?" she asked.

"Yes, but in a real city like New York or San Francisco." I grabbed a granola bar and opened it. "Don't get me wrong, I like Laketown. It will always be home. I just want *more*. I mean, how hard is it to have a successful restaurant here? I want to be the best amongst the best. You know?"

"Wow. Impressive." She said.

"Are you messing with me? I can't tell with you." I looked right into her eyes.

"No, seriously. I'm envious. I'm not really sure what I want to do. Although I am also looking forward to something *more* than just Laketown." She finished her banana and put the peel back in the Ziploc bag. I took a bite of my granola bar.

"Well, when you were little what did you want to be when you grew up?" I asked.

"Just like my father-" she paused, saw I wasn't going to react, shrugged and continued, "Well, before. So I don't know."

"Maybe finance or something?" I finished before the mention of her father made her shut down. I didn't want to stop talking to her.

"Yeah, math has always been easy for me. It makes sense. There's always more than one way to get to one concrete answer. And there is a correct answer. Oh, God, I'm rambling about math. Sorry." She covered her face with her hands and discovered more mud in her hair. "I am such a mess."

"You're fine. We're all a mess. Look at me." I pointed to myself.

"You look fine."

"Fine as in *fine?* Or just fine?" I asked, curious even though I was still with Victoria.

Sierra laughed and, I swear, blushed a little.

"So finance, huh? Well maybe you can invest in my restaurant someday." I said.

"I'll have to taste your cooking first."

"Sounds like a challenge. You should come by *The Kitchen* this weekend and see for yourself." I said.

"Actually, it's funny you should say that. I was thinking about trying to wait tables there after cross country ends," she locked eyes with me.

"Going to miss me so much that you want to come work with me?" I crossed my hands over my heart, tilted my head and smiled.

"You wish. No, I need to make enough to pay for insurance and gas for my car. Either that, or become the lucky owner of my mom's ten year old Volvo." She explained.

"Wheels are key. Seriously, you should come in. I don't know if they need anyone in the front right now but I do know they make the best tips in town."

"I know. That's why I picked it." Everyone stirred and I realized we were in the school parking lot. I didn't want to be home. I was happy talking to Sierra—stinky mud and all.

"I cannot wait to shower." Sierra said as she gathered her stuff.

"Me either," said Maggie, hopping down the bus steps.

"How's your ankle?" Sierra and I asked at the same time. We looked at each other and laughed.

"It's better from the ice, thanks. Coach thinks it's just a sprain." Maggie shrugged.

"Why don't you let me help you to the lockers," I suggested.

"That'd be great!" she sounded more excited than I had expected.

"Piggy back?" I suggested.

"Here," Sierra said, "Give me your bags." We headed up the school steps, through the door and into the hallway by the gym.

"Dave? What the hell are you doing?" I smelled the orange in her perfume. We all turned. There she stood in a tight and I had to admit sexy-as-hell little work-out outfit. Her hand was on her hip, her jaw was thrust out and her eyes narrowed. I blushed, even though I hadn't done anything wrong (well, unless you count actually enjoying a conversation with another girl as wrong). I felt like I had my tail between my legs. This was getting ridiculous, even my penis had to admit.

"Hey, V, what are you doing here still?" I asked, attempting to keep it light.

"Late practice. What are *you* doing? With *her*?" She made it sound like I was carrying a leper or something.

"I sprained my ankle at the meet and he was helping me to the locker room." Maggie explained.

"I didn't ask *you*," Victoria spat. "I asked *him*. If I cared what you had to say, I would have addressed you by name, if I could remember it."

"V, give me a break." I said. "I'm giving her a lift. I'll be back in a few."

"But I need to tell you something. *Now*!" I half expected her to stomp her foot.

I felt Maggie start to slide down my back. "It's fine, Dave. I got it from here," she said. But I hoisted her back into place.

"It will take two minutes. V, I'll be right back. You can tell me then." I didn't look back and she didn't say another word. I was relieved. I hated drama.

I carried Maggie around the corner and down the hall to the door of the women's locker room. Sierra dropped my bag by the men's entrance as we walked in silence.

"Thanks, Dave. Sorry." Maggie said.

"You're welcome. And really it's fine. I don't know why she got so pissed. Hope it heals quick," I said, nodding toward her ankle.

"See ya tomorrow." Sierra said as she helped Maggie through the door and into the locker room. "And good luck," she whispered as the door closed.

"Thanks." I responded under my breath. When I came back around the corner, Victoria was already gone. I could have looked for her but instead grabbed my bag and hit the locker room for a much needed shower. It wasn't until I'd inhaled my dinner and sat down to do some homework that I realized I didn't have my cell phone with me. I couldn't remember where I'd last had it; the bus maybe? I knew Victoria would be pissed but the truth was I hadn't really felt like talking to her anyway.

The next morning, I had a dentist appointment first thing. I wasn't able to check on my cell phone until I got to the office to sign in to school. The receptionist started when I appeared at her desk.

"Mr. Braun. Where have you been? I just tried your house," she said.

"I had a dentist appointment. Why, what's up?" I asked. She paused, blushing.

"What?" I asked.

"Um ..." she grabbed at her now splotchy neck without looking at me. "Principal Skinner wanted to see you." He popped his head out of his office.

"Mr. Braun. I need you to step in here, please." He said.

I felt that sick feeling in my stomach again. Was it my parents? My sisters? Why were they acting so strange? I stepped into his office.

"Close the door and have a seat," he sat back down behind his desk. I had only been in here once before. Our freshman year, Jack had convinced me it would be a great idea to TP our old basketball coach's house on Halloween. Couch Gomez had a temper. He verbally berated us all of the time, made us run ridiculous amounts of sprints—just another asshole on a power trip. Nobody liked Coach Gomez but he was the athletic director's son-in-law.

The day before Halloween Coach Gomez threw a chair at us in practice and barely missed clipping our point guard. When Jack mouthed off, Gomez made him run laps for the rest of practice. The school board ended up forcing his resignation at the end of that year, after he threw a girl's backpack out the third floor window for forgetting her Spanish homework. At any rate, Jack and I got called in here and reprimanded for the Halloween TP Job. Principal Skinner only knew it was us because his son, Peter, ratted us out. Peter was the ball boy for the team because he had asthma so bad he couldn't play. This also meant he was a kiss-ass. We paid for it from Gomez the rest of the season.

"David, it is your right to know that I am going to record this entire conversation for your safety and my own. Do you give your consent?" I was completely caught off guard.

"I guess, sure," I said. "What's this about?"

"You need to say yes, for the record." Principal Skinner pointed at the little recorder on his desk.

"Yes. It's fine. Is my family okay? What's going on?"

"Is this your phone?" Principal Skinner asked, holding it up.

"It could be." I said. "I couldn't find it when I got home last night so I figured it may have fallen out on the cross country bus. Let me see." I reached out but Skinner pulled it away.

"I'm not done with it." He said. "So you're saying you didn't have this phone on your person last night, around 7:18PM?" I felt like I was on an episode of Law & Order.

"I'm saying I don't know. I didn't notice it was gone until after I'd gotten home." I shrugged. "What is the big deal?"

"What time did you get home?" He asked.

"I don't know, I guess around 7:30 or so. What is going on? Did I do something wrong?"

"Can anyone confirm the time you arrived home?"

"My parents were both there. My mom warmed up my dinner. Do you want me to call her?"

"Not yet. I want to finish with your side of the story."

"My side of what story? Could you please fill me in because to the best of my knowledge I haven't done anything wrong?" I said, probably a little too loudly. I was a little pissed at this point.

"I suggest you remember where you are Mr. Braun." He leaned back in his chair and I realized he was enjoying this.

"Were you dating Victoria Spencer?" I suddenly realized I was in deep shit. My face turned red.

"Yeah, we've been hanging out, why?" I did not want to know the answer at all. This could only mean bad news. Izzy's words popped into my head, *she will squash you like a bug.*

"I don't normally butt into the relationship status of my students. I respect your privacy. But when you bring your relationship into my school, it becomes my business, you understand? Now I'm going to tell you what I think happened and you can tell me if I'm off base or not, okay?" He leaned forward and crossed his hands on top of his desk. I felt like he was trying to intimidate me but it was sort of comical because I was about six inches taller. Out of nervousness more than anything, I burst out laughing. I couldn't help it.

"You think this is funny, Mr. Braun? Because I could call the cops in on this. You could kiss any basketball or running scholarships goodbye. I'm trying to do you a favor." The bald spot on his head got redder when he yelled. I stifled another laugh. *Dude, get your shit under control.*

"Sorry Mr. Skinner. I laugh when I'm nervous." The bell rang for the end of second period. I was supposed to be headed to English, the only class I had with Sierra.

"So, I think when Victoria said you two were done, you were not happy. Maybe you tried to text her. My guess is she didn't respond because she didn't want to discuss it further. You got pissed off and decided to send the picture out to a bunch of people. Am I right?" He leaned forward again.

"I'm sorry sir, but what are you talking about? She's saying I sent a picture of her to a bunch of people?" I asked.

"Sixty-three to be exact. The entire junior class. A list I guess you have on your phone, as class vice president. And I never said it was a picture of her." Principal Skinner looked smug.

"Okay, I don't know what this picture is but I can assure you I didn't send it out. I didn't even have my phone last night."

"Let's watch our tone Mr. Braun." He pointed his finger at me.

"What is the picture of, anyway?" He stared me down for a minute as if trying to figure out my angle. "You said it yourself just a moment ago. It was a picture of Ms. Spencer. Do you want me to play back the tape for you?"

"No, but I'm telling you. I didn't have my phone. I never sent out a picture. Until you brought me in here, I had no idea any of this had even happened. I went home from the meet, ate dinner, did homework and went to bed." I said.

"And where were you this morning? Why didn't you come in until now? Were you having regrets?" He asked.

"I had a dentist appointment." I reached into my back pocket and pulled out an appointment card, tossing it onto his desk. "Here's the number. Give 'em a call if you don't believe me."

"I will. But in the meantime I need to call your parents to determine our next course of action. As you can imagine, Ms. Spencer is very upset and her parents are none too pleased either."

"Listen, I think I dropped my phone at some point yesterday afternoon or last night and someone used it to send whatever they sent." I said.

"Why do you think someone would do this?" He asked.

"I have no idea. I haven't even seen the picture. How can I possibly even answer that question? Can I go or call my parents or whatever? I didn't do it. I don't know what more you want me to say."

"Okay, I'm going to ask that you go home for the day until we sort this out. I have asked Ms. Spenser to do the same." He stood.

"What about my phone?" I asked.

"I'm afraid I need to keep it for now. It's evidence," I almost laughed again.

"Seriously? What are you going to do; dust it for prints? Why should I be punished for somebody stealing *my* phone and using it to do something wrong?" I asked.

"I'm sorry but I don't have any choice until we sort this out. I hope you can appreciate the gravity of this situation." Mr. Skinner came out from behind his desk and opened the door.

"This is total crap." I left before he could yell at me for that, too. I also wasn't leaving school until I found out what the deal was with the picture. I waited in the parking lot for third period to end and then went to find Jack on his way to PE.

"Dude, where have you been?" he said when he saw me.

"Dentist. I'm not supposed to be here so I gotta be quick. What is this crap about some picture I supposedly sent?"

"You mean you didn't send it?" He asked.

"No. I left my phone somewhere yesterday and I guess somebody took it. What is it?" I stayed behind the lockers so nobody but Jack could see me.

He grabbed his phone out of his back pocket and held it up for me. Victoria stared back, her eyes more black than blue. She flashed her bare tits in the same shirt she'd been wearing when she bitched at me the night before.

"Shit!" I leaned my head against the locker. "I'm so screwed."

"So who do you think sent it?" Jack said. He took back the phone and looked at the picture again. "Nice rack though, gotta hand it to her there."

"Great Jack. I'm getting totally screwed over here and all you can say is 'nice rack.'" I slammed my fist into the lockers and Sierra popped into my head. She would never give me the time of day after this. No girl would. "What a bitch! This is exactly what Izzy said would happen."

"What, you think Victoria sent that picture out to everyone herself? Why the hell would she do that?" He sat down on the bench to change from flip flops to sneakers.

"To screw me over. That's why. I pissed her off last night and this is her way of getting me back." I said.

"Bullshit. Really? By sending her own tits out there for everyone?"

"It's exactly something she would do. She doesn't care who sees her tits. All she cares about is making me a social pariah to every other girl in this school. Shit!" I banged my back against the locker as the reality set in. "She probably sensed I wanted to end things. She wouldn't want to be dumped by a junior so she made sure to humiliate me first." I stood.

"I'm sorry, dude. What a major twat. You want me to start a rumor she gave you crabs or some shit? I love a good payback plan." Jack smiled at the prospect.

"No thanks dude, I appreciate it, but I think I may need to just ride this one out. You better get out there. I'll catch you later." I said.

"You comin' to the game tonight?" He asked over his shoulder.

"I don't know man, probably not with all of this going on. Sorry." I said.

"No worries. I get it. I'll call you tomorrow." It wasn't until after he was gone that I realized I should have told him I was cell-less for the weekend. I went home to call Izzy before my parents got home.

Day 27 – 11/1
Biked 27 miles

It's a new month and I yelled "Rabbit Rabbit" for good luck! Ha! Nobody hears it and Lady Luck certainly hasn't come to rescue me. It sounds strange to hear my own voice sometimes. I should see how many days I can go without speaking. It will be my own personal vow of silence.

Even rinsed out, bagged and duck taped shut; tuna cans still smell. Not sure I'll make that again soon. Maybe I should make something interesting out of the recyclables. I wish I could make nail clippers. Whoever set this all up forgot a toothbrush and nail clippers. I suppose I could take to biting my nails.

Nope, tried it. It's not for me. At least if someone comes after me in here I can scratch them really good.

So I'm currently trying to read *Bridget Jones' Diary*. I think it is safe to say that her diary entries are much more interesting than mine. And based on her experiences, I'm beginning to think maybe this would be more bearable if they had given me alcohol down here, too. I could ration it out. Have a little Friday night party for myself. And such great tunes to blare, too. Let's see we've got The Beatles with *Sgt. Pepper's Lonely Hearts Club Band* (Ironic, I know); *Madonna*, her self-titled first album; Cyndi Lauper, *True Colors*; *Believe* by Cher; The Soundtrack to *The Rocky Horror Picture Show*; New Order, *Substance*; *Endless Summer*, Donna Summer, and my personal favorite; Tori Amos, *Little Earthquakes*. It's so haunting, it fits my mood most days down here. *The Rocky Horror Picture Show* skips a lot but when you have limited selection you learn to live with imperfections.

I just realized that today is also the deadline for early admissions for most of the colleges I wanted to attend. I wonder if it's still sitting on my desk at home. Unfinished; just like my last year of high school, my last cross country season. How many other lasts will I miss?

Dr. Laura Hart

Waiting for Patrick to make the drop tested my strength, but waiting for news afterwards was pure torture. Patrick was back by two o'clock that afternoon. We had purposely waited until close to one to drop the money, to reduce the window of time for pick-up.

By four we still hadn't heard anything. According to the officers posted there, the locker remained untouched. The tournament was still in full swing. The awards ceremony was not until 8pm under the lights. They suspected the kidnappers would wait for the extra cover of darkness.

"What do we do if they never come and get it? How long can we wait? Why didn't they tell us more about Sierra?" Question after question popped into my head; but I didn't voice them. I knew nobody else knew any more than I did.

So we waited. Patrick dozed off around six. I couldn't blame him. Neither of us had slept much lately and his body must have finally overruled his mind. I looked at him in envy. At least in sleep he was free from the nightmare of reality.

Day 31 – 11/4
Biked 31 miles

I have to bang on the flashlight to keep it on sometimes, but I'm hesitant to change the batteries until they are completely dead. There is only one more set; and some nights when I can't sleep after lights out, I use it to write. The words on the page are like voices in the dark.

It was Tia who first pointed out that Dave Braun had a thing for me. I had never thought of him as anything more than a casual acquaintance. His family was loaded, but known for being very generous in supporting both the school and community as a whole.

Tia had identified Dave as prospective boyfriend when she started coming to my home track meets. She could pretend she was there to watch me but tried to run into Dave. By the time our last home meet of the season rolled around, she still hadn't said more to him than (and she tracked this sort of thing), "Nice Run," and "Do you know what event is next?" The regular season had ended and there were only a few of us still training for States. Tia was worried her window was closing so she picked me up after practice for her last shot with Dave.

"Okay, I am having a complete conversation with him today if it kills me," she said as I combed out my wet hair in front of the locker room mirror.

"What's the topic of choice today?" I knew she always had a plan.

"Well I did overhear him talking about going to a Red Sox game with his dad. Maybe something about that."

"You don't know anything about baseball. Remember? You said, 'Quote, I have zero time for a sport where grown men make millions of dollars but can't even manage to avoid a muffin top, unquote.'" I made the quote sign with my fingers.

"It's true! NBA players look way hotter in their uniforms. But point taken. Okay, I could ask him about his summer plans. That is an easy open." She sat down on a bench and began to fold my running clothes into a neat pile.

"That sounds like a much better approach." I said.

"Okay, so if we see him in the hall, you'll pretend you forgot something so I can stall for time?" she confirmed for the sixth time.

"Yes," I said. "Got it, stall in the hall."

"Okay. Ready? Guys are probably way faster with the shower stuff."

We left the girls' locker room and walked as slow as possible down the hall. I felt a little ridiculous. But Tia was in luck. Dave came out right as we passed. And he was alone.

"Hey Sierra," he said. "Tia."

"Hey," I said.

"Hi Dave," she said in a strange, lilting voice. Her face turned crimson.

"Oh crap, I think I left my phone in my locker. I'll be right back." I said and jogged back toward the locker room. I went in and waited a few minutes as planned. When I came back out, I almost ran head on into Tia.

"Hey, how did it go?" I asked, shifting the weight of my bag to my other shoulder.

"Nowhere. He's clearly already completely hot for my best friend."

"Excuse me?" I asked, not sure I'd heard her right.

"Yep. Just my luck. The one guy I want is already in love with you,"

"Oh come on, you're talkin' crazy." I said.

"I am not. What is Sierra up to this summer? Did you see her race at state qualifiers? You guys are pretty tight, huh? I always see you together. Blah blah blah . . . Sierra . . . I am dead serious. How can you not know he is in to you?"

"He isn't. You are just paranoid." I said as we walked out the doors and down the steps.

"No, I'm observant. And I think you should totally go for him." She looked at me with her brows raised and a smug little grin.

"What? No. You have had your sights set on him for three months now and just like that you think I should go for him?" I asked.

"Hey, I know when to step aside. Besides I heard that Tiffany broke up with Roger Matthews and I swear I caught him staring at me in chemistry the other day. He kind of looks like Justin Timberlake. Don't you think?" She asked as we got into her car.

"You kill me. Just like that you jump on to the next thing," I snapped my fingers.

"I read in Cosmo the other day it's healthier to move on as quickly as you can. Harboring all that negativity is bad for your complexion." She put the car into reverse and bolted out of the parking lot. I shook my head, laughed, and thought *Dave Braun*?

I didn't spend much more time thinking about Dave that summer because I was quickly distracted by other pressing developments.

When Tia got home that night, she found out they were moving to California in July. She called me in tears. I didn't know how I was going to survive without Tia. She had been my lifeline throughout all of high school and the only one who really understood me and all of my family stuff. That is why when I got a call from my father less than a week later, I probably didn't handle it well. The operator asked if I would accept the collect call from the Federal Correctional Facility. I hadn't talked to my dad since Easter. Our conversations were always very uncomfortable. But he was still my dad, my former hero, so of course I accepted.

"Hey stub, how are you doing?" he asked actually sounding unusually chipper.

"I've been better." I knew I couldn't pretend with him. He always knew.

"What's wrong?" he asked.

"Do you remember my friend Tia? Her dad is the superintendent?"

"Of course I remember her. Did you have a fight?" He asked.

"No. She's moving to California in July. Her dad took his dream job at another school." I played mindlessly with the magnets on our kitchen whiteboard.

"Oh, I'm sorry. That is tough. But you can keep in touch." He suggested.

"It's not the same." I got up to look for a snack in the pantry.

"I know. Hey, at least you had an amazing finish to your track season! I saw you placed 4th and 5th at State. I am so proud of you. You can probably run circles around me now."

"Thanks." I said.

"So, I have some great news!" His voice brightened again. I tried to picture him on the other end. I only had TV and movies as a guide.

"What?" I asked, deadpan.

"I made parole. I finally have a release date." He announced.

"You mean you're coming home?" Panic gripped me. "Here?"

"Well, not exactly there. But I will be able to visit, and once I get situated . . . hopefully I can move closer so we can spend more time together." He sounded so happy. And I wanted to be happy for him. But the last thing I wanted was my ex-con dad hanging around town when my best friend was moving across the country. I had spent the last few years trying to forget about him and the *before*. And trying to make everyone else forget, too. It would drudge up all of that past mess.

"Sierra? Are you still there?" He asked.

"Yes. Sorry. I uh . . . congratulations, Dad. I'm sure you must be really excited to get your freedom back." I tried to sound happy. Looking back, I realize how selfish I was being.

"Look, honey I know this has all been really difficult for you but it will feel like a small speed bump soon enough. I think Lady Luck is going to finally shine down on me again."

"So when do you get released?" I asked.

"June 7th."

I looked at the calendar on the white board. "Wow, that's in less than two weeks!" My heart began to pound. Everything was happening too soon. School wouldn't even be out by then.

"Who's going to come get you? And where are you going to go?" I asked, secretly praying it was not too close.

"Do you remember Uncle Sam? He used to come see us every summer?" He asked.

"Your old college roommate? Sure." I said. I didn't have any real uncles or aunts because both of my parents were only children. I always liked Sam, but I got the impression my mom wasn't his biggest fan. I remembered my parents would argue a lot during his visits. As far as I knew, he had never gotten married or had kids.

"He's going to let me stay with him for a while. He lives near the Finger Lakes so I'll only be a couple hours away."

"Great." I heard a voice in the background.

"Hey I need to give someone else a turn on the phone, but I'll give you a call from Sam's when I get out and give you my contact information. Then we can make a plan to meet, okay?"

"Sure." I said, already devising a way to meet him as far away as possible.

"Bye Stub, I love you." He said.

"Bye." I hung up and immediately grabbed my cell to tell Tia the news. She made me feel better with hilariously implausible explanations for not meeting up with my father. My mom walked in the door. I hung up and shared the news.

"Dad called. He's getting out," I said, wondering how she would react. She didn't respond at first, handing me two bags of groceries and heading back to the car for more.

I started unpacking while she carried in the last two. We were both silent as we put all of the groceries away. Finally, I couldn't stand it anymore.

"Well, aren't you going to say anything?" I asked.

"When?" She took a bottle of wine out and peeled the foil off the top. My mom rarely drank unless we had company.

"Is someone coming over?" I asked.

"No," she said as she pushed down the arms of the opener and slid out the cork. "When?"

"June 7th." I said, watching her pour herself a big glass of wine.

"That's less than two weeks away." She took a big swallow.

"He's staying with Uncle Sam near the Finger Lakes." I continued.

"Sam Schwartz?" she asked, like I would know his last name. "That figures. He probably still works for the casino. That's the absolute last thing he needs." She opened the door and went out onto our little deck to sit. I put a stopper in the bottle, put it in the fridge and followed.

"When are you supposed to see him?" she asked.

"I don't know. He said he'd call when he got there."

"I'm sorry this is happening right now," she said. "With Tia leaving, I know you're already upset."

"I feel so guilty. I know he's my dad and I should want to see him, but I just, I don't know how to explain it." I looked to Mom for the words.

"Well, it's hard when someone you love lets you down. But your father loves you more than anything. That will never change. I think you're afraid that if you open yourself up to him, he may let you down again. But you also have twelve years of happy memories. I know I am not the best person to give you advice in this department, but I think as his daughter, you should at least try to have a relationship with him." She finished her glass and looked at me.

I sighed and nodded, "okay, I'll try. I know it sounds awful but at least when he was in prison, I could pretend none of it happened. But now that he can just show up somewhere, I have to think about him and face what he did. What if the town starts talking about it again?"

"We're old news. I think everyone has better things to do with their time." As if on cue, Tia burst onto the deck with a bag in each hand.

"Never fear ladies. Help has arrived in the form of ice cream and not one but two chick flicks with smoking hot men that will make your female parts quiver and your mind go blank."

"What are we ever going to do without you, Tia?" My mom asked. It was exactly what I had been thinking.

Since I didn't turn sixteen until August I either had to take a bus to meet my dad, ask my mom (which I refused to do), or have Tia give me a ride. Although I knew Tia would make a great buffer, it meant putting my life into her hands for an hour. She was by far the worst driver I knew. She failed her driver's test four times before she finally passed (probably by flirting).

Her biggest problem was she was easily distracted, analyzing people in passing cars, changing the music, or checking her phone. One afternoon after school, we were driving around listening to music when she decided to look for a CD mix. I yelled but it was too late, we slid on the loose gravel on the road and ended up in a corn field. From that point on I refused to get in her car unless I controlled the music and held onto her phone. If my mom had any idea how dangerous she was I'm sure she would never let me ride with her again.

But she was still the best choice. All I could do was hope Lady Luck was on my side for the trip. She pulled into my driveway blaring *Papa Don't Preach*, and announced she had made me the perfect CD for the trip. And we were off.

The drive went shockingly well but as we approached the McDonalds where Dad and I had agreed to meet, my stomach twisted. We parked without incident and Tia turned off the car.

"Do you want me to hang here or go in with you?" she asked.

"Honestly, I don't know." I answered. I looked through the windows but it was a sunny day so I couldn't really see much inside.

"Why don't you go in alone and text me when or if you want me to come in," she suggested.

"Okay." I said, making no move to get out.

"It's going to be fine," she said. "Remember how awesome he was as a dad. You'll fall right back into it."

"What if I remember it all wrong? Or what if he looks completely different?" I panicked.

"Sierra, remember that dance in eighth grade when I was crushing on Albert Fine?"

"Yes, though I still don't know why? He was not your usual type."

"I know, but he had helped me on that biology lab and his confidence while dissecting that pig was hot. I was sure he'd be a highly skilled surgeon someday. Anyway, remember we were at the dance and he was sitting all by himself in the corner?"

"I told you to go ask him to dance." I recalled.

"And I really wanted to, but I never did ask. Why? Because I was too chicken."

"And your point to this stroll down memory lane?" I asked.

"Well, looking back I know that I should have just asked Albert. Obviously, he was nervous about even being there. We were in the same boat."

"So you are comparing my dad to Albert in this scenario?" I smiled.

"Yes. You get my point. He is as nervous as you are, and has even more to lose. He is starting his life all over. You have a life. So, go, help him."

"Wow," I said. "When did you get so smart at relationship advice?" I got out of the car.

The smell of French fries was overwhelming as I walked through the door. I looked around to see if I could spot him.

"Sierra," I heard a yell and turned to find him waving in a booth. I took a deep breath and walked over. He grabbed me and gave me a hard hug, like he'd literally been saving it for three years. Then he held me out at arms' length and looked me over.

"Wow, you look amazing. My little girl is now ..." his voice broke and he coughed. "Sit down, sit down, or would you like something to eat?"

"Um, no I'm good. Thanks." He had a half full coffee in front of him.

"You look the same." I sat down. He really did.

"I probably have a few more gray hairs. Wisdom, I hope," he smiled. For just a moment, I felt twelve again. "Did your mom drop you off?"

"No, Tia." I said.

"When does she leave for California?" he asked.

"July 6th," I said.

"I'm sorry, Stub. That is tough," he squeezed my hand for a few seconds, then let it go.

"So what are you going to do now, dad?" I asked.

"Well, I actually reconnected with an old friend from college who is a mathematician for a technology company. She said she needed someone for a couple of projects. Math has always been my thing, and it actually pays really well if I can do it."

"What about having a record? Can they still hire you?" I asked.

"We were up front about my situation and I wouldn't be working directly with money so it shouldn't be a problem unless they have a policy about ex-cons. I should find out on Monday." He took a sip of coffee. "But I don't want to talk about me. What's new with you?"

I shrugged, "just school and stuff. Track is done so it's only final papers and exams."

"What about this summer? Are you going to camp again?" he asked.

"No I'm babysitting for one of mom's patients. He's autistic and his mom is pregnant. They want an extra set of hands to help. I'm saving for car insurance and eventually gas." I tried to find Tia out in the parking lot.

"So you already have a car?" he asked.

"Not yet, but mom is going to get a newer car and give me hers. It's ten years old but as mom likes to point out, you can't get safer than a Volvo wagon." I mimicked her voice.

"You sound just like her," he laughed. "How is she doing, anyway?"

I shrugged, "fine," I didn't feel right talking about mom with him.

"Does she have a boyfriend or anything?" he wondered.

"No." I said. "So did you still want to go do something?" I asked in a not too subtle attempt to change the subject.

"Absolutely. There's a bowling alley not far from here. You wanna check it out?"

"Bowling?"

"Yes, bowling. You used to be quite good at it. You are probably even better now." He flashed that smile that made waitresses swoon.

"I haven't been since... Would it be okay if Tia came? She's still right outside."

"Of course. I'm sorry; I didn't know she was outside waiting this whole time. Let's go."

"She's okay. She brought a book on CD just in case," I explained. We headed outside. I realized I was actually looking forward to their meeting.

Bowling turned out to be a blast. It felt really great to laugh with my dad again. Charming as ever, he quickly made friends with another father, Gill, while we got our shoes sorted out. We spent the next two hours in a heated three rounds of bowling. It was the three of us versus Gill and his two sons, Eddie and Thomas. Eddie was only twelve but Thomas was sixteen and looked like a young Matt Damon. To say Tia was in heaven was a bit of an understatement. They won the first game, we won the second, and after a very close game, Eddie got two strikes in a row to win the series. We learned that the boys were visiting their dad for the summer. Most of the year they lived with their mother in Laguna Nigel, California, just an hour from La Jolla, where Tia was moving.

"What luck!" my dad exclaimed.

I should have been happier when Thomas asked Tia for her email, but all I felt was a pang of jealousy. These random boys would probably get to see her more than I would. We all ate pizza and then Tia drove my dad to the bus station. It felt strange to ride in the back of the car behind them. They talked like they had known each other forever. I wondered if this is what it would have been like to have a sister.

My dad gave Tia a kiss on the cheek and thanked her for the ride and the fun. Then we both got out to say goodbye. He gave me another big hug.

"This was the best time I have had since you were twelve," he said. "Thank you for making it easy to pick up where we left off, Sierra. It makes me feel like you kept your promise to have fun and be happy. And I can see why you are going to miss Tia so much. But maybe I can help pick up the slack."

"Thanks Dad," I said. "I had fun, too." and I meant it.

"Well, I better go before I miss my bus. I'll call you next week, okay?"

"Okay, good luck on the job." I said.

"Thanks honey. I'm overdue for a little luck!" I watched him disappear into the station.

As I got back into the car, I burst into tears.

"Whoa!" said Tia, handing me a tissue. "What is this? I thought it went really well?"

"It d . . . id," I blubbered. "I just . . ."

"Needed to get a good cry out? Tears of joy? Tears of relief? Tears because we lost that last game to the oh-so-f'ing-hot Mr. Thomas? If you want him for yourself, I understand. It would be a big sacrifice, but I would do it for you." I knew she was trying to make me smile. And it sort of worked. The tears slowed. I blew my nose.

She put in one of my favorite albums and cranked the music so we could sing uninhibited. By the time we got home, I felt better. She turned to me in the driveway.

"Seriously, are you okay? Did you want to talk about any of it?" she asked.

"No, I'm okay. It's just a lot to process, I guess." I gathered my stuff and Tia reached over to give me a big hug. I hugged her back, thanked her for everything, and got out. As I walked up to my door in the dark, I heard her yell.

"By the way, you never told me your dad was like celebrity hot. It's like walking around with George Clooney or something."

I smiled. "Goodnight Tia," I yelled.

"Goodnight!" she cranked the music back up and pulled out.

Dr. Laura Hart

Sheryl Donovan's cell rang and woke Patrick up from his nap. It was just after seven. Patrick had made the drop over six hours ago. I held my breath and studied her reaction for any sign, good or bad.

"Okay." A long pause. "Good." That was encouraging. "Yes." Still good. "Right; thanks." Sheryl disconnected.

I realized I had an incredible ache in my jaw from the tension of waiting. I willed her to say something good.

"They are following the money as we speak. Apparently a whole team entered the locker room at once. Someone did access the locker. They have narrowed it down to four potential suspects. Our team split up to follow them all. Three of the kids made their way back to the field or their family members. One of the kids blended with the crowd, wandered past all of the fields and out into the parking lot. When he came upon a section where the lights were knocked out, he stopped to tie his shoe between a row of cars. He looked around, threw the bag in the back of a car and drove off. They are still following him. This is good. It's good news."

I looked at Patrick and he gave me a weak smile. I looked out at the swarm of reporters lighting up our lawn. *Please let her be okay* I thought.

Day 32 – 11/5
Biked 32 miles

Today I remembered in elementary school we made people out of aluminum foil. I'm going to make my friends and family and use one of the shirts and a towel to make clothes for them. I wish I had scissors or box cutters. I can try my makeshift knife; maybe duck tape vs. sewing? I'm not particularly crafty but I have made some cool digital photo albums.

The night before Tia moved to California my mom and I had her over for dinner and gave her our going away gift. I had done the work, but my mother had graciously paid for it. It was a photo book and it had turned out better than expected. It basically charted the course of our friendship from our first sleepover to a really fun day at the lake the week before. My mom had even paid the extra shipping for overnight delivery because I worked on it right up to the last possible day. I knew she was going to miss Tia almost as much as I was. She had brought light back into our life in a time of darkness. It was scary to think what would happen now that she wouldn't be around anymore.

"Oh my god! I love it!" Tia yelled and hugged us both. Then she handed my mom a gift to open. It was a book, *Online Dating For Dummies*, and a gift card to Victoria's Secret.

"Thank you, Tia. Subtle as ever." My mom laughed and gave her a hug.

"It's time to get back out there. You are way too hot to work so much." Tia said. "Besides I think we have exhausted the chick flick inventory on Netflix at this point. You are going to have to find the real deal!" She handed me my gift.

I pulled the tissue paper out of my bag to find a framed picture of the two of us from the Saturday before. It was a great shot. We had been eating lunch at the restaurant by the lake when two cute guys approached and invited us out tubing and water skiing on their boat. The weather was perfect for a change and the guys were fun without being pushy. Their Aunt invited us to stay for burgers on the grill. We played pool and foosball before they took us back to our car. We both had a long make-out session on the way and then again as we said our goodbyes at Tia's car. We didn't exchange emails or numbers. It was like we had all silently agreed to make it a fun day and leave it there. It felt so grown-up and carefree. The picture perfectly captured that feeling. We were on the boat, wind in our hair, sun sinking into the lake, sharing a look and laughing.

"Thanks!" I said.

"There's more in there," she pointed to the bag.

I reached in and grabbed a box wrapped in tissue paper. I tore it off to reveal a new iPod shuffle. "Oh my gosh, Tia, this is too much!" I said.

She smiled, "It's loaded up with your favorites, our favorites together, and a few surprises. Read the back."

I turned it over to find it was engraved *T&S Friendship Soundtrack '03–'05*. The tears started as I gave her a big hug. My mom hugged us both.

"Now you can think of me during those long runs," she said. Her voice was muffled, but I could tell she was teary too. It rained the entire day she left and for a full week after.

After Tia left, I spent the summer babysitting, running, and going to the movies with my mom. I also met my dad a few more times, but it was harder without Tia. We both had to take the bus. We went to movies, bowled, or just had ice cream and walked around. He had gotten the job as a mathematician and said he really liked it. They'd even flown him to NYC a few times. I was amazed. Only my dad could go from prison to jet setting in such a short period of time.

I still had mixed emotions about it all. He already seemed so happy and my mom still seemed sad. It wasn't fair. She never asked about my visits and he had stopped asking about her; probably because I always changed the subject at the mention of her name.

As the summer came to a close, I began to dread the return of school, especially without Tia. But at least I had cross country. Plus my babysitting job was almost over. Teddy had been very sweet but it was challenging to care for a child that was twelve in size and age but mentally only five. I had no idea how frightened people could be of someone like him. At first I got angry with people who acted strange, but eventually I realized my reaction was affecting Teddy, too. I began to ignore the stares and pointing fingers and focused on him. My last day, I gave him a new Pokémon figurine. He always had at least one in his pocket wherever we went.

"Thank you, Era," he said, giving me a big hug before running off to "introduce" it to the rest of his collection. I liked that he had a special name for me. Other than my dad calling me "stub," I didn't have any other nicknames. After a bit of small talk his mom called him back in to say a real goodbye.

I gave him a big hug. "Hey, I'll come visit during the school year okay?" I said.

"Are you going to come see my new school?" he asked.

"I'd love to," I said.

"Can I go play now?" he asked, obviously far less affected by the goodbye.

"Sure." I said.

"K, bye Era," and off he went. I hugged his mom goodbye and she handed me an envelope which I opened later and found to contain a nice summer bonus. I walked out to my bike, crying the whole way home. I felt like it was the summer of goodbye.

The first few weeks of school were uneventful without Tia around. Some of the girls that I used to be friends with *before* actually made an effort to include me again. I sat with them at lunch, because let's face it, eating alone in a school cafeteria is mortifying. But I didn't really hang out after school. They invited me, but I didn't click with any of them like I had Tia. They were most interested in make-up, hair, clothing trends, and guys.

Okay, so it sounds just like Tia, right? I can't explain it other than to say Tia was an original and these girls were like Chinatown knock-offs. I ran for sanity. I also found myself running with Dave Braun at practice. He used to run with Jack, but Jack decided to play football this year. Maggie, the only other girl on the team, always ran with her boyfriend. And I found that I actually had fun with Dave. I had kind of assumed he was a spoiled dick, but he was actually very self-effacing and funny.

This is why I was a little surprised by his choice in girlfriend. Sometime during the summer he'd started seeing Victoria Spencer. She was one of those girls that walked the halls of the high school like it was her own personal runway. With thick blonde hair, blue eyes, size D chest, tiny waist and pouty lips, I had to admit she'd have to try really hard to look anything other than irresistible. Still, Tia and I had witnessed her berating people on multiple occasions. Tia called her Vicious Spender based on her killer wardrobe. We made sure to stay out of her line of fire. She once made a freshman literally lick mud off her new Jimmy Choos after he accidently stepped on her toe at an outdoor pep rally.

I found it interesting that Dave never mentioned Victoria once during our running conversations. Of course, I never brought it up either. Tia (via email) told me this omission was further proof of his undying love for me. I wondered why he'd hook up with such a mean person when he seemed so nice (though Jack was his best friend and could be an asshole, too).

I began to suspect Tia was right after one of our muddier meets that September. He was chatty and flirtatious with me on the bus ride home; and dismissive of Victoria when we ran into her back at school.

The next morning I was ready before my mom so I decided to head out to the car and check my email while I waited. She let me drive everywhere at that point to practice for my driver's test. She had already gotten her new car but we were driving the Volvo because it was the car I'd use for the test (and I'm sure she also preferred a non-experienced driver not drive her new car). No new email from Tia but there was a message from David Braun! I remember thinking he was flirting with me until I saw the subject line: *Tit For Tat*. What the heck did that mean? I clicked to open the email and gasped as my mom got in the car.

"What's wrong?" she asked.

I stared at the screen. It was a picture of Victoria Spencer holding her shirt up to reveal her naked chest. She looked mad. "Oh my God!"

"What?" my mom asked again. "Is it Tia?"

I scanned all of the names the email had been sent to.

"Sierra?"

"Not Tia. Nobody's hurt. It's fine." I started the car and concentrated on backing out of the driveway.

"It didn't sound like nothing," she pried.

I shifted into forward and started down our road. If he'd sent it to the entire grade, I figured the whole town would know soon enough.

"Someone sent a topless picture of Victoria Spencer to the entire junior class." I said.

"That poor girl. Who sent it?" she asked.

"It's karma though." I said, feeling some strange need to protect Dave. "Victoria Spencer has been really mean to a lot of people for a long time."

"You've never let anyone take any naked shots of you, have you?" she asked.

"No mom," I snapped, blushing.

"I know that Tia has some wacky ideas sometimes. I could see the two of you messing around and-" I interrupted her right there.

"Mom, we haven't. We wouldn't. I wouldn't. Okay?" I wanted to change the subject.

"Okay good." She said. "Boy will the school board have their hands full with this one. Marianne is not the type to handle things quietly." My mom was referring to Victoria's mom. I guess I did feel sorry for Victoria. I knew that part of the reason she was such a bitch was her mom. Her dad was the most popular dentist in town but rumor had it Mrs. Spencer ruled the house. Other moms feared her like we all feared her daughter. Besides, at a school the size of ours in a town the size of ours any scandal spread like bird flu. I had been on the receiving end when my father was on trial. Life was about to suck for Victoria and for Dave.

As soon as I got out of the car, I forwarded the email to Tia and told her to call me later. We didn't text or talk on the phone much because both of us had to help pay for our plans. But a naked picture from Dave to our whole class was worthy of a call. Still, it was only quarter to six in California.

I didn't see Dave in school the day the picture was sent. Some people said he didn't dare show, but I found out later both he and Victoria were sent home by the principal. It was all the town could talk about. The following Thursday evening, the school board held a meeting to propose and vote on a new school-wide digital media policy. Marianne Spencer showed up to speak her mind and, although he listened, the new superintendent eventually threatened to dismiss her if she continued to interrupt. He was too new to fear her wrath yet.

They were never able to punish Dave because his parents backed his alibi. Nobody was going to question the word of the Brauns, the single largest donor in the area. Mrs. Spencer told anyone that would listen that her daughter had been victimized twice, first by Dave and then by the school system meant to protect her. I'd heard it was Victoria herself who finally got her mom to quiet down and let it go.

Theories about who had actually sent the email kept the school buzzing for weeks. I got the feeling most people suspected Dave really had sent it, and his parents had used their money and influence to make it go away. Being the wealthiest family in a small town made them a target. It's almost like the town expected them to do bad things because anybody with that much money couldn't possibly be nice, too.

Nobody questioned the why. Victoria had made countless enemies over the years. I'd heard everything from teachers to janitors to her best friend Rachel. Tia was convinced that Victoria had sent the picture herself to get back at Dave for humiliating her in front of us. At first I thought she was crazy, but then I reexamined the picture. She was wearing the same workout shirt that she'd had on that night. And she looked so mad in the shot. I had dropped Dave's bag in the hall by the men's locker room when we escorted Maggie to the women's. Victoria had ample time to take his phone. All she had to do was take the shot, pull up the class list, and fire away. You have to be pretty messed in the head to voluntarily spread naked shots of yourself as revenge. Plus, if she had been really smart she would have slipped his phone back in his bag or something the next morning. Instead it was found in the men's locker room by the PE teacher.

Dave and I didn't have the chance to run together until almost a week after the picture was sent. Part of me wanted to ask him about it, but I knew how it felt to have everyone around me stare without knowing the whole truth. I never brought it up and neither did he. But our first few runs were a little quieter than they'd been in the past.

Eventually, Rachel, Victoria's BFF got caught having sex with some freshman in Principal Skinner's office and Victoria and Dave's scandal became old news. As the cross country season wound down only Dave and I were left at practice. We were the only two that qualified for the state meet in November. My mom was taking off work at the clinic to attend and my dad was going to try and come as well. If he made it, it would be the first time they saw each other since about three months after he'd gone to prison.

Since there were only two of us, we rode with our parents and the coach met us there. I was a little bummed because I enjoyed my Dave time on the bus. I would never admit that to Tia, because she was already predicting we'd be a couple by Christmas. I didn't see him much during the school day. We only had one class together and he sat with the guys at lunch. So practice and the bus were the only times we actually spoke.

We pulled up to the meet around the same time as Dave's parents. His older sister Karen came to watch, too. My mom knew his parents already and he introduced us to Karen. They all found a place to sit together and Dave and I went to find our coach.

"So is your dad going to make it?" he asked as we walked. He must have noticed me looking around for him.

"I don't know," I said. "If he can find a way I'm sure he will."

"No doubt." He said.

"I don't know whether I should have him go stand by my mom or what?" I looked over my shoulder. "I don't have any experience in the divorced-parents-at-the-same-event etiquette, yet."

"There's probably a book on it." He joked. I smiled.

"Divorced Children For Dummies or something."

"Now I know what to get you for Christmas," Dave said as we approached our coach.

By the time I lined up for my 5K, my dad still hadn't arrived. I felt conflicted. I wanted him to see me run but also dreaded my parents meeting again. Right before the gun sounded I heard Dave yell "Let's go Sierra!"

I felt pretty good. The weather was surprisingly decent for early November in New York. It was overcast and probably in the upper forties but so far the rain had held off. It had snowed last year. That sucked. As I set my sights on the finish line, I heard my dad's voice.

"There she is. There she is!" I still had three girls in front of me I was sure I could take. I dug deep and kicked hard to pass the first two, but the girl from Batavia was kicking hard too. My lungs burned and so did my quads, but I wanted this. I pushed hard we crossed the finish. Batavia and I both passed another girl but I couldn't tell if I got her or she beat me.

My legs were Jell-o as I walked off to the side to catch my breath. My dad and Dave got to me at the same time.

"Nice finish Hart!" Dave yelled, handing me my water bottle.

"Thanks! Did I get her?" I asked, taking a sip.

"All I can say is WOW, Sierra. You were great," my dad gave me a big hug.

"Oh dad, I'm all sweaty," I muffled into his shoulder. I heard my mom.

"Great run, honey." She pulled me in for another hug. "Hi, Patrick."

"You look great Laura," My dad moved to kiss her cheek and she thrust out her hand like a shield. His face fell a little but he shook it gently. My mom quickly withdrew her hand and focused on me.

I tried to think of a way to fill the awkward silence but Dave got there first.

"It was close. I think it could go either way."

As it turned out, I did beat Batavia, but it still put me in fifth place, so my season was done. Only the top three individual runners or top three teams qualified. Dave didn't make it to nationals either; placing seventh. It was still a good day overall. The whole parental meeting went much better than I'd feared.

After the season ended, I applied for a position waiting tables at *The Kitchen* as planned. I didn't think I'd have a chance when I saw the hostess add it to a huge stack, but Dave found out I'd applied and promised his mom I was by far the best choice. So she hired me. I agreed to meet Dave at eleven o'clock on a Friday night at *The Kitchen* so he could give me a quick lesson in table waiting, the menu, the register, the whole deal. Tia said I was absolutely mad if I didn't realize this was all his way of getting me alone in some candlelight.

I was a little worried my mom would object when I told her I needed a ride to the restaurant at eleven on a Friday. But when I explained that it was the only time the place was empty enough for Dave to train me; she reluctantly agreed to let me go.

"I like Dave and he seems trustworthy," she said on our way to the restaurant. "I'm not sure how he got mixed up in the email thing with Victoria Spencer."

"Tia thinks Victoria stole his phone and sent it herself." I explained. "Don't worry, mom. I'm just here to train. Nothing else."

"I'm not worried." We stopped at the light and she turned to me.

"What?" I asked.

"Nothing." She said and looked back out at the road. "So do you think Victoria sent the email herself?"

"I don't know. At first I thought the idea was crazy, but the more I think about it, the more sense it makes. I could tell she was mad at Dave the night before when we got back from our meet and she was wearing the same shirt in the picture."

"It sounds like you've thought a lot about this." My mom said.

"Well it was THE topic of conversation for quite a while. I'm just glad for Dave's sake everyone has moved on to other drama. I know how it feels."

"You really like him, huh?" my mom asked. I blushed, glad she couldn't really see me in the dark.

"Really might be a strong word. He's funny. Not what I expected." We pulled up outside. I could see the tables were all empty and reset for the next day. Dave said they closed the kitchen at ten but sometimes people hung out at the bar later.

"You mean because he's a Braun?" my mom asked.

"Yeah, I thought maybe he'd be stuck up or spoiled or something, but he's just...I don't know...he's just Dave." I grabbed my purse.

"What time should I pick you up?" she asked.

"Oh, Dave said he could drop me off. Is that okay?"

"Sure, but let's not make it too late. How about you tell him you need to be home by one? I'm not going to be able to go to sleep until you get home safe."

"Thanks, mom." I smiled and got out before she changed her mind.

She got into the driver's seat, rolled down her window, and yelled, "And tell him to be careful. There are too many drunk drivers on the road at that hour."

"Yes, mom," I said, rolling my eyes.

"Love you, have fun!" she gave me a knowing smile.

The front door was locked so I walked around to the back. A Hispanic guy wearing chef pants and a coat was lighting a cigarette by the dumpster.

"Is Dave here?" I asked him.

He smiled and nodded toward the door. "Restocking," he took a big drag and blew out a puff of smoke. "Look in the walk-in. It's down to the right. You can't miss it."

"Thanks." I walked in and waited for my eyes to adjust to the bright light.

"Hey, you made it," Dave said. He pushed the walk-in door shut with his foot, a box in his arms. "I just need to finish prepping these tomatoes for tomorrow and then I am all yours." He was wearing the checkered chef pants and a white chef coat. He looked older; professional.

"Do you want help?" I asked, though I wasn't sure how much help I would be. I followed him into the kitchen where he placed the box down and grabbed a knife and cutting board.

"No, thanks. I promised my mom, no knife lessons without her here. But you can hang your stuff over there if you want," he pointed to some hooks on the wall. "Then go grab a coke or something at the bar. I think Max is still out there."

I watched as he diced the tomatoes with ease. It was kind of sexy. I blushed and turned to hang up my coat. I went through the swinging door to the front. At first I thought it was deserted, but then a handsome, gray-haired guy popped up from behind the bar.

"Hello there." He said with a very charming accent. "I'm Max," he held out his hand and we shook. His hands were warm and strong. I liked a guy with a good handshake. I got the creeps when someone gave me the dead fish.

"I'm Sierra." I said.

"Ah, yes, Dave's new girl," he said. I wondered whether that meant I was the newest in a long list of girls. I wasn't sure if it was a good or bad thing that he'd mentioned me to Max.

"Can I get you something to drink?" he asked.

"Sure. Do you have sprite?" I sat down at one of the stools.

He filled the glass from the beverage gun. I decided he must be British because he sounded a lot like Hugh Grant.

"So you're the runner right? Went to states with my man Dave?" He washed and dried glasses as he talked.

"That's right. Do you want me to help with anything?" I felt strange that they were working while I sat at the bar sipping a pop.

"No thanks. I got a system. I'm a little territorial about my bar space." He said.

"Good to know," I said.

"Have you ever waited tables before?" he asked.

"Nope. Dave said he could teach me the basics though." I shrugged.

"Ah, your biggest enemies will be the other waitresses. Especially Betty. She's been here forever, longer than me, and can be a bit of a cow. And I only say that because I love her like a sister. Be forewarned she'll ride you harder than a bull in heat." He winked at me. "Oh and don't ever take Peggy's pens. I am protective about me bar, but she is a downright mother bear about her pens. Even if you are desperate." He finished drying a glass and put it away above his head.

"Got it. Don't touch Peggy's pens and avoid Betty at all costs." I repeated.

"And respect me bar." He winked.

"Of course." I smiled. I was starting to wonder what I had gotten myself into when Dave came through the door. I noticed he had taken off the white chef coat and wore a vintage U2 t-shirt.

"Okay, I'm done. Has Max scared you off yet?" he asked.

Max laughed. "I'm calling it a night, Dave." Max said, pulling on a leather coat and reaching for his motorcycle helmet.

"Okay, Horatio left so can you make sure that back door is closed?"

"Sure thing. Sierra, nice to meet you. I leave you in the able hands of the young Mr. Braun." Max said. "Good luck." He disappeared out the swinging door.

Dave turned back to me. It suddenly felt like we had just met. "So," I said.

"Ready?" he asked.

"Ready."

He gave me a full tour of the restaurant, from the bathrooms to where we stored cloth napkins, lemons, and sugar.

"I don't expect you to remember all of this, but it's a good starting point. If you forget something, just ask. Don't waste time trying to guess. People would rather you keep things moving. A good restaurant runs like a perfectly flowing highway—like the Autobahn. If one car slows down, it can cause major back-up for everyone. Timing is key."

"Ground rules. The customer is always right. We allow menu substitutions but do not encourage them. You should take a menu home tonight and begin to memorize it. If you have any questions about dishes or ingredients just ask me and I can explain. Okay?"

"Okay," I said.

"Now let's go over serving. We still do everything the old fashion way—handwritten slips go to the kitchen for orders. My mom hates technology. Plus she thinks it's more personal. Always serve each table in the following order, guest of honor if it's a birthday or anniversary, followed by eldest woman all the way down to youngest male. Got it?"

"Got it," I said.

"So how you would serve my family." He challenged.

"Is it a special occasion for anyone?" I grinned.

"No," he said.

"Well, first your mom, then your oldest sister, your sister Izzy, your father, and last of all yours." I concentrated on the chairs at the table, rather than meeting his gaze.

"Exactly." Dave moved behind me. He smelled good." Now, you always serve from the left and clear from the right. He demonstrated with a glass, brushing my arm as he cleared. Our eyes met for a moment. He cleared his throat and approached the bar.

"We can't serve alcohol until we are 18 so any alcoholic beverages will have to be delivered by the bar back or one of the other waitresses. But don't worry about that too much starting out. They will probably have you work lunch and then bus tables at night until you have the hang of things."

"Good, honestly dinner seems a little scary to me right now." I stayed next to the table, keeping a little distance between us.

"I bet you'll be killing it by Christmas." He walked over to the waiter station.

"Come here and I'll show you the register really quick. It's pretty easy but it's also old so there are a few tricks to her." I didn't comprehend a thing he said at the register. My mind was preoccupied with every brush of his hand or chest as he stood behind me. As Dave walked me through place settings and folding napkins I kept a safer distance. My head was swimming with information. I was shocked when I looked at my watch and found it was already twenty to one.

"Wow, it got late fast." I said. Dave was getting us both a glass of ice water from behind the bar. "I promised my mom I'd be home by one." I stayed on the other side of the bar.

"No problem. I've probably thrown enough at you for one night.

So what time did they tell you to come in tomorrow?" he asked, our fingers briefly touched as he handed me the glass.

"Ten, so I can fill out paperwork and stuff." I accidently locked eyes with him as we finished our water. He turned to wash out his glass. I set mine on the bar.. He washed it, too and put them back..

"Max is pretty particular about his bar," Dave warned.

"I've been warned to steer clear." I said as we headed back into the kitchen. Dave turned out all the lights while I waited by the door. I became very aware that it was really dark except for the glow from the red exit sign. I handed him his coat. He slipped it on and we stood there, really close. He reached out his arm and for a second I thought he was going to lean in and kiss me. But he reached past and flipped the lid on the security pad by my shoulder.

"Sorry, I need to set this." He explained. "Don't open the door until I say, okay?" I faced the door so he wouldn't think I was trying to see the code. We stepped out into the cold night and the door slammed behind us.

"I'm right here," he pointed to his black SUV.

"Nice ride," I commented.

"Thanks. I'm actually paying for it myself. I was so desperate to get my mom to let me help cook here, I told her I would use the money to pay my own car expenses, including the payments."

Dave opened the door for me and I hopped in. When he started the car a Black-Eyed Peas song blasted out of the speakers. I jumped.

"Sorry," he said and turned it way down.

"I love the Black-Eyed Peas. It just scared me." I said.

"Clearly I like them a little louder than I realized." He flashed me a smile as we pulled into the street.

"I'm on Lancaster." I said.

"Yeah, I know, Small town."

"Have you eaten at *The Kitchen* very much?" he asked. "I'm always in the back so I never know who the regulars are."

"Of course, my dad and I used to eat lunch there a lot in the winter. We love the clam chowder and the tortilla soup. My mom and

I don't eat out that often but I think we've been there at least a few times."

"Have you ever had the spicy mac and cheese or any of the quiche specials?" he asked.

"I don't think so. Why?" I asked.

"My creations." We stopped at the light. "What is your absolute favorite meal?"

"My mom's mashed potatoes, my dad's pancakes, a perfectly grilled bone-in New York Strip steak and double stuffs with milk for dessert." I answered.

"Wow! That was quick. Carb-load much?" he laughed. "And double stuffs? Really Hart? Of all the delicious dessert choices out there you go with Oreos?"

"Not just Oreos, double stuffed Oreos." I corrected. "Why, what would yours be?"

"My own chicken curry with white rice, topped with peanuts, mint, and mango chutney, followed by my mom's tiramisu and a perfectly prepared dark roast cappuccino."

"Okay, now my stomach is growling." I said as he pulled into my driveway.

"Well if it wasn't so late I'd offer to make you something. You'll have to let me cook for you another day." He smiled.

"Sounds good," I said. He opened his door and I panicked, grabbing the handle. "Thanks so much for taking the time to go over all of that stuff with me." I held up the menu in my hands like a shield. "I'll try to know this by the time I get there tomorrow." He got out anyway.

"No problem. Like I said, if you're not sure, just ask." He fell into step beside me. "Let me walk you to the door." The door opened, startling us both. Our neighbor's cat, Juniper, ran past us.

"Oh, hi Sierra. Hi Dave. You scared me. I was just letting Juniper out. She must have snuck in when I was sweeping off the back deck earlier. I didn't even notice until she woke me up a few minutes ago. Anyway, now that you are here, I'm going to bed. Dave, thanks for bringing Sierra home." She popped back in the door.

“That crazy cat thinks this is her vacation home. Every time they go away, she sneaks in our house. Well, I better get some rest so I can wake up early to study the menu.” I turned toward the door.

“Hey Sierra,” Dave said and I turned back around. He stood two steps down, putting us eye to eye.

“Yeah?” I wondered if he could hear my heart racing. I knew I could.

The cat squealed, growled and then hissed near the bush by the porch. We both watched it race back toward its house. I turned back to find him looking at me. I cleared my throat.

“Well, I better go study.” I turned and grabbed the door knob. He hesitated and then turned to head down the sidewalk.

“See you tomorrow,” we said in sync and both laughed. I went in and watched through the window. I could just make out his silhouette. He sat there a minute then drove off. I couldn’t wait to tell Tia about my night.

Dr. Laura Hart

I grew restless waiting for news about the drop and found myself in Sierra's room. I opened her closet door and ran my hand slowly across her hanging clothes. Sierra always kept her room organized, though not in a sterile way. But the investigators had left things slightly askew. I walked around straightening. Sierra would feel better coming home to her room in order. On her desk, I found some of her college application materials and a spiral notebook open to her handwritten answers to essay questions.

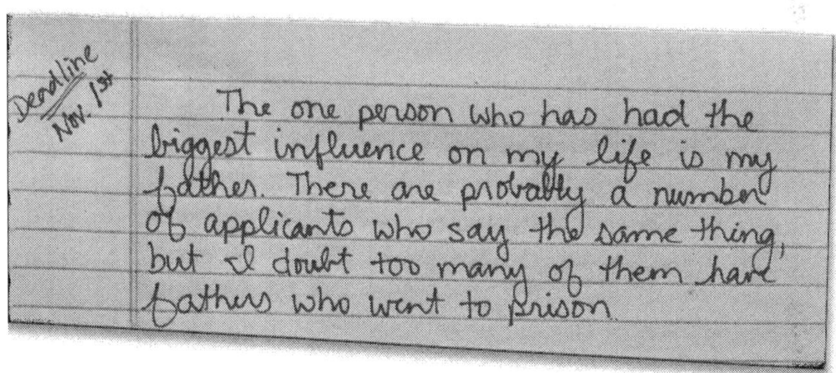
Deadline Nov. 1st

The one person who has had the biggest influence on my life is my father. There are probably a number of applicants who say the same thing, but I doubt too many of them have fathers who went to prison.

That was it. She never went further with that topic. I scanned through the rest. She'd started a number of different essays, long term goals, and greatest threats to the environment. Nothing else stood out as truly personal until the bottom of the next page:

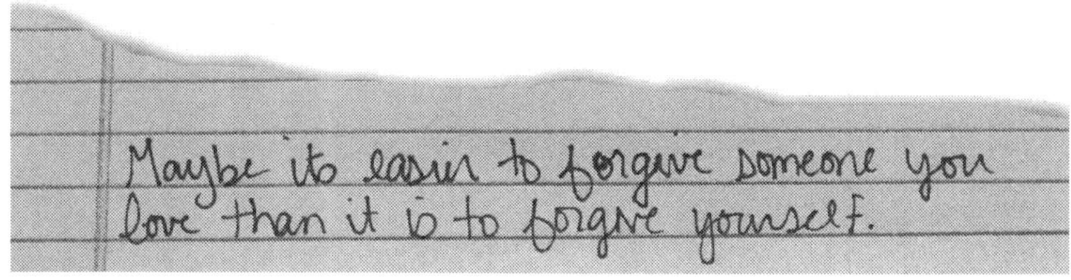
Maybe its easier to forgive someone you love than it is to forgive yourself.

Who was she referring to? Her father? Herself? Me? Should I show it to Patrick or Sharon Donovan? Could it be tied to her disappearance? I closed the notebook, put it back and went downstairs. I'd think on it a bit.

Day 35 – 11/8
Biked 17 miles.

Adding a little salsa to your tomato soup does not make it more exciting. I'm no longer alone down here! My little foil family is complete—including Tia, Dave, Gavin and little Teddy. Obviously, it's no great substitute when complete but as I crafted each person, I found comfort in the memories that flooded my thoughts. Memories are keeping me going.

My first day of work went much better than expected. Betty, the waitress Max had warned me about, had taken the day off to attend a baby shower and the other waitresses were really helpful and patient. I was assigned to shadow Peggy and made sure to stay away from her pens. Lunch had ended and we were resetting for dinner when Dave came into the dining room to get water and say "hi." His shift didn't start until four since he worked until close. He stayed at the bar for a bit talking to Max. I wanted to talk to him but didn't want it to seem like I was slacking off on my first day. Luckily, I had to go get more napkins near the bar.

"So how did your first lunch go?" Dave asked. I grabbed a stack of napkins.

"Well, I didn't spill on anyone or break anything so I guess it went okay."

"So what did I miss last night?" Max asked. I quickly walked back to the tables, my face turning a deep red.

"A true man never talks." I heard Dave say before he headed into the kitchen. I liked that he made it seem like something may have happened. Tia was convinced he would have kissed me if my mom hadn't interrupted. Things were progressing with her and Thomas (the Matt Damon look-alike from the bowling alley). They had hung out a few times and he had kissed her when he dropped her off last week. But their hour distance was a pain.

By the second week in December, I had gotten better at waiting tables and they let me fill in on some dinner shifts. With all of the holiday parties, it was their busiest season. But work did keep me from meeting up with my dad. I felt bad even though he said he understood. Then one day at work I turned around and there he was, seated in my section.

"Excuse me miss, but aren't you the sixth fastest "5Ker" in the state?" He flashed me his devilish smile and stood to hug me.

"Dad! How did you get here?" I asked, and looked around to see if anyone else recognized him.

"Well, I finally got myself some wheels," he pointed to a Toyota Highlander out front.

"Nice!" I said. "And I can legally drive it now."

"I know. Congrats on passing!" he said.

"Would you like a menu?" I was eager to get him in and out.

"Do they still have the chowder?" he asked.

"Yep," I said. "But you should try the quiche. Dave makes it, and it's incredible."

"Dave, huh?" he said. I blushed. "Well then I guess I better try it."

"Anything to drink?" I asked.

"Sure, how 'bout a coffee?" He handed me back the menu. Do you think you could sit with me for a couple minutes? There's something I want to tell you."

"Sure, when your food comes I'll have a couple minutes." What could he have to tell me?

As it turned out, I got slammed with two big groups. I barely had time to get back to my dad to clear his table. I found myself a little testy with some of the other guests when I overheard them talking about my dad. He seemed oblivious to the stares and people saying "out of jail already," and "embezzled" and "white collar prison."

"Sorry," I apologized when I finally had a second, "In the weeds. Maybe you could meet me after. I get done around five."

"It's no problem. I like watching you work. I'll take another coffee, and any dessert you recommend. You were right about Dave's quiche." He winked.

I rolled my eyes but my face turned red. "I know exactly what to bring you." I said before hurrying off to get the drinks for another table.

I brought him Mrs. Braun's tiramisu. Dave had been right; it beat the heck out of double stuff Oreos any day of the week. By the time I was able to take a minute for my dad, my shift was ending and I had six tables to reset. But he waited patiently. I was a little disappointed because that was usually when I got a chance to hang out with Dave. We didn't run together after school anymore so we barely saw each other.

I had my dad drive around back to load my bike because he'd offered to give me a ride home.

"Good thing I got an SUV," he said as he loaded it into the back. "After you, me lady," he gestured toward my seat. I laughed. He always did that when I was little.

"Thank you, sir." I said and crawled into the seat. It suddenly seemed odd that my dad and Dave drove the same car, a black Highlander. "Do you know where to go?" I realized how strange it was that my dad had never seen the new house. My own dad.

"161 Lancaster, right?" he asked.

"Yup. So what did you want to tell me?" I asked.

"Well, do you want the good news or the bad news?" he asked. My stomach dropped.

"I don't want bad news at all, but I guess I'd rather start with that and end on a good note." I responded. He stopped at the light.

"Well, the bad news is I have to be in New York for most of the next six months so we won't be able to see each other much." He explained.

"Okay, that stinks, unless that means I get to come hang out with you there?" I said.

"Well, that is a possibility. And would be really fun. But the even better news is this project will also allow me to afford my own place. Since I work remotely when I'm not in New York, I could find something closer to you." He was waiting for my reaction when the car behind us beeped. The light had changed.

"Wow, that's great. So you would want to live in Laketown again?" I asked. I know he could sense that I wasn't sure that was the best idea. Everyone here thought of him as a thief. I worried about the backlash if he were around all of the time.

"It sounds like you don't really like the idea?" I saw the hurt in his eyes and felt awful.

"It's not that I don't want to see you all of the time. I just don't want anyone to give you a hard time." I said.

"Ah you mean like earlier today?" he asked. "Do I embarrass you?" His shoulders sagged and my normally confident, charming father looked beaten down: like he had in those weeks of the trial.

"Of course not!" I said. "But why would you want to deal with that all of the time? People judging?" He turned onto my street.

"I don't really care what anybody thinks other than you. But if it will make you uncomfortable, I understand. I can live someplace else." He pulled up to the curb in front of my house.

"I'm sorry." I said. "I feel like you were all happy to tell me and I ruined it."

"No, I get where you are coming from. I do. Who wants their ex-con dad cramping their style, right?" he smiled and winked at me.

"Dad, come on. You're not cramping my style. I just-" He interrupted.

"How about we put a pin in this for a few months? I'm going to be busy in New York anyway. I can wait before making any big decisions, okay?" he looked me right in the eyes and I could see the hurt lingering.

"Okay. And maybe we could look into me coming to New York for a weekend?" I smiled. "I hear it's really nice around the holidays. And Tia said the Rockettes are a must see."

"I'd love it," he said. "We just have to get clearance from your mom."

"I can handle that," I assured him.

"Okay, see what she says and I'll look into ticket prices and stuff, okay?"

"Yes! All right, I better go. I'm supposed to be at a birthday party by seven."

"Okay, have fun! Love you." He said and gave me a hug.

"You too. Thanks for the ride." I ran into the house to get ready. I needed to consult Tia on the best way to convince my mom to let me go to NYC. Maybe she could even meet me there if it was during break.

Dr. Laura Hart

I found Sharon Donovan sitting at the desk in my home office.

"Nothing yet." When I didn't leave she looked up, "Sorry, did you need to get in here?"

I shook my head.

"Is there something you wanted to tell me?" She sat up a little straighter.

I took a deep breath and gently closed the door behind me. "Patrick is a great father. He was a great husband. Everybody loves him." I turned back. "Never mind."

"No wait. Laura. It's okay. Please go ahead."

"Before he was arrested I would never have questioned him. And I've confirmed he hasn't been gambling since he got out; but I need to know if there is anything that you know that I don't."

"Laura, I can understand how difficult this must be for you. As it stands now, we have no reason to rule him in or out as a possible motive."

"Oh God!" I sat in the chair across from her.

"Don't get upset. I can tell you we haven't found any evidence of Patrick gambling or owing money or even associating with any of those types while in prison. But Laura, no matter what circumstances led to her abduction, *your* only focus right now should be staying strong for your daughter. I need you and Patrick to be a united front. You can work through the other stuff later. Okay? You're a doctor. A very good one from what I hear. You must know how to compartmentalize well. I need you to do that now. For Sierra. Okay?

I took a deep breath, stood, and opened the door, "Of course." I ran my hands through my hair and went to make tea.

Day 40 – 11/13
Biked 40 Miles

Mixed Tuna with my mac-n-cheese- going outside the box with that one.

I've moved on to include foil Mindy, Max, and Betty; considering a Veronica Spencer and the idea of voodoo. Probably bring me bad karma though. The work of creating is calming. Having daily tasks to complete gives me a reason to get out of bed; but crafting gives me something to look forward to each day.

I realized today that I have become my mother. I used to catch her talking to herself all of the time when it was just the two of us. I guess we all have moments that we just need to hear the words we are thinking spoken out loud. Maybe it helps us to remember, or fill the silence that marks someone's absence. Maybe that's what I'm doing. Or maybe I'm talking to you.

I swear I heard someone outside today but I banged and banged with the pot and yelled and sang and played the record player on high and nothing. I wish I could see what was out there, above me. I imagine being deep in the woods.

I miss my mom. I hope my dad is taking good care of her. And funny enough I really miss Dave. I miss Gavin, too, but I guess I never thought about how much Dave was a daily part of my life for so long. Gavin still sends little ripples through my stomach while the thought of Dave gives me a sense of comfort. What a mess I am. I really wish I could talk to Tia.

I wonder what it is like to have your friend just disappear. Can she really miss me after living so far apart already? Has it had an impact at all on her daily life? I can't even cry anymore. I've tried and nothing. How would I feel if Tia suddenly disappeared? I would be sad and scared for her and want to help her family find her. But after 40 days? 60? A year? What then? Would I just go on with my life? Wouldn't I have to?

Patrick Hart

We suffered in silence as we waited to hear where the money had led them. I felt the weight of guilt and unspoken accusations thick in the air of our small house. There was no escape from the pain, the fear, or the dark reality before us. We all jumped when Sheryl's phone rang again.

"Sheryl Donovan." She looked up at us but we couldn't tell anything from her stern expression. "I want to talk to him. I'll meet you there. Thanks."

"Did they find her? Is she okay?" Laura asked.

"They didn't find Sierra, but they have identified the man behind the ransom request. His name is Emanuel Walter Pricket. Patrick knew him as Sausage."

"And they think he has her?" I asked, overwhelmed by the news that this really was a direct result of my mistakes. When would the punishment end? Why did Sierra have to suffer?

"Who is Sausage?" Laura asked.

"He was incarcerated with your husband." Sheryl explained.

"Did you owe him money?" Laura turned on me. "What have you done, Patrick?" At first I thought she was going to hit me but then she just collapsed onto our couch.

"Why was he in jail?" Laura asked, sliding forward as if she might pounce. She focused all of her attention on Sheryl, completely dismissing me. It was as if she couldn't even find the strength to acknowledge me at that point.

"He was in for armed robbery but has been in and out of juvie and jail his whole life. There's nothing on his sheet about kidnapping or sexual assault but he has a long history of abusing his four wives. He has five children. His son that picked up the ransom money."

"What does he have against Patrick?" Laura asked.

"I wouldn't..." I started to explain but Laura cut me off.

"I asked *her*." She said without even looking at me.

There was nothing I could do or say at that point. I stood quietly to the side as Sheryl explained the background.

"So now that you have him and he didn't get the money what do you think he'll do?" Laura wondered.

“I honestly don’t know. I wish I had better news, but this is all we know right now. They are bringing him to the station. I’m going to go talk to him myself.” She put on her coat and headed to the front door. “I know this has been a long, hard day. But I need you to hang tight just a little longer. I will contact you as soon as we know anything.”

Laura and I watched in silence as she pushed through the flock of questioning reporters and drove off. I heard Laura whisper a silent prayer under her breath as she left the room. I knew better than to try and follow her. We would each have to wait in our own private hell.

Day 44 – 11/17

Biked 10 miles.

I don't know why I had it in my head that if I added a mile a day surely I couldn't be here past 40. It was as if I was biking to freedom. Now that it came and went; I can't find the strength to keep going higher. I guess I should set a new goal. The closest I got today was the "new" part. I finally tried canned chicken. It wasn't too bad.

I barely remember the first time I met Gavin Ross. I had stopped by my mom's office to get her to sign a permission slip to watch *Schindler's List* in history class. If I didn't get the signature, I would have to spend the next three days of history in the library. Lame. I waited for her in the waiting room. It always made me a little nervous to visit during flu and strep season. My mom opened the door and ushered me into the back.

"Hey, how was your day?" she asked.

"Good. Sorry to bug you. It looks busy. I just need you to sign this slip." I handed it to her.

She signed it and gave it back, "Hey, I want to introduce you to someone." She said. I glanced at my watch. I was scheduled to meet Dave for a run at four. We hadn't run together since the season ended. Anxious, I followed her around the corner to the nurses' office. I knew most of my mom's nurses by name because they had been there forever. Mindy Ross was standing at a computer. Next to her was a tall guy with black hair and really intense blue eyes.

"Sierra, this is Mindy's son, Gavin. Gavin, this is my daughter Sierra." My mom said. He didn't hold out a hand to shake so neither did I.

"Nice to meet you." I said.

"Likewise." He smiled. He had a dimple.

"Gavin is going to join your school after Christmas break. He's also a junior so I thought maybe you could introduce him around. Maybe invite him to something over break so he can meet some of the guys before he starts." I snuck another peek at my watch. 3:45, and I still had to get home and change.

"Sure. I can't think of anything off the top of my head but I'm sure there will be something. Why don't you give him my email?" I suggested.

"Are we keeping you?" Gavin asked. I felt my face burn. "Sorry, I don't mean to be rude, but I'm supposed to meet someone for a run at four and I still need to stop home and change." I felt like a jerk for having made it so obvious.

"You a runner?" Gavin asked.

"Is she ever! She's been to Nationals for track and States for cross country for the past two years." My mom bragged. I rolled my eyes.

"Do you run?" I asked.

"He started just this fall and already went all the way to Nationals in cross country," his mom bragged. Now he rolled his eyes.

"Who needs PR when you have a mom?" he said. I looked at my watch again.

"Seriously." I agreed. "Listen, I'm sorry but I really do need to go. Email me and we'll figure something out." I said. "Nice to meet you. Nice to see you Mindy. Bye Mom." I rushed out before anyone could stop me.

I can only imagine what Gavin's first impression of me was. If I had known what was to come I may have paid better attention.

I was ten minutes late to meet Dave for our run. He was stretching by his car when I got to the parking lot. Our plan was to run the lake's seven mile circumference.

"Sorry," I said, jumping out of my car to stretch.

"No worries." He said.

"I had to get my mom to sign the *Schindler's List* permission slip and then she wanted me to meet someone. Do you know the name Gavin Ross?" I asked.

"Sounds familiar. Who is he?" he asked. "Shall we start? It gets dark so early."

"Sure." We headed onto the path. "His mom is a nurse in my mom's office. He's starting at M.H. after Christmas break and he's in our class. My mom was hoping I could introduce him arround over break." We fell into our familiar rhythm.

"Well, Jack and I were thinking of having a big New Year's party at his parent's cabin. Are you going to be around?"

"Yeah, sure." My heart kicked into even higher gear.

"Cool. So you could bring him and introduce him around," he suggested. My heart sank. He wanted me to come to his party with another guy?

"Sure," I said, though I wanted to scream. Was he ever going to ask me out?

"What was his name again?" he asked.

"Gavin Ross. He ran at nationals in cross country this year." I explained.

"Oh yeah. That's why I know the name. He came out of nowhere and he's really good. He ran in a different division. Why is he changing schools?" he asked.

"I don't know." I admitted. "I didn't get all of the details because I was running late to meet you."

"Gavin. Ross. Wow, I bet he'll run track, too. I guess he could be a nice replacement for Lebraun this year," he sounded a little defensive.

"So did I tell you I talked my mom into letting me go to New York City with my dad over Thanksgiving?"

"That's cool. I love the city. We used to go see the Thanksgiving parade when we were younger." A dog barked and we both instinctively looked up to see if it was contained.

"Invisible fence," I pointed out the little sign in the lawn.

"Hey, Izzy is in an off-Broadway show and my dad and Karen are going to see her the day after Thanksgiving. My mom and I have work, but you should go."

"I'd love to see Izzy perform, but do you think your dad and sister would feel weird about my dad?" The temperature drop made our breath visible.

"I don't think they'd make a big deal about it. But I can feel it out if you want."

"Okay. And I probably need to be careful about money. I don't know how much spare cash my dad has these days."

"Oh, I'll get tickets from Izzy. Don't worry about that."

"But what about dinner before? That could get expensive. My dad won't be able to go to the same places your dad and Karen can." I almost kicked myself. "Sorry, is that weird to say?"

"No, it's a fair point. Let me talk to Izzy and my dad and get back to you, okay?"

"Okay. I won't say anything to my dad until you see what they say." I was relieved I hadn't offended him.

"You're going to love it," he said. "I wish I could show you around New York. If it's nice enough you should go for a run in Central Park." He suggested. I was still stuck on 'I wish I could show you around New York.' *Me too*, I thought.

"I feel bad leaving the restaurant when it's so busy. It seems strange that you and your mom have to work and miss Izzy's show and I may get to go." Our arms brushed as we squeezed between two parked cars and I wondered if he noticed.

"We're used to it. It's part of the restaurant business. My future is filled with weekends and holidays at work so you better consider that before you decide to run off to Vegas and marry me, okay?" He flashed me that smile that made my knees jelly; dangerous while running.

I don't know if it was the running endorphins or what but I came back with a, "that's fine. Marriage didn't pan out so well for my parents. I'm thinking casual affairs are safer anyway. So maybe you could fit me in between holidays." Thank God my face was already flushed from the cold or he would have seen how I was instantly mortified by my own words. Shit, did Tia have a talking voodoo doll of me somewhere? That sounded like her words.

"Sierra, I never knew you had a wild side. Very promising." He nudged my arm with his and again flashed that smile.

"I think maybe you bring it out." I kept my eyes on the road ahead because I didn't dare look at him.

He laughed. "Come on we need to pick up our pace or we're going to be running in the dark, soon." We double-timed it back to our cars. Our pace didn't really leave room for chatter the rest of the way.

We both stretched against our own car for a few silent moments, our breathing slowly regulated. At that angle I could study him without being obvious. I liked the muscles in his upper arms. They were defined but not showy.

"Nice run Hart," Dave said, startling me. "Are you good to go again tomorrow and Wednesday?" he asked.

"Sure." I cleared my throat and avoided his eyes, "I mean, Wednesday, I work. You work on Thursday?" I asked.

"Yeah, so tomorrow it is." I caught him watching me and our eyes locked for a moment. I turned to get in my car. "I'll check with my dad on New York," he promised.

"Thanks."

He waited for me to pull out first. Either he enjoyed teasing me or he really had no interest in anything other than friendship.

Day 50 – 11/23
Biked 25 miles (to stay warm)

Ate nasty chicken noodle soup; never been a fan of soup from a can. Still, I needed a can for my new project. It's not a goal exactly but it keeps me busy. I am building houses for my foil people using recyclables. My art teacher would be elated.

It's felt colder down here over the last few days. I wear a few layers and sleep in the sleeping bag most nights. It's strange how warm it stays without any heat. At least I don't think there is any heat. Maybe that means I am really buried. Buried Alive.

Sometimes I worry my food could run out. Yesterday I spilled cooked pasta on the floor and I couldn't decide what to do. If I throw it out, will I have to dig through the garbage for it later? I put it in a sealed baggie on the counter. If I need it, it's there. But some days I get like that with everything. Should I bathe today or wait another. Will I wish back that shampoo, toothpaste, water? Nothing should be wasted. When I feel like I might go crazy with what ifs I have to focus my thoughts elsewhere. Math helps. It has one right answer.

At this point I am pretty confident that I could pass the Series 7 exam. Apparently the Keeper (as I have come to call him or her or them), wanted me to stay educated and left me with the book, *Series 7 For Dummies*. It's the test stockbrokers have to pass to get a license to trade. I would like to announce that I just took one of their test exams and aced it (again). Ring that bell—the floor is open. So maybe it shouldn't count if you've taken the same test 3 times already? But who here is going to tell me any different.

I'd love to have anyone tell me anything. Just another voice. Did you ever see that movie *Castaway* where Tom Hank's character starts talking to a volleyball? I think about that movie a lot. And since I have no toothbrush I really hope between flossing and finger brushing, I do not have to extract my own tooth like he did.

I wish I had my own Wilson. He could stay in one of my lovely residential masterpieces. I have a foil encased Kraft original duplex, the Zesta Highlife high-rise with great light from all of the windows (the penthouse even boasts a plastic wrap skylight, or the Kellog Estate complete with the empty mayo greenhouse. Just add the greens and PLEASE bring some friends!

Sometimes in the dark hours I swear someone is here. The first few times I immediately grabbed my knife and flipped on my flashlight. Nobody. But lately I think maybe whoever it is, lives only in the dark. Like a living shadow. I lay here, a sleeping bag my only protection and debate the risks of talking to the shadows. Would it mean I'm crazy? If I live through this and on to old age—screw living alone—take me to a nursing home any day. And give me a roommate.

Day 54– 11/27
Biked 12 miles.

Not very hungry. Ate crackers and finished the last jar of peanut butter.

Added the school and library to my village today; next up police station. (Irony Rocks)

Sometimes I think I hear you talking to me in the dark. Is it you? Can you see things I can't?

New York was incredible. I could see why Izzy lived there. As part of an early Christmas gift my mom and dad had secretly gotten tickets to Radio City Music Hall. We saw the Rockettes on my first night. The next day we went to the Thanksgiving Day Parade. We had a bird's eye view because my dad's college friend invited us to a party at her friend's place. I had never seen so many people and so much food. Everything was delicious. Dave would have loved it. On Friday my dad had to work so I got to explore the city a little. I went to the MOMA and, per Dave's suggestions, for a run in Central Park. Friday night we went to dinner with the Brauns at a small Indian restaurant that was surprisingly cheap. It was a hole in the wall but the food was incredible. I wasn't sure I completely understood Izzy's play but she was very good. I could tell she was born for the stage. We all waited for Izzy outside the theater and then went for dessert.

My dad and Dave's dad were at the counter and Karen was in the restroom when Izzy turned to me.

"So Sierra," she said. "I'm glad we got the chance to finally meet."

"Me too," I said, though I wasn't sure why she'd be so interested in meeting me.

"Dave talks about you so much that I feel like I already know you," she laughed. "So why don't you guys just hook up already? Are you not interested? I know he can be kind of intense and he does work crazy hours. Has he made his key lime pie for you yet? It is worth every calorie. So did you like the play? Did you get it? I know sometimes it is hard to follow."

I could not get a word in edgewise. Izzy was like Tia on speed. But it worked out because I couldn't get past "*why don't you guys just hook up already*." Great question! Before I could answer, Karen came back.

"So Izzy, how are things going outside the theater?" Karen asked.

"You mean like, how am I paying rent, or am I dating anyone new?" There was a bit of an edge to her voice.

"What? I was just making conversation," Karen said.

"I'm great. Yes, rent is paid on time every month and yes I'm still dating Zach."

"See that wasn't so hard." Karen said. "Mom and Dave were really disappointed they couldn't make it."

"Yeah," I added. "I know Dave really wished he could see it. He said it's your first production he has missed."

We parted ways after dessert and my dad and I spent the rest of the weekend seeing the usual sights and eating great food. I could see that if I ever wanted to live in New York, I needed to make a ton of money.

I called Tia the minute I got home. I knew it would be a long conversation so I saved it for a landline. She was jealous but had news of her own. She and Thomas were officially exclusive. And she was impressed that he brought it up, not her. I was happy for Tia. She sounded really happy. But it made me miss her even more. I missed just hanging out. Maybe I could see if my mom would be willing to spend our spring break in California this year.

A few days later while I was running with Dave all I could think about was my promise to Tia. After filling her in on my trip she made me promise that if Dave didn't make a move at the next available opportunity, I would.

"You okay Hart?" he asked. "You're strangely quiet."

"I am?" I asked. "Sorry, guess I'm just lost in my own head today." I said.

"Apparently my conversation skills are slipping." He joked.

"So are you and Jack definitely having the New Year's party?" I asked. We ran past the barking dog again.

“Yep. Are you still going to be able to come?” he asked.

“I feel a little bad leaving my mom home alone. We kind of have this little tradition. Well, actually it was my mom and Tia and I, but-” Suddenly I tripped and found myself sprawled on the ground.

“Whoa, Sierra. Are you okay?” Dave knelt beside me. I had saved my face, but my arm and knee were scraped and bleeding pretty bad.

“I'm okay. Embarrassed, but okay. What was that?” I tried to stand.

“Hold on. Why don't you just sit for a second and let me assess the damage.” I sat back down. Dave gently took my arm in his hands to see how it looked. He did the same with my leg. “Yep, looks like flesh wounds. Let's see how you feel with weight on your leg. He wrapped his arm around me to steady me while I stood. It felt nice.

“Does it feel like you sprained anything?” he asked.

“Besides my ego?” I asked. He still had his arm around me when I turned my head to answer him. Our faces were inches apart. My stomach flipped as he leaned in and kissed me gently. I tentatively kissed him back and he cradled my head and pulled me in deeper. The kiss intensified and I completely lost myself in him. I have no idea how long we stood there kissing. It could have been thirty seconds. It could have been five minutes. But at some point I heard a horn beep a few times and a guy yell, “Get a room already Braun!”

We pulled apart, and he smiled, “Jack.” He kissed the tip of my nose as I smiled back.

“We better get you back and cleaned up,” he said. “I have a first aid kit in my car. Do you think you're okay to run?” Dave asked.

“Sure,” I said. My voice sounded strange. “Maybe not full pace but I'm okay.”

When we got back to the parking lot he opened the back of his Highlander and had me rest on the edge so that my leg wasn't bent too far. He cleaned up my leg and arm and bandaged them pretty good with disinfectant, gauze and tape. “For a chef you are pretty proficient in first aid, Dr. Braun.” I remarked.

“Yes, well, I have had my fair share of burns, knife incidents, and occasional skateboarding wipeouts.” He explained.

"Skateboarding? I never knew. Can you do cool tricks and stuff?" I needed a safe subject to keep my mind off his hands on my body.

Dave shrugged as he finished with my arm. "I used to. I haven't done it in years. What about you Hart, any tricks up your sleeve?" I blushed when he looked at me. I could not help it. He closed up the first aid kit, and leaned into the car to put it back.

"Wow, must be pretty good to make you blush that quickly. Is there a wild child you keep hidden?" he asked. I was speechless. I felt like an idiot. I stood up.

"And now I have rendered you speechless." He said. I was between Dave and the car. He leaned in with that smile, grabbed my face with his hand and kissed me again, pressing me against the car. He tasted like spearmint gum and I could feel his heart racing against my chest. He pressed into me with the full length of his body and he deepened the kiss. I gently ran my hands up his arms to his shoulders and he shivered. *Did I cause that?* I felt a rush in the pit of my stomach. It scared and excited me all at the same time; freedom laced with danger. He slowly pulled back and looked at me. His eyes were almost solid black with just a sliver of gray. He gently ran his finger down my cheek.

"We should go." He rested his forehead on mine. But he didn't move. I will never forget the way he looked at me then. There was so much raw emotion in his stare.

"So does this mean you won't show me your skateboard tricks?" I asked. He smiled and pulled away.

"I might be convinced to bust a move or two for you, Hart. But no promises that I can even find my board." He walked me over to my car and I gingerly got into the driver's seat.

"Sorry about your fall." He said. "Probably hurt like hell tomorrow."

"I know." I said as I started my car. "Thanks for playing doctor." I said.

"My pleasure." He smiled and leaned in to briefly brush my lips with his. "See you tomorrow." he closed my door and watched me pull out.

Holy shit! I was dying to call Tia but I made myself wait until I got home. I guess all I needed to do was literally throw myself into his path to get his attention. I soon learned once I had Dave's attention, there was no turning it off.

Due to the craziness that came with the holiday season, I only saw Dave at work and school over the next few weeks. Between our work schedules we weren't able to fit in a run unless we were willing to wake up early in the morning. That may have been tempting in the spring or summer, but in the winter it was still dark. Combine it with the cold, snow and ice, and forget it. Sleep won out every time.

The Kitchen holiday party was held the Monday before Christmas. The tradition was to have the wait and bar staff cook for the kitchen staff. I was in charge of the mashed potatoes and with a little direction from Dave they turned out great. The Braun family was leaving the following morning to spend Christmas in NYC and take in Izzy's play which had been extended through the holidays.

Dave and I decided we'd exchange gifts at the party. I really struggled with what to get him because he or his parents could basically afford to get him anything he wanted. I decided to get creative. I had his mom and Hector help me collect his favorite recipes and then I used Illustrator (glad I took that graphic design class my sophomore year) to layout a cookbook for him. I had it printed and spiral bound for easy use in the kitchen. It had been a ton of work, but it came out great. I scanned the family picture from their Christmas card for the cover and included a picture of myself with a gift message on the inside back cover.

We ate dinner then exchanged secret Santa gifts. I got Peggy a four-pack of her favorite pens and Dave's mom gave me a beautiful winter scarf (clearly over budget). I loved it. The adults were all pretty happy thanks to the free-flowing wine and champagne. Max set up a Karaoke Machine and people started singing. Dave grabbed my hand.

"Follow me," he said. He grabbed a box from the kitchen counter, then led me into his mom's office and closed the door.

"Have a seat for a second." I felt like a little kid on Christmas Eve. He pulled out two candles, lit them and set them on the desk. Then he pulled out a bottle of champagne and two plastic cups. He popped the cork like a pro and poured us each a glass.

"Impressive." I said.

"Thank you." He smiled as he turned the lights off and left us in the glow of the candles. He handed me my champagne and joined me on the couch. He held up his glass.

"Merry Christmas to us," he said. We tapped our plastic cups together.

"To us," I repeated. He jumped up.

"Oops, almost forgot." He reached up and pushed play on the CD player. "It's a mix of some stuff I thought we'd both like." He said and finished his champagne. He picked up the bottle and poured another cup. "Do you want more?" he asked.

"Sure." I finished my glass and held it up. I could feel the heat and bubbles tickle down my throat and into my stomach. "Are you sure your mom won't get mad if she finds us back here drinking champagne?"

"I don't think she'll come looking. I told her I wanted to spend a little time with just you before we left." He sat back down beside me.

"I'm guessing you left out the part about the champagne?" I smiled. He ran his finger gently along my knee where I had fallen. It was still scabbed over in a few spots. I flinched.

"Sorry, does it still hurt?" he took his hand away.

"Not really. I just-" I looked up and he leaned in and kissed me gently. It made me warm all over.

"Sorry, I had to do that. You were saying?" he asked. He finished his second glass of champagne. I took a drink of mine. As one of our songs ended we could hear Max belting out *Sweet Caroline* from the dining room.

"I love this song!" I said. Even after all of the food I felt a little buzzed from the champagne. I finished my glass and he filled both again.

"So do I get my gift now? My mom said you spent a lot of time on it. I'm curious." He said, flashing that smile.

"Sure." I said. "Let me just go grab it." I stood.

When I walked to get the gift near the coat rack, I could tell the champagne had already gone to my head. Thank God I didn't have to work or go to school the next day or drive home. Although Dave was supposed to drive and he had more than me.

Max finished and they all chanted for Peggy to take the mic. I slipped back into the office and handed Dave his gift wrapped package. He must have pulled mine out of the box while I was gone. He handed me a small box.

"Ladies first." He said. I carefully tore off the wrapping and found a velvet box. It felt strange to get jewelry from anyone other than my dad. Even my mom never bought me jewelry. I almost laughed. He seemed excited for me to see what was inside.

I snapped it open. Inside was a silver heart-shaped locket with an intricate design.

"Do you like it? It's real silver so it can tarnish but I found it in this cool antique jewelry store in Rochester. Look at the back. It's the best part."

"I love it already," I said. I carefully turned it over. I had to hold it close to my face so I could read it in the candlelight. It said *For my Hart*. I almost cried. "Thank you," I whispered, feeling my face turn red.

"You really like it? So the craziest part is the inscription was already there. What are the chances? I've been dying to tell you the story. Here let me put it on you."

I turned around and lifted my hair off my neck so he could hook it on for me.

"It's perfect. I love it. Thank you." I leaned over to kiss him. He slid his hands into my hair and pulled me closer. He deepened the kiss, gently teasing my tongue with his. I felt desire race through my body like a tingly electric current. He used his arm to slide me underneath him so that we were both laying on the love seat. The bottom of my dress had slid up to my waist. He slid one of his hands from my hair down to my bare thigh and I felt another bolt run through me. I couldn't think as he ran his fingers up my leg and to my waist. I ran my hands up into his hair. He slipped his finger under the edge of my underwear at my waist and ran it back and forth. It set my lower half on fire. I had a sudden urge to feel his skin against mine. I pulled my hands from his hair and as quickly as I could I pulled his shirt from his pants and ran them up the muscles in his back. I could feel him shiver beneath my touch. I liked that I could make his body react to mine.

He moved his finger from my waist down to the leg of my underwear. Again he ran the tip of his finger around just the edge. It was tortured pleasure. I wiggled beneath him and his finger slid further into my underwear. He ran it slowly along the edges of my lips and I heard myself make a strange noise in the back of my throat. I wanted him to slide them inside but somewhere in the saner, more sober part of my head I felt like we were moving too fast. I pulled my face back from his.

"Hey, I think..." He kissed me again but slid his hand out. I tried to sit up a little.

"Sorry, I just...I..." I tried to speak but he kissed me again.

"You taste so good," he gave me another kiss, "and feel so soft." He slid his mouth over, breathed in deep and kissed my hair. He sat up, separating us a little. I pulled my dress back down so that it at least covered my underwear again. My lips were burning.

"How 'bout you open your gift now." I suggested and looked to see where it had gone. He grabbed it off the floor and tore it open like a five year old on his birthday. I watched his face as he studied the book cover in the candlelight. He smiled and I felt relieved.

"Wow, this is awesome. How did you get all of these recipes?" he asked, impressed.

"Your mom and Hector helped me." I explained.

"Oh my gosh Sierra, this was a ton of work! And will be so awesome to have in the kitchen. Thank you!" he said. He looked me right in the eyes and planted a sweet small kiss on my lips. "I love it." he whispered. The CD stopped and we could hear everyone laughing in the dining room.

"I hate to end this, but if we don't go back out there soon, I don't think I will be able to leave your clothes on." He whispered into my ear. The feel of his breath on my ear gave me chills. We opened the door, blew out the candles, and took care of the cups and the champagne bottle. There wasn't much left in the bottle. I looked at my watch. It was almost eleven. I hoped Dave was okay to drive me home. My curfew was midnight.

When we rejoined the party we were properly hazed by the group. Dave saw my beet-red face and distracted everyone by showing off his new cookbook. Max told us we were not allowed to leave without singing at least one song.

Eventually they convinced us. Dave sang, *Piano Man* by Billy Joel and I sang *Like a Prayer* by Madonna. Then we both sang *Summer Nights* from Grease. Dave was actually pretty good. I was by far the weaker link. By the time I had to go my face hurt from laughing.

Mrs. Braun wished us all a Merry Christmas and we each got a cash bonus. I felt lucky to be a part of the group. Dave and I walked out to his car and the cold air helped clear my head. I hoped it did the same for him.

"Are you okay to drive?" I asked him.

"Yeah. I ate some more tiramisu and had a coffee. I think it killed my buzz. Plus, it's been a while hasn't it?" he asked, looking at his watch.

When we pulled into my driveway, Dave killed the lights so they didn't shine in on my mom. "So I get back on Thursday night. Are you working Friday?" he asked.

"Yeah, I'm doing lunch Friday through Sunday and working a double on Saturday. I don't think I'll see you until Monday." I said.

"You wanna catch a movie?" he asked.

"Sure. If the weather is okay do you want to run first?" I asked. "I feel like I haven't had a good run since I fell."

"Sure. I'll walk you in."

When we got to the door, he took my hands in his, leaned down, and kissed me soft and slow. He whispered, and turned to go.

"Merry Christmas. Travel safe." I said and turned to let myself in the house. I waited until I heard him pull out and then headed upstairs. My mom was in her room with the light on but asleep. I walked in and turned it off.

As I walked out she sat said "did you have fun?" I turned around in her doorway and leaned against the frame.

"Yeah, it was actually a lot of fun." I said quietly.

"Did Dave like his book?" she asked.

"He seemed to." I said.

"What did he get for you?" she asked.

"An antique silver locket. It's a cool story. I'll show you in the morning." I said.

"K, night."

Dr. Laura Hart

When Patrick woke me to tell me Sheryl was here and needed to speak to us; I feared the worst. But then I took a deep breath and decided no. If she were not okay, I would feel it. I only felt numb. When we walked into the kitchen I realized Patrick's hand still held mine and gave him a grateful squeeze. I didn't let go. Though I was angry with him; I needed him right there next to me.

"I don't have any news on Sierra's whereabouts but I can tell you with certainty that Mr. Pricket doesn't have any idea where Sierra is or even who took her."

"How is that possible?" Patrick demanded.

Sheryl held up her hand. "Let me finish, okay?"

Patrick and I both nodded.

"The kid who got the bag from the locker was Pricket's son, Jimmy. The same night Sierra went missing Pricket hit his ex-wife, Jimmy's mom, a little too hard and she didn't get up. Apparently Jimmy saw it happen. Pricket panicked. When he saw you guys on the news the next day he came up with his escape plan. He'd extort enough money from you to get out of the country before anyone discovered the body. He scared Jimmy into helping him. It took us a while to get the kid to talk; he was more afraid of his father than jail time. We sent officers to Pricket's house to confirm his story. They found his ex-wife's body in the trunk of her own car. It was Jimmy who put the note in the mailbox. Nobody paid any attention to another teenager putting something in your mailbox; one more concerned classmate with a card." She looked back and forth between the two of us. Neither of us spoke as the painful reality became clear.

"I'm sorry. This happens sometimes. People take advantage of you when you are most vulnerable and desperate." Sheryl looked deflated.

"So now what?" I asked. "We wasted all of that time-" I couldn't even finish. It all suddenly felt hopeless. Now we had nothing. Nowhere to turn. Nowhere to look.

"We just have to keep talking to everyone who may have seen something that will help. We need to make sure her picture is still out there. We need to keep people looking."

I looked at Patrick for a sign of something. Anything, I don't know. But he looked as lost as I felt.

Day 64(barely) – 12/7
Haven't biked yet

I woke up a few minutes ago and had this immediate feeling I was not alone. I sat up, called out, ran my flashlight around the entire room, but nothing. I couldn't go back to sleep so I figured I'd risk some battery life to write a little.

My mother and I had a nice quiet Christmas that year. We went to the movies as was our tradition. The rest of the day we played cards and ate junk food. I spoke with my dad and Tia and Dave and everyone seemed to be happy. Tia was nervous about New Years. She'd told her parents she was staying at a friend's but she was really going to a party with Thomas and then staying at a hotel with him. They hadn't had sex yet, but she figured that was what he expected. She said she was nervous but willing "to ring in 2006 with a bang." She wanted to get the first time over with. I knew what she meant, but I wasn't sure that I was willing to go there with Dave yet. She was supposed to call me New Year's Day to tell me how it all went.

I had to work lunch on New Year's Eve. Dave was also working that shift so he could have the night off. The plan was for me to meet him at the party since I had promised to take Gavin with me. His mom was going to spend New Year's Eve with mine; two single moms having dinner and watching the ball drop. I was kind of mad that I would be going to the party with Gavin and then would also have to leave with him. All of the evening "romance" would have to take place during the party.

When Gavin and his mother showed up I was still getting ready. I wanted to look New Years Eve hot but without trying too hard. Tia had convinced me to get this blackish silver one-shoulder sequined dress. It was form fitting and came to my mid-thigh. She called it a "total fuck-me dress." I knew Victoria Spencer would be there too and I wanted to make sure Dave was looking at me, not her. My mom hadn't seen it yet and would hopefully not completely freak. That was part of the reason I made sure I didn't come down stairs until Gavin and his mom were already there; less chance for her to send me up to change. I also put on a little make-up and borrowed my mom's hot rollers. I was shocked at how much volume the curls gave my hair. I put on my only pair of heels—black pumps, and stood in front of my full length mirror to assess the complete look. I felt a little tingle of excitement. I looked so much older. For the first time, I could see I looked like my mom. I texted a picture to Tia for her opinion.

Tia: OMG Sierra, Dave is going to be blown away. You look HOT!

Me: Thx. You were right about dress. I'll fill you in later. Good luck 2nite! Send pics.

Tia: Thx. Will do. Have fun!

I took a deep breath and then walked down the stairs. I could hear my mom and Mindy in the kitchen. When I walked in, they stopped talking and stared at me. I felt my stomach sink. I'd overdone it.

"That bad?" I asked.

"No, it's just you look so-" my mom looked like she was about to cry.

"What?" I asked.

"Incredible." Mindy finished. "Sierra, you really look amazing."

"Grown up." My mom said. "I just can't believe it. I mean, you look beautiful." I could hear her voice thicken.

"Aw, mom," I said walking over to her. "I wasn't really going for tears."

She set down the wine and gave me a gentle hug, making sure not to mess up my hair or makeup. When she let me go, she grabbed a tissue. "Sorry. Just caught off guard, I guess."

Mindy finished opening the wine and my mom handed her the glasses to pour it. I heard our front door open and close. We all turned as Gavin walked in carrying a crock pot. He was wearing jeans and a T-shirt with a black suit jacket. His hair looked like it was still a little wet and he smelled amazing. I hadn't noticed how hot he was before.

"Wow, you clean up well!" he said.

"Thanks," I said. I really wanted to get to the party and see Dave. I looked at my watch. It was just after seven. The party was supposed to kick off soon but I didn't want to get there until a little later.

Gavin put the crock pot on the counter and plugged it in. "You should try this, Sierra. My mom makes the absolute best clam chowder. New Year's tradition." He stirred it, lifted a spoonful, and leaned over to breathe in the smell. "Mmm."

"Shall I get bowls for everyone?" My mom opened the cupboard.

"None for me please. I mean, normally I would love it Mindy. I'm just worried I'll spill or something." Plus my stomach was in knots. Food didn't sound appealing. "Excuse me just a minute." I said and went to the bathroom to call Dave and check myself in the mirror one last time. He should have been done with work by six but I hadn't heard from him. When I called it went straight to his voicemail. Maybe he forgot to charge it? I washed my hands, checked my make-up, and headed back to the kitchen.

My mom, Mindy, and Gavin were all sitting at the counter eating chowder.

"Are you sure you don't want any, Sierra?" my mom asked. "It's really good."

"No, thank you." I smiled.

"How 'bout I leave a bowl behind for you to have tomorrow?" Mindy suggested.

"That would be great, Thanks!" I felt awkward standing in my own kitchen while they all ate. Gavin stood and carried his dish to the sink.

"I'm all done if you want to get going." Gavin said.

"Sure." I said.

"Oh, just leave that in the sink, Gavin. I'll get it later." My mom said.

"Thanks." He said.

My mom jumped up. "Let me get my camera and get a couple pictures first."

As my mom snapped some photos, I tried to study Gavin without being obvious. I noticed how strong his hands looked and how cute his smile was with that dimple.

"Okay, now one of both of the kids." My mom said. I looked at Gavin and blushed again.

"Really mom. It's not like we're on a date or anything?"

"I know, but you both look so nice. Please, just humor me?"

"Fine," I said and stood next to Gavin.

"Closer, Sierra. I'm sure he won't bite." My mom joked. I shot her a look but moved closer to Gavin. He smelled really good. When his arm brushed mine I jumped a little and he laughed under his breath and shot me a teasing look. I felt my face turn red and heard a click. That ought to be a good shot.

"Ready Gavin?" I asked.

"Sure," he said. The moms followed and waved from the curb as we pulled out.

When we arrived, there were already a ton of cars there. But I didn't see Dave's. Just then I got a text from him.

So Sorry. Marc cut his finger badly. Been at the ER with him. He's OK but I have to cover for him tonight. Sorry. C u by 12. Promise.

My heart sunk. I didn't want to go to this party without Dave.

"Everything okay?" Gavin asked. I had forgotten he was standing there.

"Yeah. Dave just has to work late." I would have gladly gone to the restaurant and waited for him but I had promised to introduce Gavin.

"I'm sorry. But his loss is my gain." He smiled and put his arm around me. My stomach flip flopped. *Stop it!* I tried to reason with my body's reaction. "Shall we?" he opened the door.

The party was in full swing when we walked in. Jack waved me over. I was very aware of all the eyes following us as we passed—especially the girls. I have to admit it felt pretty good to walk in on Gavin's arm.

"Holy Shit Hart!" Jack yelled. "You look fuckin' hot. Dave is going to be pissed he's missing most of the night. Who's this dude?" he nodded toward Gavin.

"Thanks. This is Gavin Ross." I yelled. "He's going to M. H. when school starts again." They shook.

"Thanks for having me." Gavin said.

"No worries, my man. Any friend of Dave's girl is a friend of mine. Help yourself to food and drink. There's plenty. Cups are by the keg. Just don't drink and drive out of here, dude. If you're trashed, you crash. Got it?" Gavin had a good three inches on him.

"Got it. Thanks." Jack got pulled away to do a shot.

"So," Gavin said. "Wanna get a drink or something?"

"Sure." I said. We found the keg first. I grabbed a cup and handed it to Gavin.

"You crazy? I'm not drinking and then driving home my mom's boss's daughter." He said.

"Good point." I didn't want to drink anything without Dave anyway.

"Excuse me, Sierra," I almost dropped the empty cup when I turned around to see Victoria Spencer and Rachel standing there. "Aren't you going to introduce us to your date?"

"Gavin, this is Victoria and Rachel. This is Gavin Ross. He starts at M.H. after break." I explained.

"Pleasure to meet you Gavin." Victoria said and held out her hand for him to kiss. To my dismay, Gavin took it. He also kissed Rachel's hand.

"The pleasure is all mine, ladies." Gavin said, flashing them that dimple. Ugh!

"As head cheerleader, I feel it is my duty to give you a warm welcome and introduce you around a bit. What do you say?" She tilted her head and looked up at Gavin like a meal she couldn't wait to devour. I had to admit she was hard not to notice with her tight red dress, boobs barely contained, and big pouty lips.

"I am flattered," said Gavin, "but I'm in Sierra's competent hands already. Maybe you would be kind enough to point us to the food?" Didn't he just eat chowder?

"Sure, I'll show you both," she smiled but glared at me with her eyes. Oh great, that's the last thing I need. The wrath of Victoria Spencer raining down on me. She looped her arm through his and led us to the dining room where the table was filled with chicken wings, buffalo chicken dip, chips, crock pots of chili and mac-n-cheese. I wished I was hungry.

"Promise to come join us for a game of beer pong later." Her eyes ran the length of him. Give me a break.

"Sounds good, Victoria." I realized he was looking at me.

"What?" I asked as she and Rachel disappeared into the crowd. He smiled. "Not a fan of hers, I presume?"

"I didn't say anything."

"Your face said it all. Besides, I noticed you didn't correct her when she called me your date." Gavin smiled. That dimple taunted me.

"Whatever. She can be mean, but you should decide for yourself. I'm not going to tell you who you should like. We can't all help who we are so-" I realized I was rambling and switched subjects. "So why the sudden interest in food? You just ate all of that chowder."

"It's not for me. I thought you must be hungry. You haven't eaten anything and it's 8 o'clock." He said. "Plus, you don't want to drink on an empty stomach."

"Who says I'm drinking?" I snapped; then felt bad. He was just trying to be nice. Why was I being such a bitch? I guess I was mad that Dave wasn't there. "Sorry, that sounded rude. Maybe I do need some food."

"Why don't you get a plate and I'll find us some pop to drink, okay?" he asked.

"Sure, thanks." I grabbed a plate and tried to find the least messy food on the table.

"Hart? Is that you?" I turned around. Tim, a guy from our cross country team stood there with a friend I didn't recognize.

"Hey Tim. What's up?" I asked.

"Wow, you look really different." I took a bite of carrot.

"Is that a good thing?" I asked, not sure what he was getting at.

"Definitely! I never knew you were so …"

"Hot!" his friend filled in. I felt my skin prickle.

"Thanks." I smiled. My plate was full and I looked around in search of Gavin.

"So we are trying to round up some people to play Mexican. Do you want to play?" I spotted Gavin talking to a group of freshman girls. He didn't look like he needed any help meeting people.

"Sierra? Have you ever played?" Tim asked again.

"Oh, um, no, but maybe later. I'll come find you guys, okay?" I headed over to Gavin. He saw me approach and handed me my pop.

"Thanks." I said.

"So I take it you all know Sierra." He said to the gaggle. "Sierra, this is, let me see, Karen, Jenny, Gwen, and Mary Beth, right?"

"Hi," I said and smiled. They didn't take their eyes off Gavin.

"So, if you'll excuse us. We're going to go find a spot to eat." He put his arm at the small of my back and led me away from the girls. We sat down on a couch in the living room.

We had a good view of the beer pong table and watched the game as I ate.

"Do you play?" he asked.

"I haven't before, no." I said "You?"

"A few times; It's fun. More fun if you're drinking." He smiled.

"I'm sure you could easily convince Victoria to let you play with pop instead. If you ask *real* nice and all," I smiled up at him.

"I'm only playing if you'll be my partner." He said.

"I don't know. I'm a runner. Doesn't require much hand-eye coordination," I admitted.

"You'll be fine. Come on, it will help pass the time until Dave gets here."

I looked over at the teams playing; Victoria and Rachel versus two juniors from the basketball team. It didn't seem like a fair match, but everyone seemed to be having a good time. Victoria caught us looking and gave Gavin a little wave.

"Okay," I said. "I'm in." I finished eating and we made our way over to the table just as the girls somehow managed to win the game.

"You two next?" asked Victoria, eyes fixed on Gavin.

"That depends." he said. "Can I play with pop? I have to drive home tonight."

"Sure. As long as Sierra plays with something a little stronger."

"We don't really like beer so Jack made us this yummy punch. It's called the 2006 Mix." Rachel said, taking a sip from her cup. They all looked at me. I did want to wait for Dave, but I also wanted to have fun. It was New Year's Eve. "What the hell." I said. "Let's play."

Of course, Gavin was really good. Even with me as a partner, it didn't take us long to defeat Rachel and Victoria. They seemed to be fine with it. Once they were out, they could talk to Gavin and find ways to accidently rub up against him. It was pathetically obvious, I thought. But I don't think Gavin minded. He tossed flirtatious comments back and forth as we played.

By the second game, I was feeling pretty good. I was actually not bad at beer pong. Or in this case punch and pop pong. We won again. Next up were Jack and Todd, another one of Dave's friends. I'd checked my phone a few times but no word from Dave yet. It didn't take long before we were beating Jack and Todd, too.

"Sierra, where have you been hiding this side of you? Now I can see Dave's attraction." Jack said.

"How do you manage to even make a compliment sound like an insult?" I asked.

"Just a natural born talent, I guess." He plopped his ball into a cup in front of me. "Drink up, Hart."

"Hey, Sierra, what do you say we make this our last game?" Gavin whispered in my ear. It sent a chill down my back.

"But we're winning." I protested.

"Always better to go out on top, don't you think?" he threw the ball.

"I have to agree. It is better on top." Victoria smiled suggestively. I rolled my eyes.

I did have to go to the bathroom pretty badly at this point. I threw my ball and it landed in Todd's beer. "Okay." I said. "I need to use the restroom anyway."

We won the game, and both headed to find a bathroom. When I came out, I didn't see him anywhere. Then I ran into a few girlfriends and next thing I knew I was headed to the sauna.

The night gets fuzzy after that. I remember Gavin carrying me out of the sauna. I remember being very thirsty. Gavin brought me water. Then Dave was there, too. I heard everyone yelling and cheering. I may have kissed Dave? Gavin? No idea. Dave and Gavin were arguing. Jack was there too. They all seemed really pissed.

Next thing I remembered was puking out the side of Gavin's car on the side of the road. Then my mom, oh god and Mindy. Everybody looked worried. Then I passed out.

The first day of 2006 sucked. I woke up in my mom's bed. It hurt when I lifted my head off the pillow but I was dying for water and a toothbrush to scrape the film off my teeth. I made my way to my mom's bathroom for a drink of water. My dress was hanging in her shower. I was wearing one of my favorite oversize T-shirts. I dreaded facing my mom, or anyone else for that matter. What had happened? How did I get so drunk so fast? It was already eleven in the morning. I never slept that late. I made my way downstairs. My mom was on the phone in the kitchen. She hung up when she saw me.

"How are you feeling?" she asked.

"About as good as I look." I said. "I'm sorry, mom. I don't know what happened."

"From what I can gather; grain alcohol." I couldn't tell if she was mad. "You had us all really scared kiddo."

"What is grain alcohol?" I asked.

"Well it's basically pure alcohol, really potent and dangerous. I don't know what Jack was thinking. Someone could have died." My mom said. "I've already talked to his parents."

"Oh God. Are you serious? He's going to hate me. You didn't get cops involved or anything; did you?" I asked, fearing the worst.

"No, I know Jack didn't mean any harm. But I wanted him to be aware of how serious this could have been. His parents were glad that I called. They don't want him to end up in that situation either."

"Oh God; I've made such a mess. I didn't even drink that much."

"It doesn't take that much." She shook her head. "You should probably call and apologize to Gavin and his mom today, too. You are lucky he was there to pull you out of that sauna. I don't know what you were thinking going into a sauna drunk." She searched my face. I hated to see her disappointment.

"I don't know. I guess I wasn't thinking straight. I barely remember anything after playing beer pong. What did Gavin say?" I dropped into a kitchen chair.

"He said neither of you realized how lethal the punch was until it was too late. He couldn't find you after the bathroom and got Dave's number from Jack to make sure you hadn't left with him or something. Dave had just left work and was on his way. Finally, someone said they saw you go into the sauna with some other girls. When he went in to get you, you were passed out in there all by yourself!" my mom teared up.

"I'm sorry, mom. I had no idea. I just, I didn't know." I dropped my head into my hands. I felt like a complete failure.

"Who would just leave you in there by yourself?"

But I drew a blank. "I can't remember." I shook my head.

"Gavin said he gave you some water and you started to come around. He called his mom because he didn't know whether he needed to call an ambulance or not."

"Oh God, Mindy must think I'm such an idiot. I'm sorry, mom." I said.

"She doesn't think you're an idiot." She sat next to me at the table. "She was just scared for you. Either way, you owe them an apology." She put her hand on my arm.

"What about Dave? Did he see me like that, too?" I wasn't sure I wanted to know.

"Well, something happened between the two of them last night. Dave followed Gavin here. They were arguing on the lawn while trying to get you in the house. I told him to go home and you'd call in the morning. I know he was just worried, but the last thing you needed at that point were two guys fighting over you."

"Oh my gosh; this is worse than I thought. What do I even say?"

I knew this was extra hard on her because of her dad. She hated dealing with drunks. And here I was, her own daughter.

"Mom, I am so sorry. I don't usually drink. I just thought it was harmless punch. I never thought it would be a big deal." I started to cry and she pulled me into a hug. We just held each other for a minute or two. She pulled back and looked at me.

"Sierra, honey you have to promise me you will never drink anything that you don't know exactly what it is and what is in it. Okay?"

"Okay." I said and sniffed. She got up to get the tissues.

"Promise me, Sierra." She handed me the box.

"I promise. I don't think I'm ever drinking again." I said.

"Well, I'm sure that's not true. But I am very serious. Always know what you are drinking and never set your cup down. You never know what someone might put in it."

"Okay. I'm so sorry mom. Really."

"I know honey. Me too. I know how awful it must be to not remember. Why don't you get your calls out of the way and then we'll see if you can get some dry toast down."

"I don't know who to call first." I said. But I figured I should call Gavin to find out exactly what happened before I talked to Dave. What if I tried to kiss him or something? I had an awful feeling in my stomach. I needed fresh air. I threw on my coat and took the phone outside to dial Gavin's number. My heart pounded as I waited for him to answer.

"Hey." He said.

"Hey."

"How are you feeling?" he asked.

"Like dying," I said.

"Yeah, I figured. You were in bad shape. I'm sorry. I should have stopped you sooner."

"This isn't your fault. I'm sorry. I just don't know what happened. It was like one minute I was fine and then boom, nothing."

"Yeah, it was pretty fast, but I should have realized something was up. You loosened up while we were playing. You were saying things you wouldn't normally say."

"Oh God; to you or to like everyone?"

"It wasn't bad. You weren't mean or anything; the opposite in fact. You loved everyone. It was kind of cute. But then after you went to the bathroom and I couldn't find you, I got worried that someone took advantage of your kindness, if you know what I mean."

"Sorry I put you in that position. I am so embarrassed. Here I was supposed to help you meet a bunch of people and you end up having to rescue me from myself. Thank you, by the way, for rescuing me from that sauna. My mom said I was pretty bad, huh?"

"Don't worry about it. Everyone will forget about it all in a week." He said.

"Yeah, well. I won't." There was an awkward silence.

"Hey, um, I'm not sure how to ask this other than to just come out with it. I don't remember much but my mom said Dave seemed really pissed. Did I do something or say something I shouldn't have?" I asked.

"So you haven't spoken with Dave yet?" he asked.

"No. I... well I don't remember what happened and I just hoped you could maybe clear it up before I talk to him." I knew I sounded like a big wimp.

"Well. I guess from his perspective it didn't look so great. By the time he walked in, I had my arms around you to hold your head up and keep you drinking water. You were in a bit of shambles by then. There was a crowd of people around us. I think he just freaked. He made a bit of a scene trying to get you away from me. I tried to explain, but he was just too far gone. Pissed, you know. So when I tried to convince him to let me just get you home, he uh...he punched me."

"Oh God, Gavin. I'm so sorry. Was it bad?"

"It's fine. But then Jack came over and Dave lit into him. Wanted to know how he could let you get this drunk and stuff. Anyway, while he was distracted I threw you over my shoulder and took you out of there. He followed us back to your house until your mom made him leave. That's about it." He said.

"I am so sorry. He can be a little intense sometimes. So that was it. I didn't say or do anything else stupid?" I asked.

"Not really. You said some pretty funny stuff, but nobody heard it but me. You don't have to really worry about it." I could tell he was smiling on the other end.

"Easy for you to say. Do I want to know?"

"Well apparently you really like my eyes. They are the color of, and I quote "the water in Magen's Bay on a hot December day."

"I seriously said that?" My cheeks burned.

"And you would love to run your tongue-"

I interrupted. "Okay, okay, stop right there. Maybe we can just lock this all in a big vault somewhere and forget it ever happened."

He laughed. "Easy for you; I was completely sober so it's all very clear in my memory." Now he was just taunting me.

"Nice. Just go ahead and kick me when I'm down." The door to the back deck opened and Dave walked onto the porch. "Hey, I gotta go. Tell your mom I said thanks. I'll call her later to tell her myself. And thank you again." I said.

"K, see ya at school tomorrow." he hung up. I was horrified that Dave could see how awful I looked.

"Hey" I said. "You should have told me you were coming. I'm a mess." I ran my hands through my hair.

"You always look good to me." His tone had a chill to it.

"Wanna sit here or go inside?"

"Was that Gavin on the phone?" he remained standing next to the door.

"Yeah. I just called to apologize and thank him." I leaned forward in the chair.

"So you called him before even calling me?" He shoved his fists into his coat pockets.

"Well, I ... listen, I don't even remember most of last night. After what my mom told me, I felt like I at least needed to thank him. Sorry." I wrapped my arms around myself and rubbed my upper arms for warmth.

"Jack said your mom was really pissed; called his parents and everything. What happened Sierra? You don't even usually drink." he clenched his jaw as he studied my face.

"Well the punch had grain alcohol in it. One minute I was playing beer pong and the next minute nothing. It's like someone shut off the lights. I feel like a jerk." Avoiding his gaze, I watched a bird search our neglected bird feeder.

"Did you hook up with Gavin?" he asked.

"No!" I jumped up.

"But you said you couldn't remember anything. How do you know?" He turned away from me and wrapped his hand tightly around the railing.

I looked down at my hands, completely humiliated, "because I asked him and he said nothing happened."

"And we're just supposed to trust him?" He turned to face me.

"Because when I got there it looked like the two of you were pretty cozy on that floor." I could see the fury in his eyes. It was unnerving.

"He was just trying to make sure I was okay, hydrated and breathing. He almost called 911. It wasn't exactly a romantic encounter. He was afraid I might die." I said defensively.

"How do you think I felt? Getting that call from him, and finding the two of you like that?" His eyes searched my face.

"Awful." I whispered and looked down at my hands again. I felt tears sting my eyes.

"And then he just sneaks off with you over his shoulder like some barbarian with his prize. And when I come to make sure you're okay, I get sent home by your mom!" He kicked at the bottom of one of the chairs, causing it to bang into the table edge.

"I'm sorry," I whispered, hoping he would lower his voice. I sat down again. "Everyone was just trying to help, okay? They were worried about me and I guess you got caught in the crossfire."

He grabbed a chair and slammed it down across from me. Then he sat, took a few deep breaths and put his hands on my legs. I was wearing a long coat but I could still feel the heat through the material. He rubbed my legs as he spoke.

"I'm sorry, too. I wanted to have a great New Year's with you and I knew you were looking forward to the party. And then I got stuck at the ER and then work and then Jack sent me that picture of you and Gavin from the party and I just about lost it."

"What picture?" I asked.

"Just a shot of you and Gavin playing beer pong. You looked so damn hot in that dress and your hair and, you were smiling up at him. I raced through clean-up to get there because I just had this awful feeling that something bad would happen if I didn't. Then he called and well you know the rest." He pulled his hands back.

"I am so sorry that I worried you." I leaned forward, put my hands on his legs and looked in his eyes. "We were just playing around. Nothing happened. I swear. Okay? I'm with you. That's all I want." I grabbed his hands with mine. "And I would kiss you right now but I threw up half the night and have no recollection of whether I have brushed my teeth or showered or anything." I smiled as his whole body relaxed a little. "So you thought the dress was hot?"

"Very." He smiled and held my eyes until I looked away, embarrassed.

"Okay. Well then I have a suggestion," he stood. You go get freshened up and I'll take you to *The Kitchen* and whip you up a hangover breakfast, then we can catch a movie like we planned?

"Let me check with my mom, make sure I'm not grounded or something. And can we watch movies here instead. My mom rented a few yesterday and I haven't seen them yet. I don't think my body is up for too much today."

"Okay—new plan; I'll run to the restaurant, whip up my cure and bring it back for you to eat while we watch movies here? Sound okay?"

"Sounds perfect," I smiled and stood to go inside. I grabbed his hand. He turned to look at me. "Listen, I really am sorry." I squeezed his hand. "I was hoping it would be a great night, too. Sorry I screwed it all up."

"I know," he said and dropped a kiss on my head. "And I'm sorry I punched your friend."

"Yeah, I noticed you left that little bit out," I teased, poking him in the ribs as we closed the door behind us.

It turned out that Gavin was not the only person exposed to my ramblings. I guess in the sauna, I told everyone that I knew for a fact that Victoria Spencer had sent the naked pictures out herself. As you can imagine this became the hot gossip of the party. By the first day back, everybody was talking about it. I was dead. How many times had Tia and I tried to just stay off her radar. Now I had become target number one. This was not good.

INVESTIGATIVE INTERVIEW

Case: MPM047 **Date:** 10.11.06 **Subject:** Victoria Spencer
Officer: Detective Rock **Location:** LPS RM2

D. Rock	So you left SUNY Brockport or they asked you to leave?
V. Spencer	Does it matter? I am back living with my parents. That school wasn't right for me. I'm thinking of spending some time abroad.
D. Rock	Okay. Well let's get back to my original line of questioning. You don't like Sierra Hart very much do you?
V. Spencer	Yeah, well it's no secret. She stole my boyfriend and started nasty rumors about me. She and her dad are just a couple of thieves. The town is probably safer without her around. Hell, she probably stole a bunch of money from some place and took off with it.
D. Rock	Can you tell me what the "Fuck-it List" is?
V. Spencer	What does that have to do with Sierra Hart?
D. Rock	I'll get to that. But first I want to hear from you what exactly it is.
V. Spencer	It's nothing. It's just this thing we came up with senior year to make it more interesting, you know. Laketown High isn't exactly overflowing with exciting forms of entertainment, you know?
D. Rock	So it's a game.
V. Spencer	I guess you could call it that.
D. Rock	And it was a race to see who would complete their list first?

V. Spencer	Well it wasn't supposed to be a race exactly. We were just all supposed to try and complete it by graduation.
D. Rock	And did everyone complete the list by graduation?
V. Spencer	No
D. Rock	But you did, didn't you Victoria?
V. Spencer	What can I say? I like to win. My mom always says "What sets you apart in life is the ability to be one of the few that gets what everybody else can only dream of having."
D. Rock	"Poignant. I'll keep that in mind. So I take it that means yes, you did complete your list of tasks before graduation?
V. Spencer	That's correct Detective.
D. Rock	Is it true that included on that list was kidnapping a freshman? And, let me see here, blindfolding him, driving him out into the middle of nowhere, getting him naked and then just leaving him to find his own way home?
V. Spencer	Well I'd hardly call it kidnapping. What freshman guy isn't happy to get in a car with a hot senior girl?
D. Rock	So you admit you did this? You left some poor freshman blindfolded and naked in the woods?
V. Spencer	You make it sound like it was a bad thing. The kid should have thanked me for it. His cool factor went way up that following week when everyone got news of what happened. He was like THE hot topic, you know?
D. Rock	I see. And did you announce to the rest of the cheerleading squad at last year's State Qualifiers that, 'Since that little bitch Sierra stole Dave away from me, I've had nothing but bad luck. It's like she hexed me or something?'"

V. Spencer Really, like I remember what I said last May?

D. Rock Is that how you still feel? Do you feel like Sierra Hart is at fault for your recent streak of bad luck?

V. Spencer I was just mad. We so should have won that. We were way better than those heifers from New Rochelle. They weren't even in sync and they took zero risks. I'm sure somebody from their team knew the judges."

D. Rock But my question was do you feel Sierra Hart was to blame for your loss and other bad things that have happened in your life? Were you looking to quote teach that thieving bitch who actually runs this school unquote.

V. Spencer Who have you been talking to? You can't possibly think I did something to Sierra? Is that what you are getting at here? You have to be kidding me. I think I'm done.

D. Rock Well look at it from where I'm sitting. I've got dozens of witnesses that say you threatened Sierra on more than one occasion. And you have a history of leaving people in the middle of nowhere just for fun. And to top it all off you can't get anyone to corroborate where you were that afternoon. Doesn't paint a pretty picture for you does it?

V. Spencer I think I need to talk to my parents. Can I go now?

Day 65 - 12/5

If you mush black beans and rice into a patty, melt cheese on it, close your eyes, and picture a cheeseburger you might begin to believe. You may even forget about the mold you had to cut off the cheese. After lights out if I prop the flashlight just right I can light my recycled village from within and create the illusion of a distant town. My new neighbors are quiet, but comforting.

I finally got a call from Tia late on New Year's Day. Her plan had gone off without a hitch. She had stayed at the hotel with Thomas and her parents were none the wiser. They had sex and she said the first time was awful—but they tried again the next morning and it was a little better. But she had told him she loved him and was worried she may have scared him off. She could not believe my night and wanted me to send her a picture of Gavin just out of curiosity. I hadn't done that yet.

I saw Gavin a few times during the first day and he was clearly holding his own. He never needed any help from me. He and Dave were in a bunch of classes together and he actually invited Gavin to sit with them at lunch. So I guess that hatchet was buried. Dave's parents were going to China for two weeks and Dave was allowed to stay home alone. At sixteen it didn't seem unreasonable. Plus, most of his spare time would be spent at the restaurant to help fill in for his mother.

He was trying to convince me to tell my mom I was staying at a friend's and stay with him one night. But I didn't want to lie to my mom. We had gotten past the New Year's Incident unscathed. I didn't want to put our relationship in jeopardy again. Dave did not understand this.

We were sitting in his car outside my house. We had just finished a run. His parents were leaving that night and he wanted me to stay the following night.

"I think you don't get it because you have both your parents. If they catch you lying it's not a big deal, especially after Izzy. But for a long time it was only me and my mom. Yes, my dad is in the picture again, but it's not the same. If she and I can't trust each other then what do we have? I just can't lie to her."

"I get all of that. I do. But I just want to have you come and stay over, just once. And I can't think of another way."

"I know. I'd love to stay the night with you. But until we come up with a plan that doesn't include me lying to my mom, then I'm out. Please understand."

"Okay well, tomorrow night is the only weekend night that they are gone and neither of us has to work, so can you at least plan to come over for dinner and hang out?"

"I would love to. So is this a ponytail and sneakers or make-up and heels kind of meal?" I asked, hoping to lighten the conversation.

"I'm thinking formal. How about 6ish? Can you have someone drop you off since I'll be in the middle of cooking?"

"Sure."

"And then I'll drive you home later, K?"

I gave him a kiss and then slid out of the car. "See ya tomorrow."

"G'night," he waited for me to get in the house before he drove off.

My mom wasn't home yet so I got started on dinner and tried to decide what to wear to Dave's the following night. I knew he would want to move things forward but I wasn't sure I was ready. I don't know why. I also needed a ride tomorrow.

I was just picking up my phone to call Tia when the doorbell rang. I opened it to find Gavin standing there holding up my black pumps with his fingers.

"Nice shoes!" I said. "Are you all done with them now?" I smiled. "Come in, I'm in the middle of making dinner." He followed me into the kitchen.

"Smells good; whatcha cookin'?"

"I was craving potato wedges so I have chicken on the grill and the wedges are almost done. Would you mind just setting the shoes on the bottom stair?" I asked as I headed out to flip my chicken.

"Sure." We both got back at the same time. I noticed he was freshly showered.

"Do you want something to drink? I think there's sprite and root beer in the fridge." I opened it to check, "oh and a little 2006 mix, if you're interested?"

He laughed. "Water is fine." He grabbed himself down a glass. I pulled salad stuff out of the fridge. He leaned against the counter and watched.

"So I haven't seen much of you at school." He said. "Where do you spend all of your time these days?"

"I don't know. I'm around. I guess I've been working a lot because once track starts I will only be able to do a couple shifts a week. I'm trying to save my money."

"Ah, good plan. Well, I guess I'll see you more once the season starts."

"Probably. I take it you run mostly distance?" I asked.

"Usually. You?"

"Same. You'll be with Dave for most of your workouts. He's a distance runner, too." I chopped a red pepper.

"So I hear." He took a big gulp of water and refilled it. I caught myself staring at his mouth as he drank. Then I remembered the potatoes.

"Oh no!" I ran to the oven. In a panic to save the potatoes I reached in without my oven mitt. "Shit, Ow!" I grabbed my towel, pulled them out, dropped them on the stove and put my hand under cold water.

"Are you okay?" Gavin went to the freezer to get ice.

"Clearly brain dead, but yes, fine other than that." I said.

"Here, sit down." He grabbed my hand and put a couple cubes of ice on my thumb and pointer finger where they had touched the hot pan.

"Thanks. Hey can you go grab my chicken off the grill? The cutting board is right there and the tongs are out there."

"Sure," he disappeared out the door. After a minute I stood up to check the potatoes. They were perfectly browned. I had burnt myself for nothing. "Figures."

"What?" Gavin walked in with the chicken. The smell made my stomach growl.

"Nothing. The potatoes were fine." I pointed to the stove. The landline rang and I grabbed it from the kitchen counter.

"Hello?"

"Hey, Sierra. How was your day?"

"Good, Mom. How was yours?"

"Just got longer. I'm going to be a little late tonight so you are on your own for dinner. Sorry." I heard Gavin's cell ring and he stepped into the other room to answer it.

"No worries. Is everything okay?" I asked.

"Nothing we can't handle. I'll see you later okay?"

"K. Love you." I said.

"Love you, too." We hung up.

I decided to scratch prepping anything else for the salad since it would be just me. I had peppers, tomatoes, and lettuce. I put the rest of the veggies back and grabbed the feta cheese.

"Sorry about that," Gavin said. "I'm guessing it was your mom?"

"Yeah. Late night. On my own for dinner."

"Same here," Gavin held up his phone

"Well, I have plenty. Do you want to just eat here?"

"Sure. Thanks." he said.

"I suppose I owe you anyway." I said. My finger and thumb had already blistered so I got down the first aid kit to cover them with band aids.

"Let me help." Gavin suggested.

"I can get it." I said.

"I'm sure you can, but it would work better if you just let me help you." He closed the gap between us and took the Band-Aid from my hand. He seemed closer than he needed to be but maybe that was just me.

I held up my hand and he spread some burn cream on the Band-Aid before gently wrapping my finger. I handed him the other Band-Aid and he repeated the process. My skin tingled where he touched it. We stood there for a few seconds; him still holding my hand in his. For some reason I couldn't look away from his eyes. They really were the color of Magen's Bay on a hot December day. For a second I thought he was going to kiss me and I realized I wouldn't mind. What was wrong with me? I took my hand back.

"Thanks." I said, my voice breaking in the middle.

"I'll set the table," he suggested. "I know where the glasses and silverware are. Just point me to the plates and napkins."

We finished getting everything on the table and I put on some music before we sat down.

"Thanks for making me dinner." Gavin piled potatoes onto his plate and stabbed a big piece of chicken.

"Sure. It's the least I can do after you dragged me out of a sauna and force fed me water in an effort to avoid either death or jail time." I laughed.

"This is true."

"Hey, you were right about your mom's chowder, by the way," I said. "Don't tell Dave but I think it's better than his mom's."

"I know I could sit down and kill the whole crock pot. It's so good. Especially during the winter, watching football playoffs."

"I just realized I've never even asked you why you changed schools mid-year." I passed him the salad dressing.

"Oh, my great uncle passed away and left us his house. It needs some work but came with thirty acres and it seemed crazy not to keep it in the family. Plus, it's much closer to work for my mom."

"Weren't you sad to leave your old school? All of your friends and stuff?"

Gavin shrugged. "Yeah, I was bummed about it at first, but I knew it was a better place for my mom in the long run. I'm only around for another year and a half before college so it would have been selfish of me to make her stay."

"Wow, so grown up of you. I don't know that I could be that selfless."

"Of course you would. I've seen how you are with your mom. We are the same way. When there are just the two of you, it's different. We're a team. I actually feel pretty lucky to have what we have, you know?"

"I don't know. I guess I never really thought about it. For a long time I was really angry that our perfect little family was gone forever.

But I guess you're right, after a while we just became more like friends. When my dad got out of prison, I was worried it would get all messed up again. But it has actually been really good." I took a bite of my salad. "Sorry. I'm just assuming you know about my parents and prison and everything."

"I know the gist of it. It must have really sucked." He noticed I needed more ketchup and passed me the bottle.

"What about your dad? If you are okay with me asking?"

"I don't mind, but it's a bit of a soap opera that I'm not sure I'm up for tonight."

"No worries. I don't really like to rehash my story either."

I smiled and we stood to clear the table. He helped me fill the dish washer. There were still a few dishes that needed hand washing. I washed and he dried. I turned around to give him the last pot just as he turned to ask me where the tongs in his hand went. We did that thing where he moved to the right at the same time I did, then I moved to the left at the same time he did. We both laughed.

"Wanna, dance?" I joked. Frank Sinatra's *My Way* was playing.

"I do." He grabbed me in an awkward kitchen utensil-laden waltz while singing along to *My Way*. He dipped me back and I almost lost the pot. He pulled me back up and used the tongs as a microphone to sing the last line of the song, "I did it my way," then bowed. I laughed and threw the dish towel at him. He caught it, quickly twisted it into a whip and snapped at my leg. I grabbed another towel to get him back but when I tried to snap it, he caught it and gave it a jerk. I lunged forward and found myself right in front of him. I looked up at him and those blue eyes. He leaned down and I'm pretty sure was about to kiss me when we heard the front door open.

"Sierra? Is that Gavin's truck out there?" My mom yelled. We stepped away from each other quickly. My mom was carrying groceries.

"Hey let me help you with those, Dr. H." he said and grabbed two bags. I started the dishwasher.

"Thanks Gavin. To what do we owe the pleasure?"

"I finally brought back Sierra's shoes and since you and my mom were both working late, she was kind enough to offer me dinner." He flashed that hypnotic little dimple at us. "But I should get going. It's getting late and I still have a ton of homework." He grabbed his coat and turned to wink at me when my mom's back was turned. "Thanks for dinner, Sierra. It was even better than I expected."

I turned to help my mom put away the groceries, my mind racing. We almost kissed and I'm with Dave and what does this mean?

"Sierra, are you okay? You seem like you're a million miles away." My mom asked as she filled the tea pot.

"Sorry mom, I'm just suddenly exhausted. Do you mind if I turn in?"

"No honey, go ahead. I'm beat myself."

"G'night," I walked upstairs and fell into bed. What was I going to do? Two hot, fun guys were into me. I wanted to talk to Tia, but felt too guilty to mention it to anyone. I washed my face, brushed my teeth, and decided to sleep on it.

The next day flew by. I was preoccupied with my dinner with Dave. I'd forgotten to get a ride to his house so when he brought it up outside English, Gavin overheard and offered to help.

"Great." Dave's sarcasm was not lost on anyone as we took our seats, "but if you don't mind I'll drive her home this time, okay dude?" Gavin laughed but threw me a look. I blushed and pretended not to catch it.

By the time I got home from school I was beside myself with confusion. Was Gavin just messing with me? I decided a quick run would help calm my nerves and clear my head, but four miles later I was no better. I showered, shaved, and put the hot rollers in my hair. I had planned to wear the New Year's Dress but figured it was too Déjà vu so I dug through my closet and then my mom's. She had a ton of great stuff that she never wore anymore. I finally settled on a gray spaghetti strap dress that seemed to cling to all the right places. It came to the middle of my thighs. I threw on my black pumps again because they were all I had and my feet were way bigger than my mom's. I pulled out the hot rollers, added a little make-up and called it a day. I fingered the heart locket from Dave I had on my neck. I still hadn't gotten a picture of us together to put in it.

This seemed like a perfect opportunity. I went into my mom's office to find her camera. I didn't find it in the desk drawer, but I did notice my dad's name typed on the top of a piece of paper. When I looked closer, I found that it was actually a whole stack of papers. At first I figured maybe they were from the divorce, but I noticed the date at the top was less than a week before. She hadn't mentioned my dad other than in reference to my meeting up with him. My mom and I usually talked about everything. I only felt slightly guilty as I skimmed. From what I read it actually sounded like my mom had somebody checking up on him. I got a sick feeling in my stomach and the hair on the nape of my neck prickled. What was going on? Why was my mom keeping tabs on my dad? The doorbell rang and I looked at my watch. It was 5:40. Gavin. I put the papers back and ran to get the door.

"Hey," I said, "Come on in."

"Nice dress." He flashed his dimple smile.

Suddenly the dress seemed a little too clingy. "Thanks."

"So are we taking pictures again?" he pointed to the camera in my hand.

I laughed. "No, I'll spare you this time. I just have to run upstairs for a sec and then I'm ready. Help yourself to something to drink." I ran up the stairs and grabbed my bag. As an afterthought I stopped by my mom's room for a squirt of her perfume.

Gavin stood at the mantle looking at the family pictures. The letter popped back in my head. What was my mom up to?

Gavin kept his hands to himself and delivered me as promised. *Was I disappointed?* I pushed the thought away when Dave opened the door and I was met with such a hybrid of amazing smells. My mouth began to water.

"Oh my God, it smells like food heaven in here." I said. Dave stood there looking at me. "Um, should I come in?"

"Wow, I just, you look so . . . yeah come in, sorry." He gently pulled me inside and closed the door. He bent to give me a kiss at the same time I held up the camera to explain about the locket picture. It created an awkward moment where his nose collided with my camera.

"Sorry." We both said in sync, then laughed. I think we were both nervous.

"I can take your coat." He said and helped me take it off. When he turned back from hanging it up he whistled. "I like your dress."

I smiled and he took my hand to lead me into the kitchen. The smell was even stronger.

"I'm almost done. Do you want something to drink? I pulled out a bottle of wine to have with dinner. Are you okay with that?"

"Sure." I felt so grown-up all of the sudden. He poured us each a glass of red wine from a decanter. "Just a sec." he turned back to the oven to pull out some type of meat. It smelled heavenly. He set it on the counter, closed the oven and checked the meat with a thermometer. "Perfect," he announced. He then grabbed the glasses, handed me one and raised his. I met his glass with mine with a clink. "To an evening filled with perfect." And we both took a sip. It was smooth and made my mouth water more.

"You like it?" He asked.

"It's great." He looked relieved and led me into the dining room where the table was set for two. There were small salads already there. He pulled out my chair like a maître de. It was cute.

"Thank you, sir." I smiled up at him. He leaned in and kissed me, softly at first but then put his wine down and took my face in his hands. I felt the heat between us and leaned into him. He slowly ended the kiss and pulled away.

"Hmmm, sorry. I just had to do that, but we should eat before we get carried away. I have it timed to perfection. We begin with spinach, walnut and blue cheese salad with a strawberry reduction dressing." I took the napkin and placed it on my lap. This was like fine dining.

We wasted no time digging in. After the salad came perfectly steamed asparagus, pork tenderloin, and mashed potatoes with a yummy secret family sauce he'd made from scratch. The wine tasted even better with the food. For dessert, he'd made pumpkin spice mousse. It melted in my mouth. I was so full by the end I felt like I needed to go for another run.

"You are so going to have a killer restaurant someday." I said. "That was beyond perfection. Thank you."

He looked genuinely pleased. "Okay. Let's leave this here. I'll clean later. I want to show you something." We both stood. "Bring your wine," he took me by the hand and led me through a large great room with high coffered ceilings and a huge stone fireplace in the middle.

"This is stunning."

"Thanks." He said, leading me down a set of stairs to the basement. It looked like a hotel club or something. There was a huge, fully stocked bar with cool lighting and a big booth to sit in. Then off to the side a full fireplace with a flat screen TV above the mantle and a big wrap around couch. He led me around a corner and pulled back a pocket door to reveal a smaller room with a hot tub. There was nice soft lighting, music in the background, and another bottle of wine already opened and waiting.

"Wow," I said. "This is amazing. But I didn't bring a suit."

Dave laughed, "You are so readable. Don't panic, I snuck and grabbed a suit from your drawer the other day. Hope that isn't weird. Although, I hate to see that dress go. It's a keeper."

The thought of him going through my drawers was a little creepy. But it was also very thoughtful, right? I decided to forget about it. It was Dave. He opened a closet, grabbed a big robe, and handed it to me. "You can cover up with this if you aren't cool with what I grabbed."

I took the robe, set my wine on the side of the hot tub and went to find the changing room. Luckily he'd grabbed one of my favorites. It was solid black with high cut legs, thin straps and a low cut back.Dave had lit a whole bunch of candles around the tub. It looked really cool and smelled good too. "Wow, you thought of everything," I said. Out of nowhere, I had this visual of him and Victoria Spencer naked in the hot tub. "Have you done this before?"

"The hot tub?"

"No, I mean with other girls; you know dinner, hot tub, whatever?" I sounded jealous but suddenly needed to know.

"No, I haven't made dinner for any other girls. But I have been in the hot tub with other people. We've had it since I was a kid. I think I may have once kissed Molly Teller right over there." I laughed. Molly Teller was on the girls' basketball team. She'd been six foot tall since we were in like sixth grade. She wasn't unattractive, but she was no Victoria Spencer.

"How was it?" I asked.

"Very wet."

"Ew!" I groaned.

"Shall we get in?" he pulled off his shirt and I felt excitement ripple through me.

"Sure." He held out his hand to help me down the steps. I had to take it slow because it was so hot. He slipped in behind me and took the seat next to mine. I felt very aware of how little we were wearing and how close we were. We both took a sip of wine.

"So, how is Izzy doing? Did she get that commercial?"

"Nope. They told her she looked too young for the spot." He put down his wine and pulled me onto his lap. "But I don't really want to think or talk about sisters right now."

"No?" He gave me a quick kiss."World peace?" I asked and he kissed me again. "Politics?" I asked and he kissed me again. He set my wine to the side and pulled me in even tighter so that I could feel what he was really interested in. He moved his lips to my ear and ran his hands across my leg. He gently grazed my lips. It felt incredibly sensual and maddeningly frustrating at the same time. The longer he did it, the more I wanted him to just kiss me hard. A small groan escaped the back of my throat. I couldn't stand it anymore. I grabbed his head with my hands and crushed his mouth to mine. I felt the smile on his lips before it disappeared beneath mine. He ran his hands down my sides and slid his finger under the edge of my swim suit.

"Let's get out of here" he murmured. He stood with my legs still around his waist. I dropped my legs down and we both almost fell. We laughed with our lips still together. I pulled myself away so we could both get out. He held out my robe for me and then grabbed himself a towel. Neither of us attempted to dry ourselves. He grabbed my hand and led me over to a big wrap around sofa by the TV, flipping on the fireplace. The firelight cast a nice orange glow throughout the room.

Dave turned and began to kiss me again. I had the robe on my shoulders but left it open. He slipped his hands inside the robe, gently stroked my bare back, and pulled me closer. I could feel how excited he was and it made me feel good to know I could do that to his body. He slowly maneuvered us onto the couch. I was on my back and he was on top of me. I ran my hands down his back, feeling the strength of his muscles, the wetness from the hot tub. He slid a strap down my arm.

"Is this okay?" he asked against my neck.

I nodded. I pulled that arm free from the strap, then grabbed his wet hair and pulled his mouth back to mine. While we kissed, he used his other hand to pull down my other strap. He pulled back and looked down at me. His eyes were dark and the look sent a ripple through me. I pressed my hips into him. He kissed me again and slowly trailed kisses down my neck to the top of my chest. He slipped his tongue under the edge of the suit and I sucked in my breath. He returned to my lips with his mouth and used his hands to gently slide my suit down and pressed his bare chest against mine. It felt hot and cold at the same time. Our kissing intensified. I understood what people meant about floating on a cloud. Everything in my body felt so alive. I felt a hot tingle between my legs and a need to have him move his hands there. Instead he slid down and took one of my breasts in his mouth. I bucked with my hips and had to pull him off.

He looked up. "Are you okay? Did I hurt you?"

"No," I whispered. "I just, it felt too good." He smiled and kissed my nose. Then he slid back down and gently teased my nipples with his tongue. They grew so hard they almost ached. He moved back to my mouth and I ran my hands down his back as we both pressed into one another with renewed force. It was like we couldn't get close enough.

I slipped my hands beneath his swim trunks, cupped his smooth hard cheeks and pulled him toward me harder. He groaned and whispered my name.

He pulled himself up and looked down at me. "Sierra, do you want me to stop? We haven't ever talked about this. If we keep at this much longer I'm afraid I'll just get carried away. " Suddenly, we both heard a sound upstairs. I immediately pulled my suit back over my chest.

"Dave?" we heard a voice call out. I pulled the robe around me. He rolled his eyes and ran his hand through his hair.

"Karen." He said. "Sorry, just stay here, okay? Hopefully I'll be right back." He dropped a kiss on my lips and stood up. I could see his erection clearly through his trunks.

I gestured toward it and he wrapped the towel around his waist. He gave me a little smile and I could see his face was flushed.

"Better?"

"Pretty good," I answered and he headed off to find her. I put my arms back in the suit, wrapped the robe around me, and tied the strap, but I still felt exposed sitting there. My lips burned from kissing and my body still tingled. I could hear them talking, but couldn't make out what they were saying. I looked at my watch. I was shocked to find it was almost ten. I had to be home in an hour.

While I waited, I started looking at the family pictures on the wall. Dave had always been tall, but he hadn't really grown into himself until recently. Maybe that was why I hadn't really paid much attention to him before. As a boy he had unruly, red hair. His hair was straight now. And I did not remember him going through a chunky phase in middle school. Izzy's hair color and style changed in every photo. His sister Karen looked very serious, even when she was smiling.

I heard the door close. I went back to the couch as Dave came down the stairs.

"Sorry about that." He said. He was carrying two glasses of water and handed one to me.

"Is everything okay?"

"Yeah, she was just checking up on me. Karen likes to think she's my second mom."

"Did she know I was here?"

"Well, it was pretty obvious given the table set for two."

I blushed.

"Why are you blushing?" he smiled. "Are you embarrassed?"

"Not that I'm here, but that you went up there in a towel. The house is all dark. It looks, you know." I didn't finish my sentence.

"Like we're down here having fun?"

"Exactly," I said. He pulled me into his lap.

"At least I *hope* you were having fun." He said, "Because I was." He kissed me and rubbed his nose against mine.

"Well I hate to be a buzz kill, but it's after ten and I have to be home by eleven." I announced.

"That is a buzz kill." He smiled. "Seriously though, are you okay with everything? I didn't pressure you, did I?"

"I'm okay," I felt myself blush again.

"Damn, girl. I have never met anyone that blushes as much as you." He rubbed my back as he spoke.

"I know. I hate it. It's such a dead giveaway."

"I think it's cute." He bit my shoulder gently and let out an exaggerated groan. "I wish you could just stay here all night. I don't want you to go."

"Sorry." I said. "You said you work tomorrow night and both nights next weekend?"

"Unfortunately, yes. But we can make-out like crazy for at least thirty more minutes right now." He threw me down on the couch and I let out a little squeal of surprise. He leaned over and looked down at my face.

"What?" I asked.

"It's just crazy you know. We've been in the same classes forever, run together, lived in this small town. How did we not notice one another before?" He asked.

"It's funny; I was just thinking the same thing looking at these photos."

"Oh God, I look like a dork in most of those."

"No, well, maybe one or two."

He tickled my sides. "You're not supposed to agree!" I squirmed beneath him.

"Okay, okay," I squealed. "I take it back; you have always been totally hot!" He stopped and wrapped his arms tight around me so our faces were almost touching.

"Ah, so you admit it. You were pining for me all along. I knew it. I remember that one time in second grade when you winked at me in choir."

"You are so full of it. I couldn't wink in second grade and I can't now!"

"You can't wink? Let me see. Try it." He said.

"No way. Too much pressure." I smiled.

"Please, for me? It's easy. See?" He winked again. I tried, but blinked instead. He laughed.

"See? I told you. And now you laugh at me." I swatted his shoulder.

"I'm sorry. It's cute, really." He kissed both my eyelids.

He had been an amazing distraction. I didn't realize until I got home and saw my mom asleep on the couch that I hadn't thought about the thing with my dad the entire night. She looked so peaceful that I didn't want to wake her. I covered her up, turned out the light and locked the door. Tomorrow I would ask about the papers.

Day 68 – 12/11
Biked 8 miles

Built a church in my recycled town because it's important to have faith, right? The question is; do I have faith? Are hope and faith the same thing or more like first cousins? I can't think about it right now. I think too much down here. Physical. I need to do something physical. I bet I could make a bowling set. Cans and a foil / tape ball?

I'm sick of reading and biking and listening to the same music. I want a real toilet. Some days it really smells. I miss running. I want my dad's pizza and a toothbrush and to breathe fresh, clean air, and feel the sun on my face. God, I miss the sun. I was thinking maybe instead of just writing down all of my memories I should also write a letter to everyone I love in case by the time they find me I'm dead. Or in case the Keeper decides to eventually kill me. Of course I'm not sure that person would exactly set about making sure everyone got my letters. Huh, that would make for an interesting book; a killer who decides to actually deliver a bunch of his victim's farewell letters.

I wonder how long you have to be gone before they declare you dead and have a funeral? Wouldn't that be crazy if I could visit my own grave? And do they bury an empty casket? I guess it would be like soldiers that went missing in action. Do they have caskets? Funerals? If they find my body here later will they dig up the casket, put it in and have another funeral?

Most of the time reliving and writing favorite parts of my life makes me feel better; but sometimes the bad stuff won't get out of my head until I put it down on paper. It's like my brain is trying to rid itself of toxins; in addition to being held hostage I now suffer from a bad case of memory flu.

The morning after my dinner with Dave, I came downstairs to the smell of pancakes. I was surprised because my mom hadn't made them since the many failed attempts after my dad left. I was even more shocked to walk into the kitchen and find my dad seated at the table with my mom and a huge plate of pancakes.

"Dad?" I said. "Did we have plans?" I gave him a big hug.

"No, not at all; your mom and I just wanted to talk to you about something. I figured you might like some pancakes, too."

My stomach knotted. The last time we had a family meeting it was to discuss their divorce.

"Why don't you get some tea and have a seat." My mom suggested. I skipped the tea.

"What is it? Is something wrong?" I asked. I could hear the panic in my voice.

"A few months ago, I found a lump in my breast."

"You have cancer?" I interrupted. I felt a wave of nausea wash over me.

"It's going to be fine, honey. I just need a simple surgery and some treatment and I'll be fine." My mom explained. I didn't bite.

"Mom, there is nothing fine about any of that. What is the diagnosis? What did they say? Is there a chance you could-" I couldn't say it. I felt tears slip down my face. She came over and gave me a hug and then kneeled next to me.

"I have great doctors and a good treatment plan. We are going to fight this. Hundreds of thousands of people survive breast cancer."

"If it's all going to be fine; then why is dad here?" I asked.

"Between the surgery and the treatments, your mom just thought it might be a good idea if I were around more to help out." He explained.

"What about New York? I can take care of mom."

"We were thinking maybe he could stay here in the guest room for a while. At least through the surgery," my mom explained. She had her hand over my dad's.

A strange feeling came over me. "Have you guys been seeing one another? Like dating?" My voice got all funny and I felt my face flush with anger.

My mom said, "No." My dad looked uncomfortable. I suddenly felt like the third wheel. Had I been so blind?

"Honey, we're just trying to do what we think is best." My mom said. She looked really tired; run down. Why hadn't I noticed this before? I felt guilty and humiliated.

"How long have you guys been sneaking around?" I knew I sounded mean but I couldn't help it.

"We've hardly been sneaking around, Sierra. Your father has been helping me come up with a plan with the doctors, and we just-" She looked like she was going to cry.

"Sierra, your mom and I have a long history. I know it is hard for you to understand."

"No, I get it. Mom didn't think I could handle this so she went to you; the one who let her down in the worst way. I was here when all her happiness drained out of her, until she was nothing but earth tones and flat hair and pretend smiles. And you get to just come back?" My father looked like I had just slapped him.

"Sierra, you're upset. Don't make this more than it is," my mom tried to reason with me. But I felt ambushed.

"I gotta get out of here!" I grabbed my phone, my keys and my coat, and ran out the door. I pulled out onto the road and realized I didn't know where to go. I looked at my watch. It was 10:18. Too early to call Tia. Dave was already at the restaurant. I dialed Gavin's number.

"Hey," he said.

"Where are you?"

"Are you crying?" I could hear a voice in the background.

"I'm sorry. You sound busy. Never mind." I hung up and drove toward the lake. My phone rang. It was Gavin.

"It's okay." I said. "I'm fine." But my voice caught in my throat.

"Sierra. You're obviously not fine. Where are you?"

We agreed to meet at the dam. I pulled in, turned off my engine and went to sit where I could look out at the lake. It was cold and the air smelled like snow, even though it was the end of March.

The sky was gray, which matched my mood. I threw rocks down the embankment until Gavin pulled in. I stood and felt a pang of guilt that it was not Dave making my heart race as he approached.

"Hey, what's up?" he asked. I burst into tears and he wrapped me in his arms. I sobbed into his down covered chest and he let me cry; his chin rested on my head. I don't know how long we stood like that, but by the time the tears slowed I felt completely drained.

"Ca...can we sit?" I managed.

"Sure," he said. We sat shoulder to shoulder, looking out at the cold, calm lake.

"Smells like snow." He said.

"Yeah." He handed me some tissues from his pocket. I blew my nose and let out a jagged sigh. "I must look awful." I was still wearing my pajama bottoms and T-shirt under my jacket. I hadn't even brushed my hair or my teeth.

"You've looked better." He said, nudging me with his elbow.

"Gee, thanks." He put his arm around me and pulled me in for a half hug.

"I still wouldn't kick you outta bed for eating crackers." He said.

"What?"

He shrugged. "It's just something my friend Ted used to say. So are we going to continue gabbing about your un-brushed hair or are you going to tell me what's really going on?"

I took a deep breath and told him everything, struggling to get through it without crying. He seemed to catch most of it.

"Wow, that's a lot to take in all at once," he said. "I'm really sorry to hear about your mom. That's scary. Do you know how bad it is?"

"Not exactly. Bad enough for surgery plus treatment," I said. "I just heard cancer and couldn't swallow much after that."

I threw another stone toward the water but it fell short and landed on the dirt.

"I just feel so ... betrayed. And then I feel guilty when my poor mom is the one going through hell. But how could she choose him over me? After everything that happened? It makes me so mad. I know I probably sound selfish."

Gavin squeezed my shoulders.

"Am I crazy?"

"No. I think this is perfectly normal. You just found out your mom has cancer and asked her criminal ex-husband to help her before even telling you, her own daughter."

"Harsh, right?" I said flatly.

"Harsh." He agreed.

"Why do I feel a 'but' coming?" I looked up at him. He looked back and then out at the lake, throwing a rock over the bank.

"But, you need to put yourself in your mom's shoes. She has cancer. It sounds serious. She recognized you should not have to handle this alone. Imagine how hard it was for her to reach out to your father for help after what he put her through. But she did that for you."

I started to cry again. "I am such a bitch."

"No you're not." He slid around and lifted my chin with his hand so that I had to look at him. "You're just scared. Who wouldn't be?"

I wiped the tears from my face and looked at his blue, blue eyes. "Thanks." I whispered. He smiled and moved back beside me.

"So this also kind of explains the stuff you found in your mom's desk. She must have been making sure he was on the up and up before she brought him back into your home."

"I'd kind of forgotten about that. But you're probably right. And it explains why she didn't tell me about it." I sighed. "I guess I need to go back home with my tail between my legs."

"I'm sure they understand. But are still probably worried."

"Yeah," I stood. "I should go." We walked back to our cars and stopped beside mine. I opened my door and turned to say bye. Gavin seemed really close. My heart jumped a bit. He reached down and ran his thumb gently over my cheekbone, his eyes searching mine for a few seconds. Then he turned to go.

"Call me if you need anything. That goes for your mom, too." He called over his shoulder.

"Thanks Gavin."

My mom's "little surgery" turned out to be not so little. She was scheduled for a double mastectomy the same day as our first track meet of the season. We argued about where I needed to be and I won. How was I supposed to race when my mom was in the hospital? Arguing became all too frequent that winter. Apparently, Jack drove past when Gavin and I were at the dam and told Dave we looked awfully close. Of course, Dave got even angrier when he found out why we were talking. He said I could reach him at the restaurant anytime when it was important. He was really hurt I didn't go to him first. I had started something awful. During practice, Dave and Gavin became pretty competitive with one another. They didn't exchange words but there was an underlying tension in the air when all three of us were together. Meanwhile, I couldn't really focus on much of anything. Even running didn't seem to help me stop thinking about what would happen if I lost my mom.

I had thought having my dad move in with us would be strange, but it felt right somehow. Of course, a part of me wanted them to get back together. But I also worried about how that could turn out. What if my dad let us down again? I don't think either of us could forgive him twice.

Dad took over the guest room and we created a small office for him in the corner of our living room. My mom came home from work completely exhausted in those few weeks before the surgery and my Dad was great. I had not realized what a great cook he was. Maybe it was part of my attraction to Dave.

Then there was Dave. Looking back, I think I pulled away from Dave during my mom's battle with cancer. I felt guilty having fun or laughing when I knew my mom was fighting for her life.

My mom's surgery went well and she was home within a few days. But I don't think any of us were prepared for the months that followed. It was strange to see her in such a weakened state. When she started chemotherapy, things got really tough. She lost all of her hair, couldn't keep food down, and slept most of the time.

I realized just how right my mom had been to call on my dad. There is no way I could have balanced school, track, work, and my mom. She had drainage tubes, medications, and her incisions had to be properly bandaged. I would have been overwhelmed but my dad was amazing. He was gentle and patient and seemed to know just what she needed.

I remember one morning I went into my mom's closet to get her something to wear. I ran my hands along the beautiful dresses she used to wear on those date nights with my dad. The material felt so silky and beautiful in my hands and I recalled brushing her thick hair as she got ready. I dropped down on to the floor of her closet and sobbed. It didn't seem right. My mom had done nothing wrong. She had always been such a good person; the doctor that took care of everybody else. My mom had requested no tears. "Don't give cancer the satisfaction," she'd said. But my dad found me crying there and said, "Sometimes we all need a good cry."

I don't remember much from that stretch of time. Even the track season was a blur. By June my mom was done with her chemo and had gone back to work. I was so proud of her. She still had the reconstructive surgery ahead of her, but the doctors were confident that she was going to beat the odds.

One early summer day, I got an invitation in the mailbox from Dave. It was on cool stationary:

For the first time in a long time I was excited to go do something. Dave and I had barely spent time alone since our last dinner, the night before I had learned about Mom's cancer. It seemed fitting that I celebrate the doctor's good news with a second dinner.

Dr. Laura Hart

Cancer sucks. There is no doubt about it. When you have to face your own mortality, your perspective on everything changes. As a mother, my number one concern was how this would all affect Sierra. It was her senior year. She seemed to have finally come into her own. I'd seen glimpses of the woman she would become. I was proud of her for finding her way back to happy.

And now I was going to screw it all up again. I knew I couldn't do it alone and I knew there was only one person I could ask to help. Patrick was wonderful about everything. He did not hesitate for a second and never made me feel guilty for shutting him out all those years. I felt, given how this could end, complete and total honesty was a must. I told him I had hired a PI to make sure he hadn't been gambling. He later joked that in addition to intel on his potential criminal activity perhaps I'd also been checking to see if I had any female competition. Who knows, maybe I had been curious about that too.

I don't think I allowed myself to realize how much I'd missed Patrick until cancer forced me to take a hard look at my life choices. He is difficult to resist. I forgot how good it feels to share laughter with someone who can make a regular Tuesday feel like a holiday. Those little gestures that round out a relationship; no sugar on my cereal, never enough in my tea, socks for sleeping but not for gardening, red wine served cold, water with no ice, daisies not roses; the ability to kneed free that one stubborn knot that haunts my right shoulder. Patrick even remembered to carefully wrap every bottle with a paper towel before recycling to spare me the skin-crawling sound of glass hitting glass. I'm really glad Patrick came home.

I know I owe him an apology and an explanation, but I don't know if I'm ready to talk about it, yet.

Day 70 – 12/13
Biked 10 miles

I think I'll order Chinese tonight. When I play the record player quietly, it sounds like I do have neighbors. Maybe I should have a party for them. What would I wear?

For my date with Dave, I decided to dip into my savings to buy myself a new dress. I didn't have Tia to help me this time so I had to wing it. I found an off-the shoulder sage green number that clung nicely to my hips and came down to just above my knees. The color brought out my tan and the green in my eyes. It felt good when I put it on. It happened to be on sale, so I also treated myself to a new bathing suit. I didn't normally wear a bikini but I thought it would be a nice surprise for Dave. The bikini was black and made my boobs look twice their actual size. It was a keeper.

I was actually nervous when Dave picked me up. He seemed to like the dress and kissed me like we hadn't in ages. I finally had to pull away so we could get out of my driveway before my dad found us there half-naked or something. Once again we had his house to ourselves. He made yummy fish tacos, Mexican rice, and homemade tortilla chips with fresh guacamole. It was incredible. He also made us some tasty Margaritas. By the time we hit the hot tub, I was pretty buzzed. I have since learned that tequila makes me a little more impulsive.

I changed in the bathroom and came out wearing the fluffy robe. Dave was already sitting in the hot tub when I came back.

"I got you some water." He must have realized I'd had enough.

"Thanks." I said. "So I got a new suit."

"Really?" he asked with that killer smile. "Well let's see it."

I blame the tequila for feeling the need to do a little striptease for him. I let one shoulder slip down a little, turned my back to him, undid the tie, and let the other shoulder slip down while looking back at him over my shoulder. He seemed to enjoy the view. Then I slowly shimmied the robe down my back to about my waist, still with my back to him. I glanced back, and let it drop.

"A bikini. Nice."

I smiled and turned around with my arms spread. "Tada." Man was I buzzed. Looking back I feel like an idiot even describing it. I stepped into the tub.

He grabbed my hand to guide me to his lap, laughing. "I think that tequila went straight to your head."

"Maybe just a little," I ran my hand through his hair and leaned down to kiss him.

"Mmm." He murmured against my lips. "I've missed you."

"Me, too." Our kissing grew more intense and he slid me tight against him so that I could feel how hard he was beneath me. That only excited me more. He ran his hands under my bikini bottoms and cupped my bare cheeks. He kissed the side of my neck, nibbthat. He ran his hands down ling at my ear, and I felt chills spread through my body.

"Are you cold?" he whispered.

"No," I whispered and dropped little kisses along his jaw line up to his ear. I gently bit his lobe and tickled the edge with my tongue. He let out a small groan in the back of his throat, grabbed my head in his hands and brought my lips to his again. I was overwhelmed with a need to feel his skin against mine.

"Let's get out." I whispered. We never seemed to last long in the hot tub. We grabbed towels and made our way to the roaring fire. He had a big blanket stretched out in front of it. We lay down, his body straddling mine. He looked so good, his chest damp, his eyes so alive, the firelight dancing along his muscles. I ran my hands up his chest, kissed each of his nipples and gently bit one.

"Tequila makes you crazy." He said and rolled me on top of him. I looked down and smiled. He rested his hands on either side of my waist. As if proving him right, I reached behind me and released the hook on my bikini top and slid it off. I pressed myself against him, skin to skin. It felt so good. I kissed him again, gently at first, but then he deepened it. He rolled us so that I was beneath him again. His hands found my breasts and teased at one nipple then the other until they ached. I ran my hands down his back and slipped a hand beneath his swim trunks. I slid it back and forth along the waist band. He groaned again. I could feel his whole body react to my touch. The power was intoxicating. I untied his trunks and slid them down. I wrapped my hand around him and gently stroked. He put his mouth over one of my breasts and ran his tongue in circles around my nipple until I thought I would scream. I ground my hips up against his.

"Sierra," he said into my hair. He moved so that he was looking into my eyes. "Do you want to?" He punctuated his question with a gentle kiss on my lips.

"Yes, I mean-" my voice sounded huskier than normal.

"Have you ever?" he looked serious.

"No." I admitted. My face grew red.

"Hey, don't get embarrassed." He said. "I'm glad you haven't." I smiled and kissed him again. He slid off his trunks and my bottoms so that we were completely skin to skin. The feel of his excitement against my leg made me nervous. It felt so much bigger than I'd imagined. He kissed his way over my ribs and down my stomach, sending little waves of tingle through my body. He kissed my hip bone and I grabbed his head with my hands. I'd meant to pull him up but he took it as a sign to go deeper. He ran his tongue along me and I groaned out loud. He flicked his tongue quickly back and forth and I felt myself lift up to meet his tongue. I felt a streak of heat run down my inner thigh and rest in the balls of my feet. I wanted him to stop but not stop all at the same time. He slipped his fingers inside me and I cried out.

"You okay?" he whispered.

I couldn't answer. I just nodded. He went back to work, teasing me with his fingers and his mouth. I couldn't think. I could only feel. Every nerve in my body seemed to pulse against my skin to get out. It felt like my inner thighs were on fire. My nails dug into the back of his arms and my whole body seemed to convulse with small ripples of pleasure. I let out a small whimper. He moved back up and kissed me gently on the head. I couldn't open my eyes or move. I just laid there for a minute while he gently stroked my arm with his hand. When I did open my eyes, he was looking right at me. He smiled. I smiled back.

"Did you like that?" I didn't trust my voice so I just smiled and kissed him.

"I'll take that as a yes." He rolled over on top of me so that we were pressed together again. I felt my heart beat between my legs. I was wet and throbbing and I felt him hard against me. He was gently positioning himself between my legs. I could feel the tip of him against me. I heard him open a condom and the sound sent a chill through me. I breathed in deep. It suddenly seemed wrong. I panicked and pulled away.

"Wait." I managed. My voice sounded groggy. He pulled back.

"You want me to stop?" I saw disappointment flash across his face. I thought about going ahead with it. He was a nice guy. He just did all of this for me. Couldn't I give him this? Shouldn't I? I pushed my way up so that I was sitting beneath him.

"I'm sorry. This is further than I've ever gone." He wrapped his arms around me.

"It's okay. It's okay." I wondered whether he was trying to convince me or himself. He kissed the side of my head. I could still feel a throbbing between my legs. I felt exposed. It must have been obvious because he grabbed a towel and wrapped it around my shoulders. He used it to pull me into him. He put his forehead against mine. "Are you okay?"

"Yeah. I'm sorry. It was a little intense and I don't think I'm there yet." I felt silly and young. I knew he and Victoria Spencer probably did stuff like this all of the time. It made me feel stupid that I couldn't even do it once.

"Hey, it's no biggie. I'm not going anywhere. We can do it when you're ready, okay?" I searched his eyes to see if he looked upset or annoyed, but he just looked like Dave. He smiled and my heart jumped a little.

"Thanks." I said. I looked down and saw that he was still ready to go. I felt a pang of guilt. "Um, I'm going to use the restroom." I said. I gathered the towel around me and headed to get dressed. I thought maybe it would help if I wasn't naked anymore.

When I came back he was dressed. He had folded the towels, picked up the blanket and was sitting on the couch drinking water. "You look hot, like you've been properly mauled."

I sat next to him. He put his arm around me, pulled me close and dropped a kiss on my head.

"Hopefully my parents won't see that, too." I looked at my watch. I still had another half an hour. It felt good just to snuggle next to him. I rested my head on his shoulder and breathed in the scent of him. He smelled good; fresh with a hint of chlorine. "Thanks again for dinner."

"I love cooking for you. I just wish we could do this more," he said.

"Well, hopefully it will get better now that it's summer and my mom is doing well. She has another surgery in July, but at least we know what to expect this time. And she won't have to follow it up with chemo."

"Jack is going to have his Fourth of July party again this year. And he has sworn off any grain alcohol. Do you want to go?'" he asked.

"Sure," I said. "Is it usually a ton of people or just your friends?"

"This is Jack. It's go big or go home. Although he may tone it down a notch. His parents have been on his case since the New Year's party. I guess you weren't the only girl who got a little sick from his 2006 Mix. Hey, I almost forgot dessert." He announced. "Come on."

We went upstairs for chocolate covered strawberries before he took me home. Luckily, my dad was half-asleep so I didn't have to worry about him noticing that freshly mauled look.

Patrick Hart

After the fake ransom demand; it was difficult to know what to do to find Sierra. I tried to take my mind off things with work. Laura went back part-time; but she was struggling with more than just Sierra missing. I'd catch her watching me.

One morning she fell asleep sitting on the couch. We had been circling one another like reluctant boxers for weeks and I longed to feel her warmth next to me.

I joined her on the couch, and when she didn't wake; moved close enough to gather her into my arms; her head against my shoulder. She never woke. Eventually I dozed off; until she called out.

"Stop, daddy, please just stop." She sat up straight and looked at me with fear and anger.

I gently stroked her back. "It's okay. It's just me. You had a nightmare."

It took her a few seconds to realize where she was and how close we were.

"Patrick, I..." then her cell rang. I'd lost her again.

I tried to get her to talk later, but she lied and said she couldn't remember what she'd wanted to say. I felt like both the people I loved the most had gone missing.

Day 72 – 12/15

Biked 8 miles

Due to the 2006 Mix incident my mother insisted she pick me up from Jack's Fourth of July party at 12:30AM sharp. I wasn't planning on drinking anyway since I had to work the next day, but a bunch of the guys, including Dave and Gavin, planned to sleep over so they started drinking at two in the afternoon. To escape the heat and humidity, Jack let people use the 4-wheeler to drive back and forth to the lake. By late afternoon, I was the only sober driver.

I didn't really mind. Most of the afternoon we'd spent in or by the water. Dave and I dominated in chicken fights—we even beat Gavin. But to be fair, his partner, Jill, was pretty drunk.

Dave fell asleep under a tree and when the cooler needed replenishing, I couldn't wake him to help me.

"Anyone need a ride back to the house? I'm doing a beer run." I threw the cooler in the backseat and got in the 4-wheeler.

"I'll go. I forgot my phone up there." Brad, Jack's cousin, hopped in.

I felt a rush of heat when Gavin grabbed shotgun. "Want some help?"

"Sure. Thanks." His tan enhanced his blue eyes.

We rode in silence as we shook and bumped our way up the path. I shifted down at the base of the big hill.

"You're a pretty good wrestler for a runner, Hart." I felt his eyes on me.

"What do you mean?"

"Earlier, the chicken fights."

"Oh!" I laughed but focused on the path ahead. "Yeah, well, I think I had the sober advantage today."

"I did have to basically pour Jill back onto her towel."

"I think she would have liked to pour you next to her." It came out harsher than I'd meant but at that moment the 4-wheeler stalled. We began to roll back down the hill and I slammed on the brake.

"That's odd." I tried restarting.

"Why we stopping?" Brad asked.

"Not gonna start Hart. Look." Gavin pointed to the illuminated gas light. I hadn't noticed it in the bright sun. I set the E-brake.

"House or Lake?" Gavin asked.

"Lake's closer" I said.

"I gotta get my phone. Later dudes." Brad hopped out and headed up the hill.

I hopped out. "Ow!" The path was covered with little prickers.

"Where are your shoes?"

"In my bag, currently Dave's pillow."

"Well you can't walk without shoes. Hop on." Gavin bent down.

"You can't give me a piggy back all the way to the lake." He had no shirt.

"Get on Hart. It's downhill, we can get gas at the lake. We have thirsty drunks to nourish." I wrapped my legs around his waist, and my arms loosely around his neck, very aware of my chest brushing his bare back.

"You're going to have to hold on tighter than that" Gavin turned his head, our noses bumped and I pulled back quickly.

"I don't bite." He laughed, "Seriously, hang on."

I tightened my grip. My face was so close to his neck I could smell his sun block. We made our way down to the lake. I wondered if he could feel my heart racing.

Gavin tried to set me down on a big rock, but when I stepped on it, it tipped just enough to throw off my balance. I grabbed him to steady myself and pulled us both down. We burst out laughing.

"Sorry," We untangled ourselves and sat up.

"You're not supposed to take down your own man." Our faces were inches apart.

"I thought I was your man." Dave approached on the path. I quickly jumped up.

"Hey, you're awake." I reached out to fix his tussled hair but he ducked away.

"What have you guys been doing?" he looked at Gavin.

"The 4-wheeler ran out of gas." I stepped between them.

"And Gavin just happened to come to your rescue again." he glared over my head at Gavin. "It feels like every time I turn around you have your hands all over her." Dave's body blocked the sun, casting a shadow across me and making his face hard to see. It was intimidating.

"She tried to get you, but you were passed out." Gavin's voice had an edge to it. Dave clenched his hands into fists.

"I worked 60 hours this week. I was asleep." I put a hand on his chest.

"Hey, let's go ask Jack where to get gas." Neither of them moved. I could feel Dave's heart racing beneath my hand.

"Ow!" I yelled and sat down, holding my foot in my hand.

"What's wrong?" Dave asked.

"I think something stung me." I lied.

"Why were you driving barefoot?" Dave bent down to take a look.

"You passed out on the bag with her shoes, Rumpelstiltskin." Gavin scoffed.

"Gavin, why don't you go ask Jack about the gas?" I tried to plead with my eyes.

"Why are you being such a dick?" Dave stood up.

"You passed out on your girlfriend, but I'm the dick?" Gavin held up his hands.

I stood up between them again. "Gavin can you please just go get the gas?"

"That's right Gavin, *my* girlfriend. So why don't you fuck off and leave us alone." Dave moved to stand beside me.

Gavin's eyes narrowed in anger and he took a step toward us. I braced for him to lash out but instead he laughed. "Okay, okay. Relax. I'm just messing with you. I'll go find Jack and you can keep Sierra all to yourself." He winked at me and jogged off before Dave could respond.

"Why does he think he can make me feel like I'm the one out of line when he's the one hitting on someone else's girlfriend?"

"I don't know, but let's not let it ruin our day." I turned to face him.

He searched my face with his eyes.

"Please?" I pulled his head down and pecked his lips.

He finally sighed, kissed me and grabbed my hand. "Come on, it's hot, let's cool off."

I avoided Gavin all afternoon and focused on having fun with Dave. He cooked dinner for everyone over the bonfire. It was some of the best potatoes and corn I'd ever had. By the time the fireworks started, I felt like Dave was himself again.

I went inside to get us a drink and when I returned Victoria Spencer and her posse were on our blanket. Dave faced the fireworks as Victoria sat close to him studying his profile. I hung back and watched.

"Where's your little publicist, Dave? She tapped her fingernail on his shoulder. "Out spreading more lies about me?" She ran it down his arm.

"What do you want Victoria?" Dave shoved her hand away.

"Remember last year?" She leaned in close to his ear but spoke loud, "In that back bedroom? How did you say it? 'I didn't know sex could feel this fuckin' good!" She turned and looked right at me.

Dave pushed her away. "Fuck off."

Victoria stood. "Your beer bitch is back anyway." Dave turned as I approached.

"Careful with my leftovers," She gave me a wicked grin. I only felt slightly vindicated later, when I overheard Gavin ask her what a recent grad was doing at a high school party. She and her posse huffed off before the fireworks even finished.

When there was just a small group left, Jack broke out the new karaoke machine. He had us all laughing with his hip hop skills. Then Gavin began singing *Jessie's Girl* by Rick Springfield. Dave walked out of the bathroom just as Gavin sang the part about wanting to make his friend's girlfriend his.

Everyone looked at Dave. I made my way over to him.

"Hey, let's go sit by the fire. " I whispered in his ear. He remained focused on Gavin's smug smile. I slipped my hand in Dave's, but he pulled away; making a fist with it instead.

Gavin fixed his smile on the two of us as he sang "…I want to tell her that I love her, but…" and before I could stop him, Dave tackled Gavin. They smashed into an end table, breaking the lamp and sending solo cups, chips and beer sailing. Jack and Brad pulled them apart and pushed Dave outside to cool off.

I followed him. "What the hell, Dave?"

"Seriously Sierra? '*I wish that I had Jessie's girl*'. He's singing about wanting you. Right in my face."

"So ignore him; who am I with right now? Who was I with in there?" The dying bonfire snapped behind us.

"I've seen you look at each other."

"I don't want to fight."

"You think he's hot, don't you?" the intensity of his expression was unnerving.

"You're drunk. Let's talk when you're sober." I turned to go back inside.

"Don't go, Sierra," He grabbed my arm hard.

"Ow! Dave that hurts," I yanked on my arm. He released it.

"Sorry, I don't know what my problem is. I act crazy when it comes to you, I'm sorry. Are you okay?"

I rubbed at my arm with my hand.

"Do you want to go down to the lake?"

I checked the time. "My mom will be here soon."

"I don't want you to go." He pulled me close for a kiss and almost fell over. I steadied him.

"You should sleep here, too." He kissed my nose.

"Maybe my mom should take *you* home; keep you out of trouble, Rocky,"

"Let's sit." He pulled me down next to him on a wet blanket. "You're so pretty. You know that?" He reached toward my face but didn't connect.

"You're being weird."

"I'm sorry. I'm wasted." He flopped back. I lay back next to him and looked at the stars.

"I just can't stand the thought of you with somebody else, you know?" He leaned over me, blocking the stars. The intensity of his stare, gave me a little chill. He leaned closer and kissed me hard on the lips." The full weight of him and his sloppy kiss were too much. I felt a rush of panic, pushed him away hard and took a deep breath of fresh air. He was so drunk he simply fell back on the blanket.

"Thanks for being my girlfriend." He said and took my hand in his. I heard a snort and realized he'd passed out.

I got some of the guys to help me get him to a bed. Before I left, I made Brad, who was basically sober, promise to keep checking on him.

I went outside to wait for my mom because I didn't want her to see how drunk they were. I sat on one of the wet blankets to take in the night sky and found the Big Dipper and the Summer Triangle. Then the hair on my neck shot up, like someone was watching me. I stood and looked around, but it was seriously dark without the fire.

"Hello?" I called out and turned in a half-circle until I backed right into someone. I let out a little shriek.

"Sorry." Gavin's voice caught me off guard, "Didn't mean to scare you."

"What the heck are you doing out here?" I turned and put a little distance between us.

"The bathroom was occupied." I couldn't quite make out his expression.

"What about you, Hart? Why are you out here all alone?" He tsk tsked. Light temporarily lit his face and my heart leapt at the way his eyes held mine.

"That's my ride." I nodded toward the approaching headlights.

"Sorry about earlier." He said, never breaking eye contact.

"Dave over-reacts sometimes." I looked behind me as my mom pulled into the driveway.

"No, I'd have probably punched me, too." I tried to read his expression but his face was shadowed again. *What was he saying?*

"I hate fighting."

"Yeah well, it wasn't really a fight; more of a tackle and roll."

"Well hopefully he got it out of his system."

"How's your foot? Sting go away?" He flashed a sardonic grin.

"Sierra?" My mom called out.

"I gotta go." I bolted for the car.

Dr. Laura Hart

When Sierra began dating, I tried to stay calm. I liked Dave, but I remembered the thrill of flirting, the pain of finding out my crush only had eyes for girls with quick zippers, and then that magical moment when you and the guy you like click so well that the rest of the world fades away. My physician side knew Sierra should have the chance to feel all of that, too; but the mom side wanted to save her from any heartache.

When I saw Gavin and Sierra in my headlights, my "mom radar" went off.

"Nobody else needs a ride?" I asked as Sierra hopped in and closed the door.

"Nope. All good." She gave me a quick forced smile and turned to look out the window.

"Was that Gavin I saw?"

"Yeah. He's staying over."

"Did you have a good time?" I tried to catch a glimpse, but her gaze remained fixed.

"Yeah, it was so hot and humid, the lake felt great."

"So I guess Gavin fits in okay with the group?" I hoped I was being subtle.

She snapped her head around. "Why?" I felt her trying to read my expression in the dim light. "Did you think he wouldn't?"

"No, I guess I just thought it was a hard time for him to move; junior year, mid-way through. But it sounds like he's doing well."

We rode in silence for a bit.

"I'm a little surprised Dave didn't walk you to the car." I stopped at a red light.

"He fell asleep and I didn't want to wake him." She leaned back in her seat with a sigh.

"Everything okay with you two?"

"Yeah. It's fine. How are *you* feeling? You should have had dad come get me. You need rest."

"I'm fine. I took a little nap earlier. Besides, I wanted to come."

Sierra gave me a once over like my body might say different.

"So does Gavin date anyone? Mindy hasn't mentioned him lately."

"Not really. Victoria Spencer hangs all over him every chance she gets." Sierra wrinkled her nose.

"Was she there?" I turned onto our street.

"Unfortunately; but Gavin blew her off and she left," Sierra grabbed her bag from the floor as we pulled into our driveway. "Why all the Gavin questions? Did his mom say something?"

"No. I saw that he walked you to the car." I wasn't completely lying.

"He didn't walk me to the car." Her tone was defensive. "I ran into him on the way out. Right when you pulled up." We parked and Sierra hurried to the door.

"Oh. Well, I'm glad you all had a good time." I followed her into the house. She said a quick goodnight to us both and headed to bed. I could tell there was more to the story, but I let it go for the moment.

Patrick Hart

I was relieved when Laura came through her first reconstructive surgery with no problems. Within a week the drains were removed and she was back at work. Sierra and I tried to get her to take more time, but she insisted.

I worried she'd ask me to leave again now that she didn't need my help. She had one more surgery but not for months. She smiled easily again and I hoped I had a little to do with that. We hadn't talked about *us* outside of logistics and healthcare.

I wanted to know what she was thinking; how she felt about me. Had she forgiven me? But I was too afraid I might not like the answers. When Sierra left for college would it be the two of us again or would we go our separate ways?

I took Sierra with me to New York in August so we could combine my meetings with college tours of Columbia and NYU. Then we drove to see Syracuse University and Cornell. It was the longest we'd been alone in a while.

"Hey Dad, this is our exit. Aren't you going to get over?" Sierra looked up from her phone just in time.

"Sorry about that. Guess I was someplace else."

"Did your meetings go okay?" Sierra asked.

"Yeah, fine. I was thinking about your mom."

"She's good; I just texted her a few minutes ago." Sierra looked back down at her screen.

"Do you think she seems happy?" I set my cruise control.

"Hold on," Sierra smiled down at her phone as she texted. "Sorry, do I think mom is happy?"

"Yeah?" I tried to look at both her and the road.

Sierra looked at the road ahead. "I haven't thought about it as much lately, but yeah, I do." Sierra looked at me. "She was singing in the shower earlier this week. I forgot she used to do that." A new text took Sierra's attention back to her phone.

I wanted to ask Sierra if she thought Laura had forgiven me, said anything about me staying for good, but I knew it wasn't fair to pull her into the middle.

"Who are you texting with that has you smiling like that?" I asked.

"Oh, just friends," she said without looking up.

I probably should have pushed her for specifics but I turned up the radio and let it go for now.

Day 73 – 12/16

Biked 9 miles

Cheerio stuffed pasta shells—soft on the outside, crunchy in the center. I timed it and it took me only 23 minutes to stuff them all. Neighbors won't answer me about the party. I think they may be shy or possibly afraid of us. I made them party hats and everything.

For my seventeenth birthday, my parents took me on a surprise trip to Nantucket. My dad bartended there summers between college and my parents spent their first anniversary there; probably why he'd chosen the spot. My mom's doctors had given her the all clear so we went.

We spent Saturday at Surfside beach. My mom had gotten limited exercise since her battle began and insisted we all rent bikes and buy a picnic lunch at Henry's Sandwich Shop. My mom did great; she looked like her old self again.

The beach was busy, but beautiful; everything we needed after a difficult spring. We biked back and after a quick nap and shower it was almost time for dinner. My mom had given me a new sundress and my own set of hot rollers for my birthday. I felt pretty good when I stepped onto the porch. My dad had rented a cute little house in town from a co-worker.

"Wow," my dad whistled. "Look at my birthday girl. I am going to be the envy of every man on the island with the two of you this evening." He dropped a kiss on my head. My mom had tears in her eyes. It scared me at first.

"Are you okay?"

She sniffled a little. "Sorry." She said. "Just having a moment." She patted her tears with her drink napkin. "I'm going to mess up my make-up before we even leave."

We hugged and my dad joined in.

"Okay ladies. Enough tears. Let's have some fun!"

As we walked to dinner, I studied my mom. Her hair had grown in thicker and darker. The shorter hair emphasized her eyes and cheekbones. She looked really happy. "You look really pretty, Mom."

She squeezed my hand. "Thanks, Sierra. I feel good."

You can imagine our surprise when we ran into Gavin talking on his phone outside the Boarding House, our dinner destination.

"Gavin?" my mom saw him first. My heart leapt. He looked freshly showered and dressed for dinner. He ended his call.

"Dr. H, Mr. H, and look at you, Hart!" he shook my dad's hand.

"What are you doing here?" I asked.

"I actually have a client here, Mr. Benson. I think your mom knows his wife, Elaina."

"Right, I heard they spent summers here." My mom confirmed.

"Wow, Gavin," my dad said. "I didn't realize your business had you on the road, too. Pretty impressive."

"Thanks. I helped them in Laketown and they asked me to set up their network here, too."

"Are you eating here?" my mom asked.

"We were, but their kids and grandchildren surprised them with a visit. That was Mr. Benson on the phone inviting me to join them for a cook-out. But I don't want to interrupt."

"You should just eat with us." I suggested and threw my dad a look.

"Of course, come help celebrate Sierra's birthday." My dad agreed.

"Oh, that's right." Gavin gave me a wink. "Happy Birthday."

"Thanks."

My mom had a forced smile on her face.

"You okay, mom?"

"Hungry, let's go in."

Dinner was delicious. My dad ordered wine for the table and nobody said a thing when they poured it in all of our glasses. My dad had us laughing with stories from his summers on the island. By the time they sang *Happy Birthday* and served cake, we were all ready for a walk. The wine had gone to my head and it felt good to step out into the fresh salty air. My dad wanted to take my mom for a nightcap.

"What about Sierra?" my mom asked.

"I can walk her home," Gavin offered.

"But it's your birthday." my mom took my hand in hers.

"And it's been great; you and dad should go have fun."

"We could sit on the porch. We have wine." My mom suggested.

My dad looked torn.

I squeezed my mom's hand and whispered. "I think Dad would really like you to himself."

My mom looked at my dad and sighed. "Okay." Then she spoke mostly to Gavin, "We won't be late."

He thanked them for dinner and we went our separate ways.

"I wish we could walk along the beach." I said.

"Why can't we?"

"Well there aren't good beaches near town."

"We could grab a cab."

"My parents would probably freak."

"Leave a note at the house. If you text, they can say no. I find forgiveness is easier than permission."

"I don't know. Stress isn't good for my mom."

"It's your birthday. Come on. We'll probably beat them back anyway."

I could blame it on the wine but if I'm honest, I didn't want my birthday to end yet. "Okay, surely if we're back in an hour, my mom won't care." We passed a bachelorette party. I noticed them checking out Gavin.

"Your mom looks great, by the way." Gavin said.

"Yeah, I think she's happy again."

"That couldn't have anything to do with your dad, could it?" he flashed that dimple.

"I don't want to jinx it, but I don't think it's a coincidence that my dad picked their first anniversary spot for my birthday trip."

"It must feel good to see them together and happy again." He grabbed my hand as we quickly crossed between cars in the street.

"It does. But I'm hesitant to believe in the happy family. I don't think I could forgive him twice."

He squeezed my hand.

"Everybody deserves a second chance."

Dr. Laura Hart

When we walked away from Sierra and Gavin, I felt torn. It felt nice to spend time with Patrick in such a magical place; but I worried about Sierra. We found a bar near the water and ordered a drink.

"To second chances," Patrick clinked my glass with his.

"And raising a great person together," we locked eyes as we drank. I looked out at the ocean.

"What's wrong?" Patrick asked. "You seem distracted."

"Sorry. Do you think it's strange that Gavin just happened to be in Nantucket the same weekend we are? Then alone at the same restaurant we had dinner reservations?"

"What are you saying? Do you think he and Sierra planned it?"

"Sierra? I just meant Gavin."

"They definitely have chemistry; but Sierra didn't even know we'd be here. How could he?" Patrick rubbed my arm gently.

"I don't know that I want them dating. He's a lot more, uh," I couldn't think of the right word.

"Experienced?" Patrick suggested.

"Yes. They didn't move just because of the inheritance. Gavin had been secretly seeing a single mom that lived next door. He babysat her son. One evening Mindy stopped by with Gavin's phone. The little boy was in front of the TV and they were in her bedroom."

"How old was this woman?"

"Twenties, Gavin was 16. Weeks later, when the boy's father got released from prison, he jumped Gavin. It was an ugly scene. Anyway, the move gave them both a fresh start."

"But Sierra wouldn't do that to Dave." Patrick interlaced his fingers with mine.

"I should text her."

"And say what? We don't want you to date Gavin?" he raised his eyebrows, challenging me. "Sierra has a good head on her shoulders. Let's trust in her. Okay?" he squeezed my fingers.

The guitar player returned from a break and announced, "I had a request for this one." He began playing *Wonderful Tonight*, our song.

"You?" I tilted my head toward the guitarist.

Patrick winked. We shared a smile.

“Care to dance?” Patrick stood and offered his hand.

“Here?” I looked around. Every table was filled with couples or groups enjoying late dinner or drinks.

“Yep,” He pulled me into his arms. I laughed and followed his lead. I felt myself relax as cheek to cheek we glided into a place I’d really missed.

Day 74 – 12/17
Biked 12 miles

I keep waking up in the middle of the night convinced someone is rubbing my feet. It's terrifying. I get hot when I stay zipped in the sleeping bag, but I don't want my feet exposed. And every time I turn on the flashlight I hear the *Jeopardy* jingle counting down the time until it goes black for good. I turn it off and the presence returns. I try to take myself back to a better moment.

Gavin paid the driver and we stepped out of the cab. I realized I had left the house with no money, no ID, nothing but my phone, a bottle of wine, an opener, and a blanket.

"Sorry, I'm such an airhead I didn't even bring money."

"No problem." He said. "It's your birthday. I wouldn't let you pay anyway."

"Thanks. And by the way, this isn't Surfside Beach."

"I know, it's called Steps Beach. Mr. Benson told me about it. We walked down the steps and closer to the water to spread out our blanket. We lay side by side and looked up at the stars. The rhythmic sound of the waves was relaxing.

"Lying at the beach this afternoon, I wondered if life could get any better? But this is pretty sweet too." I said.

"It is." We lay there, listening to the waves.

"Shall we open the wine?' I asked, sitting up.

"Sure." He opened it while I watched a group of people down the beach. I could just barely hear their music and an occasional voice.

"Guess we weren't the only ones who thought it was a good beach night." I said nodding toward their silhouettes.

"We forgot another important thing." He handed me the opened bottle.

"Glasses," I realized. "Sorry. Oh well, I don't have cooties if you don't" I took a swig.

We passed the bottle back and forth and talked about college and moms and our desire to graduate already.

"So I didn't realize your business was this successful," I said. "You're already being flown to Nantucket."

"Yeah, well this is a fluke. Most of my clients are moms who can't figure out the basics. Sometimes I feel like I'm taking advantage of them. I don't even know a fraction of all there is to learn. I wish the school offered more technology classes. I've found a few online, but I'd rather start college now."

"Oh I love this song." I heard *Crazy* by Gnarls Barkley float up from a gathering further down the beach. I stood up and danced "Come on."

"I'm enjoying watching you."

I plopped back down when it ended. "You don't like that song?"

"Country boy; remember?" he handed me the bottle again.

"That's right." I took a drink. "So country boy, do you know how to swim?"

"Are you suggesting we do that now?"

"Gorgeous night at a Nantucket beach; there's probably a law." I teased.

"Really? I don't know. You seem a little buzzed. Are you sure it's safe?"

"I'm fine; besides I won third place in the backstroke twice." I bragged.

"And you were how old?"

"Eight and three-quarters."

He laughed, "Oh okay, well now I feel much better about it."

"Oh come on. It'll be fun." I begged.

"I have no doubt it will be *fun*. It's the *safe* part I'm worried about."

"Okay. I have an idea. How 'bout you give me like a sobriety test? If I pass; we swim. If I fail; we stay here and finish the wine?" I pointed to the bottle in the sand.

"You want me to give you a sobriety test?"

"Yeah, if I pass then I must be okay to swim, right?"

He laughed. "You have no idea how completely adorable you are, do you?"

"Flattery will get you nowhere. Come on test me." I stood up with my hands on my hips.

"Okay fine, but you have to perform all of my tests without question." He held out his hand and we shook on it.

"Okay. First, stand on your right leg and without taking your eyes off mine, touch your nose with your left pointer finger."

I did as he suggested flawlessly.

"Very nice, Hart. Okay, now tell me what you were wearing the first day we met."

"What?" I asked. "That's not a sobriety test, that's a memory test."

"You're stalling." He said with that dimpled smile.

I closed my eyes and tried to remember. "It was at my mom's office, after school…" I opened my eyes. "How do I know *you* remember?"

"You'll just have to trust me." He said with a shit-eating grin on his face.

I sighed and closed my eyes again. "I had on jeans, a gray sweater, and converse."

"What color converse?" he asked.

"Black." I grinned.

"Correct."

"Ha, that's two down. One to go?" I asked.

"That is at my discretion. Okay. Now I need you to do a cartwheel." He took a swig from the wine.

I stepped to the side of the blanket, put my feet together, took a breath and did a perfect cartwheel.

"Nicely done, Hart." He clapped. I curtsied.

"Okay, now I need you to stand, put one hand over your heart and the other in a salute and sing the National Anthem."

"The entire thing?" I asked.

"Do you want to swim or not?" he asked.

"Fine." I started to sing. "Oh say can you see…"

"Louder. I can barely hear you."

I rolled my eyes, but complied, "by the dawn's early light, what so proudly we hail…" and suddenly I realized I wasn't singing alone. From over in the dune we could hear a man's voice singing with me. I gave Gavin a look but kept going; by the time I got to "Oh say does that star spangled…" the other people further down the beach had joined in. Gavin even stood and sang "and the home of the braaaave!!!" When we finished the mystery guy from the dune fell silent but the group on the beach cheered and yelled "God Bless America!"

"My dad said crazy things always happen here."

"That was classic." Gavin laughed.

I took another drink of the wine. Then I pulled my dress over my head, tossed it on the blanket, and ran for the ocean. It was like bath water. I swam out just far enough to feel covered but not far enough to worry Gavin. He ran into the water and swam out to meet me.

"That was cheating," he said when he popped up next to me.

"Sorry, but you are going to thank me, check this out." I waved my arms through the water and it created a blue light in my path. "Isn't that cool?"

Gavin did the same. "The locals call it phosphorescence but it's actually a non-stinging jellyfish. When you move the water it makes them light up like fireflies underwater."

"Wait a minute," I asked. "You knew about this?"

He flashed me that dimpled smile. "It's why I told the cab driver to come to this beach."

"So you had planned on us getting in the water!" I jumped, put my hands on his shoulders and pushed him under water. He grabbed me around the waist and pulled me under with him. We both came up for air. We moved our arms back and forth in the water, making the jellyfish light up.

"This water is perfect." I floated on my back. The stars were endless. I noticed it seemed even quieter and saw that the group was leaving. Gavin grabbed me quick from behind and I let out a squeal. He pulled me back against him. I could feel the skin of his chest against my back. Both of our hearts were racing. Chills ran down my arms as our skin kissed in the water.

"We're all alone now." He whispered in my ear in what I think he meant to be a joking scary voice. But it sent another batch of chills through me.

"Are you actually cold?" he asked me.

"No." I said and swam away from him a little.

"Well if you aren't cold, Sierra Hart, then what is giving you those goose bumps?" he asked and flashed that magnetic dimpled grin.

"Must be the jellyfish."

He swam back over to me, grabbed me by the waist and pulled me against him again. My body responded accordingly.

"Really? Still sticking with the jellyfish?" he teased.

"Gavin. I can't...Dave..." he brushed his finger across my lips.

"I know. Dave is a nice guy. I get it. But he's not here now. It's just us. Who will ever know? This isn't going to go away unless we do something about it. Maybe if we test the waters, get it out of our system, we can all move along."

"Just like that. We make-out, then go home and act like nothing happened?" I asked.

"Do you have a better idea?" He rubbed my arm and it sent a new wave of chills.

"Dave would never do this to me."

"You're probably right. But if Dave had an interest in another girl; how would you feel if you knew in his mind he was always wondering about someone else?"

"So you think I spend a lot of time wondering about you?" I asked. "Rather presumptuous of you, Gavin Ross."

"You are deflecting. I'm serious. Wouldn't it be better to just know if there is anything to what we feel?" he asked.

"I don't know. I'd rather not think."

"Then don't." He reached out and pulled my face to his.

When he kissed me I felt the last of my resistance slip away. I clung to him. I felt like I had been holding back and suddenly couldn't get enough of him.

He wrapped me around his waist and carried me back to our blanket. All that was separating our bodies were my bra and underwear and his boxers. We removed the last little barriers as quickly as possible and wrapped ourselves back up in one another.

"You are so fuckin' hot," he pulled up and looked at me. "And the best part is you have no idea." He buried his head in my neck. I kissed the side of his face, down his neck. My hands traced the muscles in his back. I wanted to explore every part of him. I rolled so I was on top of him and ran kisses down his chest. I closed my hand around him and I heard him suck in his breath. I wanted to make him feel as crazed as I did. I moved lower and ran my tongue up and down the length of him. He broke out in goose bumps. I felt him arch against me and put his hand on my head. I put my whole mouth around him and slowly moved him in and out until he pulled me back up to his lips.

"Sierra, you're making me crazy." He said and rolled me beneath him. He captured my breast in his mouth and sucked, then nibbled. It sent a wave of pleasure through my body. I felt my hips grind up against him. I couldn't get close enough to him. He brought his head back up and kissed me again. I shifted beneath him and felt him between my legs. I was overwhelmed with a desire to have him inside me and I grabbed his butt with my hands and pulled him toward me. He complied and I felt a hot pain sear through me as he entered. I cried out and dug my nails into his back in both pleasure and pain. He let out a little sound that may have been my name and his entire body tensed on top of me. Then he collapsed his head on my chest. We were both breathing heavy. My body tingled everywhere he'd touched me.

"I'm sorry Sierra." He propped himself up on his elbows and looked down at me. "I just got carried away. Are you okay?"

"I'm good," I said, though I knew we didn't even use a condom or anything. All of those talks with my mom, lectures at school. And my first time I just ignore it all and dive right in.

"Are you sure?" he rolled to the side and looked at me. I saw him grab his boxers to wipe himself off. They were white and he saw the blood.

"Sierra," his tone changed. "Oh God, Sierra this wasn't your first time? Please tell me I didn't just devour you like that your first time, did I?"

"It's fine. I... it didn't hurt really..."

He pulled me to him. "Oh, Sierra, I am so sorry. I just assumed that you and Dave had... you are so amazing." He said and kissed me.

I kissed him back and let him pull me into his warmth. He reached down and wrapped the blanket up around us. "Wow," he said. "I feel like honored or something. I just wish I knew. I wouldn't have rushed you like that. I got caught up in it and you felt so incredibly good."

"It's okay." I said. "Stop apologizing. Really, it was nice. I kind of got carried away myself. I wanted to do it. It felt . . . right. Stop worrying." I put my hand up to his cheek and looked him in the eyes. He put his hand on mine and moved it to his mouth to kiss my palm. We put our clothes back on except the wet undergarments. Then he wrapped himself and the blanket around me as best he could without getting any blood on our clothes. I leaned back against his chest and he sighed into my hair.

"I wish we could just stay here like this; it's like we're the only people on Earth." I looked out at the ocean and thought *yes, it would be far less complicated that way.* My phone beeped and I looked to see I'd missed a number of texts from my mom:

> *Are u okay?*
> *Still at the beach?*
> *It's late!*
> *Call me.*

I grabbed it and texted her back:

> *b home soon, sorry. Lost track of time swimming.*

I looked up at Gavin. "Reality check. We gotta get back."

He kissed me and said, "Everything good must end."

Dr. Laura Hart

Sierra's birthday weekend in Nantucket seemed to mark a change for us all. I felt like Patrick and I had finally reconnected. It was the perfect place to try and make a fresh start. Since we weren't sure how Sierra would react, we decided to take things slow and discuss it with her when we were more comfortable with plans for the future.

But just as Patrick and I pulled things together, Sierra's world began falling apart. The morning we left Nantucket, she seemed quiet and uncharacteristically grumpy. We'd had words when she got back from the beach. It wasn't like her to go places without asking first. Like anyone, Sierra has her moments, but that morning she was particularly moody. I didn't want anything to spoil the happy mood Patrick and I had created so we just gave her extra space.

Her miserable mood continued over the next few weeks. From what I remember, she didn't spend much time with either Dave or Gavin. I tried to talk to her about it one evening and she just brushed me off, telling me she was working through some stuff. That was it.

When she went missing, I wished back that conversation. I should have gotten her to talk about things. But I didn't. And then it was too late.

Day 75 – 12/18
Biked 10 miles.

Made my own trail mix with the rest of the cheerios, raisins, and peanuts.

I made a mirror out of foil; but when I saw myself I repurposed it as an ice skating rink for my village. Sometimes it's hard to look at your own reflection.

When we got back from Nantucket to find Dave sitting on our steps, I felt sick with guilt. My parents said hello and disappeared inside.

"Hey, how was it?" He said, giving me a hug.

"It's a beautiful place filled with beautiful people. Almost felt unreal, you know?"

"You must have fit right in."

"Always with the flattery, this guy." I said, not sure how to act. "So do you have to work tonight?"

"Nope, and neither do you. I checked the schedule. I thought maybe we could catch a movie or something unless you're too tired."

"You know, in theory that sounds great, but my parents let me have wine last night and I got a little carried away. I am pretty tired." I felt awful when I saw his disappointment.

"We could watch a movie here if you like. That way if I pass out on you, I'm already home." His smile returned.

"Great, well I'll let you get settled back in, finish my run, and come back later with a movie. Should I pick up dinner too?"

"No, my dad wants to make pizza so there should be plenty. You are more than welcome to join, maybe around 6?"

"Great, see you then." He leaned in to kiss me. I could barely return it. He gave me a strange look but didn't say anything before going back to his run.

I went straight up to my room and made a face at myself in the mirror, "bitch!" I fingered the locket from Dave, collapsed onto my bed, curled up in a ball and fell sound asleep.

Almost two hours later, I awoke to a text.

GAVIN: *Did last night really happen or was it just an amazing dream?*

The text made me smile. But then I thought of Dave and felt like crying. I wasn't sure what to do. I couldn't just pretend everything was fine with Dave, but I couldn't tell him what had happened without hurting him.

ME: *Amazing? Yes. Dream? No. D was here waiting when I got here.*
GAVIN: *Did you tell him anything?*
ME: *No.*
GAVIN: *Are you going to?*
ME: *Do you think I should?*
GAVIN: *Doesn't matter what I think. I will follow your lead.*
ME: *So you think we should pretend it didn't happen.*
GAVIN: *I will respect your decision.*
ME: *I can't do this. I'm not built to lie / hide /cheat.*
GAVIN: *Then it was just a dream. I can live with that.*
ME: *I don't know that I can.*
GAVIN: *So what then?*
ME: *I wish I knew. D's coming for dinner & movie, maybe it will be clearer when I spend time w/ him*
GAVIN: *Good Luck. I'm here . . . dreaming*
ME: ☺

I jumped in the shower. By the time I'd dressed and dried my hair, Dave was already downstairs talking to my parents. I went down to join them. As soon as I saw Dave, I realized what I had to do. The weight of it just killed me. I really liked Dave, but all I could think about when we ate dinner was "I had sex with Gavin."

My parents left us to watch our movie and settled outside on the deck with drinks and cards. I still couldn't figure out if they were together or just enjoying one another's company. Still, I had enough relationship trouble of my own so I just put theirs to the back of my head. As soon as they were out of earshot, Dave spoke up.

"Is everything okay? You seem upset. Did I do something wrong?" he asked.

We were on the couch, his arm around my shoulders. I turned to look at him and held his hand in mine. "I had a lot of time to think while I was away and-"

He interrupted, "Are you breaking up with me?"

"I just think I need a little time to myself." I said.

He gently pulled a loose hair from my face. "Is this because of the other night? Because we can slow things down. I don't need anything more. I've never felt so comfortable with anyone in my life. It just feels right, you know?"

"I do and I don't. Yes, I love spending time with you and it has always been easy. I just think that there is a part of me that isn't sure how deep my feelings go. Maybe we'd make better friends." Tears threatened when I saw the pain in his eyes. I felt like a monster.

"Sierra, I know I've never said it, but I love you." He started to cry. "I can't imagine anyone else I'd rather cook for, or just run with. What can I do differently?"

"We'll still run together, and see each other at work and school. I just need to take a step back from the dating side of things and be on my own."

"I thought things were great. I don't understand why you are suddenly pushing me away. Is it because of your dad? I would never hurt you."

"No, it's not that. You are an incredible guy, and I love you, too. I just don't think that I am *in* love with you. I just don't want to end up hurting you more."

"So that's it. We're just done?" He looked crushed, running his hands through his hair. "Fuck, Sierra. How am I supposed to see you everywhere and know that I can't be with you?"

"I know this is hard. But do you have any idea how many girls like you? You'll probably be dating someone else in no time." I said.

"You don't get it do you? I don't want anyone but you Sierra. Ever since sectionals two years ago, you have been the girl in my head. I can't just walk away. I can't just say 'oh well, that didn't work out.' And the fact that you can just crushes me. God, Sierra. I have to get out of here." He stood. "Fuck, I can't believe this is happening." He walked toward the door and opened it. I followed. He turned and looked at me, tears streaking both our faces. "Just swear to me there is nothing I can do to change your mind."

I didn't trust my voice so I just shook my head. I reached out to hug him goodbye but he pushed my arms away. "I can't." he said. "I just, I can't. Tell your parents thanks for dinner." When he left, I slid down the door and cried. It was true, I did have a great time with him, but the way I'd felt when I was with Gavin made me feel like Dave had been just a warm-up. I felt terrible, but who can control their heart?

INVESTIGATIVE INTERVIEW

Case: MPM 047 **Date:** 10.07.2006 **Subject:** David Braun
Officer: Detective Rock **Location:** LPS RM2

D. Rock	When did Sierra break up with you?
Dave	August 6th
D. Rock	Did she say why she wanted to end the relationship?
Dave	She said she needed time and space.
D. Rock	How did you react to this news?
Dave	How do you think? I wasn't exactly happy. And it felt like it came out of the blue. Right before she left for vacation things were going really well between us.
D. Rock	Do you think she met someone during her trip?
Dave	I asked her, but she said no.
D. Rock	Did you believe her?
Dave	I did at first. Sierra isn't one to play games, you know. She's pretty straight forward about that stuff. But she acted so strange around me after that.
D. Rock	Strange how?
Dave	I don't know. Like she couldn't even stand to see me. And we had been friends for a long time so it seemed weird.
D. Rock	Did you do anything about how you felt?
Dave	What do you mean?

D. Rock	Well, last time a girl broke up with you it didn't go too well, did it, Mr. Braun?
Dave	You're going to bring that up? I was glad when Victoria broke up with me. I was already interested in Sierra anyway. And I don't think Victoria is the kind of girl guys get too upset over, if you know what I mean.
D. Rock	No, I don't know what you mean.
Dave	That whole thing was just BS. I never sent the picture. Obviously everyone agreed because nothing ever came of it.
D. Rock	Yes, well your daddy and his money made sure of that.
Dave	Whatever. Can we get back to Sierra? I'm only here because I want to find her. I will do whatever it takes.
D. Rock	Sounds like you really have it bad for this girl.
Dave	Is that a question?
D. Rock	Your buddy Jack said you were obsessed with her. That you started following her around after she broke up with you. Is that true, Dave?
Dave	I just couldn't understand how she would go from hot to cold so quickly. I know there was a reason. Sometimes I checked where she went to see if I could figure anything out.
D. Rock	And did you figure anything out?
Dave	Just that, for someone who wanted her own space, she seemed to spend a lot of time with Gavin.
D. Rock	Gavin Ross. He's the new kid at school. Hot-shit runner, right?
Dave	That's him.

D. Rock	I thought you guys were friends.
Dave	We were. We are. I just saw them alone sometimes, talking all hush hush.
D. Rock	Did you ask her about Gavin?
Dave	She said nothing was going on.
D. Rock	Did you believe her?
Dave	(shrug)
D. Rock	You know what I think? I think maybe you were mad that Sierra dumped you for your buddy Gavin and you wanted to get back at her. Only this time you got a little carried away.
Dave	(scraping of chair) Screw you! You don't know anything about me or Sierra. It wasn't like that with us. I would never hurt her. Ever.
D. Rock	I seemed to have hit a raw spot there. Would it surprise you to know that we have an eye-witness placing your car in Sierra's driveway around the time she went missing? And when we checked with the school they said you signed out for a doctor's appointment at 11:00AM and didn't come back the rest of the day.
Dave	It's true. I was in PE when I saw her drive out of the school lot. She had been sick recently so I decided to go make sure she was okay. Only she didn't go home. I pulled into her driveway and waited for a few minutes. When she didn't show, I drove by the dam. I knew Gavin wasn't in school that day and thought maybe they were together. But she wasn't there either.
D. Rock	Why didn't you return to school?
Dave	(shrugs): I don't know. I guess I was too depressed.
D. Rock	So where did you go?

Dave	Home. I went home and cooked.
D. Rock	Cooked? You couldn't find Sierra so you went home and cooked?
Dave	It's what I do when I'm depressed. Cooking makes me feel better.
D. Rock	Was anyone at home with you that can verify you were there? Your mom? Dad? A maid? Anyone?
Dave	We don't have a maid. And no, both of my parents were at work.
D. Rock	So you have no alibi for the window of time in which we believe Sierra went missing.
Dave	No, but you are wasting your time with me. Please. You need to focus on other leads or you'll never find her.
D. Rock	Fine Mr. Braun we can be done for now, but don't get any ideas about skippin' town with daddy's money.
	(Subject, David Braun, slammed door and left the room.)

INVESTIGATIVE INTERVIEW

Case: MPM 047 **Date:** 10.10.2006 **Subject:** Gavin Ross
Officer: Detective Rock **Location:** LPS RM1

D. Rock	When did you last see Sierra Hart?
Gavin	Thursday at practice. I saw her getting in her car.
D. Rock	You didn't see her at school on Friday?
Gavin	I was home sick all day.
D. Rock	Did you leave the house at all?
Gavin	Around 11 or so I went to Panera to get some soup, and stopped at the drug store for some cough drops and cold medicine.
D. Rock	Can anyone verify that?
Gavin	Whoever was working at both places, I guess.
D. Rock	And what time did you return home?
Gavin	I don't know. Around 12 or so.
D. Rock	So you remained at home from noon on Friday until when?
Gavin	Um. Until Dr. H called later that evening looking for Sierra.
D. Rock	What time was that?
Gavin	Around quarter to eight or so.
D. Rock	And what did you tell Dr. Hart specifically?

Gavin	Just that I hadn't seen her since practice the day before. She wanted to know if I had any idea where she might go.
D. Rock	So what did you do?
Gavin	The same thing everyone did. We all went looking for her.
D. Rock	Do you know anyone she had a problem with?
Gavin	Well, there were people before that had been mad at her.
D. Rock	Before what?
Gavin	No, I just mean in the past. Victoria Spencer for one. She wasn't exactly a fan. I wasn't living here yet, but I guess Victoria went out with Dave before Sierra did.
D. Rock	Dave Braun?
Gavin	Yeah. I guess some naked pictures of Victoria floated around.
D. Rock	Yes, I am aware.
Gavin	Well, I guess Sierra told a bunch of people she thought Victoria sent the picture herself to frame Dave.
D. Rock	Interesting. And how did Victoria react to this?
Gavin	That's the strange thing. Sierra was worried Victoria would do something to get her back, but I don't think she ever did.
D. Rock	So you think Victoria may have been involved in her disappearance?
Gavin	I have no idea.
D. Rock	What is the nature of your relationship with Sierra?

Gavin	We're friends. Our moms work together so she introduced me around when I moved here in January.
D. Rock	So you have never been romantically involved.
Gavin	We are just friends.
D. Rock	What was it the two of you did at the dam when you met there?
Gavin	Her mom has been sick and she just wanted someone to talk to.
D. Rock	She called you, and not her boyfriend, Dave Braun?
Gavin	Well they broke up, and she felt like I understood her better. We both grew up with just our moms.
D. Rock	Did she break up with Dave so that you two could be together?
Gavin	Is that what Dave thinks?
D. Rock	I'm asking you if that's what happened.
Gavin	Dave took the break-up hard. He needed someone to blame.
D. Rock	Have you two ever gotten into a fight over Sierra?
Gavin	Not really.
D. Rock	So he didn't punch you in the middle of a New Year's Eve Party and later at another party?
Gavin	Yes, but it's not how it sounds. He just punched me because he misunderstood the situation. I never punched back and we were fine the next Monday at school.
D. Rock	Can you tell me why you were on the island of Nantucket from August 3rd through August 6th?

Gavin	Working for Mr. Benson. He has a summer house there.
D. Rock	And you work with computers, is that right?
Gavin	Yes. I was making sure his home network was secure.
D. Rock	Did you and Sierra plan to be on Nantucket at the same time?
Gavin	No. It was just a coincidence.
D. Rock	A coincidence?
Gavin	Can I get some water?
D. Rock	So you're telling me you and this pretty girl end up in a beautiful romantic spot together and nothing happens?
Gavin	I had dinner with her and her parents. That's about it.
D. Rock	Did she ever mention why she broke up with Dave when she got back from the trip?
Gavin	She said she needed space. Are we almost done here? I have homework.
D. Rock	Do you think Dave would ever harm Sierra?
Gavin	Dave? No. I don't think so. The guy is nuts for her.
D. Rock	Okay, well, don't run off on us, okay? And if Sierra gets in touch for any reason, you need to give me a call. Here is my card.
Gavin	Yes, sir.

Day 77 – 12/20
Biked 11 miles

I accidently made too much corn, beans and rice. I've eaten it for lunch and dinner for two days, but I don't dare waste it. Waste. Haste. Toothpaste. My shampoo and conditioner are almost gone. Guess I'll wash my hair less frequently. I mean who cares anyway, right? It's not like the neighbors are going to complain.

The last few weeks of the summer I went to work, ran, and hung out with my parents. I wanted to see Gavin but I couldn't do that to Dave. Every time I saw him at work, my heart ached. He looked truly miserable. And the entire staff seemed angry at me for breaking his heart. I began to dread going, but the money was too good to quit. Besides, I deserved it.

My parents were very supportive. They didn't ask a lot of questions, but I could tell they were worried. Tia thought I was crazy, but she was so in love with Thomas that she couldn't understand why the whole world wasn't in love. I envied how easy she had it.

When cross country season started every practice became a competition between Dave and Gavin so I went back to running with Maggie. I have to hand it to Gavin, he respected my space. The night I broke up with Dave I called to explain what had happened, and told him I needed time. I missed him, but stuck to my resolution.

The first week of school I got a stomach bug. We were running sprints and I felt dizzy and nauseous. I had to run to the bushes and throw up, which brought Dave and Gavin racing to my side. They both offered to drive me home but I insisted on driving myself. I felt better, but I was really tired. I went to bed without dinner and my mom made me stay home the next day even though I didn't have a fever.

A couple of days later in PE, I had a sickening thought. My boobs started to hurt when playing soccer. I suddenly remembered I hadn't had a period in a while. I skipped them fairly often thanks to my rigorous running schedule, but with all of the other symptoms I was a little freaked out.

At lunch, I drove one town over to the pharmacy. I kept telling myself that surely I couldn't get pregnant the first and only time I'd had sex. I mean it couldn't have lasted more than six minutes. Wouldn't it have to take longer? I knew the basic science, but it just didn't seem like it could have happened that fast.

I made myself wait until after dinner to try the test. The directions said early in the morning was better, but I had to know. I placed the pee-soaked stick on a washcloth next to the sink in my bathroom and waited outside. I swore if the results were negative I would not have sex again until I was 21. I listened to two songs to make sure I'd waited long enough; then I took a deep breath and opened the door. The two lines were a clear equal sign. Cheating on your boyfriend equates to pregnancy. My dad's theories about Karma and Lady Luck never felt more true to form. I sat on the floor, thinking *there is no way I am having a baby*. Obviously, I needed to find a clinic. I guessed I was about five weeks along. According to the internet, it was the size of a sesame seed and didn't have a brain yet. That made me feel better. *I can do this*. I called Tia.

"What's up?"

"I'm pregnant." I could feel the tears rise in my throat.

"What? How? I didn't think you and Dave ever sealed the deal."

"It's not Dave's." My voice shook.

"Hello? Is this my friend, Sierra? Who did you sleep with and why am I just hearing about it now?" I felt a little pang of guilt.

"It was Gavin, in Nantucket. I cheated on Dave. I wanted to tell you but I felt like if I never talked about it, I could ignore it. Clearly this is Karma's way of getting me back." I pulled my pillow off my bed and squeezed it to my chest. There was no turning back now. I'd called her.

"Gavin?"

"I really wish that I could just be with him but I don't want to hurt Dave. Now I'm pregnant and my life is one hot mess."

"Oh, Sierra. It will be fine. Seriously. What do you want to do? Have you told Gavin?"

"No. I just took the test. I can't have this baby. Do you think I should even tell him?"

"Well, who will go with you to the clinic?" I heard knocking.

"Guys, not now! Go watch TV. Sorry, I'm watching the twins. Are you going to tell your mom?"

"God no! I thought I'd just go by myself." With no witnesses, it might be easier to forget.

"You can't go alone. I wish I was there." I squeezed the pillow tighter.

"Me too. God, I can't believe this. Who gets pregnant the first time they have sex?"

"Apparently you." She responded. "Hold on a sec, look in the couch cushions!"

"You need to go, and I guess I should call Gavin."

"Yes, call Gavin. And make sure he helps pay for it. It's not an inexpensive thing."

"You speak like a woman with experience." I wondered if there were things she'd kept from me, too.

"Yeah, Thomas and I had a pregnancy scare a few months ago. I did a fair amount of research. It turned out to be nothing but I went to Planned Parenthood and got on the pill."

"I don't care if I ever have sex again." I threw my pillow across the room.

"Trust me, you will. It gets better."

"Okay, I better go." I didn't want to hear any Tia sex stories right then. "Thanks for listening. I had to talk to someone."

"Always here."

"I know. I miss you being *here*."

"Me too. But we will be together again soon. You can do this. Call Gavin. Love you."

"You too. Bye." I looked at my swollen teary face in the bathroom mirror. "You did this to yourself, you selfish idiot." Should I tell Gavin over the phone or in person? It was seven. I texted him.

> ME: *Any chance you could meet me at the dam in 15?*
> GAVIN: *Sure. You OK?*
> ME: *Not really.*

Gavin was already there when I pulled into the parking lot. I jumped into his car.

"Hey, what's up?" He asked before I even closed the door.

It had been so long since we had been alone together, I pulled his face to mine. For a few minutes, I forgot why I had even called him there. It just felt so good to kiss him. And he smelled so good. But then it all came rushing back and I burst into tears.

"Hey, it can't be that bad. The first time I kiss you again in months and it brings you to tears?" This made me cry harder.

"I'm pregnant." I said. He wrapped me in his arms and let me cry for a while. I felt relieved to share this with someone who wasn't 3000 miles away.

"Hey, it's going to be okay, Sierra." He rubbed my back through my coat. "I have money saved and everything will work out. You'll see." I wanted to believe him.

"I can't tell my parents—not with everything going on with my mom."

"There is no rush, Sierra. It hasn't been that long, right?"

"I think about five weeks." I sniffed and he opened his glove box to hand me some napkins. I blew my nose and wiped my face.

"I need to make an appointment at Planned Parenthood." I said. "Maybe I should do it in like Rochester or Syracuse so I don't see anyone I know." I looked up at him. Those damn Caribbean blue eyes looked back. They were easy to get lost in.

"I missed you." I said.

"I've missed you, too." He kissed me gently.

"I just needed some space and time to be sure."

"I know. Though I don't think Dave feels any differently about you."

"I feel so bad for him. God, if he ever found out about this, it would kill him." I said.

"You can't hide it forever."

"Why not? Nobody needs to know but you and the doctor, right?" I asked.

"Wait. You're not keeping the baby?" His jaw clenched and his face grew dark.

"What did you think I was talking about? Just getting a checkup?" I asked.

"Yes. You can't seriously think that I would be okay with an abortion? I can't believe *you* would be okay with this." He opened his door and got out of the truck, pounding the hood with his fist. "Jesus, Sierra."

I followed him out. "Gavin, we're 17. We're a frickin' reality show." I started to cry again. "I can't have a baby right now."

"Why not? I make great money; you could still go to college. I could watch the baby while you're in class and you can watch him while I work." He held me by the elbows.

"You're serious?" I shook his hands off of me, and stepped back. "And where are we going to live that you can work and I can go to college? Think about it Gavin. There is no way. I don't want this."

"Our families would help. We wouldn't be alone. And this baby, our baby, would be amazing. I just know it." He put his hand to my stomach and a wave of nausea rippled through me. I walked away and closer to the edge of the dam embankment. I looked out at the slight ripple to the water. I couldn't let myself think about the pregnancy as a person.

"Gavin. Look I really care about you, I do. I want to see where things go with us, but we can't go from sex on the beach one drunken night to marriage and a baby. Life doesn't work like that. I don't work like that!"

"I'm not saying it's the perfect scenario, but sometimes life doesn't make sense. You're the one who is always talking about signs and Karma and Lady Luck. Maybe we are meant to be together. Don't you see that?"

"No Gavin, I don't. All I see is punishment for cheating on Dave. I am not having a baby, I will not change my mind. So you can either take me to go do this or I will go on my own. It's your choice." I walked back toward my car.

"Not much choice in it for me, is there? This is a baby, Sierra. How can you just toss him out like garbage?" His voice chilled me. The tears started again.

"It doesn't even have a brain yet. I checked. It's a sesame seed." I got back in my car and he kicked his truck door closed. I'd never made anyone that mad. I rolled down the window.

"I'm calling tomorrow for an appointment. I'll text you the time and date and you can let me know if you can take me or not." I pulled out before he could say anything else, not daring to look in my rear-view mirror.

When I got home, I avoided my parents, ran upstairs and threw myself on my bed. My eyes were already swollen, but I couldn't stop crying. How had everything gotten so messed up? I wished I could talk to Dave about this; but his was the last shoulder I could cry on. Would it have made any difference if it was his baby? No—I didn't want to be a mom yet. I wanted to go to college and have my own life.

As I went to shower before bed, I noticed someone pull in my driveway. The front porch light went on. It was an SUV. Dave? As soon the light went on, the driver drove off. I heard our front door open and then close. My dad called up the stairs.

'You're here, right Sierra?"

"Yeah, why?"

"There was someone in the driveway. I thought it was Dave. Were you expecting him?"

"No. I don't know why he would have come by."

"Are you okay?"

"I'm fine." I cleared my throat. "Just tired."

"Okay. Well you better get some sleep."

"K. G'night."

"G'night. Love you."

When I texted Gavin the time and date of the appointment, I didn't hear back. I assumed that meant he was not going with me. But he was standing by my car after practice.

"Hey," he said.

"Hi." I wanted to be distant but a part of me yearned for him to wrap me up in his arms. I wished we could just go back and start over.

"How are you feeling?" he asked.

"Okay. It kinda hurts my chest to run and I'm nauseous off and on, but I haven't thrown up again." I heard the gym door open and I turned. I hoped Dave wouldn't see us talking.

"Listen. I got your text. I don't agree with your choice, but I can't let you go by yourself. If you insist on doing this, I will take you." I'd never seen that look in his eyes.

"And after?" I asked.

He looked at me with no hint of emotion. It was unnerving. "Honestly, Sierra, I don't know. It breaks my heart that you would do this to our baby. I just don't know."

I tried to reach out but he stepped back. "So we will both have to miss practice on Friday. I'm going to call in sick. What are you going to do?"

"I already told coach I had to miss practice to do something with my dad."

"What about your dad? Won't he wonder why you're home early?"

"He's going to be in the city Thursday and Friday. And you know my mom. She won't get home until 7. But I am a little worried about people seeing my car at home when I'm supposed to be at school."

I watched two girl scouts walk out the door wearing their little sashes. Gavin followed my gaze but didn't speak.

"Why don't I drive to your house? You guys don't really have neighbors and your mom gets home late, too."

"But then you're going to need to drive home later. What if you don't feel up to it?"

"It'll be fine. I'll be fine." I said, even though I wasn't sure. I just wanted to get through it and move on as soon as possible.

"Guess you have it all figured out. I'll see you at my house at 11:30 on Friday," he turned to go. I heard the gym door again. This time it was Dave and Maggie.

"I'm sorry, Gavin," I said quietly.

"Me too, Sierra." He said and headed to his truck. I opened my door to get in and watched as Maggie flirted with Dave. As I turned onto my street, I noticed Dave's car was right behind mine. When I pulled in to my driveway, he pulled in too. I got out.

"Hey, what's up?" I asked.

"That's what I want to know, Sierra. I thought you broke up with me because you needed space and time. But it looks to me like you're spending a lot of your time in Gavin's space. I just wanted to come hear it from you. Are you with him?" his face was flushed.

"Dave, calm down. No, we are not together. I am all alone. Trust me." I said with more bitterness than I'd intended.

"Then why all the serious discussions?"

"What are you even talking about? Just now after practice?"

"And at the dam. I've seen you guys there a few times."

"What the hell, Dave? Are you following me now?" I sighed and changed my tone. "Look, I know you're hurting. And you'll never know how sorry I am about that. Truly. But you need to give me space."

"Don't you miss me?" suddenly for a tall fit guy he looked like a kid.

"Of course, Dave. But that doesn't mean we should be together. I think in time we can go back to being friends but for now we just need to take a break, okay?" I saw hope flicker across his face.

"So you're not with Gavin?" he asked. "I ran into Victoria the other day and she said she heard you dumped me for him but wanted to keep it a secret."

I felt my face flush. "Victoria Spencer? What is she doing home?" I asked.

"Who cares? That's not the point."

"Consider the source," I said. He followed me up the walk. I unlocked the door and let us both into the house. I turned around to find him staring at me. "Dave?"

He pulled me to him and kissed me. It caught me completely off guard. For a few seconds, I kissed him back. Then I pushed him away.

"You should go." I felt tears threaten and turned so he wouldn't see. *What was wrong with me?*

He put a hand on my shoulder. "Please, Dave. Just go." I said. "Please?"

He looked crushed, but went out the door. I heard him peel out of the driveway and gun it down the road. I felt like I'd stumbled into someone else's life. When had mine gotten so complicated? And how had Victoria Spencer gotten wind of the Gavin situation?

At dinner, I noticed my mom looked especially happy. She was doing great. She had one more surgery the following week to complete her reconstruction. Then two tattoo sessions to create new nipples (who knew?). She told us she was thinking about getting another while she was there. Apparently before they were married, she had almost gotten a butterfly tattoo on her hip at a Jimmy Buffet concert. But the artist's wife went into labor right before it was her turn. My dad (who hadn't been a fan of the idea) convinced her it was a sign. So she never got it.

I felt envious of the ease between my parents. I'd had that with Dave and sent him packing. I would be glad to put this hormonal roller coaster to rest. I noticed the spark was back in my mom's eyes. That dinner was the last really happy memory I had. I would revisit it again and again when I needed to cheer myself up.

On Friday morning I considered not going to school at all, but I didn't want my mom to worry about me all day. She and I left at the same time and she backed into the garbage on her way out. The trash had gone all over the place. The smell kicked my nausea into high gear and I had to pretend I'd forgotten something to run to the bathroom. I brushed my teeth and headed back out again. Last day, I thought. I can do this. I dreaded the hour drive with Gavin. I hated how he looked at me like I was literally a murderer. But I had no choice. He'd understand some day. The morning seemed to tick by. By 11:00 I all but ran out to my car. When I got in, I found a small package in the front seat with a simple typed note:

Triple stuffed especially for you – if two is great, three has got to be better. Don't give up on us yet.

I opened the box and inside were three double stuff cookies, except someone had added a third cream filling to each, making them triple stuffed Oreos. I smiled. Had to be Dave. I guess it was his way of apologizing for the day before. I ate them as I drove. I had planned to swing by *The Kitchen* for my paycheck. It would hopefully pay for about a third of the cost. I had already taken some money out of my account but I didn't want it to be too obvious. My mom could see my activity. She would want to know what it was for.

When I ran in, Max said I looked really pale and insisted I have something to drink. There is no arguing with Max, so I drank some water while he ran back to get my paycheck from the office. I did feel a bit better, thanked Max, and hurried back out to my car. The way they fussed over me I felt like everyone knew I was pregnant. But who would have told them? Only Tia and Gavin and I knew. I looked at my watch, it was 11:20. I didn't want to be late. I went straight to the bank drive-through, cashed my check, and then headed to Gavin's house. I felt a fresh wave of nausea course through my body. *Oh God,* I thought, *not now.* Luckily, I wasn't far from my house so I headed there. I turned into my driveway, opened the door, and then everything went black.

Day 80 – Dec. 24th Christmas Eve!

Biked 8 miles (hey, it's a holiday)

There's no place like home for the holidays. I can't believe it is Christmas Eve and here we are still trapped for no apparent reason. I didn't want to get up this morning. If my bladder hadn't forced me up, I don't know how long I would have just stayed in my chain bed. I just keep thinking about what we should be doing. My mom would be working and my dad would be cooking. They always closed the office at one on Christmas Eve. I assume my mom had to go back to life as usual. Surely she couldn't just abandon her patients. Christmas Eve. Mmm green bean casserole, turkey, mashed potatoes, and pumpkin pie. My stomach is growling. We order Chinese for dinner because we cook all day. And then we watch *White Christmas*. Right before bed we hang our stockings—a tradition. I can attest to the fact that "homesickness" really does make you feel sick for home. I swear I can literally feel pain in my chest.

Okay, Hart, get a hold of yourself. We can get through this. We'll just focus on making it feel Christmas-y down here. I will plan the perfect Christmas dinner for tomorrow. It will be okay.

Still Christmas Eve...

I was really trying to rise above this. I was. But then two hours ago everything went black. I've tried all of the power items. Nothing. Either this place lost power or somebody cut it off. I probably should not be using my flashlight to write this but have you ever sat in complete pitch darkness before? It gets really creepy. Your mind starts imagining things. I have no idea what this could mean. Is there a storm? Did the generator run out of gas? Is my keeper trying to send me a message? Will he or she open the door? Is "my stay" over? Or is this it? Is this when someone comes in and does whatever they planned to do all along. Is this some sort of religious thing? It's Christmas and I'm playing the part of the not so virgin Mary?

Part of me just wants it all to be over—one way or another. Just end this nightmare. So much for Merry Christmas. I am going to preserve batteries just in case and keep my make-shift knife close. I guess it's a cold dinner tonight. According to my watch it is almost two-thirty in the afternoon. That's a long dark time to fill before going to bed. That is if I can fall asleep. Merry Christmas.

CASE REPORT

Case Leader: Sheryl Donovan

Subject: Sierra Hart

DOB: 8/1/1989

Brief Description: Long Brown Hair, hazel eyes, 5'7". Last seen wearing black leggings and a beige sweater–possibly purple winter jacket with faux fur lined hood.

Missing: 32 hours

- The sex offenders list has been a big nothing. Two more alibis to confirm but neither seem likely.
- We've confirmed the last people to see her for sure were Max, the bartender, and Betty, a waitress at *The Kitchen* right downtown here. That was around 11:15 AM.
- We know she then went to the bank to cash her check. She left there about 11:22AM. We got a shot of her car from the bank camera and she is heading down West Main which would be away from the school but toward her house.
- We have no idea if she ever reached her house if that is where she was headed. Laura Hart confirmed her house remained locked and just as it had been when they left that morning.
- **Sierra's Computer:**
  - According to her computer Sierra has a small circle of friends and family she regularly communicates with:
    - Her parents
    - David Braun who she was dating until early August
    - Gavin Ross, friend or possibly more, we aren't clear
    - Tia Myers, her best friend who lives in California
    - Three or four other girls from her class but very infrequently and not at all in the three weeks prior to her disappearance

- A number of strange dating profiles on free dating sites. One was male and two were female. None have been active in over a year.
- There were a few chain emails from co-workers at *The Kitchen* but all harmless and none were just sent to or from her.
- There were two emails between her and one of her teachers but it was regarding a college recommendation only. The teacher is a 58 year old grandmother of two married to a retired navy pilot who does contract work for an aerospace company. We didn't see any reason to dig deeper here.
- Her browser history had been erased but the techs will look further

- **Sierra's cell records**
    - Again she mostly communicates with her parents, Dave, Gavin, and Tia.
    - There was one incoming call from a number for the Planned Parenthood in Rochester, NY on October 5th at about 10:30AM. It lasted less than a minute. We didn't find any other calls to or from Planned Parenthood. But we should see if they have a record of her as a patient. They may give us a hard time on that one so let me know if we need a subpoena or anything.
    - Texts—this is interesting. Her number of texts per day averaged about thirty-five to forty for the last six months or so. But in the days leading up to her disappearance there are about half as many. In fact the majority of texts in the recent memory appear to be to and from her parents. It looks like she may have been deleting most of her texts. Except there are two from Dave he sent three days before she disappeared. In the first he apologizes and says he will try to give her more space. The only text the day she disappeared was one from her father, Patrick Hart. He simply wished her Good Morning, told her to have a good day and he'd see her that evening around 8. That came in at 8:50AM and then nothing.
    - Her phone either died or was shut off at 11:32 PM the morning she disappeared. According to the report, the last ping put her near her house.

- **Patrick's computer:**
  - contained mostly work related emails and correspondence.
  - There is a woman he communicates with frequently in New York: Maureen Shapiro; at first we thought there was a relationship there that could be something but she has a steady girlfriend. She said she and Patrick were old friends from college and she'd helped him get his job after prison. Apparently the guy is very good with numbers.
- **Possible Leads**
  - Sausage—this guy didn't like Patrick on the inside. Put him in the infirmary a couple of times. His real name is Emanuel Walter Pricket. We are still trying to track him down. He was in for armed robbery this time but he has been in and out of juvie and jail his whole life. There's nothing on his sheet about kidnapping or sexual assault but he has a long history of hitting his wives. He's had four. He has five children ranging in age from 5 to 18. He may be looking for money or revenge.
  - David Braun has no alibi for the time during which Sierra went missing. We have confirmed he left school around 10:50AM and Sierra's neighbor spotted his vehicle in Sierra's driveway around 11:00AM until 11:10AM. When questioned David admitted he had been there, then claimed he drove by the dam looking for her. When he didn't find her there he claimed to have returned to his home where he remained the rest of the afternoon cooking until he went to work around 4:45pm. Nobody can confirm his story.
  - Gavin Ross also has no solid alibi for the time during which Sierra went missing. He stayed home sick from school, grabbed take-out from Penara around 11:00AM, was in the Laketown Family Pharmacy from 11:15-11:25. Then he claimed he drove home where he remained the rest of the day; sick. Receipts and employees confirmed his story but nobody can confirm his whereabouts from 11:25 until his mother arrived home from work around 5:20pm.

Dr. Laura Hart

When I got the call that someone had broken into the office on Christmas Eve, I didn't really think too much about it. It was hard for me to feel anything but numb at that point. If it wasn't Sierra on the phone, did it really matter? It was Christmas Eve and Sierra was still ... gone.

They said that a homeless girl had broken in and may have taken some drugs from the supply cabinet. They'd rushed her to the hospital but to treat her most effectively, they wanted me to go do a quick inventory to determine what might be in her system. I was grateful when Patrick offered to drive. Our relationship was strained at best. Although we both lived in the same house, we rarely spoke. The holidays had made Sierra's absence even worse. I didn't even bother to decorate the house. I just couldn't bring myself to think about celebrating anything. I went to work. I made sick kids well. I ate some. I slept very little. I spent hours online talking to other parents with missing children. But none of it seemed to help. Looking back I can't even remember what we ate. People dropped off food for a while, but eventually everyone moves on with their life. But we were stuck, waiting, looking, and hoping. I scoured the news for found bodies or other missing teen girls. It didn't matter if the story came out of Oregon or Louisiana. I followed them all, hoping it would somehow point me in the right direction. I felt in my heart of hearts that she was still out there somewhere. I would feel it somehow if she wasn't, right?

After a silent drive, Patrick and I walked up to the front door of the office. An officer was planted outside. I felt like I should know every cop on the force at this point because I had spent so much time with them in the last few months. The door itself was broken. It looked like the girl had broken the window to get into the office.

"Sorry to bring you down here on the holiday, Doctor, but the girl acted like she had taken some kind of drug. Can you take a look and see if you can tell what is missing?"

"Of course." I said.

"We need to go around back so we don't mess up the scene."

"How old is the girl? Was she conscious?" I asked as he escorted us to the back door.

"Not sure. Maybe 16 or 17. Likely a run away or homeless. She passed out again before we could get her to say much. She seemed pretty out of it and threw up, too." He explained as I walked into our supply room. A number of the cabinets were thrown open and the room was littered with bottles and boxes.

"Wow," I remarked, taking it all in. "I'll see what I can figure out; but I hope that the ER can get her stabilized without the information. This is a mess."

"We noticed you have a security system, Doctor. Do you have cameras anywhere?"

"No, but maybe I need to get some." I said, looking around.

Patrick and I began trying to piece together what could be missing. We worked in silence.

"Uh, doctor?" I recognized Officer Pageant as he filled the doorway. He had a young daughter I'd treated recently for an ear infection. She looked just like her father.

"Yes?" I picked up the last of the boxes on the floor.

"They need both of you to go to the ER." He said, looking unsure.

"Why?" Patrick and I both asked.

"Well, the girl is saying she's your daughter."

"I, did you say, she said she was our daughter?" I looked at Patrick to see if I was crazy. He looked confused as well.

"Sierra? The girl says she is Sierra Hart?" Patrick asked. We ran for the door.

Sierra Hart

When I tried to open my eyes, I couldn't. They were just too heavy. I tried to recall what had happened. I'd been asleep and heard my cans. Someone had opened the door. I'd felt the fresh, cold air. I'd heard someone say something under his breath. A man. When I tried to grab the knife, I accidently cut my own finger and cried out. Then I felt a sharp pain in my arm. I remember trying to see but it was still pitch black. I dropped the knife but began kicking and hitting the person. He didn't make any sounds. Then my body just stopped working right. As if the signals from my brain weren't reaching my limbs. I felt him lay me back on the bed. *This is it.* I'd thought. *This is how it ends.*

But here I was. At least we were still alive.

"Miss, are you okay?" said a man's voice. I could hear the crackle of a walkie talkie and the man spoke into it. "I'm in exam room 3. I have a sick girl in here. She looks like she may be homeless. Have you checked the rest of the place?"

"Miss, why did you break in here? Do you need a doctor?" the man asked. He looked like a police officer.

"Oh my God." I said. "Where am I?" I asked. I tried to sit but it felt like some crazy invisible force was holding me down. My head felt like it weighed a ton. I heard the crackle again.

"Looks like someone broke into the medicine supplies. It's a big mess in here. Hard to tell what is missing, but I don't see anyone else on the premises. I think she may be alone."

"Miss did you take some drugs? What did you take?" the officer leaned over my face. The crackle again. "Hey, we better call in a bus. I don't know if she took something or not."

"I… I'm…" I tried to talk but it was like there was a pillow in my mouth. I saw a bright light, felt like someone was squeezing my head with a vice and then nothing.

Dr. Laura Hart

A million scenarios ran through my mind during the drive to the ER. We didn't say a word to one another. I think we were afraid if we spoke, our hopes would be jinxed.

We parked illegally and ran into the ER. I walked up to the desk and yelled "Sierra Hart. Is she here? I'm Doctor Hart, her mother. Is she really here?"

"Just a moment-" I saw an officer standing outside one of the triage rooms. I opened the door and ran down the hall, ignoring the protests from the woman at the front. Patrick was right beside me. I saw it was Officer Jeff Hall. "Jeff, is Sierra in there?" I asked. "Is it her?" I wasn't waiting for a response I just continued toward the door of the room. He reached out to stop me with his arm. "Hold up, Dr. H. Detective Rock is in there. He needs to get a statement."

"Jeff, is it Sierra? If it is then I don't give a damn who is in there with her. I want to see my daughter!" I pushed past him. I had to know it was her and that she was okay. Three surprised people looked up at me but all I saw was the girl on the bed. My girl. My Sierra.

"Mom!" she yelled and burst into tears. I ran over and hugged her to me. I didn't want to ever let go. I finally pulled back to look at her.

"Are you okay? Are you hurt?" I tried to do a quick visual assessment. She was dressed in a hospital gown. Her hair was wet, her face fuller. Her nails were longer than normal, but her color was good—maybe a little pale. She looked different. She looked healthy. She looked…

"You're pregnant!" She'd been gone 80 days. Was that enough time to look this pregnant? Who had done this to her?

"Hey Stub. You are…" Patrick couldn't choke out the rest. He simply embraced Sierra from the other side of the bed. "I'm so sorry. You guys must have been so worried." She leaned back into her pillow. We all looked up as the doctor came in with Detective Rock and asked if he could speak to us for a minute outside. Neither of us wanted to let her out of our sight again but the doctor insisted. And Detective Rock promised to stay with Sierra.

"I just wanted to assure you that before we cleaned Sierra up, we did a thorough examination. The good news is she seems to be in perfect health. There are no signs of trauma. The tox screen only showed Doxylamine Succinate.

"What's that?" Patrick asked.

"It's prescribed for morning sickness. It's also found in most over the counter sleep meds." I answered.

"But the amount we found was too high for a typical dose. It appears as though someone wanted her incapacitated. I'm sure you noticed, Dr. and Mr. Hart, that your daughter is pregnant." He said, very matter-of-fact.

"Yes." I said. "Do you know how far along she is? You said there was no noticeable trauma . . ." I couldn't finish my thought.

Patrick came to my rescue. "Have you or the police discussed where she has been and what happened to her?"

"Only that she was held against her will by an unknown person and the person never hurt her in any way. She said she was pregnant before she was abducted. I've ordered an ultrasound to check on the fetus but the heartbeat is strong and so are Sierra's vitals. She can go home with you tonight. Why don't you go ahead in and talk with her. I'll be back in a few minutes to do the ultrasound."

Soon it was question after question. I couldn't provide any helpful answers. No, I had no idea how I ended up in my mom's office. No, I had no idea who had taken me. No, I had no idea where exactly I had been held. A root cellar or basement or something? Yes, I had plenty of food and water. No the person never hurt me as far as I knew. I never saw my keeper. No, I did not know how the person transported me or drugged me for sure. Possibly an injection. I remembered a sharp prick earlier that day.

I kept asking for my parents. They said they were on their way. And then there they were. That's when I lost it. I couldn't hold in the tears anymore. I couldn't believe I was here and fine. We were alive and safe. It was so good to see them but I could see what my absence had done to them. They were both so worn down. Our reunion was cut short by the doctor and Detective Rock who needed to finish my statement. My parents reluctantly followed the doctor out the door and Detective Rock continued his questions. Again I had no great answers for him.

He pulled out my journal. I'd almost filled a 5 subject notebook.

"Where did you get that?" I tried to snatch it out of his hands. He pulled it away.

"It was beside you when we found you. So technically it's evidence. You wrote that you thought it could have been a friend of your dad's from prison or your ex-boyfriend, Dave."

"You've been reading my journal? Is that even legal?" I asked.

"Look, miss, I'm trying to help you. If I cross into some uncomfortable areas I apologize, but I need to figure out who took you and why. We don't want this happening to someone else, do we?" Everything about him just rubbed me the wrong way. No wonder nobody found me sooner with this guy on the case.

"Fine!" I sighed. "I had a lot of time to think while I was down there and I couldn't come up with a reason."

"Okay." I agreed.

"What about Dave? You mentioned him, too. Did the person who took you sound or smell like him?"

"No, I really have no memory of anyone taking me at all. But I think it was just one guy. At least that's all I remember or could kind of see. But

I'm sure it couldn't have been Dave. I mean, have you met him? What would be the point?"

"How do we know that you didn't just run away and decide to just show back up with this crazy story when you couldn't make it? Maybe you were scared your parents would find out you were pregnant."

"You know what? I know you're a cop but, screw you. I don't want to talk to you anymore without my parents with me!"

That is when my parents walked back in the room, followed by Sheryl Donovan. She explained she was from the FBI and had been investigating my disappearance. At first, I wasn't sure I wanted to talk to another cop, but she was actually nice. I could tell by my mom's body language that she liked her, too. After I agreed that I wanted my parents to stay in the room this time, I went through all of the questions again.

"Sierra, I know that you are already feeling vulnerable and this may be uncomfortable for you to discuss with your parents right here, but I have to ask. Did you know you were pregnant when you were abducted?"

I couldn't stop the tears. I looked at my mom. "I'm so sorry. My birthday night in Nantucket I just..." I took a shaky breath.

"Gavin?" my dad sounded shocked. My mom raised her eyebrows at him and a flash of guilt preceded the angry set of my dad's jaw and fists.

"It was only one time and I feel like such an idiot for getting pregnant. And then I wanted to you know, not have her, but then we spent all of that time together down there and she was like my Wilson, you know? I talked to her all of the time and I felt her move. That day I was taken, I was going to Planned Parenthood for an abortion. I just wanted to put it behind me and focus on school and college. I wasn't ready to be a mother. And those first weeks down there I was so angry with myself, with whomever it was that put me there, at everyone. It wasn't fair that I would have to keep this baby. God, I even thought about trying to figure out a way to get rid of her myself. But I couldn't come up with any way that wouldn't hurt me, too. I couldn't risk anything because I was trapped. I was completely trapped."

I paused to blow my nose and wipe my face with the tissues my dad handed me. "But being alone like that with no other person to talk to... It starts to make you crazy. I just didn't want to feel like I was alone anymore. And then I don't even remember how it started but I found myself talking to her. And I say her but I don't really know, of course. I just, that's what I picture in my head that she's a girl. And I never... I just didn't understand how it would feel to have this living being, this little person inside you that you are responsible for protecting. And eventually all that seemed to matter was making sure we made it through whatever this was alive and healthy. I was so scared that whoever was keeping me there would figure out I was pregnant and hurt us or maybe they would never let us out and we'd both starve or run out of water." I took a deep breath. "I just, I'm so happy we're going to be okay. And I'm sorry." I took a breath and looked up at my parents.

My dad leaned down and took me in his arms. "Stub, you have nothing to be sorry about. You've been through hell. All we care about is that you're okay. You're safe and you're home. Both of you." My mom also bent down and gave me a hug. "I'm so sorry this all happened to you, honey. But you're safe and you're going to be okay. After everything we've been though, a baby will be a welcome challenge."

I let out the breath I hadn't even realized I was holding. I couldn't imagine not having their support. I heard a little cough and looked up at Sheryl Donovan. I had completely forgotten she was there, too.

"I'm sorry; I really need to keep going with the questions if you're ready. Important details start to fade quickly."

I blew my nose again and sat back up in the hospital bed. "I'm ready. Let's keep going."

"So you did know you were pregnant when you were taken. Did anyone else know? The father, maybe?" Sheryl asked.

"Yes, and my friend Tia. I'm actually surprised they didn't tell someone when I went missing." I said. "Have you spoken with Tia?"

"Detective Rock spoke with her, but she didn't say anything."

"That explains why." I said. "If he treated her like he treated me, she probably wouldn't say much." We all looked up as the door opened yet again. This time it was a woman pushing a machine.

"Sorry to interrupt, but the doctor insisted we get an ultrasound." She held her hand out to me and I shook it.

"I'm Carol. Would you like any of these people to step out before we proceed?" she asked looking only at me still.

"Um …" I wasn't sure how to respond.

"I'll give you some privacy." Sheryl said.

Carol placed the ultrasound stick thing on my stomach and started moving it around a little. I could feel her respond in my stomach.

"Okay, you can see the head and a hand." Carol explained as she slowly moved it around on my stomach.

"Looks like she's sucking her thumb." My mom pointed out. I could hear tears in her voice. It was so cool to see this little person moving around inside me.

"I think she looks like me." My dad joked and we laughed. It felt really good to laugh.

"Can you tell if she's a girl?" I asked, curious. Carol moved the joystick thing again a little lower. She pointed out the heart. I was transfixed.

"Well, I'm pretty sure you're right. She looks like a girl." Carol announced. I knew it. I had just felt it.

"I'm going be a grandpa!" my dad said. For just a moment, it seemed like this was all a perfectly normal situation; my parents and I happily viewing my daughter on an ultrasound.

"Look," I said, before either of them said anything. "I know this is not what any of us had hoped or planned for me. I still want to go to college but-"

"We're not giving her up." My dad said, surprising us all.

"Oh, thank God you agree," said my mom. She started to hug him but stopped herself. Something was wrong between them, but I had to table that for later. Right then all I wanted was to go home.

But when I walked back into my house, it felt different..

"Are you okay?" my dad asked.

I nodded. Everything was as it had been when I left. Same couch, same fireplace, same pictures on the mantle.

"Why don't you just sit and take a moment." my mom suggested.

I sat and realized I was running my hand over my stomach. "I'm okay." I said. "I just… everything just seems different. The same; but different."

"I'm sorry it's not more festive." My mom apologized. "We sort of ignored Christmas this year."

"I forgot tomorrow is Christmas." I glanced at the mantle clock. "Which is in less than an hour.

"I thought I'd whip up some pizza since none of us really had dinner. Sound okay?" my dad headed toward the kitchen.

"Honey, are you okay?" my mom rubbed my back as I began to cry.

My dad came back to sit on my other side and they wrapped me in a group hug. I thought. There are four of us now. We'd been three, then two, then three again, but now we were four. It felt so good to be here; to feel safe.

"So you would prefer burgers, instead?" my dad broke the silence. We all laughed.

"No, I have been dreaming about your pizza for weeks."

The next day, I received a sorely needed phone call.

"Hello?" I was sitting on my bed, trying to figure out how to sneak past the media frenzy for a walk. I had been trapped inside by the keeper for months and now I was trapped again by the media. I had every window open, but the curtains pulled. It was January and cold, but it felt so good to breath fresh air. It made my dad crazy. He was so worried that I'd be taken again.

"Seriously, like what did I do? I mean, you *never* call me anymore!"

"Tia. You have no idea how good it is to hear your voice."

"Merry Christmas! How are you doing? Are you really okay?"

"Yes," I started to cry again. 'Sorry. I am okay. Merry Christmas to you, too. I don't know why . . . I . . . I'm crying."

"Let's see. You were abducted and held hostage in some cellar or something for months and then just wake up at your mom's office, pregnant, and drugged. I mean, I just found out that George Clooney has made yet another lucky woman his girlfriend and it is not me. I should be the one crying. Get it together already."

"I can't believe you kept my pregnancy secret from everyone."

"Was that the right thing to do? I just didn't know if you were still pregnant or if you'd already had the abortion. I didn't feel right being the one to say something. I figured if Gavin hadn't said anything you must have gone through with it already. And that cop Rock. What a major dick. I really didn't want to tell him jack, you know?"

"I know. I can't stand him either. Do you know he accused me of running away because I was too scared to deal with being pregnant?"

"Total moron. So what's it like?" she asked.

"Running away?" I asked.

"Being pregnant. What does it feel like? Can you feel the baby move yet?" I heard a small thump. "Sorry, dropped the phone. I'm painting my nails."

I imagined Tia, back against her bed, casually cradling the phone, knee bent, painting her toes. I realized I didn't want to talk about *her* with Tia. "Yeah; it's hard to describe without sounding strange I think." I loved her humor but I couldn't handle jokes about my baby right now.

"What did you do that whole time in a room? You must have gone crazy."

"Sometimes. But I just tried to keep busy with the things that were there. There was a bike I had to ride for ventilation. There were books and stuff." A rush of heat washed over me, sweat surfaced on my neck, upper lip, and forehead, my heart catapulted into triple time; and vomit threatened at the back of my throat. I dropped the phone, ran to the bathroom and just made the toilet. I couldn't stop shaking.

"Sierra? Are you still there? Are you okay? Sierra?"

I felt every mile of distance between Tia's voice and me. I couldn't get up and go to her right then. I used my foot to close the bathroom door, crawled over to the open window and rested against the wall beneath. The fresh air relaxed my breathing, slowed my heart and turned the heat to a cold dried sweat.

Dr. Laura Hart

The first couple of days after Sierra came home we didn't want to leave the house. Our yard was a minefield of reporters; but in our despair Patrick and I had neglected grocery shopping. Poor Sierra craved fresh oranges, apples, cottage cheese and cucumbers. We had little to offer. Patrick volunteered to face the vultures and get enough to last us a few days.

I took advantage of his absence to return to the conversation I should have had with Sierra last fall. I found her in her room, with all of the windows open. The winter wind rippled her curtains as she sat at her computer. She wore one of Patrick's thick wool sweaters, fingerless gloves and a knit hat.

"Patrick went to get your list of food requests." I saw her jump a bit at the sound of my voice. "Sorry, didn't mean to sneak up on you."

She turned around in her chair to face me. "It's fine. Just a little jumpy, I guess." Her smile didn't quite reach her eyes.

"How are you feeling?" I sat on the edge of her bed and wrapped her extra blanket around myself.

"Sorry, do you want me to close 'em?" she gestured toward the windows.

"No, I'm good," I pulled the blanket tighter. "How about you; are you feeling okay?"

She looked down at her stomach and rubbed it gently with her hand. "Yeah, I guess. Maybe a little restless. I wish I could take a walk or go to the movies, window shop on Main Street; go somewhere."

"We can if you really want, but we thought it would be better to lay low for a few days."

"I know. You're probably right." Sierra ran her finger along the edge of her keyboard. "Tia called."

"It must have been good to hear her voice."

"Yeah, but it's hard, too." Sierra picked up a photo book from beside her computer. I couldn't see the picture she was studying. "I don't know exactly how to describe it. It feels like a giant hand reached out of the sky, plucked me from this like conveyer belt of life, and held me in its fist for months. Then just as abruptly dropped me back onto the conveyer belt. Only the belt kept moving for everyone else and now I don't feel like I belong on the same belt. Uhhh, I sound crazy," she dropped her head into her hands.

"You don't sound crazy at all. In fact you make a lot of sense. I know it doesn't feel like it now, but you'll catch back up. And because of what you've been through, and the baby, you may find you suddenly feel way ahead of everyone else." It was hard to see the pain in her eyes.

"But I don't want to be ahead either. I want to be *with* everyone else. I want things to go back to how they used to be." She held up her hand. "I know, I know they can't; I'm just saying I wish they could." She fell back against her chair.

"I wish they could too, sweetie. But we've both been here before. Maybe everything we had to go through with your father was in some way to help us prepare for this." I suggested.

"Maybe." She flipped the page of the album in her lap.

"You know we never really talked about what happened between you and Dave and Gavin. I wish I would have tried harder to talk to you before."

"You did, mom." Sierra focused her eyes and hands on pulling a loose thread from her glove. "I think at the time I was so ashamed of what I had done to Dave that I couldn't talk about it. I felt like the pregnancy was a punishment for cheating." Sierra's voice thickened with emotion.

I crossed the room, set the album on her desk, and hugged her to me. When I released her, I placed my hands on either side of her face. "Sierra, we all make bad choices sometimes, but that's when you're supposed to trust in the people who love you to help you through it. You can tell me anything. We can always find a solution. Okay?" I gently wiped away a stray tear with my finger.

Sierra turned to get a tissue off her desk; "Yeah, right. Like you ever make bad choices." "Oh Sierra, I've made plenty of bad choices."

"Like what?"

"I dropped out of med school, I refused to be in my friend's wedding because I didn't like her groom; the list goes on. And some day I will share those with you, okay? But I don't want to talk about me right now."

"You dropped out of med school?"

"For a period, yes."

"Still, when Dad screwed up, you got so mad that you divorced him." Her words were a slap to my face. I stood.

"That was different. You're my daughter. I would never..." I wasn't sure what to say. I had no idea my actions had such an impact on Sierra. She blew her nose and I paced the room.

"I'm so sorry, Sierra. I guess it may have appeared that I divorced your father because of the stealing. In reality it was more of a catalyst. My overreaction to his mistakes was fueled by heartache I've been carrying around with me for years; heartache that was festering under the surface before I even met your father. When he got arrested, I exploded. He was on the receiving end of years of repressed anger toward my parents. Horrible memories came flooding back. I panicked, reacted, and then felt stuck. Finally, Mindy convinced me to see a therapist. I am so sorry." I hugged her to me again. "Your dad was a casualty of my emotional breakdown." I spoke into her hair. "I just wish we'd have talked about this sooner."

"So you aren't mad at dad anymore?" She pulled back to look at my face.

"Wait, how did this become about me?" I stood. "We were talking about you."

"So you *are* still mad." She threw a used tissue toward her garbage.

"It's complicated." Out the window, two reporters split a sandwich on our lawn.

"What happened while I was gone? That last family dinner you were both so happy. Do you know how many times I re-lived that meal when I was homesick?"

I turned back from the window to look at her. "I'm sorry, honey. It's not fair to drag you into our issues. We need to work this out as a couple. Do you understand?" I searched her face. She thought for a moment and rubbed her stomach.

"Can you please at least promise not to push him away again? You are both miserable apart." And just like that, my daughter had become an adult. I didn't trust my voice so I simply hugged her to me.

The door slammed downstairs and Patrick called out for us. Sierra stood and as we headed out the door she asked again, "Promise?"

"I promise."

It wasn't until we'd unpacked the groceries that I realized Sierra had diverted our conversation again.

Dave Braun

When I heard that Sierra had come back, I wanted to race to the hospital. I wanted to see with my own eyes that she was okay. But I knew there would be lots of people and cops and media crowding her. And she had asked for space the last time we spoke.

So I waited. Even when the story broke: *Missing Teen Found Safe but Pregnant*; it hurt all over again; but it only made me want to see her more. What had she been through? I thought of how nervous she'd been when we came close to having sex. She must have been terrified if she'd been forced by a stranger. The thought made me sick. What kind of monster would do this? I needed to see her. I waited another day and then drove by the frenzy outside her house. I couldn't eat. I couldn't sleep.

By the third night, I couldn't take it anymore. I went for a run and found myself on her street. I cut through back yards and ran up to the back of her house. I jumped the fence and stood below her bedroom window. I could tell it was open even though she had the curtains drawn. Did I dare approach? I didn't want to scare her, but I wanted to see her for myself.

I ran home, wrote a note, and stood beneath the open window again. I had used a rubber band to wrap the note onto a tennis ball. I took a deep breath, aimed and threw. It hit the window frame and bounced back. I held my breath as I watched for any movement within the house, but all I could hear was the winter night. The reporters had packed it in for the day.

One more try. If I miss, it's a sign that I should go home. This time it hit the curtain and dropped. I had to assume it was in her room. Now the ball was in her court, I smiled to myself at the pun. She loved puns.

Sierra Hart

I don't know when he threw it in my window. I probably should have been freaked out, but for some reason I wasn't. Dave was safe. I knew he couldn't have had anything to do with what happened to me. I smiled at the delivery method—a tennis ball. I've kept it all these years in the same box with my necklace and his other gifts:

Sierra,

Hopefully this delivery method didn't scare you. I figured this was safer than the stones they throw in the movies. The last thing I want to do is make you feel unsafe. I wanted to let you know I've been thinking about you. I don't know what you've been through. I'm just happy you are home. Before all of this you said you wanted space and I'm trying to respect that, but everytime I run my feet bring me to you. I understand if you can't see anyone right now. But if by any chance you can - I'd <u>very</u> <u>much</u> like to be one of them.

Maybe you could return my serve ☺. I can't retrieve it until after work so maybe wait a bit. (Wouldn't want some dog running off with your response). If you need to say "no" I understand. I've missed you.

-DAVE

the Kitchen

Dave Braun

I raced over to Sierra's after work. It had started to snow and I worried that a note might get lost. I jumped the fence and looked for signs of life in her room. The window was open, but no light peeked under the curtain.

I looked around. Great, I thought, her parents will see my footsteps here in the morning and think someone was after her again. But then I found it. She had considered the snow. The ball was wrapped in a plastic bag and closed tight with a bread tie.

Dave,

So my big question is how many times did you have to throw the ball before you got it in the window? I understand the need for contact more than ever. and I missed you, too. I have had a lot of time to think about everything. I know I owe you answers to questions you have every right to ask. But as much as I want to see you, I dont know that I can give answers yet. So, here is what I propose. If you still have it off, come by Monday evening around seven - reporters are mostly gone by then. My parents will let you in the back door. If you can promise not to ask questions, I can promise to try and open up if I feel I'm up to it.

Love,
Sierra

PS: They are under strict orders to only open the door if you come with Tiramisu.

TAKE NOTE

Sierra Hart

I was in the kitchen when I heard a knock on the porch door. Dave was not only at the wrong door, but early. It was 6:35. I couldn't tell if the feeling in the pit of my stomach was nerves or a tiramisu craving. I checked my reflection in the toaster and opened the side door.

"Hey," My heart skipped a beat when I saw Gavin standing there.

"Wow, hey yourself." He stepped through the door and wrapped my in his arms. I buried my face in his chest, felt the steady rhythm of his heart and breathed in the musky scent of his soap. I couldn't hold in the tears. Gavin must have sensed it because he pulled me even closer.

"I'm so sorry this had to happen to you." He said in my hair. After a moment he pulled back to look at me. "You look amazing."

I smiled. "Thanks. Sometimes I'm amazed by this new body but sometimes I just feel fat and ugly."

"I think you look beautiful." He leaned in and kissed me. I reached up and pulled him closer. It felt so good to have this intense human connection after the extended absence of intimate touch.

"What are you doing here?" We jumped apart at the sound of my dad's raised voice.

"Sorry, sir; I needed to see she was okay." Gavin explained.

I swayed on my feet and my mom suddenly appeared at my side.

"I think you should go." My dad said.

"Are you okay?" Gavin asked me.

"I'm fine. Just got a little dizzy."

"Gavin." My dad moved between us.

"Dad, it's okay. I'm okay." I locked eyes with Gavin. "He's leaving in just a minute."

"You should sit down." My mom handed me water.

"Please, just give us a minute." I said. They exchanged a look, but finally left us alone. I felt like a child with too many babysitters. But I bit my tongue. I understood why everyone was so reluctant to let me out of their sight.

"Guess they know, huh?" Gavin nodded toward them.

"Yeah, but we haven't really talked about it yet. Probably why seeing you hit a nerve. Sorry."

"I'm sure you are sick of the questions, but I have to ask. Were you hurt in any way? Did you see who took you?"

Sweat peppered my chest and back and I had to bolt for the toilet. I opened the bathroom window and the fresh cold air was a welcome shock.

"Sierra? Are you okay?" Gavin knocked on the door. "Do you want me to get your mom?"

"No, I'll be okay in a minute." I stood and looked at my pale face in the mirror.

"Now will you go?" I heard my dad outside the door.

"Not until I know she's okay." Gavin held his ground.

I ran cold water over my wrists like my mother had showed me and opened the door. "I'm fine." I stepped between the two men standing guard. A knock on the back door made me jump. My mom popped out of her office.

"I got it." She stopped and turned, her hand on the door handle. "Are you sure you're up for this?"

I took a deep, shaky breath, glanced at Gavin, and nodded. "Yeah, I'm okay." I put a hand on my dad's chest. "I'll walk him out." My dad moved to the side.

"Let me guess, Dave?" Gavin asked as we walked to the side door. We heard Dave knock again. My parents were stalling for me.

"So I guess Dave is okay, but not me?" Gavin didn't sound angry but his jaw was clenched.

"They just need a little time." I said.

At the side door, Gavin made no move to leave. I could hear Dave talking to my parents. "You gotta go."

"Tomorrow?" he opened the door.

"Hopefully," I said. As I turned, he popped back in. "Sierra," he whispered and pulled me in for a kiss. I felt a tingle that I hadn't felt in months. It was like having someone breathe life back into me. Then he released me and dashed out the door. I was so stunned I didn't even hear Dave and my parents come into the kitchen.

"Sierra?" my dad said. "Are you okay?"

They were all looking at me. My mom held the tiramisu. I could tell she was trying to read me. Was I happy? Sad? Scared? But I couldn't even describe it myself.

"Sie… rra." Dave's voice stuck in his throat. He moved toward me, reached out , and abruptly dropped his arms, "Is it okay if I hug you?"

Only Dave would ask permission first. "Yes," I hugged him. It felt good, although my body didn't react like it had with Gavin. It felt like coming home. "I missed you."

"You have no idea." He reluctantly stepped back. "It's good to know I was missed, too." We all stood in silence for a few moments.

"Well, I better get the chicken on the grill if we want to eat tonight." My dad said.

"And I really need to finish up a few more things in the office." My mom put the Tiramisu on the kitchen counter and disappeared. Dave and I sat in the living room.

"So, how's The Kitchen?" I started off with a safe topic. A half hour later, my dad announced dinner was ready and we moved to the table.

To an outsider, things would look completely normal. I could tell Dave was animated and comfortable back at our family table; but I caught him studying me a few times. It was a little unnerving. He and my parents discussed his plans for attending the CIA in New York City next year. I felt lost on that conveyer belt again.

We cleared the table and my parents took their coffee out onto the back deck.

"Sierra?" Dave took me gently by the arm and walked me into the living room. We sat down on the couch. His demeanor resembled a pre-prom proposal, only we both knew this was far more involved.

I waited.

"I know you asked me not to ask questions. And I haven't, but-" he shifted to grab both my hands.

I swallowed hard, I knew what I was about to say was going to hurt him. "I know. I'm sorry. There is no great way to say it."

"It was Gavin. You and Gavin were together, weren't you?" he sounded calmer than I would have imagined, but the hurt in his eyes persisted. "Before you were taken. He was in Nantucket, too? When I first saw the headlines I worried you'd been-"

"No. The keeper never touched me." I interrupted.

"I'm glad."

"I'm sorry."

He made it easier, saying it for me. Tears streamed down my face. I'd never felt more ashamed in my life. "I'm so sorry. It wasn't a planned thing. It just…"

He interrupted, "kind of happened."

I nodded. "I wish I could understand myself. Trust me when I tell you I have had a lot of time to think about this. The choices I made-" I took a deep breath and slowly let it out again as a wave of nausea slid from my stomach to the back of my throat.

"And?" he asked.

"And I don't think you're going to like what I realized." I cringed as his shoulders slumped and he looked away.

Dave dropped my hands and began to pace the room. "So you love him. Not me."

"It's not that simple. My whole world has been turned completely sideways. I can't just think about me anymore." I smoothed my shirt against my stomach.

"Let me guess; Gavin doesn't want anything to do with your baby. He isn't even going to own up to his mistake?" I'd never heard such vitriol in Dave's voice.

"Don't call her a mistake. And no, just the opposite, actually. I mean we haven't talked about anything since I've gotten home.

"Sierra. Everything okay?" My dad called out from the office.

"Everything is fine, dad."

I lowered my voice. "Look, the morning I was taken, I left school to go get an abortion. I wasn't ready to be a mom"

"He was going to let you go alone?" Dave asked.

"No. He was going to go with me." Admitting Gavin's disapproval felt like a betrayal so I kept that to myself.

"And now? What are you going to do? Get married, have a baby? What about NYU? What about college?"

"Dave, I don't know. My parents and I haven't even talked about it yet."

"I just need to know. Is there any chance for us? I mean, you and I, we could figure it out. With my trust fund, money wouldn't be a problem and we could both still finish school. And our parents could help."

"Dave. Stop. God, I so appreciate that you would be willing to do that for me, but I can't answer those questions yet. I need to have some hard conversations with my parents, with Gavin. I've only been home a few days."

"Sorry. I... you're right. I'm sorry." He sat next to me on the couch. "I don't want to push you. I just wanted you to know that I'm not going anywhere. Okay? I want you in my life."

I took a deep breath. "Of course. Can we just say we'll figure things out as we go along?"

"Sure." He straightened his shoulders. "We can do that."

I stood. "I am so glad you came, but I am tired. Would you be mad if I kicked you out so I can go lie down?"

"Sure, no problem. I have to stop by the restaurant anyway." We walked down the hall to the back door.

"It's so strange having everyone sneak in and out of here. I'm home but I'm still trapped. I just want everything to go back to normal." I opened the door.

"I just wish everything could go back," he gave me a tight hug. "Is it okay to call you?"

"Sure. I'll text you my new number." I said. He dropped a kiss on my head and left. My parents came out of the office.

"Everything okay?" my mom asked.

I nodded.

"You look exhausted."

"I think I'll just go right to bed." I headed for the stairs.

"Okay, but your dad and I think we should sit down and figure out a plan in the morning."

"Okay." I knew they were right. It was time.

The next morning I was shocked to see it was 9:20AM when my phone woke me up.

> GAVIN: *My mom said we are lunching at your house today. All of us?*
> SIERRA: *News to me. Just woke up.*
> GAVIN: *Talk first?*

"Sierra, are you awake, honey?" my mom called at the door.

> SIERRA: *Can't now. Later.*
> GAVIN: *K. Later.*

"Yeah. I'll be down in a minute." I said.

The combination of vanilla and butter enticed my senses and I knew my dad's famous pancakes were waiting for me in the kitchen.

"Sierra," my dad leaned back in his chair. "We need to make some decisions."

"I know." I said.

"We've invited Mindy and Gavin to join us for lunch," my dad said.

"We felt it was important for us all to discuss options. Having a baby is hard enough without the stress of school and everything else." My mom added.

"You don't think I can handle it?" I felt a flash of anger.

"That's not what we are saying at all," my dad refreshed my mother's coffee.

"We want you to know that we are here to help. We also need to know what Gavin and Mindy are thinking."

"Why are you are so mad at Gavin, anyway? It wasn't only his fault." I looked down at my plate.

"I know, but you're *my* baby. He grabbed my mom's hand. *Our* baby. And he took advantage of you when you were drunk."

"It wasn't like that."

"Okay." My mom said. "This isn't helping anyone. How we got here isn't important right now. How we handle everything moving forward is. Decisions need to be made."

My father folded his arms and leaned back in his chair. "You're right, sorry."

"We don't know how you feel about this, but we suggest you don't return to school. You can get your GED and then explore college options.

I began to cry. Of course, I agreed. I had thought about it a lot in that cellar, but it still hurt to hear it out loud.

"I'm sorry sweetie. This is not what we would have chosen for you either. It's going to be hard; but it'll all work out." My mom rubbed my arm.

"We also would like you to live here so we can help you with the baby." My mom explained. "Do you agree?"

I nodded, looking down at my stomach.

"So much for NYU, huh?" I said.

"Maybe just a little further down the road, stub." my dad said softly. "Sometimes life has a different plan than we do."

That afternoon when I answered the door Mindy grabbed me into her arms and hugged me tight.

"I'm so glad you are safe. We were all so worried." She spoke into my hair. And then she pulled away and looked at me and my stomach. "You look beautiful." She smiled.

"Thanks," I said.

Gavin approached my dad. "Listen, sir, I know you're pissed at me and I get why; but I respect and care for Sierra. I am excited to be a dad and take care of them," He threw me a look. "if she'll let me."

My dad looked a little uncomfortable. "I appreciate you saying that,

Gavin." He cleared his throat. "You're going to have to give me a little time to get used to all of this. Okay?"

"Yes, sir," they both stood their ground until my mom ushered my dad and Mindy into the kitchen to get them something to drink. Gavin came over to me, dropped a kiss on my head and then my stomach.

"So, I guess everything is out in the open now."

"Dave, too?"

I nodded.

"I'm sure he wants to kick my ass, huh?"

"I don't think so. He's mostly just hurt." He wrapped his arm around my shoulder and we joined our parents.

During lunch, Mindy brought up the first elephant in the room. "So have the police made any progress?"

"Not really. Sierra is supposed to meet with Sheryl and some psychologist after the holidays to see if there are any memories or clues that she is suppressing," my dad explained.

"They haven't been able to find any connection to other cases, which is good because nobody else should have to go through this." My mom squeezed my hand.

"But it's also bad because they think that means I was a specific target." I took a deep breath and swallowed some water. Hair tingled at the nape of my neck.

"I thought we were here to talk about the future. Not the past." Gavin rubbed his hand up and down my arm.

"I'm sorry." Mindy said. "I wasn't thinking. Yes, let's talk about the future."

"Well, we all talked this morning and agreed Sierra shouldn't go back to high school here. She's missed too much to catch up with the regular curriculum. She's going to take her GED and start a few college courses online this summer."

"This way I am still working toward the same goal I've always had. It just might take a little longer."

"We could do a wedding at the house!"

"Whoa, hold on." My dad said. "Sierra's not..."

"Oh, I'm not..." I looked at my mom.

"Mom." Gavin shot Mindy a dirty look. "Sierra and I haven't discussed anything, yet."

"Marriage seems a bit...sudden but I think maybe you two need to talk." My mother looked at us.

"But not about marr…" my mom silenced my dad with a hard look and a hand on his arm.

"We are here for you in whatever capacity you need." My mom said.

"I agree. I'm just so excited to be a grandmother." Mindy said.

I looked at Gavin.

"Do you think it would be okay for us to go for a drive? Maybe dodge the reporters long enough to find a nice quiet, safe, place to talk?" Gavin suggested.

My parents exchanged a look, "Sierra, is this what you'd like to do?" my mom asked.

I did and I didn't. But for reasons that I didn't want to share with the group.

"I'll keep them safe. They won't be out of my sight for a second." Gavin promised.

"But what about the vultures?"

"I parked a street over." Gavin said. "So maybe someone could leave from the front to distract them while you and I sneak out the back and walk to my truck."

"Actually, if your mom and I walk out with Mindy, with a jacket over her head, they might assume it's you Sierra. Then they will follow us. That should keep them guessing long enough for you to get somewhere private." My dad almost seemed to enjoy the thought.

"But," my mom added. "Gavin, can you please have her back here before it gets dark?"

"Of course." He agreed. He looked at his watch. "We'll be back by 4:30, okay?"

I looked at my watch. What were we going to do for 3 hours?

"Great." My mom confirmed. I felt like I was eight years old again.

"Let's go." I grabbed my coat from the closet. The plan worked perfectly. The walk from my house to his truck felt great. Just to be outside, the cold air on my face. I missed running.

He had the country music blaring and turned it down as we drove out of town.

"Where are we going?" I asked.

"Some place safe, quiet, and fitting." He said with that dimpled smile and put his hand on my leg. It was comforting and distracting at the same time.

"This is crazy, but can I roll down my window and we'll crank the heat?"

"Sure." He smiled. The air felt amazing.

Thirty minutes later he pulled into the empty parking lot of an elementary school.

"Tomorrow is New Year's Eve." I realized.

"A lot has happened in a year, huh?" he opened my door and helped me out of the truck.

I stood in front of him, my hand still in his. He leaned in to kiss me. It took my breath away with its fierce hunger. I felt that familiar ripple of pleasure roll from my stomach to my very center. I returned the kiss with the same hunger and desire. We stood there, completely connected and lost in the moment until a police siren wailed. I jumped.

"Sorry." I said. "I'm still a little jumpy."

"I hate that you've been scared. Hopefully it will fade." He ran his finger along my cheek. "But it's just as well. We need to do more talking and less kissing." He walked us over to the swings.

"So, I think I made myself pretty clear on my vision for the future. But while you were missing, I realized maybe you would have understood my reaction better if I had explained more about my family. It wasn't really fair for me to freak out on you."

"It's okay. You know, we both said some things."

"Well, you asked me about my dad before and I just wasn't ready to talk about it. But I think if you let me tell you now, you'll understand me a little better. Okay?" He grabbed my hands in his.

"Sure." I said. "Of course."

"My mom and dad started out as high school sweethearts. My mom came from a pretty conservative and strict Catholic family. She was the fourth and youngest child. My grandfather died when she was still a junior in high school. My grandmother couldn't afford Catholic school so she had to switch to public. My mom was thrilled. My dad, on the other hand, came from a very different background. His dad had been in and out of prison, his mom had five kids, all with different fathers. They were all on welfare. You get the picture." He twirled a stick in his hand.

"Apparently it was love at first sight." He grabbed my hand and squeezed it.

"Let me guess, they got pregnant with you." I smiled.

"Not exactly, though she did get pregnant. As you can imagine, it did not go over well with my grandmother. She told my mom to give the baby up for adoption or she was on her own. Well, she was in love with my dad and they wanted to keep the baby, so they decided to make a go of it. My grandmother went a little mental and somehow tricked my mom into having an abortion. She's never told me all of the details but it was some under the table situation." He bent over to pick up a little pink bow.

"This must be a good sign, right?" he smiled.

"You've been hanging around my family too much. But continue; you weren't kidding when you said your family history was like a soap opera."

"I know. I warned you. So my mom and dad were devastated. They ran off together and eventually got married. My mom got her GED and went to nursing school. My dad worked construction. They tried and tried to have kids but it never seemed to work. She had four miscarriages. She got her nursing degree and found a good job. When they had a little more money, she finally went to a doctor and found out that the abortion had permanently damaged her uterus. She wouldn't be able to have children."

"Your poor mom." I grabbed his other hand so we were facing one another.

"I know. She grew really depressed. I think they both did. But eventually they decided to adopt. My dad wasn't as into it as she was. He really wanted to keep trying to have their own. She said she couldn't take any more loss. Finally, he gave in." He did a little bow. "Hence, yours truly."

"You're adopted?" I realized he was really nervous sharing all of this with me.

"Yep, but when I was about two, my dad broke my mom's heart. He had fallen in love with another woman. She was pregnant with his child, and he wanted a divorce. My mom let him go and held tight to me. And we've been a team ever since." He picked up a rock and threw it into the chain link fence surrounding the grounds. "So in a lot of ways, I never really had a dad."

"Wow, and she isn't in contact with any of her family? Even now?"

"Except my great-uncle, until he died. He was gay so he suffered similar treatment."

"Do you ever want to find out who your real parents are?" His jaw tightened.

"Never," his voice was harsh and he closed his hands into fists at his side. "If they didn't want me, why would I want to know them? My mom is my mom. Always."

We were silent for a moment.

"Why didn't you tell me this before?"

"I don't know. I was just so shocked that you would even consider an abortion, I wasn't really thinking straight. I was just disappointed that maybe you weren't who I thought you were." The words stung.

"The fact that I could have an abortion changed who you thought I was?"

"In a way, yes. Look at it from my perspective. I am only here because my birth parents decided to give me up for adoption versus an abortion; your mom is a pediatrician. It's her job to keep babies alive and healthy. I guess when you mix my family history with your background it led me to assume you wouldn't ever consider it."

I took a deep breath and began to swing. I was angry. But after everything that had happened it was hard for me to remember exactly how I had felt before. He began to swing next to me and we just moved back and forth in silence for a bit with only the sounds of the winter birds in the big pine tree above. He broke the silence first.

"Now that I've given you all of that to swallow; I want to talk about us as a family. I have no idea where your head is after all you've been through. How do you feel about us? About Dave? About our baby? I know this wasn't the choice you wanted to make."

"Our baby. That sounds so strange to say out loud. I've spent so much time with just us that I didn't really think about her as anything other than *my* baby. We were a team. Now I'm back out here in the big world and I already feel so connected to her, more than I've felt toward anyone in my life. I mean, she's a part of me in there. I'm sure I sound crazy." I kicked at the dirt under the swing with the toe of my boot, making a little pile.

"Crazy? No. A mom, yes," he said.

"Thanks." I flashed him a smile. We sat in silence for a moment. A dog began barking as a chainsaw started up in the distance.

"And what about the other stuff. What about us?" he asked.

"That is a harder question to answer. We've never really had a chance to be an 'us.' We went from flirtation to parenthood with not much in between. I don't know that we've spent enough actual time together to completely understand our feelings."

"So, you want me to take you out on dates?" he asked with a bit of a smile.

"Are you making fun of me?" I asked, not sure whether to laugh or cry.

"No, no, not at all." He grabbed the chain of my swing. "You are just so damn adorable, all pregnant, and thinking through everything out loud. I understand what you're saying. And you're right. Let's spend more time together. I guess what I am wondering is more of a big picture question. Can you imagine us getting married, raising our daughter together?"

I looked up at him. He usually acted like he had life by the short hairs, but I could see in his eyes that he was really worried. I felt the full weight of his need. "Gavin, you are talking to a girl who hasn't ever really thought about marriage. I'm not saying I never want to, but I'm still trying to get used to the idea of having a baby. Can you understand that?" I saw a flash of anger cross his face as he tightened his grip on the chains, but just as quickly it transformed into a smile.

"Of course. I'm pushing too hard too fast. I'm sorry." He took a deep breath. "So now what?"

"I don't know. I guess we try spending time together. And you obviously can be involved in all the doctor appointments. Even if things didn't work out with us, we'll always have her together, right?" Again, I saw the flicker of anger, but he swallowed it.

"How about this? I will court you, just like in the old days. We will spend our free time together and then after she's born, have this discussion again?"

"Okay. We can do that." I agreed.

"But I want you to know I do hope we get married and raise her together. I'd really hate for my daughter to grow up like us—without a dad. Okay?"

"I understand. If it works for us, I agree that would be best. But I hope you can understand why I can't make that decision right now."

"I do. I can be patient. Besides, give me a few weeks and you won't be able to resist me." He used the chains of my swing to pull me in for a quick kiss, pushed away and began to swing. I did the same. Swinging felt great. The higher I got, the lighter I felt; each pump taking me further from the weight of approaching adulthood. We fell into sync, swinging side by side.

"Didn't you girls used to call this double dating in middle school?"

I laughed. "Actually this would just be called dating. If a third person was in sync it would be double dating. And if you and I stayed in sync for a certain number of swings we'd say we were married."

"Your dad would say this is a sign from Lady Luck, I believe. Do you think we're swing married by now?" Gavin raised his eyebrows at me.

I rolled my eyes and leaned back and stretched my legs out straight. I had always loved the feel of my hair flying out behind me. I looked up at the sky. "I think it's going to snow."

"So what are we going to tell our parents?"

"That we are going to leave things as they are for now. Hopefully, after a while, the right choices will become clear."

He jumped off his swing as it was in mid-air. "Be careful leaning back like that mama, we don't want you falling off."

I pulled myself back and smiled. The first few flakes of snow began to fall.

"Guess it's time to go, huh?" I said, reluctant to leave this childhood flashback.

We went straight home since the snow was sticking to the roads. When we explained the plan my parents both looked relieved but Mindy was clearly disappointed. I thought it was strange how comfortable both Mindy and Gavin were with the idea of the two of us getting married with so little history.

Dr. Laura Hart

The next few months went by quickly for all of us. When we didn't give them anything to report, the vultures moved on. Day by day it got a little easier to let Sierra out of our sight, but for the most part she was never alone. Either Gavin, Dave, or one of us went with her everywhere.

Detective Rock wouldn't let the case go, and we were grateful, but I just wish they would have let another investigator handle it. Neither Sierra nor Patrick were very fond of him and that made every step more difficult. It was only after Detective Rock received the psychiatrist's report on Sierra that he was convinced she had definitely been abducted and held against her will the entire time.

Months went by with no answers and no good leads. They had determined that she had probably been held in an old bomb shelter. But all of the shelters they found on record turned out to be dead ends. We all just slowly had to go back to living. After all, we had a baby coming and a lot to figure out. Sierra had her good days and bad days. In truth, we all did. As a late Christmas gift we bought a treadmill. We all knew running would be important therapy for Sierra. If the sidewalks were clear of snow and ice, she and Patrick or one of the boys would run outside. Those were the days she seemed the most like the old Sierra.

She took a class and did very well on her exam to get her GED by the end of March. If everything went well with the baby, she planned to take a few classes online to get started on college. We were too nervous to have her attend any on-campus classes alone. I wondered if we'd ever feel comfortable having her out of our sight?

Sierra Hart

Everything happened so fast. I woke up at 3:15AM on May 1st and knew you were coming. Labor was a lot like running a well-paced race. I listened to my coaches (nurses), used my strength, stayed the course and was rewarded with a beautiful, healthy baby girl at the finish. I had been frightened about the pain but everything went smoothly. At 9:26AM I gave birth to you, Maycee Kay Ross.

"Isn't she just perfect?" I asked as I looked up from your sleeping face into my dad's. He looked tired but happier than I'd seen in a while.

"You were great, stub. Really great." He rubbed my shoulder and dropped a kiss on my head. "She may have her daddy's eyes but that is your cute little ski slope nose."

"Can you believe we are parents?" Gavin handed me my water and held the straw so I could drink without disturbing you in my arms. I had the strangest feeling rush over me and instinctively pulled you away from him. I didn't want to share you. I felt like the two of us had been through so much together. When Gavin asked to hold you, I couldn't.

"She looks so peaceful. Let's just let her sleep." I said. "She's had a big day."

I saw that familiar flash of anger cross his face but then just as quickly he smiled it away. "Of course, you're right. I can wait. It's enough just to look at her for now."

A few moments later the nurse suggested everyone let the two of us get some rest. I was never so grateful in my life. When they all left, I gently placed you in your little baby bed and we both fell into a deep sleep.

Dr. Laura Hart

When we brought May home from the hospital I felt like we all had been born again. She seemed to magically transform our household from a tense, gray hide-out to a happy sun-filled home. She was the long-awaited rain for our desert of despair. This was especially true for Sierra and Patrick. They both seemed like their old selves. And May was such a happy baby. She rarely cried and loved to smile.

One morning I took May so Sierra could sleep. Looking at her innocent sleeping face I felt overwhelmed with emotion. I'd held countless newborns in my practice and Sierra, of course; but holding my granddaughter in the first rays of morning sun, awoke within me an intense love and connection with Patrick. We'd started this. She was a product of a love we'd embraced and grown. I'm not sure I can properly capture it with words; but when he walked in the room moments later, I held his hand in mind and the words I'd struggled to find, finally came. We sat side by side on the loveseat; me cradling May.

"Like everyone in my small Pennsylvania town I grew up thinking my dad was a hero. As the chief of police he kept our town safe and orderly. He expected the same at home; everything had its place. My mom's "place" was usually her bed—especially on the weekends. She rarely left the house, which meant my dad took me to birthday parties or the park. When he had to work, he took me to the station while mom rested. Almost every weekend he brought home flowers or gifts for my mother; but she didn't seem to like them. I wished again and again for a normal mom who would appreciate my dad.

But then the summer I turned eleven I came home early from a sleepover because my friend threw-up. When I got home I started up the stairs to tell my parents when I heard my dad yelling in a strange voice.

"You are pathetic. Get up. Why do you keep making me do this, Evelyn?" I froze on the stairs. "Do you know how hard I work all week just so you can have a good life? Then I have to come home to this? You know I don't allow magazines in the bathroom." Then I heard a sick thud quickly followed by a small shriek and a moan. My throat went dry, my heart raced. *I'd* left the magazine in their bathroom."

Tears streamed down my face. Patrick squeezed my hand and nodded for me to continue.

"I didn't know what to do. Normally when I was scared, I ran to my father for comfort. I crept back out the door and slept in my old tree house. When he left for work the next morning, I slipped back inside and up the stairs. I took a breath and slowly opened the door. The room looked as it always did; orderly and dark. Their bathroom door was open and through the glass shower I could see a smudgy image of my mother. Stooped over like an old lady, she gingerly dabbed herself with soap as she sobbed. I cringed at the purple and yellow bruises covering her torso.

I quietly snuck back to the tree house overcome with sick shame. How many times had my mom suffered for items I'd carelessly left out of place? The man I'd worshiped was not the enviable father I thought he was. He was the kind of scum he'd always told people *he* wouldn't tolerate in our safe, happy town. My whole childhood was a lie. But my father was police chief. Who would believe me? I was a kid and he'd convinced everyone my mother was a depressed recluse. He had us trapped."

"What did you do?" Patrick asked gently.

I dropped my head in my hands. "Nothing. I walked in the door like I'd just come home from the sleepover. When my father came home with flowers for my mom I realized all of those gifts had been apologies. How disillusioned I'd been about my world."

"Did you ever tell your mom you knew?"

"We never discussed it; even after he died. But I think she knew I knew because I became obsessive about order and stopped doing things with my dad. Plus, he stopped hiding the fact that he drank. When I was younger he must have hidden the bottles, but by middle school I stayed up too late. Clank after clank I'd hear him drop them into the recycling. He wasn't only a wife beater; he was a drunk.

"What about the beatings?"

"They continued until high school when he started sleeping with a nurse at the hospital and rarely came home at night. The town looked the other way. Who could blame a man with a depressed recluse for a wife; especially when he kept our town so safe?"

"With him not around, my mom came out of her room but she didn't leave the house. Before I left for college I helped her get comfortable going to the store. When my dad was killed in the line of duty my freshman year we buried everything about him. My mom sold the house, and moved to Florida. I stayed at college year-round."

Patrick shifted on the couch so we were face to face. "Why didn't you tell me any of this before?"

"I couldn't. I'd pushed it out of my head. Then when you got arrested, something came loose and everything I'd fought to forget came rushing back. You suffered the brunt of all that anger. I'm so sorry. I shouldn't have pushed you away. I should have fought for us." It felt so good to finally explain myself.

"Hey, as for us, it's okay. We found our way back. I'm more concerned that you sound like you still feel responsible for your mom's abuse. You know none of it was your fault, right?" He looked me right in the eyes.

"I'm working through it. I stopped going to therapy when I started chemo and then Sierra was gone ..."

He cradled my head in his hands and gave me a gentle kiss.

"Well you found a way to tell me. That's progress. But yes, you need to do whatever it takes to let go of the guilt. You're an amazing mom and now grandmother. If you won't do it for you, do it for them. You've seen how therapy has already helped Sierra to heal. She sometimes goes two or three nights in a row without any nightmares."

"Well, that could be "May therapy" as well," I smiled. "But, I know, I will go back once we get Sierra through this first month."

"Promise?"

"Promise," I looked into his eyes and he gently kissed me.

"Am I interrupting?" Sierra whispered from the door with a big smile.

"Not at all," Patrick opened his arms, "I think your mom could use a group hug though." Sierra wrapped her arms around us and Patrick crushed us both with his embrace.

Sierra Hart

I have to admit I was a little sad and jealous of Dave and Gavin during their graduation ceremony. My parents and I quietly tried to attend but our appearance created such a frenzy of well-wishers that we had to leave. It seemed unfair.

Summer was emotional for all of us, too. Gavin and I fought over his acceptance to RIT. I felt he should go but he chose to stay nearby and do a combination of online and community college classes. I was mad at Mindy for taking his side. She felt he belonged with his daughter.

At least Dave and Tia were still following their dreams. Tia called deliriously excited about her acceptance to USC. She and Thomas would be together again. Dave stuck to his plan to attend the Culinary Institute of America. We were all going to miss him (well maybe not Gavin) but I was happy for him.

I will admit a part of me was crushed when August came and went and I didn't get to escape to college, but then you'd do something amazing and I knew I was right where I was supposed to be.

My mother's test results came back excellent. She was officially cancer free. The combination of you, my return, and this news seemed to bring back a little lightness to her life. The hardness in her face and posture slowly melted away over the summer and fall. My dad tried really hard, too. They began to go out on dates. It made me so happy to see them working to be together again.

There were a number of date nights at that time. Gavin insisted on courting me. We went to dinner or the movies. But sometimes our evenings ended very tense because he often brought up marriage. In September, we had a particularly big argument and I told him I would not agree to another night out unless he promised to drop the subject for at least two months.

He agreed and let it go for a while. One afternoon after a little Christmas shopping and dinner, I convinced Gavin to go see the movie *Juno*. I had heard rave reviews and I thought the story was pretty fitting. I loved the movie. Gavin hated it.

"Sierra, I don't understand why you would think that is a happy ending. Here is another kid that is going to grow up without a father. Why?

Because both of his possible dads were too selfish." Gavin slammed the truck door.

"I completely disagree. Yes, it is nice to have a dad *and* a mom; but having someone love you that intensely; even before you are born. That boy is never going to feel like he is lacking."

"You can't know that. What if something happens to that mom? That kid is all alone."

"True, but I would pick one unconditionally committed, loving parent over a couple in an unhappy marriage."

We rode in silence until I realized he wasn't headed to my house.

"Where are we going?" I asked.

"You'll see." he said and reached over and rubbed my leg. I felt the familiar tingle. I was glad that even though we'd disagreed about the movie, he was quick to let it go. I felt pretty content just looking out the window as we drove. The light was fading as the day crept away. We passed one of my old favorite running spots and I realized we were going to his house.

"I told my parents we'd be back after the movie."

"I know." He said. "I texted them and told them we would be a little later. They said it was fine."

"What about-" He cut me off.

"May was great. She had a good nap, and took her bottle no problem."

I had just weaned you off from breast feeding and you sometimes refused the formula.

"What about-" he interrupted me again.

"They took her for a walk in the stroller and were just about to feed her a little dinner. They have it covered, Sierra. They raised you and you turned out great."

He pulled into his driveway. I suddenly felt a little nervous. "Is your mom here?"

"Not until later. She went to a church thing." He guided me through the door.

"Sit here for a minute, okay?" he kissed me quickly on the forehead. I was too restless so I looked around the living room at the pictures on the wall as I waited. There were pictures from throughout Gavin's childhood. I had a sudden vivid flashback to doing the same thing in Dave's basement. It felt like it was a memory from another world. So much had changed. I missed Dave. We texted but it wasn't the same. Still, I knew he was really happy working on his dream.

“Okay.” I jumped when Gavin spoke. I hadn’t heard him come in.

“Follow me.” He grabbed my hand and I followed him back outside and around the house to the barn. When they first moved in, he had converted the barn to his office. The inside was mostly high tech. However, he had a love for all things country so he had cleaned and kept lots of antique farm tools. I was impressed by his decorating skills. He had managed to make it feel down-home country and high tech. I’d teased him about changing his major to interior design.

He covered my eyes, slid back the door and walked me in. When I opened my eyes it took me a second to take it all in. He had transformed his office into a romantic barn using old fashioned lanterns and little white Christmas lights. He had moved a cozy little love seat into the middle of the room and had a projector pointed at a wall he’d painted white.

“What are you doing, Gavin?” I asked, but I had a pretty good idea.

“Let’s sit.” He gestured to the love seat. He wrapped one arm around me and grabbed a remote with his other hand.

“I want to show you a little presentation. I know we haven’t known each other that long. But I like to think of our time together in a more qualitative than quantitative perspective.”I suddenly felt really nervous. He smiled at me, tilted his head, and winked.

“Now in our time together I have learned a thing or two about you. You love numbers and math, running, movies—especially of the romantic nature, our daughter, sweet baby May, of course; and well I hope I can confidently add me.” He put his hand to his chest.

“So, I have made for you a movie of the romantic nature, including all of the things you love, like me, (and again he put his hand to his chest) and if you’d like to watch it, I would love to show it to you; but you must promise to hold all comments until you have watched it in its entirety. Agreed?” he asked holding out his hand.

I laughed and shook his hand. “Agreed.” He pushed play. And as images from our separate childhoods, our past few years together and some relatively sophisticated animation filled the white wall before me, his voice over went like this:

“1 lonely boy named Gavin fell in love with a beautiful girl named Sierra. When the 2 of them got together their love was so intense it blossomed into 3, creating their miracle sweet baby May. But be4 that love could be sealed together 4 ever; that girl that loved that lonely boy said they all had to take 5 and make sure that 1, 2 and now 3 could and would always equal a well-balanced 6 (Which lonely boy knew to be beautiful girl's favorite number). So right now this lonely boy was wondering if you Sierra Hart would agree that our 1+ 2+3 could 4 Ever move from this Take 5 to your favorite number 6? On 6 (your favorite number), 7 (my favorite number) 08 (also the symbol for infinity or in this case forever). Will you, together with our sweet baby May, do me the honor of becoming my wife?"

The movie ended with a picture of the three of us and the proposed wedding date, 6.7.08.

I was blown away. With tears threatening, I turned to look at him. He slid to his knee on the floor before the love seat. Just as I opened my mouth to speak, his voice came on the movie again. "Oh, and I know I didn't exactly incorporate running into this proposal so I hope to hell you aren't about to get up and do that right about now!"

I laughed and it actually made the tears finally spill over and slip down my cheeks. Gavin let go of one of my hands and gently wiped away the tears. I bit my lip. My head spun with doubts but then I looked back up at that image of the three of us happily playing together at the beach and it just felt right. Family should be together, right? I looked back at Gavin, gently brushed my lips across his and whispered "6 it is."

"Yes!" he yelled as he grabbed me up off the couch and spun me around. Then he gently placed me back on the floor, took my face in his and kissed me hard. He pulled back, looked into my eyes with that grin and said, "I can't wait to tell May, her mom said yes."

Dr. Laura Hart

When Gavin came to Patrick and me and asked for our blessing to propose to Sierra, we weren't completely shocked. But I don't know that you can ever be prepared for that question. Gavin was smart about it. He told us he didn't expect us to answer without a discussion.

After he left, Patrick poured us each a glass of wine and we sat at the kitchen table.

"I keep going back to that evening in Nantucket. It's like you knew something big was about to happen. Do you remember?" Patrick asked.

"There was electricity between them. The way she looked at Gavin when he spoke; she looked so happy and I don't know…" I struggled for the right word.

"Alive?"

"Enamored." I took a sip of wine. "It scared me a little."

"Turns out you were right to be nervous." Patrick's eyes reflected my concern.

"Yeah, and I guess the hardest part is, I see that same enamored look on Gavin's face, too. But it's not as much with Sierra as it is with May or when Sierra is holding May."

"So you don't think he loves Sierra?" Patrick looked horrified.

"No, I'm not saying that. I do. I think he does love her, but I guess I wonder. If it weren't for May, would he still want to marry her?"

"I see what you mean. But there is no sense in wondering because May *is* here." Patrick put his hand on mine. "Do you think if we do agree, that Sierra will say 'yes'?"

I took a sip of my wine and thought over the past year. I knew Sierra had asked Gavin to stop bringing it up a while ago. Since then she'd been more relaxed around him. We'd chatted while she was getting ready to go out with him recently, and I could tell by her happy, nervous chatter, she was excited; "Possibly."

"You know he will ask her either way. This 'blessing' is part of his continued effort to get in our good graces." Patrick made little quotes in the air.

"I know. So the question is how do we feel about Gavin being our son-in-law?"

"If I'm honest, I have been secretly rooting for Dave."

"Me, too," I nodded.

"But it's probably better for May to grow up with her mom and her dad. I know how important that is." Sadness flickered in his eyes.

"I just wish they were older. Everything has happened so fast." I sighed.

"I know. But as we both know; love follows her own path." He linked his fingers through mine.

I sighed. "Let's call Gavin and welcome him to the family."

Patrick Hart

As a father, you have this vision of what you think your daughter will be when she grows up; beautiful, smart, happy. When I walked Sierra down that aisle, I was overwhelmed with love and pride. Gavin may not have been my first choice, but I watched her face as she walked down the aisle toward Gavin and I saw that look, what Laura called "enamored." She was glowing with happiness. I knew that she and Gavin wouldn't have it easy, but I was confident she could handle whatever life threw at her.

We kept the wedding small and quiet. Both the service and reception were at Mindy and Gavin's barn. He transformed it once again into a romantic haven. When I reached out to take Laura's hand as we followed them back down the aisle, I waited to see her eyes when she looked back up at me. I so deeply wanted her to return a look of love and trust, the look she had given me on our wedding day. It felt like an eternity as I held my breath, crossed my fingers, and prayed to Lady Luck.

Dr. Laura Hart

Sierra and Gavin's wedding was pure bliss. The sky was brilliant blue with just a few full white clouds. At 75 degrees Fahrenheit, you couldn't ask for a more perfect temperature. Everyone she loved was there, Tia with her boyfriend Thomas, who really did look like Matt Damon; Dave, Mindy, Dave's immediate family, most of the staff from *The Kitchen*, May, and us. It was exactly what she'd wanted.

I was so in awe of how much she had grown in the past year. Sierra, Tia, Mindy and I spent the morning getting ready. I'd given her my wedding day pearl choker as her "something old." I was touched she remembered it from our pre-date nights when she was a little girl. It had been the perfect finish to her simple, strapless, A-line gown.

As we all stood in front of the mirror I remember being struck by her beauty and strength. No matter what, she would be okay. As I listened to them exchanging vows I couldn't help but reflect back on my own wedding day. I'd felt unstoppable, like the world was at my feet. Patrick Hart not only turned heads everywhere he went but he was kind, fun, intelligent, a great cook; and he had chosen to spend his life with me. I wondered if people had looked at me like I did Sierra. But at the first sign of real trouble I gave up on our marriage. Luckily, Patrick never gave up on me.

When I turned to take Patrick's hand and follow Sierra and Gavin down the aisle the moment seemed pregnant with bigger meaning. As I reached for him I looked up and what I saw reflected back filled me with an overwhelming sense of relief and love. Without even thinking, I reached up and pulled his lips to mine. He kissed me back gently and we continued down the aisle to the hoots and hollers of our surprised friends and family.

Sierra Hart

Our wedding ceremony was magical, simple and included everyone I loved. Gavin transformed the barn with lighting, flowers, burlap, lace and antique farm equipment to create a look that impressed even Tia. She described it as "Romantic Country Chic." And even though my parents frequently expressed concern in the months leading up to the wedding, they looked genuinely happy for us.

Dave's speech brought tears to my eyes (and his) and a little fist-clenching from Gavin. I calmed him by subtly pointing to the ring on my finger. Luckily, Tia's speech had us all laughing. Dave helped May catch the bouquet. The wedding cake was Mrs. Braun's tiramisu and Dave's parents generously donated catering as our wedding gift. The group dwindled as evening turned into night. When my parents took May home with them for the night, I struggled. We had never spent a night apart. I was a little teary eyed when I headed back into the barn to rejoin the party.

"Hey, are you okay?" Dave was carrying a round of beer back to everyone.

"Yeah, May just left with my parents." I dabbed my eyes with a tissue.

"Well, lucky for you, we have the perfect cure."

"Beer?" I asked as we approached the group and he handed out the fresh round.

"No," Dave motioned Tia over. "Sierra needs a cure for the baby blues."

She gave me the once over and immediately yelled, "Mindy, Sierra and I are up first!"

While I was getting May settled with my parents Mindy had gotten Gavin to set up the Karaoke machine she'd bought for my bachelorette party. When Tia and I have a little liquid courage we tend to act as if we can sing like rock stars.

Dave was right, singing with Tia was a pretty good cure. After a particularly energetic rendition of *Dancing Queen* we both headed to the bathroom.

"Do you think I'm crazy Tia?" She took her turn at the toilet and I washed my hands in front of the mirror.

"Think? Honey I knew you were crazy that first day we met—also in a bathroom, I might add." she flushed for punctuation.

"You know what I mean. Having a baby and getting married before I'm even legally old enough to drink?"

Tia stood next to me at the mirror and washed her hands. "You know what I think? All that matters is what you think. You *look* happy. Do you feel happy?" Her reflection asked mine.

"I do, but ever since what happened with my dad and then being taken, I'm terrified to completely give into happiness, you know? Like if I let my guard down everything will turn sideways again; does that make any sense?"

"Of course it does. Girl, you have been through a lot in your two months shy of nineteen years. I think anyone would be a little happy-shy. But just enjoy it for tonight, okay? Just let go and feel happy." Tia hugged me until we heard Gavin belting out *Friends in Low Places.* We laughed and headed back to the fun.

Gavin stepped down from the makeshift stage, surrounded by hay bales. They had moved the antique lanterns around to create a spotlight on the brave singers. Gavin grinned and handed the microphone to Thomas, Tia's boyfriend. "Let's see if you can sing as well as you can dance." Thomas and Tia had dominated the dance floor earlier. Then he headed straight for me.

"Hello wife." He planted a big kiss on my lips. "Feeling better?"

"Singing helped."

"Good." He looked really happy, too. Thomas picked *Sweet Caroline* and everybody sang along. He hopped down and approached Mindy.

"I believe you are the only song bird yet to sing." Thomas held the mic out for her.

"Mom, are you still looking through that list?" Gavin teased. Mindy held the booklet of songs in her hand.

"I'm looking for a particular song. I can't remember what it's called. It's right at the tip of my brain."

"Who sings it?" Tia asked.

"Donna Mills?" Mindy looked at us for help. "No she was an actress. Donna something."

"Summer?" Dave guessed.

"Yes. Donna Summer." Mindy pointed at Dave. "I knew I liked you."

"Here, let me see the book. I'll find Donna Summer songs." Tia said.

"You know what? I know." Mindy handed the booklet to Tia. "Hey

Gavin, remember that box of old albums your uncle left here?" She pulled off her reading glasses and turned to Tia. "It was a strange mix, but Gavin said they were pretty typical gay favorites."

Gavin jumped out of his chair, knocking over a few empties. "Mom, I just remembered that antique table is still sitting outside from earlier. We need to get it back in the house. It's supposed to storm tonight."

"You're right. I would have forgotten." She stood. "I just wish I could remember that song. I know it was on one of those albums." She gathered the empties to take with her.

"Mom, just leave it. We can clean in the morning."

"What did we do with that box?" Mindy looked again at Gavin as he ushered her toward the door.

"Goodwill, I think."

Dave stood up."I'll help with the table."

"*Last Dance*?" Tia suggested, as all three headed toward the door.

"No." Mindy shook her head.

"*Hot Stuff*?" Tia asked but they were gone. "She'll probably wake up in the middle of the night singing it. You know how that goes."

Mindy yelled triumphantly from outside "Donna Summer's Endless Summer. 1979. And the song was Bad Girls. That's it Bad Girls." She began to sing. "Bad girls . . . bad girls . . . such a dirty bad girl."

I've read that smells can trigger profound memories. I can tell you when you have been through a traumatic experience, the music you heard can trigger a full blown panic attack.

I heard Mindy singing that Donna Summer song; the same song that I had played 100 times while trapped in that bomb shelter. I was right back there.

"I think I'm going to be sick." I warned Tia, then bolted out the barn door, dropped to my knees, wedding dress and all, and heaved all over the damp night ground. I felt Tia next to me immediately, rubbing my back.

"You're okay sweetie, just too much celebrating." She said in a soothing voice; then yelled, "Thomas can you please go get Gavin and some water?"

"That song. What was Mindy saying about old albums?" I asked her.

"I don't know sweetie; something about the gay uncle's collection? Are you okay? You want me to help you up?" Tia asked.

I shook my head and threw up again.

"That's okay. Get it out." Tia said still rubbing my back. Then Gavin was there with some water.

"Hey baby, are you okay?" he asked. "You want me to take you inside to the bathroom?"

I shook my head again; unable to answer yet. *What had Mindy said about a box of old albums and Donna Summer.* I needed a clearer head.

I saw Thomas' shoes. "Hey Tia maybe we should go and let the newlyweds have their night." He suggested.

"I don't want to leave Sierra like this." Tia said.

"It's okay Tia," Gavin said. "I got her. We've done this once before haven't we, baby?"

"Sierra, do you want me to stay?" Tia asked. "Or leave you to your husband? How crazy does that sound? Your husband. So grown-up." Tia squatted down so her head was next to mine. I managed a weak smile.

"Here baby," Gavin handed me a napkin. I took it, wiped my mouth and sat the rest of the way up. A wave of dizziness hit me and I leaned back into Gavin. "It's okay, I got you." He said.

"Tia, come on. Gavin's got this." Thomas said.

"Are you good, Sierra?" she asked me again and this time I nodded. Wow, I didn't drink that much. The world felt like it was spinning.

"Okay, we'll see you tomorrow." Tia said. "You were beautiful today. Just let go honey, okay? Let go and be happy. You deserve it." She bent down and kissed my hair. "Please thank your mom for us, Gavin. Congratulations!"

"Thanks, Tia. Thanks for coming you guys." Gavin said. And she and Thomas left.

"Let's get you to bed." Gavin scooped me into his arms to carry me back inside.

"Hold on." I said and squirmed to my own feet just as Mindy and Dave came out of the house.

"Forgot my glasses." Mindy explained.

"Mindy, what other albums were in that box you were talking about?" I asked.

"Sierra, I should get you to bed." Gavin said. "Come on." He tried to guide me toward the barn again.

I pushed him off.

"What's wrong, Sierra?" Dave asked, looking from me to Gavin. "Did you get sick?"

"Oh honey, are you okay?" Mindy turned toward me quickly and tripped on a cord in the grass. Both Dave and Gavin reached to steady her.

"What were the other albums?" I screamed and they all turned toward me in shock.

"I don't know. Um, I think there were a couple more current ones, a Tori Amos album, Madonna, Cyndi Lauper, or . . . and that one that was a play and a big cult movie . . ."

I looked at Gavin in horror "How could you? You, you . . ." I couldn't even think.

"Sierra." Gavin took a step toward me.

"What's wrong?" Dave asked and for a moment it shocked me that he was even standing there.

"Gavin, what's going on?" Mindy asked.

"Sierra?" Dave looked from me to Gavin.

"I need to go home. Can you take me?" I asked Dave.

"You are home." Gavin said and stepped between us.

"Gavin, what is going on?" Mindy sounded like she might cry.

I turned to go, but Gavin grabbed my arm. "Let's talk about this, Sierra."

"The Oreos." I pulled my arm away from Gavin and turned toward Dave. "The day I went missing. Did you put triple stuffed Oreos in my car?"

"I didn't know they even made those. What is going on Sierra?" Dave looked from me to Gavin.

"How could I be so stupid?" I couldn't hold in my tears.

Gavin reached out and I pushed him away. "Don't touch me." His eyes went black, he clenched his jaw. "You belong here, Sierra."

I turned to go, but he caught my arm again.

"Let her go, Gavin." Dave took a step toward Gavin.

Gavin turned on Dave. "This is none of your business, Dave."

"Let her go." Dave demanded.

Gavin formed a fist with his free hand. Mindy placed a hand on her son's shoulder. "Let's just all go inside and talk this out."

I yanked my arm free from Gavin and ran toward Dave's car. All three of them followed. I got in the passenger seat but I struggled to pull my wedding dress in and Gavin grabbed the door before I could shut it.

"Think about May." He held the door open. Dave jumped in and started the car.

"Let me go, Gavin." I said and pulled on the door.

He held it open. "We need to talk about this Sierra." He tried a softer voice.

I put on my seatbelt and turned to Dave. "Go!" I demanded, looking straight ahead.

"Look at me Sierra." Gavin continued to hold the door, running along beside us, until Dave accelerated to the point where he had to let go.

"We're a family." Gavin's voice broke as he yelled into the night. I couldn't look back.

"Are you okay?" I asked, but Sierra was wrapped in her own arms, tears streaming down her face. She simply rocked herself in the seat. We drove in silence until I couldn't stand it anymore.

"Should I pull over?" I asked.

"No, I need to see May. Please just keep driving. I'm sorry. I can't… I can't talk."

We pulled up in front of her parents. The dash read 12:13AM. "I'll walk you in." I opened my door and came around to help her out. She used her key. Nobody stirred.

"I need to see May." She whispered. I wasn't sure if I was supposed to stay or go. I sat on the couch and waited until Sierra reappeared, dressed in a T-shirt and sweats, carrying a sleeping May. I stood but she motioned for me to sit. She settled herself with May at the other end of the couch.

"If I decide to tell you something, you have to swear on our friendship, swear on, on baby May, that you will not tell anyone else or do anything about it unless I ask you to. Do you think you can do that?" she asked.

"Of course. Whatever you need me to do. I promise."

"It's big. And if you did go back on your promise and tell, I don't know that I could forgive you or trust you ever again. Do you understand?" I'd never seen her look so sad.

"I swear. I understand." I turned to look her straight in the eyes. "I promise."

She took a deep breath as if she were deciding whether or not to believe me. She stood and paced the room, gently rocking May.

We both looked up as Laura came rushing down the stairs.

"Oh thank God!" she put her hand to her chest and dropped into a chair. "When I saw her empty crib" she exhaled with relief, "what happened? Where's Gavin?" Laura looked from me to Sierra.

"Oh mom," Sierra began to sob and Laura stood to wrap her in a hug. Patrick came down.

"Is everything okay?" Patrick took in the scene and stopped on me. "Where's Gavin?"

Sierra released her mother and took a deep breath. Patrick handed her a tissue.

"Let me take May," Laura held out her arms.

"No, I'm okay." Sierra gently stroked her sleeping bundle. "Actually, I need you all to sit. I need to tell you something important. And I need you to promise me you will let me handle what happens next. If you have any faith in me at all, please promise you won't do anything about this until I've thought it all out."

"Of course, Sierra. Just tell us already. You're scaring me. Did something happen to Gavin? Is he okay?" Laura asked.

"Did he hurt you?" Patrick narrowed his eyes and moved to the edge of the couch like he was ready to bolt.

Sierra sat down in the rocking chair across from the couch and looked at all of us. "It was Gavin who took me. He did it so I wouldn't be able to have an abortion. He wanted me to keep May and I…" her voice broke and she pulled May tighter to her chest. "I wouldn't have kept her," she finished through tears. We all leaned forward but Laura moved to try and put an arm around her shoulders.

"No, please, don't. I… I can't," she continued. "I don't want comfort right now. I just. I need a sounding board, okay? I need you to listen as I talk through it."

So she talked and we listened. The reality of what she was saying took a while to sink in. Gavin had taken her, had put her and her family through 80 days of hell. For that I wanted to run out of the house, find him and hit him until I couldn't hit him anymore. And looking at Patrick with his fists and jaw clenched, I'm pretty sure he felt the same way.

"Sierra, we need to go to the police. He drugged you, held you hostage in a cellar, and stood right in this living room, lying to our faces. He saw us go through hell, attempt to pay an extortionist. And he did nothing. What kind of sick…" Sierra cut Patrick off.

"I know Dad, and I will never forgive him for what he put you through, but he's also May's father. And if he hadn't done what he did, there would be no May." Sierra choked on her own words and began to sob again. This time she let her mother hug her.

"What about what he put *you* through? How can he hear you scream out at night or watch you panic in an elevator and just ignore the fact that he caused all of it?"

"I wish I'd never introduced you. I knew he might be trouble." Laura shook her head.

"And I should have listened to you in Nantucket, Laura." Patrick shook his head.

"Stop it!" Sierra yelled, startling May awake.

“Momma.” May looked up at Sierra.

Sierra stroked her hair. “Hi, sunshine, it’s okay. Go back to sleep.” She looked over her head at us. “None of us can wish back any of it. Think about what you’re saying.” And she gestured down at May with her chin.

I began to feel like a fifth wheel in the conversation. I assured Sierra that I wouldn’t say anything to anyone or do anything to Gavin or go to the police, and left them to discuss their future as a family.

I really wanted to beg her to leave Gavin, marry me, and raise May together. And God, I wanted to kill him; but I understood her pain. As much as that made me want to hurt him even more; I knew why I couldn’t. I knew why she wouldn’t. And I completely understood why she made us promise. This wasn’t about her. This wasn’t about Gavin. And this certainly wasn’t about me. This was all about May.

Dr. Laura Hart

The next morning when Sierra asked if we'd watch May while she went to talk to Gavin, we were completely caught off guard.

"Absolutely not!" Patrick stood between her and the door. "And definitely not alone!"

"Sierra, we don't know what he's capable of. Look at what he's already done." Laura protested.

"Yesterday I married this guy. We all-" her voice caught, "we all loved him. We welcomed him into our family. He is still May's father. He did all of this for her. Trust me, he is not going to do anything to jeopardize a relationship with May." She grabbed her car keys from the hook.

"We do trust you, just not him. Let me ride with you. I'll stay in the car. I swear." Patrick was practically begging.

"I know I am asking a lot of you. I'm sorry to put you in a position where you have to worry about me again. But please if you want to help me; take care of May and let me do this." She opened the door.

"We love you." I said.

"I love you, too." She hugged us both. As we watched her leave, my stomach knotted with fear that I may never see her again.

Sierra Hart

I texted Gavin to tell him I was coming so when I walked into his barn, he was waiting for me on our love seat. To see him made my heart physically hurt in my chest. I'd been so happy the night he proposed to us. But now I couldn't even bring myself to sit that close to him. Standing was better anyway. He must have sensed that he needed to let me speak because he didn't say anything.

"When my dad went to prison I was just as mad at my mom as I was with my dad. Sure my dad had stolen the money, committed the crime; but in my twelve-year old mind I believed it was my mom's fault, too. For not knowing her own husband was gambling, stealing and depleting their savings accounts. How could she not know? They were *married*. And when they decided to get divorced I blamed them both again—my dad for breaking her trust; but my mom for just giving up on him. He'd been this amazing dad and husband for so many years; how could she just let him go?" I stopped by his desk to grab a tissue to wipe my face and blow my nose.

"Love is so much more complicated than we are ever led to believe as children. Love is a tricky temptress. She can lead you down dark paths, cloud your judgment and entice you to make rash decisions that lead to lifetimes of pain and regret. As her mother, I want to protect May from feeling the searing pain that only love can cause, but I know more than ever nobody can protect you from love or the choices it brings you to make. I have gone over all of the "what ifs" in my head. What if you'd never moved here. What if I'd stopped running after my dad went to prison. What if I'd said yes to Dave and no to you? What if you and I had never been on Nantucket at the same time? What if I'd never eaten those Oreos. What if they had kicked in sooner and I'd crashed my car? We could play the game all day. What if my boyfr … no *husband* hadn't kidnapped me and trapped me in a bomb shelter for 80 days? But it always comes back to the same thing. I can't wish for anything to be different. Right? Because to wish for any of those things to change is to wish away May. And I can't do that. I won't do that. Of all of the cruel things that love has dragged me through, the best thing love has ever given me is her. I got May. No actually *we* got May." I blew my nose.

"Sierra, can I say something now?" Gavin asked. His eyes were darker than I'd ever seen them. He started to come toward me.

"No." I said. "Sit. I'm not done. I can understand *why* you kept me but what makes it even crueler is the fact that you allowed my parents to attempt to pay an extortionist, a situation that led my parents to believe my father's past may have caused all of this. Do you have any idea what that did to my parents? On top of the torture they went through wondering if their daughter was alive or dead; you almost destroyed them a second time. You made my mom question my father again. And the fact that she had doubt—that nearly broke him."

"Sierra" he tried, but I wasn't done. I was so angry I could barely breathe.

"You, of all people, who has built your life around the love and trust of one other person; can you imagine how you would feel to learn your mother had been deceiving you all along in the worst possible way? How could you do that to them? They had come to accept you as a son."

"Sierra. Please just give me one second, okay?" He got off the couch, came to where I was standing and dropped to his knees. "You are right, but if I had stopped the whole thing when they found that note, it would have ruined everything. You'd been there less than two weeks. I... we would have lost May." He looked up at me with pleading eyes.

I walked to the other side of the room.

"Sierra, I swear on our daughter. I care about your parents, too. I felt downright evil watching them suffer; but I knew what I had to do to save May. Can you really fault me for saving our baby? No, I didn't go about it in the best way. And yes, I know it hurt your family for a period of time, but in the end we got May. Isn't she worth it?"

Before I even realized what I was doing I was on him. I started with a hard smack across his face and then I couldn't stop myself. It was like all of the fear and anger and love and hate just poured out of me all at once and I just kept hitting him. "I hate you Gavin Ross. I hate you for taking me, I hate you for torturing my family, I hate you for leaving me rotting underground for 80 days." With every hate I hit him again. "I hate you for everything." I was out of breath. I dropped to the floor, sobbing, "and most of all I hate you for making me feel like a monster. You've made me a monster to myself and probably to my own daughter. How is she ever going to love me when she finds out if it had been in my control, she wouldn't be here? How do we overcome that?"

Gavin just let me hit him and rage and then he slowly put his arms around me. I pushed him off again but he grabbed me again and pulled me hard to his chest. For a moment I just wanted to stay there. I wanted to pretend none of this had happened. It was somehow easier when a stranger had taken me. If a stranger had taken me I didn't have to think about the choice I had made because it seemed like fate had taken choice away from me. But to know that he had taken me meant he had in some way saved May when I wasn't going to. Now everything was a big mess. I pushed him away again, stood up, and gave myself some distance.

We both caught our breath. I could hear a pounding rain outside and thunder in the distance. He was the first to break the silence. "Now what do we do?" he asked.

"I have some thoughts." I said.

"Do your parents know?" Gavin asked.

"Yes." I said.

"Well I guess I should be grateful that you didn't show up here with the cops." I didn't respond. I wanted him to worry that maybe they could still be right outside.

"Sierra for what it's worth I did this because I love you. I knew you'd love our child and I knew you'd be a great mom." Gavin's words were hollow to me.

"Gavin, as far as I'm concerned, with the exception of my parents and my daughter, love is just another four letter word. And I think you gave up your right to ever use that word with me the minute you decided it was okay to make decisions on my behalf. That's all I came to say, for now, I need to go." I said and headed for the door.

"Wait, are you going to the cops? What happens now?" he asked.

"You might want to tell your mom what you've done. She's tried calling our house all morning."

"But what about us and May and…" I took a little pleasure in seeing him look so helpless.

"When I'm ready, I'll contact you. Don't contact us. I mean it. Now, *you* can wait and wonder." And as I walked out of that barn and into the rain I realized with blinding clarity that I could never stay married to Gavin. I cried the entire drive home. Not because of what I had lost, but because of what you had lost.

After I left Gavin, I couldn't go home. I drove aimlessly. The landmarks I passed flooded my mind with memories like a bizarre movie montage of my life in this small town. As I rounded the lake I realized that for the first time since my abduction I could safely go for a run on my own. I pulled to a stop at the dam and got out. Luckily, I was wearing running clothes and shoes. The storm had subsided, leaving behind a gray sky and crisp clean air.

At first I tried to blank everything out and just listen to my body, my breathing, the sound of my feet on the pavement. The rhythm of a run was the exact therapy I needed. Each mile seemed to come with a fresh round of emotions. I was angry with myself for not realizing it was Gavin when all the signs were right in front of me.. It made sense; the food, the vitamins, the water, the text books. He made sure I took care of myself; but most important, May. I was sad and hurt that Gavin wasn't the person I'd thought he was. Love could truly be blind. I worried about how this would affect May. And how could he have done this to my family? By the time I came to a stop in front of my car I was emotionally and physically exhausted but ready to talk through everything with my parents. I just hoped they supported my decisions.

Epilogue

May,

I've carried this story, your story, in this bulky fireproof safe from Laketown to Hoboken and finally, Brooklyn. Every year, I pulled it out and wondered when you would be ready to read it. Last week, you brought Tara home to me in tears, and it became clear it was time.

Tara may not always be the nicest friend to you, but you were completely empathetic and compassionate when she found out she was pregnant. It says a lot about who you've become as a young woman that out of your whole group, she chose to confide in you. You made me incredibly proud and honored that you then chose to seek my advice. If it hadn't been for you, I don't think she would have been brave enough to tell her own parents.

I hope you can find that same compassion inside of you for all of us. I know some of this may have been difficult to read, but my ultimate goal in pulling it together was to help you understand the delicate nature of your relationship with everyone you love. When your life is suddenly turned sideways, the rippling effects can last for a lifetime. Hopefully this honest portrayal will in some way calm a few of those ripples for you.

I'm sure you noticed your father's voice is missing. He agreed to share all of this with you in person when the time came, but felt it was safer if he didn't put his words on paper. I've never gone back to fill in the blanks from Laketown until now. Most of the important stuff you already know, but in the interest of full disclosure, I thought you may want to know how your father and I managed to go from devastated in Laketown to peaceful in Brooklyn.

After I left your father in the barn, I made him suffer for a week. Poor Grammy Min was devastated, ashamed, and apologetic to all of us; but I made her give us space, too. I needed that time to do some research, discuss options with my parents, and make a lot of decisions that charted the course for the life you've had so far.

The day we finally asked to meet Grammy Min and your father to discuss your future; I was so proud and thankful for my parents. They were able to push aside all that had happened and focus on what was best for you. We promised we would never report what your father had done if they agreed to the plan. First, I wanted a divorce; a decision I didn't make lightly. I knew it could make life easier for you if I forgave your father and stayed with him; but I couldn't forget what he'd done to my parents. And it took time for me to figure out how to have a relationship with him at all.

I also announced we'd be moving to New York City and requested your father and Grammy Min do the same. I couldn't raise you in a small town and keep you from learning about your past. My mom joined a new practice and helped Grammy Min find a job. I insisted your father grant me full custody. You must understand I didn't do this to punish him. After what he'd done, I didn't trust his judgment. If there was ever an issue when raising you, I had the legal right to make the final decisions. He really struggled with signing those papers; but luckily I have never had to use them. I also made a hand shake promise to allow him to spend equal time with you. Hopefully, we've done a good job of raising you together, but separate. I can't think of an important event in your life that hasn't included both of us.

My final demand was for all of them to agree to help me put together what you just read. I insisted we do it right then, before we moved to New York; before we moved forward. And I enlisted the trust and help of "Auntie Tia" and "Uncle Dave." They have been my main supports through this sometimes terrifying but overall amazing experience I have had raising you.

I know this is a lot to take in and we run the risk of you hating one, both or all of us after you read this. But it was a risk we all agreed to take because we love you. Each and every one of us; your father, your Nana and Poppie, Grammy Min, Dave, Tia and of course me.

I remember a time when I thought living through my dad going to prison would be the hardest thing I'd ever have to do. And then I remember a time when I thought surviving those 80 days would be the hardest thing I'd ever have to do. When I first put this together for you years ago I thought the hardest thing I'd have to do is live with the knowledge that if Gavin hadn't kept me locked in that bomb shelter, I wouldn't have had you. But now I think the only thing that could be harder than all of that, would be if you were so devastated by this knowledge that you decided you couldn't be a part of my life.

Whatever happens going forward, I know telling you is the right thing to do. You know what came before—all of it. If you still have any questions, you can come to any one of us and ask. I know it isn't exactly a pretty fairytale; but this is your story. You are now an informed part of where it goes from here.

I feel blessed for what Lady Luck brought my way—the absolute best wish I never even knew I'd made—you. I love you and hope you will never question that. I know in writing this I say some pretty awful things about love. And I can't promise that love won't possibly play her tricks on you one day. But what I can promise you is that there is a love that exists that is so indescribably wonderful you'll only know it when it's wrapped in your arms. I know I do.

Love,

Mom

Acknowledgments

Without the following cast of characters, not only would this book not exist but my life would be a blank page, too. Thanks to my husband for his unyielding encouragement and championing all my efforts, my children for their support and the flavor they undoubtedly bring to my writing; my parents for being behind me from birth, my sister for being my first reader and my most fierce and loyal defender since childhood; my brother for supporting all of my crazy endeavors and visiting me as I wandered; Nana, PopPop, Cap & Meek for cheering me on and offering helpful and encouraging suggestions; Mike for reading my book when he never reads any. A special shout out to my hometown in WNY for everything it has given me from friends for life to the perfect backdrop to my stories. I am humbled to say I cannot name all of the friends who have supported me in fear of inadvertently leaving off someone I hold dear. Instead I'll simply say Cuba Girls, SU sisters, Nantucket Nancys and Knights, Boston Beauties, Williamsburg Women, St. Thomas Sisters, and my Swiss Misses.

My little CW writers group has been invaluable—especially LJ's precise editorial eye. Special props to Kiele Raymond; she is truly a book sculptor. Her expert editing and storytelling savvy helped me to chisel away unnecessary segments, and refine the fine details that truly brought my characters to life.

The concept of this book haunted me until I put it down on paper. And to that point I'd like to add a special note of appreciation for anyone out there who has taken the harder path in the name of love. I live in awe of you, your courage, your selflessness, and above all your ability to rise above for love.

If you liked *The Keeping* I would love to know!

Visit RochelleRansom.com
Write a review on Amazon
Tell a friend or six or the world on FB, Twitter or GoodReads
Send me an email at 2TellRochelle@gmail.com

Made in the USA
Middletown, DE
14 June 2016